John Slater: The Journey.

By Dave Furlong

Published in 2012 by
Dalyn Publishing.

British Library C.I.P. A CIP catalogue record for this title is available from the British Library.

Dalyn Publishing
Dalyn House
270 Lower Hillmorton Rd
Rugby
Warwickshire CV21 4AE
www.dalynpublishers.co.uk

email and manuscript submission guidelines:
dalynpublishers @ talktalk.net

Dedicated to Truck Drivers everywhere

.

Drive carefully Guys. Come Home safely. May your God always ride Shotgun with you and yours.

ONE: THE END

Dying seemed easy.

It was living, just earning a basic crust, that was hard. Sometimes it seemed I had spent my whole life just waiting to die. And, like most people, I had given passing thought to just how that life would end.

Top of the list was going like my Grandad did; nice and peacefully in his sleep. Not screaming and scared like the passenger in his car. I also thought about the many other ways I might depart. Some were nice; others not so nice.

The second favourite was a quick painless heart attack whilst making love to a beautiful woman. Then there was a heroic demise, selflessly sacrificing myself for others. Bottom of the list was dying alone, uncared for, wasting away with an incurable and excruciatingly painful disease.

In between was a whole gamut of probable and improbable ways that I could go.

Which was why, when it came, my death was a bit of an anticlimax, a bit of a let down, and not quite the way I would have chosen.

*****

When people asked me what I did for a living I told them I was a trucker. I said it with pride but most people didn't seem to think it was anything to be proud of.

Truckers seem to have a bad reputation. Never mind that the country would grind to a halt if there were no trucks to deliver goods to shops, take export goods to the docks and return with imported necessities, luxuries and even the most basic of commodities. No, most people would be glad to see the end of all those big smelly trucks from the roads. To be able to drive without their rear view mirror filled with a large grille and the knowledge that there was 40 tons of metal just waiting to pulverize them into the road.

But, to a trucker, it meant something else. It meant pride in a job that required driving skills beyond those attained by lesser drivers in their cars and vans. It meant days away from loved ones as the dissolution of European borders made the distances between collection and delivery points further and further apart. It meant language skills, clerical expertise, map reading abilities and the toughness to cope with the sheer physical and mental effort to arrive at those destinations with both truck and load intact. So, yes, I was a trucker and damn proud of it.

Trucking is not just a job: it is a way of life. And it had been my way of life for twenty six of my forty six years.

I had started on UK work. Learnt my craft and moved on to better jobs and bigger trucks. For the last seven years, I had been on continental work driving my own truck. Taking my loads to where ever the paperwork told me to go. During those seven years, I had learnt German, French and Spanish. Along with English, those languages were all I needed to get by anywhere in Europe.

I had never been married. No one to call me ‘Darling’ or ‘Daddy’. Trucking is hard on marriage; long distance most of all. Being single was sometimes lonely but the sensible solution. Now, my truck was both my life and my home.

Truckers are a breed apart.

This particular trucker was driving on the M2 down to Dover docks and the ferry. 14th September, 2009: fourteen days from my forty sixth birthday. Destination Hamburg. I had plenty of time so there was no urgency. The speedo said 55mph but that was my usual cruising speed anyhow. On the continent, the official speed limit was 80kph/50mph for trucks: most truckers settled for just under 90kph/55mph and the traffic police accepted this as the unofficial limit.

Traffic was light and I had already settled into motorway driving. My Renault Magnum truck was left hand drive and this made overtaking a little harder in the UK. It also meant I had to keep careful watch on the right hand side of the truck for any unnoticed motorists who were overtaking. Generally though, it was not a problem. I was used to switching to either side of the road depending whether I was in the UK or Europe.

Gradually, I lapsed into auto mode. Most professional drivers do this without knowing that they do so. The mind switches off and allows the body to drive with an automatic sensor on standby. Any problems and full awareness kicks in instantly and takes charge.

Most drivers have had that feeling of "where the hell am I?" or "I don't remember passing that junction" moment whilst driving and hadn't realized they had been on automatic pilot.

Anyway, somewhere in the back of my mind. I was keeping tabs on traffic and traffic conditions. I knew that a XJ Jaguar had just passed at near warp speed and that a foreign truck was pulling out a little way back preparatory to overtaking. There was nothing immediately in front of me in the inside lane and both of the other lanes were reasonably quiet.

The only large vehicle to keep an eye on was a coach that was traveling uncharacteristically slowly about a quarter of a mile ahead. I was desperately hoping that I wouldn't have to get any nearer to that particular vehicle.

It was full of schoolkids who were probably going abroad on a school trip. How did I know that? Earlier on I had been stuck behind it on a long uphill drag that it lacked the power to cope with at any speed. Traffic was heavy enough that I hadn't been able to overtake safely and, contrary to public opinion, I didn't want to use my size and bulk to force a gap in the next lane. So there I was: front window to back window with a bunch of gurning schoolkids who took a delight in making me squirm.

Believe me, there is nothing worse than a bunch of over-excited children pulling faces and giving me one and two finger gestures. Obviously they hadn't made the connection that my UK registration plate should have led them to and just saw a left hand drive truck with a foreigner driving it. Right hand drive trucks got a much better reception of smiles, waves and phantom air horn blowing .It took ages to crest the incline and for the coach to slowly pull away. During that time, I had nowhere else to look but the back of the coach and be fun-fodder for their overactive little minds: bless them! So, no, I didn't want a repeat exercise. The trouble was that the safe distance between us was slowly diminishing. I hadn't backed off, so it must have been the coach.

I signalled to overtake and pushed harder on the go-pedal. The effect was not immediately noticeable and I didn't expect it to be. I was fully laden and, even with 500bhp on tap, it took time before I got near enough to start my overtaking manoeuvre. Plenty of empty road behind so I put on the indicator and pulled into the middle lane. The kids saw and recognized me and gathered at the back window for the next installment of Bait the Foreign Trucker.

There was a motorway exit signposted a mile up ahead, Junction 6 to Faversham,and nothing coming up on the outside lane. I caught up fairly quickly and realized that the driver was having problems. I could see in his mirror that he was wrestling with the steering wheel and the vehicle seemed to be juddering. The next moment, the front offside wheel came right off and went bouncing away towards the central reservation.

The coach dropped onto the front axle and veered into the middle lane. Right into my path. What happened next was entirely instinctive.

I wasn't thinking "I don't want to run into a coach full of kids"; I wasn't thinking at all. Instinctively, I wrenched my wheel to the left and away from the back of the coach.

As I rocked back into the inside lane, I was dimly aware of the coach sliding along the steel barriers of the central reservation. I was more aware that I was headed straight for the base of the bridge and that I couldn't do much about it. My brakes were locked and I could feel the back of the trailer sliding round into a jack- knife situation. I could either release the brakes to avoid the trailer swinging alongside the cab and swatting other motorists aside or I could carry on braking and cause possible carnage. I made my choice and took my foot of the brake pedal. Desperately, I tried to keep trailer and unit in a straight line. Unfortunately, that straight line was taking me straight for the bridge support. It got nearer and nearer. My last conscious thought was 'Oh bugger, this is going to hurt".

TWO: The Beginning

My first conscious thought was the fairly predictable 'where am I?' followed by 'why is it so foggy?'

All around me was a bank of white fog that was damp and smelt of wet laundry. I couldn't see around or through it. Where I was, therefore, was difficult to establish. My mind was slowly becoming sharper like wakening after an operation. A bit slow at first and then, through the anesthetic afterglow, gradually becoming aware of my surroundings. Except I wasn't in a hospital bed and I didn't remember having an operation.

I was standing upright on legs that felt steady enough. I glanced down and saw that I was fully dressed in my usual jeans and t shirt outfit –admittedly, not the best dressed trucker but clean and tidy – with my heavy driving shoes firmly laced. I flexed my arms and legs and they seemed ok. They worked and there was no stiffness other than what I normally got after too long behind the wheel.

That started off the train of thought that reminded me that I was a truck driver and that I was...................had, just crashed into a motorway bridge abutment. So, where the bloody hell was my truck and why was I just standing around in a fog bank? Why wasn't I hurt and why was there no wreckage? Were there any other drivers injured? Just what was going on?

I was starting to get angry by this time. Perhaps the fog had stopped the emergency vehicles from getting to the scene but surely some of the other drivers could have got out to help? And, just what was with this fog anyway? It was like no fog I had ever seen not even the London fogs or smogs as they were called in the 50's cinema footage This was like......like cotton wool?

I stuck my arm out and, yes, it felt just like cotton wool. Thick and just penetrable but still light enough to push out of the way. I decided to walk through it to get some help or, better yet, some answers. Actually, it wasn't like walking through; it was more like swimming through. I grabbed handfuls and sort of pulled myself forward About that time, I realized that there wasn't a hard road under my feet. I should have been on a concrete motorway and yet it felt more like grass. Had I been thrown into a field by the force of the impact? Naw, I might have been a bit groggy but I could still remember that bridge getting nearer and nearer as my truck veered across the road. No way I could have been thrown into anything other than reinforced concrete. Yet here I was, swimming through cotton wool with my feet in grass and not feeling anything other than a bit confused.

I carried on grabbing handfuls of fog and pulling myself forward. The ground was level beneath my feet and progress was fairly easy. After a few minutes of fairly fast forward motion I realized that my handfuls were getting smaller and less dense. Eventually I began to see a suffused light ahead and increased my efforts. Sure enough, the fog thinned and the light got brighter. Within a couple of minutes I could see the edges of the fog clearly and what looked like sunshine ahead.

I broke through into a green meadow that was studded with daisies and shimmered under the warmth of the sun that was directly overhead in a cloudless sky. Bloody hell, thats better. Being able to see clearly and out of the cool fog was great. It still didn't answer the question of where I was though.

I had looked over motorway embankments many times at the fields of Kent on my way to Dover. And, believe me, this wasn't Kent.

Behind me was the fog bank stretching up into the sky like a whiteout curtain and ending in a trench of green. Ahead and around was green grass, big sky and, just visible in the distance, a big building. No fences, no motorway, no animals, no people, no vehicles. Just me and empty space.

People may call me many things but a stupid trucker and a quitter, I'm not. There were still many questions I wanted answered but there was nobody around to ask . But, buildings meant people and, rather than doing nothing, I felt that the long walk to the distant building might provide some answers.

There was no road so I headed across the meadow directly for the faint outline on the horizon. By this time, I was feeling ok. Still confused but strong enough to set a good pace. After about an hour, I could see progress. The outline became clearer and my immediate thought was that it was a BIG building. Like the fog, it seemed to go up and up. I knew there were big skyscrapers but this big? And in the middle of nowhere?

Just what was going on? Where was this place? About this time I had another more immediate concern. I was really, really thirsty. Just as I wondered where I might get a drink, I walked into a stream that seemed to materialize beneath my feet. I could have sworn that there was nothing but flat meadow in front of me but there it was. A stream of clear water running from left to right and flowing into the distance. I must have been more confused that I had thought.

I lay flat on the ground and scooped handfuls of the cold water into my mouth. I have drunk water all over Europe but, never in my life, had I tasted water like this. It was cold, it was clear and it felt so good on the back of my throat. But the taste, …. how to describe that taste?

Think of every drink you have ever had; tea, coffee, beer, spirits,…whatever. Think of your favorite, all time best drink and multiply that tingle on your tongue a hundredfold, a thousand fold and you still wouldn't get close to how the water from that stream tasted. I drank and drank and still couldn't get enough.

I must have dozed off because when I opened my eyes I experienced that 'where am I?' disorientated feeling again. Still in the meadow but, and this was the strange part, there was no stream. Obviously, I must have walked away from it but I couldn't remember doing so.

And, the building didn't seem any nearer. I didn't know where I was but I did know one thing. This was a very strange place.

Truckers are built for speed whilst sitting on their backsides. I reckoned I had walked for a couple of miles and I was feeling the effects of this unaccustomed exercise.

The landscape remained endless green, flat horizons and little else except for the tall building that was my destination. Slowly, it became clearer and more attainable. What I had perceived as white was in reality a light grey or maybe just dirty white. Either way, it became less majestic the closer I got. It had gone from a shimmering pure white edifice to a less appealing Tower Hamlets type of tower block but without the windows. It was still the biggest building I had ever seen though.

Finally, after another hour of increasingly harder effort, I stood in front of it. There was no courtyard, no paved surface. The grass ended where the walls began. There was one door set in the middle and , as I stood in front of this, I looked up….and kept looking up. Damn, this was one high building. It must have been an optical illusion because I could have sworn that it kept going upwards until it reached the sky and then continued from there.

If you ignored the height and lack of windows, it was a typical tower block building in width and appearance. It's construction was of stone block rather than poured concrete and, judging by the weathering on the stone and mortar joints, it was old. The heavy wooden door looked more in keeping with a fortified building than anything else. Once, this building must have looked imposing, regal even, but now it just looked neglected. Maybe it was better inside.

I pushed open the door and walked in. I suppose I had expected some type of foyer. Some sort of meet and greet area where there were people to answer questions and tell you where to go. A Rent a Cop sitting at a desk who might deign to talk to you once he had finished perfecting his tough expression in the mirror on his desk. Maybe a cleaner or janitor.

There was nothing and no-one. No occupant notices or post boxes on the walls, no furniture, no graffiti, no indication of human occupation. Just a bare space enclosed with bare walls and ceiling: except for one metal door at the far end and one button to press. I pressed it.

I half expected a bell to ring out somewhere like in the old movies when the lost characters chance upon a dilapidated house in the middle of nowhere. Instead a voice boomed back 'Name?' Not just any voice but one that sounded like Barry White with a heavy cold. Thick, deep and with the kind of timbre that sent a cold shiver down your spine.

By now, I was too immersed in the strangeness of this place to wonder why Barry needed my name and not just open the door.

'John Slater' I replied equally briefly and not quite as deeply. The Button digested this information. After a few seconds, it responded.

'Age? Date of birth?'

'What? Why do you need my age?'

'Age, date of birth' Barry growled back

'46. 28th September 1963'

'Wait'

As if I had a choice. Turning my back on the door, I surveyed the building. Nope, nothing had changed. Just BARE.

A squealing behind me set my teeth on edge. Turning quickly, I saw that the door had slid noisily opened. Didn't they believe in oil in this place? Barry said nothing so I guessed it was ok to go through. It was no surprise to find that the same building theme applied to the little room I walked into. I had half expected a lift or maybe even a stairway. But it was just a small room with, you've guessed it, bare walls, no door but one small button on the opposite wall.

'Press' Barry said.

I did. I didn't expect the whole room to rocket upwards at Mach Whatever. I never have been one for thriller funfair rides. I get seasick on every ferry crossing. And, I wasn't enjoying this one little bit. G Force kept me pressed in one place and, presumably, my stomach contents in their place. It was a close thing though. I have an Inner Ear problem that makes even crossing puddles a challenge and this wasn't Motion Sickness; this was Extremely Rapid Motion Sickness. I hung on whilst the room/lift warped ever higher like Voyager trying to get away from a Borg assimilation party invite.

I felt the blood drain from my head and, just as I started to feel seriously lightheaded, the floor slammed into my feet and it was over.

The door juddered noisily open and I staggered out. I suppose I was expecting more of the same. Bare rooms, empty buildings and endless grass. I had given up even trying to wonder where I was or what was happening. If Janeway or Picard had appeared and told me that I was needed to drive their ship, I probably would have just accepted it.

The first thing I noticed as the door rolled back was the noise. It was a wall of sound that hurt my ears. It was the busiest open air market you had ever visited, it wa a rock concert, it was Last Night of the Proms rolled into one After several hours of silence – except for Barry – it was probably the most welcome sensation I could imagine. Normality. People talking, walking, talking in groups. I stood just inside the doorway and took it all in.

The first description of the place that popped into my head was ‘airport departure lounge’. It had that kind of look and feel about it. The marble floors, the pillars supporting the upper concourse, the people milling about, tannoy announcements, the roped off sections for the queue lines and the line of desks that were at the head of each queue. Above each desk was an information sign in several different languages. I read the one nearest to me: New Arrival Information Desk. The next one was for Accommodation Allocation; after that, there was Work Assignments. Definitely not an airport departure lounge then.

The people themselves could have happily posed for a United Nations advert. They were black, white, yellow and all the off-shoot variations that you would expect in a Human Race Convention. Clothing was equally diverse from suits to sari’s, dresses to dungarees, jeans to jumpers…well, you think of the combinations for yourself. They were all there. Long people, short people, fat and thin; dressed in every combination of colour imaginable. I am not good in crowds. I don’t get on all that well with large groups of people. I become agitated, tongue-tied and generally get away as quickly as I can.

Probably the reason I became a trucker in the first place. Cocooned in my own little space that protected me from the masses but still allowed me to be a participant.

Frankly, my first instinct was to press the Button and get away from this place. I was seriously contemplating this when Barry's gravelly voice told me to report to the New Arrival Information desk. Coward or Curious? Wimp or Warrior? I made my choice and stepped into the crowd.

It was only a short distance to the desk I wanted. Sitting behind it was one of the most gorgeous girls I had ever seen. She was blonde with big blue eyes and the kind of figure I had only seen in my Wet Dreams. She had a white dress on that was snug in all the right places and a face that you could look at all day and never get bored.

I don't get on all that well with lovely ladies either. Normally, I become all shy and simple. But not today though. Today was definitely not a normal day. I effected a John Wayne type of macho walk and approached the desk.

As our eyes met, she smiled the SMILE. The SMILE would have melted glass, uncoma'd the comatose: it was the best . Her lips parted and she spoke. Her voice was like the rest of her. Just PERFECT. It was low and husky, warm and inviting, it made the hairs on the back of your neck -and something further south – stand on end.

'Good Morning' this vision said. 'Welcome to Heaven'

'It certainly looks like it from where I'm standing' I smiled back in my deepest voice. 'But, where am I exactly' I glanced at the name tag perched precariously on her left breast 'Celeste?'

She looked puzzled. 'I just told you' . She looked at me a little warily as if I wasn't ticking over on all cylinders. 'You're in Heaven'

'Yes, I heard you but where exactly is Heaven?' thinking that maybe Celeste's brain wasn't as developed as the rest of her.

'Heaven is.....well, Heaven just is' she explained.

' But whereabouts?' I persisted ' I was driving to Dover. I was involved in an accident, woke up, walked for miles, got into some sort of lift and ended up here.'

'That's how most people get here, in the Ascension lift, I mean, not by having an accident' She was obviously struggling now. 'What did your Guide tell you?'

'Guide? What bloody Guide? I haven't seen anyone for hours. Not until I walked out of the Ascension thingy'

'Please don't swear here'

'Sorry but I am getting just a bit annoyed now. The Guide?' I reminded her

'You really weren't met?' she asked. 'You came out of the Cleansing Mist and there was no one there? And you walked all the way across the Plains of Adjustment and into the House of Ascension by yourself?'

'Well, Yes' I agreed. 'But I thought of them as a fog, a meadow and a run down tower block'

'Shit' she exclaimed. 'I'll kill that bloody Chris' Suddenly she realized what she had just said, blushed a deep red and looked furtively around.

'Language' I reminded her

'Sorry, I just forget sometimes. I've been here six months now and still the odd swear word pops out. I just hope HE doesn't hear about it"

'HE? Chris?'

'HE is the Boss/CEO. HE is just…is.' She finished lamely. 'Chris is Christopher, you know, the Patron of Travellers. If I have got it right, you are down for a Grade 2 welcome.'

'What's a Grade 2 welcome?'

'Personal executive Meet & Greet, Lada Limo, Guided Tour and Extended Explanation' she read off a clipboard.

'Sounds great, apart from the Lada' I joked. 'So, what went wrong?'

'Chris probably forgot. He's getting on a bit now and doesn't always remember to check his list. I can only apologize. Still, you are here now, so no harm done. You won't want to report him, will you?'

'I suppose not. This place doesn't seem very organized, does it?' I glanced around at the chaos

'You should see it when we're busy. This is reasonably quiet' Right, back to business. Let's get you sorted' Celeste grabbed her clipboard, crossed her Go On Forever legs and gave me her 1000 watt smile. 'Can you confirm your name?'

'John Slater'

Celeste wrote that down slowly, her tongue sticking slightly out as she mouthed the letters. 'Occupation?'

'Trucker'

'Does that have one U or two?'

'Celeste' she looked up from her labour. 'How about I fill in the paperwork and you can fill me in ?'

She looked dubious then, deciding it would probably be ok, handed over her clipboard and pen.

I grabbed it and read the form. It was on gold paper with the heading New Arrival Details. On the first line, Celeste had written down Jon Slatter. I crossed it out and rewrote my name. Filled in the next two spaces Trucker. 28/09/1963.

'Celeste?' she put her nail file down ' What do the next two lines mean? Date of Demise and Reason for Demise?'

She leaned over the desk and gave me a view of her cleavage. It was an effort to tear my eyes away. She saw where my eyes were and gave me that universal 'Humph Men!' look.

'Today's date is 14th of September 2009 and the next line should say something about giving my life so a coachload of kids could live or something like that' she explained and, suddenly, there were tears in her eyes.

I have never had a bucket of cold water thrown in my face but I can now imagine the effect. My jaw dropped and I went cold. The room seemed to spin and I held onto the desk for support. Celeste reached out her hand and I grabbed it as tightly as I could.

In a flash, everything became clear. The crash, the mist, the meadow and the building that reached into the........

'Then I'm dead and this really is.....?' Celeste looked me in the eye and slowly nodded. 'Yes John. Welcome to Heaven'.

'But, how, why?' I blurted out as I struggled to understand just what had happened. Celeste must have seen something in my face that worried her. She got up, came round her desk and put her arms around me.

'Take your time John' she whispered in my ear. 'I know how you feel. I've been here just over six months now and I'm only just getting used to it myself. We all are. Take a look around' She indicated the crowds. 'All these people are new here as well. Some knew they were dying and were prepared. Most died unexpectedly. Accidents, murder, whatever. One moment they are living their lives and the next...well, You know just how they feel.'

'All these people? All these people have just died?' I asked incredulously. 'How many? Where do they go?'

'This is about an average day' she explained. 'It's not something you give much thought to when you are living. Sure, you read of people dying everyday. Probably you have lost relatives, friends and people personal to you. But, think about it. All over Earth, people die. And, most of them end up here. Only the really bad ones go straight to……well, you know, the Other Place'

'Hell, you mean?'

She looked around quickly. 'Uh John, we don't say that word here. It makes people nervous. Makes us look bad'

Hell makes Heaven look bad? This was a bit of a body blow. Something that was at odds with what I had fixed in my mind.

My first school was St Ignatius, a Jesuit Preparatory. And, you know what they say about Catholic schools: once they get you, they have you for good. I first learnt about Heaven, Hell and Purgatory from Brother Simon. He had years of experience in teaching little kids about what was in store for you. Live a good life and you went straight to Heaven and lived happily ever after with the Angels. Be bad and you went straight to hell to suffer for all eternity. In between was the half-way house called Purgatory where the close calls lived until God made up his mind just where to send them. As I said, once the Jesuits have you…..

Of course, as I grew older, and naughtier, I had to go to Confession. Get a Penance. Say prayers, Go to Mass every Sunday. Growing up in a Christian family isn't much fun for a child. You get racked with doubts about everything you do. Is this a Sin? Do I have to Confess this? Is there anything you can do without going to the Eternal Fires of Damnation?

And, like most people, I promptly forgot all of my Catholic ideals and Can do/Can't do list once I got to hormone kick-in age.

But, like most Catholics, those ideals never left me.. They were never purged completely from my hard drive but lingered in the Lost File and Where the Hell Did That Go? section of the computer that is my brain.

From about 15 years old, I had stopped going to Mass. At first my conscience bothered me –for at least a week - then, as time passed and I grew older and more world weary, I gradually became an Agnostic. Somehow, I couldn't reconcile reality with a Hereafter. A mythical place called Heaven couldn't logically exist. God and Paradise were what priests used to keep themselves in a job and us under their thumb. Now, those long lost teachings came flooding back. And, as Celeste hugged me tightly, I remembered them and was even more confused.

'But Celeste' I said as I reluctantly untangled her arms and looked into her eyes. 'What about Ascending into the Kingdom of Heaven to sit at the right hand of God? What about suffering in Hell? How can Hell be better than Heaven?'

'Well, things have changed a bit since then' she agreed. 'Look, I can't go into it now. Let's get your accommodation sorted out and I'll have a word with Counseling to see if they can bump you up the list a bit. You are Grade 2 after all and that still counts for something…….probably'.

"What's with this Grade 2 stuff?'.

'Grade 2 is dying that others may live. Grade 1 is for martyrs, priests and anyone who has lived a pure and religious life. Grade 3 is for people who previously led a bad life but turned it round and devoted the rest of it to doing good'.

'What grade are you?' I asked as I digested this information. Grade 2 eh? Brother Simon would be upset. He reckoned I wouldn't amount to anything.

'I don't have a Grade' she said. 'I didn't do anything spectacular with my life. Most of us' she indicated the crowd of people around us 'just queue up in the Cleansing Mist until there is enough of us to send a bus for'

'Yeah, I'm Grade 2 and I had to bloo…..well.. I had to walk' I reminded her.

'I am sorry' she saw that I was teasing her and smiled. 'Take this Grade 2 Pass and go straight to First Accommodation. Angelica is on today and she'll look after you.' She looked quickly around and leant over. 'Once you get settled in, give me a call and we can maybe meet up for a drink later?' she asked as she scribbled a number on the back of a card and handed it over.

Not bad Slater. Talk about Christmas. First day in Heaven and already you have pulled a cracker.

I took the card and gave her hand an extra squeeze, smiled my Big Bad Trucker smile and walked over to First Accommodation and Angelica.

Waving my Pass, I walked right up to the head of the queue. Not surprisingly –or maybe surprisingly, given the location – there was a bit of muttering but no-one actually protested out loud. This was Heaven after all. More likely, everyone was still slightly confused and unsure of the way things were run.

Angelica was an Angel. Well, maybe she really was. I didn't know. I couldn't see any sign of wings but maybe Angels didn't have any in this version of Heaven. Wings or no wings, I wouldn't have crawled over her to get down and dirty with Haley from Coronation Street.

'Morning, Can I help you?' she asked in a bored voice that matched the bored expression on her face. . Just then the phone on her desk rang. She picked it up, listened for a moment and replaced it and the bored expression. 'That was Celeste. She's my room mate and I have to look after you' she explained with a Rock my World and Melt my Socks smile.

'Apparently, I have to get accommodated' I replied and tried to replicate her smile. I felt that I had failed miserably but struggled gamely on. 'Any chance of a vacancy in your place?'

'Grade 2 opens a lot of doors but, unfortunately, not my door.' She said somewhat primly but with enough of an expression in her eyes to show that the idea wasn't entirely offensive. 'I'll have a look to see what is available in your Grade.'

As she looked at her monitor, I looked at her. She was a redhead –no hair just a red head. Sorry, old joke - with the palest of skin, luminous green eyes and Scarlet Johansson lips. Her flaming locks fell onto shoulders that were encased in a white tee shirt that clearly showed the red bra underneath. 'Humph, bit racy for Heaven' I thought really primly. Yeah right. Truthfully, I thought I would like to see what was under that red lace. Redheads weren't normally my type but this Ginger Ninja was definitely in with a chance.

And, that was strange, wasn't it? Here I was in Heaven lusting after this angel –well, she was, whether she was or not- without getting The Guilt or The Conscience about it. Maybe it was because I was new that I could get away with lewd thoughts.

Like most women, she could read murky minds. Or maybe it was just my tongue hanging out that gave the game away. Whatever, she gave that little satisfied smile that they all have as standard equipment and pecked away at her keyboard.

'Any preferences?' she asked. ' There isn't that much choice but there is always a little leeway for a Grade 2.'

'Um, I think I would prefer a detached house somewhere quiet' I decided.

'Wouldn't we all? Something detached and quiet? Now, that really would be heavenly" she laughed.

'I'll have to share then?'

'John, we all have to share here. There are no single dwellings. There are no semi-detached dwellings. There are just accommodation blocks. Heaven is bursting out at the seams. It's full'

'But what about the Land of Milk and Honey? The place where everyone is happy, contented and rewarded for living a good life?' I was beginning to think that Brother Simon hadn't known what he was talking about.

'I think it was like that …at first. At least, if you talk to the old timers, that's how it was in the beginning. Everyone had their own little house, green fields all around, plenty to eat and the Afterlife was really good. It just isn't like that anymore'.

She went on to explain how, as the human race grew increasingly larger, so Heaven began to shrink as more and more people died. At first, people had to share a house. Then all the green fields began to be replaced by housing. Housing became tower blocks. Tower blocks became bigger and bigger until, eventually, even these were replaced with Astro blocks which went even higher. The housing for the Management went underground in an effort to provide something slightly different and marginally more exclusive.

I know when I am having my leg pulled so I kept silent and waited for the punch line. After all, you only had to look around this place to see that there was plenty of space for everyone. Angelica stopped speaking and, seeing my expression asked what I was finding so funny.

'Nice one.' I laughed. 'You almost had me believing you there. Almost'

'But, it's true' she insisted. 'Look, let me get your keys and I'll show you'.

She walked over to a large metal cabinet and selected a set of keys from the large collection hanging there. I couldn't help noticing her skin tight jeans and long shapely legs. Or the logo on the back of her white tee shirt …Angels Do It Divinely.

Angelica definitely wasn't your stereotype Heavenly body. There was a bit of attitude to this girl as evidenced by the Doc Martin boots. Catching my admiring look, she laughed. 'Eat your heart out Slater. We Angels only put out for Grade 1'

'I thought Grade 1's were priests, martyrs and really holy men. I queried.

'They are and they don't if that is your next question'

It was but I left it at that. I decided I would follow that train of thought once I got a bit more acclimatized to this being dead and in Heaven situation.

Holding the keys, Angelica returned to her desk, told the people waiting that it was her lunch break and that she would be back in an hour. They took it extremely well and this, if nothing else, more or less convinced me that this was indeed Heaven and not some drug induced or coma related dream. I mean, in the real World, can you see anybody waiting in a long line, calmly accepting a Queue Jumper and then being told it was lunch time and there was no replacement staff ? Neither could I.

Grabbing the coat from the back of her chair, Angelica handed it to me and then turned round expectantly. Always the gentleman, I held it whilst she put it on. As I brushed away the hair from the back of her collar, I caught her scent. I don't know if it was her shampoo, perfume or just the smell of Woman but I could have stopped there all day just inhaling her.

'Come on, come on. I don't have all day' she admonished, grabbing my arm and pulling me across the concourse. No doubt about it; she knew just what effect she was having on me. I think it was when my hand got to sweaty for her to hold that she made up her mind.

'John' she said softly as she turned to face me. 'I like you, I really do but that's it for now. I could try to explain but I would probably make a mess of it. It's not out of the question but you really have to see a Counselor first. And, I promise you, I'm not leading you on or giving you ideas intentionally. If anything I'm just reacting to you the same as I would on Earth but this isn't Earth and different rules apply' She reached out to hug me and softly, gently, kissed my cheek. I just held her.

Breaking away, she continued guiding me towards a pair of large glass doors directly ahead. These were coated in something that let the light in but you couldn't see clearly out of. Just beyond, as indistinct shapes, I could make out some buildings.

As we dodged around people and got closer, I suddenly had a moment of dread, fear…some instinct that squeezed my heart and left me breathless.

Angelica sensed my mood and, giving me a 'Don't worry, it'll be all right' smile, led me directly towards the doors. As we approached, she flashed her badge and they opened. In comparison to inside, the light beyond those doors seemed darker and I held back. Breathing erratically, my heart pounding, I summoned what little dignity and courage I had and, with a weak little smile at my companion, crossed the threshold.

Outside it was dark. Not pitch black but that subdued light you get just before dawn or a few minutes past twilight. I had no real idea what the time was and looked up at the sky to get an indication from the sun. Overhead I could just see a sliver of blue sky and an illusion of sunlight.

At my feet was pavement. A bit cracked and uneven but definitely solid and ending about five feet away in kerbstones. A road started or ended – depending upon whether you were arriving or departing – just past the Arrivals Hall and snaked down a low incline to the buildings that stretched from horizon to horizon and, it seemed, from the ground upwards. And upwards and upwards……

'What the hell is that lot?' I asked Angelica as I stared at a collection of the ugliest buildings I have ever seen together in one place.

'That's not He… what you said' she replied matter of factly. 'That's Heaven' I searched her face for the slightest indication that her statement was a joke. A let's play games with the newbie act that all new arrivals had to endure. If it was an act, I wouldn't have played cards with her. Not a twitch, not a glimpse of amusement in those big green eyes.

'You're serious: right?' I said. 'That is the Promised Land. The Land of Milk and Honey. Paradise.?'

'I told you things had changed' Angelica looked right back at me and there was sadness in her voice. 'I told you about the overcrowding. The population explosion. I understand how you feel. I felt exactly the same way. But you live with it because you don't have a choice. And, believe it or not, it's not so bad. You can have fun. It's like living in a big city…………..'

'Yeah, just the biggest dump of a city in the world' I finished for her. 'Or. should that be universe?' I looked down at the ground and felt tears in my eyes. Anger in my heart and the feeling that I had been royally cheated and misled. Bloody Brother Simon.

'Come on. Trust me. Once the initial shock wears off, You'll love living here'

'I have a choice, do I?' I almost shouted. Almost, but it wasn't her fault, was it?

She grabbed my arm and led me away. Down the road to the place where I was destined to spend all Eternity. Oh Great, I couldn't wait.

'Wait, Angel, wait" we both turned round and there was Celeste waving and tottering on high heels as she came towards us. Her cheeks were flushed and her eyes sparkled. "Oh, I'm glad I caught you. I've just got off and was hoping I'd see you. Have you told him?' she asked.

'Yes, she's told me' I replied resignedly. 'I thought it was a joke but it obviously isn't. I thought you might have told me or at least warned me what to expect.'

'Sorry, I'm no good at stuff like that. I have some good news though. Counseling has moved you up the list and will see you at 9 am tomorrow. Isn't that wonderful?' she queried with a smile.

'Wonderful' I agreed. 'Coming with us? Celeste is just going to show me my new home. It's by the beach, she tells me'

'But, we don't have a beach….. Oh you! You're having me on aren't you? Glad you're not too depressed by… you know' she trailed off and just nodded in the direction of downtown Heaven. Funny thing was , she was right. The sort of day I was experiencing, nothing seemed real or worth getting upset about. I'd just died, gone to Heaven, got a Grade 2 –I was really chuffed about that – met two beautiful and really nice girls and was just off to see my accommodation. What was to get upset about?'

I held out my hand. Celeste laughed, grabbed it and, with Angelica holding my other one, we set off down the road. For no reason other than that I was holding two

beauties -what better reason? - I felt the need to burst into song 'Heaven, I'm in Heaven'..................

THREE

Peter Tiler liked the night shift. He must do because it had been his preferred option for just over 5 years now. Currently he was driving his Scania truck down the M2 towards Faversham. in Kent. Once there, he would drop off his 40foot curtain sided trailer, pick up an empty one and return to his base at Crick, just off junction 18 of the M1.

Routine and therefore boring work. But with good pay and not exactly taxing on mind or body. Traffic could still get heavy on the motorway networks even during the night. Generally though, that traffic consisted mainly of fellow truckers. Truckers who, like himself, worked this dark shift so that the population now sleeping snugly in their beds could go to the shops in the morning and not find depleted shelves of milk or cornflakes or whatever else was needed.

And, beside the truckers, there were the support teams. The warehouse staff who unloaded the convoy of truckers who invaded them each night. The shelf stackers who distributed the transported goods onto the correct shelf of the supermarkets ready for the customers who – with the advent of all-night shopping – seemed almost as numerous at night as in daytime.

Six years ago, Peter had retired. With 10 years to go before he was-officially a pensioner , he felt it was time. A recurring back problem, dodgy knees and a wife who constantly reminded him that it was time to take it easy and spend more time with her had been the catalyst.

The first week, the unaccustomed luxury of his own bed every night and a lie-in every morning, had been great. Pottering around the house and catching up with the myriad repairs, decorating and improvements to the marital home had kept him busy. Shopping with his wife had been interesting. But, once the To-Do list was complete and shopping became boring he found himself with more time on his hands that he could cope with.

He found himself rising earlier and earlier each morning and just moping around the house. Elizabeth, his wife, became more and more annoyed with him always being in the way. Finally, after one monumental row over something trivial, they sat down and decided that maybe Peter would be better off working again.

His former employer couldn't offer him his old job back but did have night shift vacancies. Four nights on; four nights off. It seemed the ideal solution even though he didn't initially find the prospect of night driving very attractive. As he got into the rhythm of the job, that changed. Now, with nearly six years of nocturnal trucking under his belt, he couldn't envisage anything else. Daytime sleeping wasn't a problem and he still found plenty of time to do other things. On his four nights off , he and Elizabeth got along great. Hell, he'd even got himself an allotment and discovered a talent for growing things.

As he pulled off the motorway and into the depot, he was deciding that he would plant some Sweet Potatoes this year and see how they did. Pulling up at the gatehouse, he powered down his side window and greeted the security guard.

'Hi Pete boy, how's things?' He asked in his broad Norfolk accent as he handed over his documents.

'Can't grumble, Stu, you?'

'Be glad to get home and have my four days off'.

'That was a nasty crash earlier on wasn't it?'

'What was that then?' Peter took the paperwork back. 'What bay do you want me to back onto?'

‘21 and you’ll be picking up your return trailer from 16. There was a bad accident on the M2 earlier on. A coach lost a wheel and a trucker swerved to avoid it and smashed into a bridge support...Traffic was held up for quite a while . Took them ages to clear the wreck away. Driver died straight away, they reckon. Coach hit the central crash barrier. Got tore up pretty badly but no-one got hurt. Coach was full of kiddies off to France. Police said on the local radio that if the trucker hadn’t swerved to avoid them, it could have been really nasty.’

‘No, I hadn’t heard anything and there was no sign on the motorway that I noticed” Putting his truck into gear, Peter pulled away and drove round to Bay 21. Reversing between the adjacent trailers, he gently eased backwards until he made contact with the loading bay. Getting out of his cab, he stretched his six foot frame and retrieved his number plate from the rear of the trailer. Wound down the legs, disconnected his airlines and electrics, pulled the safety lever that kept the jaws on his turntable securely locked on to the trailer kingpin, climbed back into his cab and pulled slowly away.

Driving the unit round to Bay 16, he reversed onto the trailer and felt the jolt as the turntable slid under and locked onto the trailer kingpin. Jumping down, he clipped the fifth wheel safety clip into place on the locking mechanism, wound up the trailer legs, re-connected his air and electrical leads, secured the number plate in it’s holder and returned to his cab.

Pulling away from the loading dock, he drove back to the exit. As he drew level, Pete handed him a plastic cup of coffee, operated the barrier and Peter raised the cup in salute and drove down the access road.

Sipping the coffee, he replaced the cup in the cup holder and concentrated on the road ahead. Just before he joined the motorway, he pulled into his usual lay-by, parked and shut off his engine. Finishing off the coffee, he climbed out of his cab, put the cup in the waste bin and urinated against the rear tyre. Back in the cab, he climbed into the bunk, stretched out and prepared to sleep. Two hours should do it, he thought, then up to Crick and job done. Life could be really good sometimes, he decided.

As Peter Tiler slept, motorway life continued. Trucks, vans and cars sped up and down the nation's concrete veins. But mainly truckers. Truck drivers from Europe and going to Europe. Many way over their legal hours but desperate to catch a ferry or get to a destination on time. Separated from family and loved ones but doing it because of them. Doing the job because truck driving was in their blood; because of the money, the adventure or wanderlust. The Call of the Road was a Siren Call that claimed many men and, increasingly, women and was not something that could be readily explained. You either heard the Siren music and danced to the Rhythm of the Road or you didn't. Driving was a chore or a choice. If the latter, then you were always wanting new roads, new horizons and never finding them. Truckers were modern day explorers always seeking and never satisfied.

Exactly two hours later, Peter Tiler opened his eyes, yawned and climbed back into his seat. He drywashed his face with his big hands and ran them over his thinning hair. Within minutes, he was on the motorway and heading home. As he settled into both his and the truck's rhythm, his inner pilot took over as his mind began to ponder things other than the job in hand.

Now nearly 60 years old, he was just beginning to feel his morality. Still fit with his six foot frame reasonably slim, he reckoned he had a few good years left before he met his Maker or whatever happened at the end of life. And, like most people, he looked back on his life with a mix of pride, regrets and What Ifs.

What If he hadn't left his native Norfolk and come to the Midlands? What if he had taken that job instead of the other one? The list of What Ifs was infinite. The regrets of his chosen path were few. The pride he had in his achievements to date was sufficient that he slept well and was mainly at peace with himself and his life's work.

Probably that poor trucker who died earlier felt that he had a few years left as well, he mused. If nothing else, it showed how quickly and unexpectedly the Grim Reaper could strike. If he had time to feel anything at the end, Peter hoped that the departed trucker felt that his life in exchange for those of the kids on the coach was a fair exchange. 'Truck on Good Buddy and may your next journey have good roads and far horizons'. Peter saluted his fellow trucker with sadness and pride.

The Truckers Code was important to drivers like Peter Tiler. It wasn't written down in black and white but every good trucker knew it. Look after your truck, guard your load, be courteous to other road users. Take pride in your skill and always help other truckers. Those were some of the rules that distinguished the professional driver from the rest. Some came with practice, others with experience, some you taught to others but most came from within. Driving, Peter reasoned, was probably the only skill that never stayed the same. You either got better or worse and the distinction came from the individual and his or her personal pride in a job well done.

As he embarked on this train of thought, he thought of the one truck driver he knew who was the template for the ideal trucker.

In 1989, Peter was driving for a now long gone haulage company. It was mainly day work with a few overnight journeys every now and then. A local kid had badgered him to let him come out in the truck. Glad of the company, Peter had obliged. The odd trips became more frequent and, during school holidays, the pair were traveling together every day. During those journeys, the kid learnt his geography, his navigation skills and the myriad levels of expertise that a trucker needed. A good listener and a quick learner he learnt the road craft and the Truckers Code essential to a professional truck driver.

At 18, with Peter's help –both practical and financial - his apprentice took his rigid truck driving test and passed first time. With his mentor's recommendation, the firm took the newcomer on and never regretted it. Three years on rigid vehicles then his next driving test and the leap to articulated trucks. Pretty soon, he was a top driver and exceeded his teacher's skills. But, he was also ambitious and was enticed into his dream job of continental driving by another company who made him an offer he just couldn't refuse. But, he didn't forget his friend either. Every time their schedules worked out he and Peter spent a week together on the continent. Pupil and master together again but with the latter now firmly in the passenger seat –albeit still on the right hand side - and John Slater at the wheel of his left hand drive truck.

'I'll have to give John a ring this week-end' Peter Tiler promised himself as he exited the motorway and drove to his depot. Once there, he parked up, did his paperwork and walked to his latest pride and joy, a Ford Ranger doublecab pick-up.

Climbing in, he started the big diesel engine, grinned to himself and thought 'Yeah, its not a bad old life, boy. Just wait until John Slater sees this beauty'.

A short journey home to Rugby and he was already planning his day. Breakfast, sleep, allotment, work. Pulling into his drive, he was surprised to find Elizabeth waiting for him. Normally she would be on her way to work and he wouldn't see her until she returned. One look at her face and he knew it would be bad

‘The Kent police have been in touch” she informed him with a wobble in her voice. “I’m so sorry, love. He’s been in a bad accident and he died.’ She sobbed as she held him. ‘He’s dead, Peter …..John Slater is dead.’

FOUR

'John Slater! If you don't slow down this minute, I'll never talk to you again' Celeste threatened as she walked warily across the uneven pavement in her high heels.

'Should get some proper footwear girlfriend' Angelica taunted her, raising up her clunky boots for inspection.

'What and look like you? Some of us have to look smart for our jobs'.

'Now, now ladies. Let's be nice.' I stopped and allowed them to catch up. Looking around, I wondered why I was in such a hurry. The closer I got to Heaven, the more it looked like Hell. Look up and all you could see were the slab sides of buildings. And, you could look a long, long way up. There were buildings on every side of us with narrow alleyways between them. Every sixth block, the alley became a road no wider than a truck width across. Not that you could judge the distance that accurately because there were no trucks. No cars, no motorbikes or pushbikes. No wheeled vehicle of any kind.

'Is this normal?' I asked the girls as each grabbed my arm. 'Where's all the traffic, the people? Is it always like this?'

'There isn't any private traffic, just a few maintenance vans and a few small distribution vehicles" Angelica replied. 'As for the people, why they are all at work, silly'

'But this is supposed to be Heaven. People shouldn't have to work in Heaven for Christ's sake!'

Both girls went pale and looked nervously around. Holding my arms tightly, they practically frog marched me down the alleyway and into the door of a dilapidated looking building. It wasn't a hard thing to do; walk me into any one of the buildings in this place and it would be dilapidated.

'John, listen to me. I'm being serious now'. Celeste pulled me round to face her and I could see in her face that she meant it. 'Never, ever, ever use the 'C' word here. I know you're new and it just slipped out but you really are going to have to think before you say anything. No 'C' word, no 'J' word, no 'G' word, no 'H' word.'I was still trying to work out what the letters meant. Obviously, I knew what the 'C' word meant but I hadn't actually said that, had I? And, where was the 'F' word? Or the 'N' word? Were there any black angels here? Celeste obviously saw my confusion. Leaning close, she placed her lips next to my ear –I shivered with anticipation – and whispered 'Christ, Jesus, God, Hell'

'Oh, I see'. I was going to have problems. I don't swear in the normal sense. No Frank-uncle-charlie-kate or the other more obvious ones but the newly forbidden ones? Jesus Christ, how in God's name, was I going to remember not to say those? Bloody Hell!

That little faux paux had put a dampener on things. I looked around. The hallway of the building we had entered was dimly lit. Probably just as well because it half hid the rubbish piled up under the stairs, the Army camo-green paint-peeling walls and filth covered floor. What couldn't be hidden was the smell. A combination of urine/faeces/damp and unwashed bodies that was strong enough to bite the back of your throat and make you look around for something to puke into.. My escorts looked around with interest and no apparent sign of respiratory distress..

'This isn't bad, is it Ang?'

'No it isn't Cel. I've been in worse.' Angelica pronounced. 'Anyway, come on John, your own little piece of Heaven is just out here'.

Just ‘out here’ was down to the end of the hallway, out of a door and into a little walled yard. I suppose it measured about 30ft by 40ft. The floor was bare earth littered with rubbish. The enclosing walls were around six feet high and had barbed wire running around their tops.

Wedged in at the far end was a caravan. A caravan that had seem more bad than better days with most of its windows replaced with cardboard or wood panels. A caravan that sagged in the middle where the chassis had given up. A caravan that had green mould decorating it’s walls and roof. A caravan that even Claude Greengrass would have had a conscience about renting to his worst enemy. A caravan that I was getting a very bad feeling about.

‘Here we are then’ Angelica smiled with a magician’s flourish as she handed me a keyring. ‘Home, sweet home’.

‘Ohhh, isn’t this exciting’ Celeste exclaimed as she did a little leg stamping dance and clapped her hands. ‘You are so lucky John Slater. I’d give anything for a place of my own. Come on, come on, I just can’t wait to see inside’.

I could but didn’t get much chance to resist as my Heavenly Honeyies practically dragged me to the door. Using the key, I reached up and opened the door. It promptly collapsed against the wall of the caravan and hung there on one hinge.

‘Minor detail’ Angelica decided. ‘Big strong trucker like you should have it fixed in no time. I imagine that you are very good with your hands’

She looked directly at me as she said it and winked. Celeste put her hand in front of her mouth and giggled behind it. Just what was it with these two? Talk about blowing hot and cold.

There were no steps so I grabbed Celeste around the waist and, ignoring her protests, swung her inside. My fingers nearly touched around her slender waist and she was light as a feather.

Angelica decided she didn't want my help and started to pull herself inside. Holding onto the door frame as high as she could reach, she cocked first one leg then the other inside the van. That position put her bum virtually in my face and my reaction was pure male instinctive. As she pulled herself inside, I put my hands on that ravishing rump and, true gentleman that I was, pushed. She jumped as if she had been electrocuted, gave a little squeal and, once inside, turned round accusingly. I gave her my best 'Aw shucks Ma'am, only trying to help' smile and tried to look as if I wasn't bothered whether I caressed her buttocks or not.

She must have decided I was pretty harmless because she held out her hand to help pull me inside. I pulled the door into place. Given the sort of day I was experiencing, I should have been immune to any further shocks. I wasn't.

The interior of that seemingly grotty caravan, was the exact opposite to it's exterior. Sure, it was dark inside but that was due to the lack of light outside. And, once Celeste had found the main switch and flicked the lights on, it was like the sun coming out from a bank of storm clouds.

It positively gleamed. The walls and floor were clean and litter free. The floral print curtains that covered the glass, wood and cardboard windows blocked out the depressing outside view. The furniture looked almost new and the interior smelt like a bracing 'fill your lungs with that sea air, son' walk along Brighton promenade. Even my mate Peter Tiler would have liked it and he hated caravans.

I was a bit overcome, truth be told. I'd had a rotten day so far. You know, died, gone to Heaven, found out conditions were different than I had been led to believe but now this. I put my head outside the door. Yep, same old DEPRESSING. Inside it was clean, calm and contrastingly different. I felt a lump in my throat and tears in my eyes and pretended to blow my nose. My two angels were studiously looking elsewhere but kept sneaking glances my way. I sniffed and held out my arms. They came and, with their arms around me, I let go and cried my heart out.

I cried for myself, Peter and Beth, my other friends, everyone I had left behind. I cried for everything I had lost in my life. Hanging onto Celeste and Angelica, I cried for everything that Had Been and what Could Never Be.

My two angels comforted me as best they could and gradually my sobs died away and I dried my eyes. Burying my face between theirs and my arms around them, I sought their strength. Finally, I drew away and kissed each one tenderly and fully on their lips. 'Thank you' I whispered.

'It's what you needed John' Celeste replied as she also wiped her eyes.

'Yes, the sooner you get it out, the sooner you can move on' Angelica confirmed.

'Does this happen to everyone?' I asked as I struggled to regain my composure.

'Pretty much, sooner or later' Celeste agreed. 'I was devastated for weeks. I got knocked down by a bus just after I had bought a new designer dress . I was so busy thinking about the new dress I was carrying – you should have seen it; it was to die for – that I just stepped out into the road. One minute I'm in Oxford Street, the next in Heaven. And, do you know what really pissed me off?'

'No, what'

'Well, I never got to wear that dress?' she said in all seriousness.

I couldn't help it. I just burst out laughing. Once started I couldn't stop. I collapsed on the floor and laughed so much it hurt.

Celeste looked at Angelica, her top lip trembled and, within seconds, we were all rolling about the floor laughing our hearts and our hurts out.

When I got up, I dusted myself down – both literally and figuratively – and helped my companions to their feet.

“Better give you the guided tour’ Angelica grinned.

There wasn’t that much to show. Living space with leather couch, easy chair and table with two chairs. The end bedroom had two single beds. These were both made up with Playboy’s Heavenly Bodies duvet covers, pillows and yellow sheets. The small kitchen had a worktop and a strange looking appliance set into a small alcove. No sign of any pots, pans or anything to cook on. I reached up and opened the small overhead cupboard. Just a Gideons bible. What else?

Past the kitchen was a partitioned off area which I took to be the bathroom. It was. White tiles, a shower cubicle and what I presumed was a toilet; albeit a strange looking one. It was basically a white porcelain stand with an eggcup shaped seat and a red button at the side. There didn’t seem to be any water plumbing. The other thing missing was a hand basin although there was a U shaped pipe sticking out of the wall.

‘You better show me how everything works’ I asked.

‘Well, it’s probably a bit different from what you are used to’ Angel replied. ‘This’ she pointed to the pipe sticking out of the wall ‘is a sonic hand wash. There is no water; it uses sound waves. Same for the shower. The toilet is a vacuum system. Do your business, press the red button and everything gets sucked away.’

‘How can you wash without water’ I queried.

‘Ultra high modulating sound waves remove the dirt without you getting wet. It’s a strange sensation at first but it works really well. Most people adapt to it quickly and generally prefer it. It saves having to dry yourself afterwards and works whether you take your clothes off or not. Most of us just jump into the sonic shower in the morning with our clothes on and get them cleaned at the same time.'

'Well, yeah, but it can't be the same as a good long soak, can it?'

'Long soaks in a hot bath with bubbles, a book and bar of chocolate. Ooh, I really miss those' Celeste said regretfully

'Unfortunately, there is only a very limited supply of water in Heaven' Angel reminded her.

'What , no water?' I couldn't believe that. 'How do you make a cup of tea? What about cooking?'

Walking back into the kitchen, Angelica stopped in front of the strange recessed machine. 'How do you like your tea ?' she asked. I told her 'Tea, white, no sugar' she said . The machine made a series of bleeping noises and, right before my eyes, a cup with steam coming out of it appeared. She grabbed it and handed it to me. It was tea and, after the first tentative sip, probably the best cup of tea I had ever tasted.

'Anything you want to eat or drink, order from the Replicator' Angel told me.'

'Anything? Just like that? Free?'

'Umm, no, not free. You get credits and you use those credits for food, drink, entertainment, shopping etc. Sort of like money but you don't have to carry it around'

'You said "not free"' I reminded her.

'Well, no. You have to work to get credits. You'll be seeing Work Allocation tomorrow after you have seen Counseling. Until you start work, you get free credits'

'Does it do alcohol?'

'It produces Syncohol which is a replicated alcohol that gives the effect of a drink without the hangover. Like sonic washing, you soon get used to it and most people like it. You must have seen all this on Star Trek or other sci-fi programmes?' I probably had but hadn't thought that I might be using sci-fi equipment in my lifetime. But, then again, I thought ruefully, I wasn't: I was using it in my deadtime. I put my cup of tea down, walked to the Replicator and, in my best Captain Picard impression, ordered three double vodka and cokes.

They went down a treat, so we had three more..........

You know when you have been drinking and you suddenly get the Munchies? I hadn't had anything but tea and I don't remember how many Syncohols since I got here and I was ravenous. I went to the Replicator and ordered steak, chips, eggs and peas. 'You want anything girls?' I asked. They obviously didn't. Both of them were suitably relaxed in a heap on the floor and weren't feeling any pain.

Seated at the table, eating my replicated meal –it tasted superb by the way – I took stock of my day. Driving to Dover, driving into a bridge, dead, heaven, caravan, drink and a meal. Quite a day by any standards. Time to end it.

I picked up the girls one by one and put them on the bed, covered them – fully clothed, of course. Oh yeah, I did think about it but it wouldn't have been right, would it? – with the duvet and left them to sleep it off.

I had a digestive transit in my super dumper toilet. I half expected wrapped and scented crap but, no, it still smelt as bad as ever. I did, however, forget Celeste's warning before I pressed the red button. Ever put your bum cheeks in a gigantic vacuum cleaner? I have and have got the bright red ring to prove it. Must remember to get off the seat next time before activating the Dump Suck, I thought as I lay down on the couch and closed my eyes.

I opened my eyes and, not seeing a top bunk and the back of two truck seats, knew I was in a strange place. As I awoke fully, I realized that was probably the most stupid thought I had ever had: this strange place was the strangest place I had ever been in or probably ever would be.

At least the couch had been comfortable. I got up, saw that I hadn't undressed and went to the replicator and ordered a cup of tea. Strange how some things you got used to in a hurry. I could have done with one of those in my truck. Laying on the worktop was a folded piece of paper. 'Thanks for putting us to bed last night' it read. 'And thanks for...you KNOW! Your Counselor appointment is at 9 in Arrivals. See me and I'll direct you.' It was signed with two lip imprints.

Finishing my tea, I walked over to the shower. Remembering Angelica's advice about clothes, I pushed the red button. I didn't hear anything but it was the weirdest sensation. I tingled all over and then the button returned to its normal position. I stepped out of the cubicle and saw that my clothes were clean, pressed and smelt… well, heavenly. I sniffed under my arm and smelt only a clean little trucker..

Stepping out of the caravan took me back to reality. The contrast with the tidy, calm interior and the shabby exterior couldn't have been greater. The dark yard, the compressing effect of the myriad Astroblocks only seemed to emphazise just what a major turn my life had suddenly taken. Crossing the yard, I entered the building and walked to the outside exit.

Out on the pavement, things seemed exactly the same as yesterday. No vehicles, no pedestrians, nothing but neglect, squalor and gloom. It struck me as I made my way back to the

Arrivals Hall that, apart from Angelica and Celeste, I hadn't actually seem a living – make that a dead – soul since I had left the chaos of that hall. Where the Hell was everyone? I must remember to substitute Hell for Heaven, I reminded myself. Where the heaven was everyone?.

Getting to my destination proved harder that I had thought. Normally, I have an excellent sense of direction. Put me in a strange place, spin me round a few times and I could stop and instinctively know where the points of the compass were. It was a very useful and necessary skill for a trucker to have. Here, with all those identical buildings pressed around me and very little light, I couldn't. I didn't have the little direction pointers that I subconsciously used to plot my course. No street signs, no shops, no traffic lights, none of the usual things that you remember when you are going to a place and that you reverse-order to get back. I was starting to get a panicky feeling when I spotted Angelica walking towards me.

'I'm glad to see you' I said. 'I was having difficulties. How did you know to come and get me?'

''I didn't' she confessed after giving me a quick kiss on the cheek. 'I was going back to the caravan to get it ready for the next Firstnighter'.

'I thought the caravan was my place?'

'I should have explained it all last night. I remember thinking I would do it after my first drink. I forgot after that. The caravan is a sort of refuge for new people to spend their first night in Heaven. The Boss realizes that everything is a bit strange, a bit weird so there are similar vans all around. You get to relax, have a meal, a drink, a good sleep and the next day, things don't seem so bad'.

'Bugger. I was getting to like it. So where will I be stopping permanently?'

'I don't know. That will be decided once you have seen Accommodation. It will depend on a few things. Whether you have relatives here, what job you get…many things. Speaking of which, shouldn't you be getting a move on?'

'I was lost' I confessed. 'Point me in the right direction?'

'Head straight back up this alley until you come to the end. That's where the Habitation stops. Turn left and you'll see Arrivals. Don't worry, a couple of days and you'll get the hang of it.. Sorry, I have to rush. I have to make sure everything is just right for my new Firstnighter. You'll never guess who it is?'

'Probably not, can't you just tell me? And, will I be seeing you again tonight?'

'I don't think so. I'm going to be busy doing the same thing as I did last night. Helping my Firstnighters get settled is my job. But, I will see you again, I promise'.

With a little smile, she turned around and left me. I was a bit miffed. I thought we had hit it off ok and I had plans to turn my angel into a devil. Suddenly, I was just a job. Was it going to be the same with Celeste?.I headed up the alley and suddenly remembered that she hadn't told me who her new Firstnighter was.

Back in Arrivals, eventually, I made my way to Celeste's desk. Things inside the hall seemed as chaotic as ever. People milling about, queuing at the desks, all looking as confused and helpless as I had been. One little old lady was just leaving the Arrivals desk and I waved to Celeste. She help up her hand with the five minute gesture and I grabbed a nearby seat. When she had finished her paperwork –it obviously wasn't her strong point – she headed over.

'Hi, how are you? Did you sleep ok?' she asked as if she really cared. With a quick look round, she leant in close and planted a quick kiss on my lips. 'You'll never guess who's arriving today?'

'Celeste asked me that as well. She seemed a bit preoccupied. Ok, tell me, who is coming today?'

'You've seen her? Was she ok? She's been so excited since she found out. It's meant to be a secret but I'll tell you. It's only Celeste's favourite actor from her all time favourite film. She told me she had seen Ghost over fifty times'

'Demi Moore is her favourite actor?'

'Not Demi, silly, Patrick Swayze. Today is 15th September isn't it?' she asked then carried on anyway. 'According to the Arrivals List which came in first thing this morning, he will die of cancer today. Isn't that exciting?'

'I don't suppose he is too pleased about it' I pointed out.

' No, I suppose not but it's great for us. I wonder if he'll open a dance studio here. He used to be a ballet dancer, you know. Look, I have to get back and you have to be in Counseling in five minutes. It's just over there; the room with the red door. Can I meet you for lunch?' Without waiting for an answer, she hurried back to her desk and yet another confused and frightened client. Well, at least she hasn't gone off me, I thought. Patrick Swayze indeed. Humph, I bet he isn't a Grade 2

The red door had Counseling written on it in faded gold lettering. I knocked and, getting no answer, walked in. It was a non descript office so I won't describe it. Suffice to say, it was shabby, run-down and didn't inspire confidence. And that pretty much summed up the little man seated at the large desk.

'John Slater, isn't it?' he asked in a bored tone of voice. 'I'm……'

'Morning Brother Simon' I greeted him. 'Paradise? Boy, did you mess up'.

FIVE

'Faversham Police. Can I help you"

'Hi, yes. My name is Peter Tiler. Someone from your station rang my wife regarding John Slater. He is…was the truck driver killed in a crash on the M2 yesterday. Can you tell me what has happened to him….his body?'

'Are you a relative?'

'Well, no but I was down as John's contact for emergencies. He stays with us when he isn't in his truck. That's why my wife was contacted. I presume our number was found in his wallet?'

'Yes Mr Tiler, what can I tell you?'

'Basically, where is he? When can we start arranging his funeral?'

'At the moment, he is awaiting a post mortem. It's pretty obvious that he died from his injuries but we have to be sure. His blood will be tested for alcohol or drugs…."

'John never took drugs and never drank if he was driving'

'That may be so Mr Tiler but the law requires us to make sure. Look, can I make a note of your number again so I can contact you when his body is released?'

Peter gave his home and mobile number and also obtained the contact number for a local undertaker. He arranged with the undertaker for his friend's body to be collected as soon as it was released. Ordering an oak coffin, he paid a deposit using his credit card and agreed to pay the balance when he came to take his friend home.

'I can quote you for the journey to Rugby in one of our hearses' Mr Findlay of Findlay and Sons Funeral Directors assured him.

‘That won’t be necessary Mr Findlay. John will be going home in style’.

SIX

'Please have a seat Mr Slater. I see you haven't changed.' Brother Simon said a bit warily as if I was going to get even for all the detentions and canings he used to give me so regularly and enthusiastically.

I sat down opposite him. He hadn't changed. Literally. He was exactly the same as I remembered him from my prep school days all those years ago. Still the same chalk flecked cassock that the Jesuits wear. The white collar with his scrawny neck poking through it and his little head waving above. Like one of those big Galapodos Island tortoises you see pictures of. His comb-over still made me wonder why he bothered to brush hair up from the back of his neck and plonk it on his bald head and think it looked entirely natural.

'This is all a bit different from how you used to describe it' I said waving my hand around the dingy little room. "Where's all the milk and honey. The green pastures and all the rest of the Paradise you promised me?'

'Things may have changed slightly' he agreed.

'I ought to charge you under the Trade Description Act" I just loved seeing him squirm. 'Anyway, why am I here?'

'My job is to make your Crossover, Transition or whatever you like to call it a little easier , to explain how things work here and to work out your emotional issues' he intoned as if reading from a script. 'From what I hear, you seemed to settle in quite quickly. Angelica and Celeste were both late for work this morning. You're not on Earth now, Mr Slater'

'I worked out my emotional issues last night. Those two girls helped me do that and I won't have them punished. They didn't do anything wrong and neither did I, much as I would have liked to. I can't seem to make the transition from Milk and Honey to Astroblock and Grot. Perhaps you could counsel me with that?'

Brother Simon stood up. 'Have you any idea of just how many people die each and every day, Mr Slater' He wandered up and down the room as he talked. Exactly as he did in the classroom. 'The last population census on Earth was in February 2006. At that time it stood at 6.5 billion. In 1700, world population was estimated at 600 million. In 1800, at 900 million. By 1900, it had grown to 1,500 billion. The population of earth was 6.5 billion in 2006 and, in 58 years from now , it is estimated that world population will double. Are you with me so far, Slater?'

Bloody heaven, talk about being back in class. But, give the old bugger his due, he was an excellent teacher and he obviously hadn't lost his touch.

'The world birth rate is 21 births per 1,000 people. Thanks to improvements in medical science, the world death rate is 9 per 1,000 people. Before these improvements in medicine , science and diet, the death rate was much higher. There are still wars going on all over Earth. People die in accidents, there is disease. The Black Death, for instance, nearly wiped out half the Earth's population. All these deaths, since the human race crawled out of the slime. Where do you think all those souls end up.?'

I very nearly stuck my hand up and said 'brother, brother'. I didn't. 'I guess you are going to say Heaven?'

'Not quite. Many, the really bad ones, go to the Other Place. I'm sure you know where I mean?' I nodded. 'But, I am sure you can see why Heaven is so overcrowded. At first, it meant sharing houses, then sharing rooms. Then accommodation blocks were built. Then tower blocks. All getting higher and higher. Eventually, in the mid 1800's, there was a massive redevelopment programme. All low level buildings were torn down and replaced with the first Astro-blocks. The first were a thousand storeys high. The next phase, in the early 1900's – to cope with the death rate from the two World Wars – were an extra 500 storeys higher. Can you imagine, Mr Slater, buildings 1,500 levels high? The engineering that was required taxed the expertise of every building engineer and architect we had. Engineers who had built pyramids, castles, the early American skyscrapers, tunnels under mountains, dams; they were here and we used them. The next Astro-blocks are planned as two thousand storeys high. And even they will not accommodate the all souls that come to Heaven. And, Mr Slater, what about food, heating, clothing? Everyone has to work for credits to obtain all these things. Replicators create the food and the clothing. Fortunately, clothing does not wear out in Heaven so everyone has only two sets of clothes; work clothes and relaxing clothes. You might not believe it but this cassock is thirty years old and' brushing at some chalk mark on his sleeve 'is still as good as new. My relaxing cassock is just the same as this one but in even better condition.

But, and here is the point, replicators and heating use energy. And where does that energy come from Mr Slater?'

'The sun?' I surmised.

'Some of the solar energy is used for heating but the bulk of Heaven's energy comes from prayer Mr Slater. From prayer. The more people on Earth who pray to Go…..the Boss, the more religious energy get stored in our Accumulators. What do you think of that, Mr Slater?'

'I had no idea. But why then do people have to work here? If the energy comes from Earth's prayers, then what do people do?'

They repair things , they build things, they regulate the energy, they Meet and Greet, they fill in their days with meaningful labour. When you go on holiday Mr Slater, how long before doing nothing gets boring and tedious? How long before you actually look forward to getting back to work? Why? Because, you have nothing to do and get bored. Everyone works or does something on Earth; apart from footballers wives, politicians, so-called nobility and a few other parasitic species.

So, everyone needs something to do, something to fill in their time. Something to keep them occupied for all eternity.'

I shook my head. This was taking some believing. Grotty accommodation, overcrowding, having to work forever. No retirement, no holidays… nothing. And this was Heaven? What must the other place be like? I asked the question.

'I'm afraid I don't have any further time to discuss that subject. All I will say is that things are more, er, relaxed. No doubt, once you get working, your work mates will answer all your questions. That is the end of your counseling. I hope you feel better and looking forward to your time here ?'

If I say no, will the old bugger give me detention? I thought. 'Yes, thank you Brother Simon. I feel so much better now'.

'Good, my fee is four credits. These will be deducted from your first salary'.

'I assumed this session was free' I protested.

'Never assume Mr Slater. That makes an Ass out of U and Me. I have to work and get paid as well, you know. By the way, I *now* know that it was you who placed those drawing pins on my chair. They were very painful when I sat on them. And, just to satisfy your curiosity, I had one hell of a shock when I arrived as well'. He stood in front of me, held out his hand and gave me a shy little grin 'Goodbye John, I do hope we meet again. Despite my worst fears, you turned out all right. You have my greatest respect for saving those children'.

'Goodbye Brother Simon' I shook his hand firmly. 'It was nice meeting you again'. And, you know what? I really meant it.

Outside the Counseling office, the Arrivals Hall was as busy as ever. People were moving from line to line, wandering about in a trance like state, talking to each other, praying, arguing with the staff. I needed a coffee.

Finding Celeste's desk, I waited until she was between customer/client? What did you call the people lining up to see her? "Any chance of a coffee?'

'Couple of minutes. Go and wait by that door over there' she pointed to a gold door by the far wall. I went, I waited.

As I waited, I observed. Truckers tend to do a lot of that. Truck driving entails a lot of waiting; waiting to load, unload, stuck in traffic jams, whatever. You sit in your cab and watch the world go by outside.

What I observed in Arrivals was that the new people, the recently dead, came in the myriad shapes and sizes you would expect to find in the general population. But, the staff –those at the desks or working in the hall – were, for the most part, all young.

Certainly, all the females were young, perky and pretty. They weren't all out and out drop dead gorgeous but all had that firmness and prettiness that girls in their mid-teens to mid twenties have. They didn't all have model figures but the general female population mix between "could definitely lose a few pounds" to stick thin.

The guys tended to be older, around late twenties to early thirties. There were a few much older men –like Brother Simon – but mainly that age range. Coincidence? I didn't know. I would have to ask someone.

That someone came sashaying across the floor looking like a wingless angel. Celeste grabbed my hand and dragged me through the gold Staff Only door. 'Oh, some people' she moaned. 'Are you sure it was my time to die? It is so inconvenient' she mimicked in a British upper class accent 'I could have killed her'.

She walked over to a replicator and ordered two coffees. 'How did Counseling go?' she asked as she flipped off her shoes and sprawled in a chair.

'Not bad. I knew the guy. He was one of my old prep school Jesuit school teachers.'

'Yes, Counseling and the other top jobs all go to Grade Ones. Did he explain everything ok?' she sipped her coffee and raised an eyebrow. 'Bloody Hel…Heaven' she corrected hastily. 'I wanted a latte and this is instant. Instant! Bleeding replicator is on the blink again.'

'Tough morning?' I guessed.

'Annoying. Just as Patrick Swayze came to my desk, that cow in VIP Arrivals snatched him away. I didn't even get to welcome him to Heaven. Then I get all these Moaners, Groaners and Bitchers. Some people don't know just how lucky they are to be dead.'

'No, they could be living in their detached houses in the country. Instead they get to live in an overcrowded, over populated and overwhelmed place like this.' I agreed. 'Some people eh?'

She got my sarcasm and grinned. 'Ok, I'll stop moaning. Any questions you'd like answering?'

"Thousands but they can wait. Oh, there is one thing I've noticed. Why are all the staff so young?'.

'Err…actually most of them aren't'. Seeing my confusion, she put her cup down and sat up straight. 'How old do you think I am?'

Guessing a ladies age is always a dangerous game. I reckoned Celeste was around 20/21 but decided to play safe. 'About 18?'

'Not bad Slater, very diplomatic. Here, I am 20 years old. On Earth, I was 68 when I departed'.

She saw my "Go on! Pull the other one" look and grabbed my arm. The look on her face was the most serious I had ever seen.

'It's true. One of the really, really good things about Heaven is that people get to choose the age they are going to spend eternity at. How cool is that?.

She put her arms around me and pressed her firm young 68 year old body against me. 68? Hell, it was like having the hots for my gran.

'You just have to think differently here' she warned as she felt my reluctance to hug back. 'The other really neat thing is that you never get sick. You get the chance to live forever at the age you felt most comfortable with'.

'Let me get this straight. You pick whatever age you fancy, don't get any nasty bugs, virus' or disease but still have all the memories, experiences, feelings and sensations you picked up in your Earth lifetime?'

She nodded. 'Yeah, it's great isn't it?'

That explained the ladies but why were the men older and by choice?

'We girls tend to be at our best body-wise around 17 -25 years old. We are out of the spots stage, we are confident with what we have got and at our sexual peak. With guys it's different, they tell me. They are past the stage of walking around with a permanent stiffie, hormones have settled, spots have gone and they are experienced enough with the ladies to make the moment last. You should know. What age would you choose?'

I decided that it required a lot of serious thought. I had a more immediate thought on my mind.

'You mean that people still make out here? You know, have sex, hide the sausage, grease the ferret, make love?'.

'Of course. It's only natural after all. It's just that things are a bit more organized. We girls don't get pregnant. We don't even have periods here and that is a real blessing. I used to dread my monthlies, all those cramps, the nausea….'

'Yeah, but' I broke in, still having a bloke's normal reaction to talk of periods. 'doesn't that encourage promiscuity? If you can do it without fear of pregnancy, what stops you doing it 24/7 with anyone?'.

'What kind of angel do you think I am?' she responded a little primly. 'Even on Earth, I only did it with people I cared about. Here, even more so. Here in Heaven, it's kinda special. More intense, more…..' she groped for the right word

I had another kind of groping on my mind. 'Heavenly?'

'Meaningful. It lasts longer, feels 100 times better and…oh, you'll just have to try it and see'.

Was that an invite? Just as I was going to make my move, Celeste stood up, put her coffee cup on the table and stretched. She nearly tripped over my tongue as she made for the door. There was a mischievous glint in her eye. 'Down boy. You have to get a place to stay yet. Accommodation is three doors down. Jump the queue, you're Grade 2 if anyone says anything'.

I jumped the queue. I did hear one upper class lady protesting but Grade 2 is Grade 2. Can't argue with that.

By now, I didn't expect anything different. I wasn't disappointed. Accommodation was another dismal little office although someone had placed a vase of flowers on the desk to brighten the place up a little. According to the nameplate, someone was called Astra – didn't anyone here have ordinary names? Maybe you got to choose a new name as well – and she was another stunner. Of course, now that I knew why the staff were such lookers, it didn't have quite the same impact. She was a brunette with large, luminous brown eyes, a tilted up nose and an eminently kissable mouth. A green blouse, brown skirt –a tight brown skirt – and black high heels completed her chosen work outfit. Astra wasn't in the same class as Celeste and Angelica. She was in a whole different class. She was the kind of girl that melted your big brain and firmed up your little brain. The kind that rendered you speechless and drooling. She looked up and smiled. 'Don't tell me, John Slater right? Celeste told me to expect you. She didn't say you were quite so dishy. I just wish we had room for you in our place. I share with Celeste, Angelica and Molly. You haven't met Molly yet have you?'

I hadn't and wasn't quite sure I wanted to meet anyone with such a boring name. Boy, was I turning into a Grade 2 snob or what?

'Obviously, you know about our little overcrowding problem?' I nodded. 'So, you know that you have to share right?' I nodded. 'I've checked our records and see that you have several relatives here. But, most of them already have a full complement of people living with them. So I've decided to put you with a couple of people you have already lived with.'

My mind raced backwards. I had lived with a couple of girls for a short time but it hadn't worked out with either of them.

Must be blokes then. That wouldn't be so bad would it? All lads together, out on the town. I nodded.

'Are you always this quiet?' I nodded. I didn't want to speak because it is embarrassing to have drool pouring down your chin.

'Right, I won't spoil the surprise then. You can meet them after you have been to Supplies, Clothing, Ageing and Language. Fortunately, they are all in the same room, saves space, you know. Just next door. Any questions or anything you want to say before you leave?'.

I nodded, swallowed and, in a dry, squeaky little voice, blurted out 'Any chance of a date?'.

Her face clouded over. 'I'm sorry John, I don't go out with truckers'.

'Oh' That was a bodyblow. 'I'm ok. I've been house trained and everything. Even eat with a knife and fork. You shouldn't believe everything you hear about truckers. Try me, you might like me'

'Astra wasn't my Earth name, John. In November,1980, I was a student at Bradford university. I met a truck driver there. He definitely wasn't a nice person. He's the reason I'm here. You may have heard of him. His name was Peter Sutcliffe. He was also known as the Yorkshire Ripper. So, sorry, John but no. I don't go out with truckdrivers, however nice they seem to be'.

There wasn't a lot I could say to that. I got up and left.

Supplies,Clothing, Ageing and Language was indeed next door. It was in a large, light and airy room decorated in bright colours and smelling as fresh as a stroll along Brighton beach. You really believe that? Of course it wasn't; it was the exact opposite. It was typical Heavenly Drab.

The only bright spot in the whole room was the person behind the long counter. After meeting only stupendously beautiful staff, it was a surprise and almost a relief to find a normal person.

You know what Dawn French looks like, right? Almost the first word that springs to mind when you see her is – sorry Dawn, no other way to say it - large. Then, suddenly, she isn't so large. She is funny, charming, captivating and beautiful. I don't mean drop dead gorgeous but she has that inner spirit, character and joy of life that almost transcends classical beauty. You just know that if you spent a bit of time with her, she would capture your heart, make you laugh and leave you wanting more.

The girl behind the counter was like that. Overweight sure, but such a beaming smile that I couldn't help smiling back. And, as I got closer, I could only see her clear skin, white teeth and sparkling eyes. Short black hair framed her face and just touched the shoulders of the yellow - well, smock was the first word that sprang to mind and I couldn't think of another – outfit she wore. Even without the name tag, I knew who she was.

'You must be Molly' I grinned. Somehow, you couldn't see yourself doing anything else with this girl.

' That's me' she laughed. 'Plain old Molly. I did try to think of another name, a more sophisticated one but, I'm never going to be anything other than plain old Molly so I decided to stick with it'

I didn't know how old she was but she would never be plain. I told her so.

'Go on, you silly trucker. I've heard all about you from the girls. Celeste is smitten, Angelica thinks you're really cool and Astra? Well, Astra has her own personal demons with truckers but, once she gets to know you, will come round. She was really impressed that you got the other two collapsed-on-the-floor drunk, put them to bed and didn't take advantage. Must have been hard?' she twinkled.

'It was and it was' I laughed at her play on words. 'You have no idea how hard'.

'I can see we are going to have to watch you. Right, to business. Everyone gets a standard Supplies pack. Everything you need for washing and personal care. You only get the one so look after it. Nothing wears out here so it should last a lifetime.'

It wasn't that funny but her laugh was so infectious that I joined in.

'Any ideas for Clothing?. You need standard day/work wear and something more exotic for going out. I get the feeling that you are happy with what you are wearing so I've put out jeans -32inch waist, 29 inside leg – with leather belt, tee shirt, casual shirt, a nice leather waistcoat I think you'll like, good shoes and socks, vests, knickers and handkerchiefs. You won't need a coat as it never gets cold here. Any ideas for evening wear?'

'You tell me. You seem to have got everything right so far. You must have a file on me?'

'Yes, of course. I have a file on the likes and dislikes of everyone who comes to this department. Two outfits might not seem like much but it does simplify things. No quandaries about what to wear, no competition or clashing with anyone else because we all know what everyone else will be wearing. I would recommend a nice pair of grey trousers, white dress shirt, dark blue tie and a nice fitting blazer. That'll cover any occasion and you can mix and match with your work stuff. You know about using the sonic shower for cleaning your clothes? Wonderful invention. Clothes are always clean and pressed and nothing ever wears out.'

'You are an angel' I let her know that I could word play with the best of them.

'Yep, on both counts' she giggled. 'They'll be delivered to your room some time this evening. Sorry, can't do it any faster. We're a bit busy at the moment. No, make that busy all the time'.

'How many people do you see in a day?'

'This department averages about 1,500 people a day' she informed me proudly.

'You can't do' I was expecting another leg pull. 'I've been here what, five minutes? That's twelve an hour. 24 hours times 12 is only 288 people at five minutes a time.'

'Yep, normal time' she agreed. 'But, in the Arrivals Hall, time isn't normal. It is a lot, lot slower than normal. As soon as you get outside the Arrival doors, time speeds up to normal. If it wasn't for the Time Displacement Rift, we would never ever catch up.'

Time Displacement Rift? This was getting more and more like an episode of Startrek by the minute. I grinned back. 'Yeah right'.

She shrugged her shoulders. 'You'll see. Right, Ageing. What age would you like to be? Have a think about it whilst I sort out the Language pill'.

Given the chance, what age would you choose? Childhood, Troublesome Teens, Teriffic Twenties? What was your best decade? I was reasonably happy being 46. Old enough to have experienced life, young enough to enjoy it.

I suppose if I was a woman, it would be that time when I had got rid of my virginity, could handle men and everything was firm and perky enough to attract them. Probably late teens to mid-twenties.

For men it was different. Male teens were a nightmare of chasing and trying to bed women, in constant competition with other males and deciding what you wanted out of life. The male twenties were a time of development, finding work in an area that gave satisfaction and the promise of security. The male twenties were a detour whilst you sorted out your life. I decided on 35 years of age as a nice age to be. Settled, confident, healthy, handsome and still with hair, hopefully. Whilst I still had the first four ticks, I could remember my 35 year old head of thick curly locks with fondness and regret. Not that I was bald but I was definitely thinning and not that happy about it. 35. Yep, definitely 35. I might even grow my moustache again.

'Good choice, Slater. Women like older men. They know what they want and they know how to give as well. I see that you already have language skills but you might as well have the whole package.. Give me a minute whilst I programme your pill and then you can swallow it and return to Accomodation'.

'She returned in under five minutes and handed over a shiny metallic capsule. 'Swallow this and, by the time you wake up in the morning, you'll be ten years younger and speak every language there is. Also, you will be able to find your way about outside, thanks to the GPS sat nav programme built into it. GPS stands for God's Personal Satellite, by the way'

I took it gingerly. 'What's in it or shouldn't I ask?'

'Nanoprobes' she said matter of factly. I didn't even bother to ask the question. I had seen enough sci-fi to know that nanoprobes were tiny robots that were programmed to undertake all sorts of tasks. And, once inside the body, they carried on working, multiplying and getting cleverer. I just popped it in my mouth and swallowed. Somehow I just knew it wasn't a joke.

The capsule didn't taste of anything, went down ok and didn't instantly poison me. I waited for a reaction. Nothing. I looked at Molly.

'I told you, it works overnight. You won't feel anything until the morning. Right, off you go. Tell the next person to come right in. See you around?'

I leaned over the counter and planted a big wet kiss on her cheek. 'Get off me, you silly bugger.' She sounded cross but the twinkle in her eyes gave her away.

I walked out the door. The man waiting outside was accompanied by a – you've guessed it – gorgeous young lady. He glanced at me as I told them to go in. He looked familiar but I couldn't instantly place him. They both went in and as the door closed I could hear Molly's voice. 'Patrick Swayze! Come in, come in, you have no idea of just how much I have been wanting to meet you'.

Humph, Patrick Swayze. I wonder what age he was going to choose. Probably about fifteen so that the ladies would want to mother him. I stomped back to Astra.

She was in a dither as well.

'Do you know who was just in here?'

'I suppose you are going to tell me it was that Ghost bloke' I played along.

'Oh, he's so fit. I am going to show him around his accommodation as soon as he comes back.'

'Does he have to share? Anyway, I thought he was going to the caravan tonight. You know, to settle in'.

'I just happened to have a suitable place come empty. The other three girls are coming over later.'

Bang goes my plans for the evening. I asked about my accommodation.

'It's on level 1,494 Archangel Gabriel House. Apartment number 666'

That's a bloody good start, I thought. House of the Angel, flat of the devil. I asked about my room mates.

'I would rather leave it as a surprise' Astra said with a chuckle. 'All I will say is that they know you and are expecting you. Oh, whilst I remember, here is your FAQ book. Frequently Asked Questions. This will answer most of your questions about Heaven. I'll get someone to guide you there. Until your navigation programme comes on-line, its probably safer. By the way, you were due to go to Work Allocation next but they have an emergency VIP allocation to sort out and can't see you until tomorrow at 9 am"

I picked the book up and shoved it under my arm. I was beginning to have the suspicion that my Grade 2 accommodation and work allocation had just been upgraded to VIP status. There didn't seem much to say. I waited for who ever was going to show me to my new home.

I didn't have long to wait. Within a few minutes, a small boy was tugging at my sleeve. He looked to be about ten or eleven. On reflection, he was the first small person –how PC am I? – I had seen in Heaven. He was dressed smartly in grey trousers, blue shirt and maroon blazer. His blue tie with yellow stripes, taken with the rest of his attire, probably meant school uniform.

'Where you going mate?' he enquired with a pronounced East End accent.

'Archangel Gabriel House, level 1,494. apartment number 666'

'Oh, the rough end. What you gone and done, eh?' he smirked.

'What do you mean, the rough end? I thought everything was a bit rough up here'.

"Yeah, well there's rough and there's rough. All the problem families get put in Gab House. That's in the English section'

'English section?

'Yeah, all the different countries have their own sections. So you get the Froggies, the Spics, the Krauts, all the others, in separate areas.. Tell you about it on the way'.

As I walked through the Arrivals doors, I experienced a light headed feeling. It only lasted a few seconds but was enough to be noticed by my gobby guide.

'Don't worry mate. It's only the Rift in the Time/Space continuum' he said matter of factly. 'You've been spending too much time in there. You'll soon feel ok. What is your name anyway?.

'John. John Slater' He was right. I did feel ok again.

'Righti ho, John John. I'm Alfred Howley-Smythe' he caught my look. 'Yeah, I know. Brought up in the East End, Me old man wins the jackpot on the Lottery and suddenly, we're bloody rich and posh. I gets taken out of me old school and all me mates, and put in this posh school with a new double barreled surname. Too posh for me old mates and too bloody common for those tossers in me new bleedin' school'.

'Must have been hard' I sympathized. 'How did you end up here then?'

'Got into a fight with one of them. Big bugger he was. I was doing all right though until he frew a lucky punch and knocked me down. Trouble was I hit me 'ead on a wall and that was it. Lights out and then 'ere. It's ok 'ere though'

By now we had reached the end of the road and were about to enter the Habitations. Talk about depressing. Still no vehicles, no pedestrians and, I suddenly realized, no animals. Didn't animals get to heaven then? I must find out later. In the meantime, I was having trouble keeping up with my guide.

'Going too fast for you guv?'

'How do you find your way? Everything looks the same'

'It's this map thing in me head, innit. Once yours comes on-line, you won't have no bovver.'

It was a strange and unsettling experience for me. Normally I am good at finding my way. Give me an address and I'll generally find it with the help of a map and asking directions. Here, I was totally lost. No map, no-one to ask directions and reliant on a small school boy who seemed intent on losing me.

Alfred obviously knew where he was going though. He ducked and dived through passageways, alleys and even through buildings. My problem was that everything looked exactly the same. Each grey and dingy Astroblock looked exactly like the last one. Each alley, each passageway, each grimy little yard all looked similar. A couple of the enclosed yards we went through had caravans in situ and the sight of them brought on an attack of nostalgia. Showed how bad my mental state was didn't it? Pining for a grotty caravan. Eventually, - after what seemed like miles but was probably only a few blocks – we stopped in front of one of the seemingly endless buildings. The sign on the front read .r.. Ang ...riel..ouse. Home sweet home! I could hardly wait. We pushed through the front doors. What do you think we found? Bright lights and sweet music? Tastefully decorated walls with rich carpeting on the floor? If you did, then you obviously haven't been paying attention.

Dismal grey concrete everywhere. The floor and the walls had that rough unfinished Jerry built look about them. Step into the middle of the small entrance area and there were two corridors left and right. I could see down each for about five doors and then no more. There were no overhead lights to pierce the darkness. The corridors could have gone on for miles or metres. There was no way of knowing.

Alfred walked over to a set of doors on the far wall. He pressed the button and they slid reluctantly back. 'Hope the bleeding fings working' he said as he walked in. 'Bloody long climb otherwise'. I crossed my fingers. 'Say a little prayer then. Naw, on second forts don't. Got told orf about that the other day. Apparently sudden prayers make God jump'

He pressed the appropriate buttons for Floor 1494. 'Doors closing' a familiar deep voice boomed back. Barry! I almost shouted. I don't think I would have got the words out if I had done.

You know when you are in a plane waiting on the runway to take off? Suddenly the brakes are released and the plane hurtles down the runway. Well, multiply that feeling by about a thousand fold and imagine that the plane is going straight up. That will give you the tiniest indication of what that lift felt like.

I could almost feel my bones compressing as I seemed to slam into the lift floor. I grabbed the rail and hung on, my eyes tightly shut and waited and waited for it to stop. It did. Slowing instantly from a thousand, billion, trillion miles per hour to full stop in a heartbeat. I just hope for the sake of all you Earthlings that Alton Towers doesn't get the opportunity to buy one of these Barry White Special lifts.

Speaking of Barry, his booming bass voice rang out 'Floor one thousand, four hundred and ninety four. Please disembark'.

Actually I didn't need the prompt Barry, thanks all the same. I floundered out of that lift like a drunken Brains from Thunderbirds.

Still on rubber legs, my guide and I –seemingly unaffected by the Lift from Hell/Heaven? – made our way along a long, long corridor. Finally we stopped in front of 666. With more trepidation than anticipation, I knocked on the door. I could hear grumbling from the other side as someone made their way to the door. I could hear multiple bolts and locks being pulled back and turned before the door finally opened. A complete stranger stood there with an enquiring look.

He was in his early twenties and dressed in fifties Teddy Boy gear. Drainpipe trousers with blue brothel creeper shoes –complete with thick crepe soles – Edwardian frock coat in velvet, white frilly shirt and bootlace tie. His sideburns went down deep on either side of his narrow face and atop of all this splendour was a greased and styled hairdo complete with a quiff that Quiff Richard himself would have envied.

'Err, Accommodation told me to report here. It is flat 666, isn't it?'

'Yes it is. Come on in, John' He put his arms around me. 'You've changed, mind it's been a while hasn't it?'

Been a while? Who was this guy? He was already making his way down the corridor. I pushed Alfred in first as protection and tagged along behind.

Inside, it was quite pleasant. Nice wallpaper on the walls and a decent thickness carpet underneath. We entered what I presumed was the living room. Again, a nice surprise - if you like fifties era décor. Yellow and green walls, leather armchairs and sofa, pictures on the wall and, obviously in pride of place, a jukebox stood in regal splendor against the far wall.

A petite girl got up from one of the armchairs. She was in her late teens I suppose and quite a looker. Nylon low neck blouse, flared skirt with layers of petticoats underneath and black pumps on her feet. She came across the room with her arms open wide. I backed off a little. I mean, just who were these people? Astra said that I had already lived with them but, for the death of me, I couldn't remember when. The girl finally got her arms around me and, stretching up on tiptoe, planted a long lingering kiss full on my lips. I kept my eyes on the Teddy Boy, half expecting a razor to suddenly appear. Instead he looked on with a fond little smile on his face. Had I wandered into some sort of Swingers Heaven by mistake?

'Come on John' she said. 'That isn't any way to treat your old Mum. Hasn't he grown Mike?' she asked. 'Sure has, Jean' Mike replied. 'Grade 2 eh? You've done us proud John'

Jean? Mike? Those were my parent's names. The parents I lost when a building collapsed on them when I was thirteen. But this couldn't be them. I mean, my memory was a bit hazy but I always remembered Mum as a plump little woman and my Dad as a bald headed middle aged man.

'Whoa, hang on a minute. There is obviously some mistake. My parents died when I was thirteen and they were both in their forties then. That was thirty three years ago. How can you possibly be them?'

'Haven't they told you about ageing then?' Mike/Dad asked.

The penny dropped. 'You choose to be this age?'

'Too right. Best years of our life; me and your mum both. Just after the war, plenty of energy, our own money, great gear and the best music ever.'

I didn't know whether to laugh or cry. My parents were younger than me! The next minute we were in a group hug and I suddenly found that I could laugh and cry at the same time.

"Can I go now then' little Alfred asked. I had forgotten all about him.

'Sure you can Alfie' Dad –that sounds so strange – told him.

'Ok then, I'll be back in the morning, about 8.30?' He cast an enquiring look at me. I looked blankly back. 'Job Allocation at 9?' he reminded me.

'If it's all right. Hang on a minute though. I thought you said my sat nav doda would be online by the morning?'

'It should be but I'll drop by in case it aint. Show you ow to use it, like. Here, Mr Slater, a little joke for you. The Vatican has just brought out a new low-fat, low-calorie, low-cholesterol communion wafer. Guess what its called? I Can't **B**elieve it's Not Jesus'.

'Get on with you Alfie. Give my regards to your Mum'. Dad escorted him to the door. He was still chuckling when he returned. 'Cor, he's a little bugger that Alfie. Good kid though. Nice he's back with his mum. She passed over last year. Before that, he was living with his grandparents. Right son, you must be hungry. What's for tea, Jean?'

Talk about weird. These two were strangers and yet, they weren't. My parents –my Earth parents, I reminded myself – had died thirty three years ago and, truth be told, I barely remembered them. Yeah sure, when I thought about them I had flashbacks of a jolly plump woman and an out-at- work all day Dad who didn't say much. And, back at the room where I stayed with Peter and Elizabeth Tiler –when I wasn't in my truck – I had a photo album that I hadn't looked at in years. And yet, as I shared a meal of egg, chips and beans with these two young and vibrant people, I kept getting glimpses of their older, future, faces peaking through. They were my parents but I was older than them. Confusing or what?

After the meal, we talked. I learnt that this Astroblock contained most of our relatives stretching back through the generations. I learnt that Heaven was a bit like Earth in that it was separated into different countries. There was no physical land or sea divide between the countries, like on Earth, but a sort of No-Man's land between the Astroblock Nations that served as a border.

There was no Heavenly decree that prohibited the natives of each country from entering another country or State as they were called. However, most people stayed within their own State by choice. Perhaps they were clinging onto the familiar sights and sounds, cultures they knew, what they were used to.

Even immigrants, who had lived and died in a foreign country, maybe for many years, usually elected to return to the land of their birth.

So, despite the billions of souls that inhabited this one Heaven, they were fragmented over many Heaven States and there was little or no traveling or communication between different States. A bit, I suppose, like people from the 13th or 14th Century who knew vaguely that there was a big wide world out there but who seldom traveled outside of a 20 mile radius of their own village.

From what I was being told, Heaven existed for the locals within the very small boundaries of their own and neighbouring Astroblocks.

As we talked, I found myself really liking Mike and Jean. Obviously I loved, had loved, them because they were my parents but now I liked them as individuals. The young, vibrant and exciting kids they were before marriage, parenthood and responsibility had worn them down, kicked them in the teeth and robbed them of their youth, looks and energy.

'What about work? What do you do?' I asked.

'I'm a chippy, a carpenter' Dad declared proudly. 'I work on the Astroblock Maintenance Programme. Usually I am repairing things or putting up more partitions to make more room for Newcomers. Your Mum's in Hydroponics. She grows fresh vegetables in liquid without any earth. It's an important job. Any job in Foodstuff is. The replicators can make lettuce, cucumbers and the like but it isn't energy efficient and they taste like crap.'

They told me more. Of the constant building and rebuilding of the Blocks. Higher and higher, bigger and bigger. The need to utilize every centimeter of useable space.. The battle to provide lodgings and fresh food for a population that grew by the thousands every day, every week, month, year until...........?

'There won't be any where left to put another Astroblock anywhere on Earth Heaven?' Dad warned. 'Then? Then The Boss will either have to create another larger Earth Heaven or we have to go to Alien Heaven'.

'Alien Heaven?' I asked. This was a new one. I had been taught that there was only one Heaven – yeah, forget all that Milk and Honey crap – and that everyone ended up there. I still wasn't sure that I totally forgave Brother Simon for filling my

head with all that other nonsense. But, hey, maybe he hadn't been told the whole story either.

'All the other planets, all those that support life that is, have their own Heaven. There is Venus Heaven, Saturn Heaven, Mars Heaven, all of them have their own version of Earth Heaven. Same problems, same overcrowding. I tell you, son, Heaven has gone to Hell'. Mike smiled at his own joke.

'Leave him now Mike. He must be tired and it's all too much to take in one go anyway. He'll find out for himself. Come on John, I'll show you your room'

My room was barely big enough to contain a narrow bed and small cupboard. Mum turned down the Aston Villa duvet cover –I hadn't supported them for years – and opened the cupboard. Obviously my new clothing had arrived before me. Good old Molly.

'I'll show you the bathroom. You know about the Sonic shower and Vacuum bog I guess? That's about it then. I'd try and get some sleep. I remember just how strange everything was the first couple of days. All those beliefs and expectations shattered. It's not so bad here. It's nice not having any aches and pains, no worry about making ends meet, all your relatives nearby, so it's ok. One thing everyone likes is the entertainment. That's out of this world' Jean laughed.

'Entertainment? What, you mean the telly?'

'No telly up here anymore. It got too expensive to make all those tv sets, maintain them and such a palaver about getting the programmes. Every State wanted their own tv shows and there just weren't enough satellites to cover everything. Anyway, the Boss reasoned, all these dead entertainers, who needed tv? And, as usual, He was right. Most nights we go out to see a show, hear some music, watch a play. All free. Couple of nights ago, Mike and I saw Elvis Presley. Can you image that? Actually seeing Elvis perform. He was supported by Billy Fury and Buddy Holly.

John Lennon and George Harrison were in the audience and they came on stage and it turned into quite a jamming session.'

'I'd have loved to see that'. Elvis had always been a favorite of mine. Suddenly I could see the possibilities. I began compiling a list of dead artist as I got into bed. I kissed Mum goodnight - although it was still a bit weird kissing someone you would prefer to snog the face off – and closed my eyes. As I got comfortable, I carried on with my list. Elvis, of course, Buddy Holly, Roy Orbison, Red Sovine, Jimmi Hendr……………

SEVEN

Peter Tiler had taken a few days off work. After hearing of John Slater's death, he felt that he wouldn't have been safe on the road. Too many memories to distract him.

He remembered John as a thirteen year old who came to live with his middle aged aunt and uncle after his parents had died. Both of them at the same time. Out shopping in Rugby and suddenly, the façade on the top half of an old building had collapsed on them. Suddenly orphaned, the teenager had kept to himself for a long time. Gradually, he appeared more and more in the close where Peter and Elizabeth lived with their son and daughter. Once, Peter remembered, he had brought a new truck home to show off. Looking out the window admiringly, he had spotted John Slater at the side of the truck. Quickly going outside, probably fearing vandalism, he saw the look on the youngster's face. He knew that look. He unlocked the door and proudly showed the truckstruck kid the interior.

John had climbed up and, seated at the wheel, had looked around and confidently announced that he was going to be a trucker one day.

When John first asked if he could come out with him one day, Peter hadn't been too keen. Probably he had felt that his own son should have been the one but he wasn't interested. After putting John off many times, he had finally relented. Going round to his neighbour's house, he had asked if it was ok for their nephew to come out for the day with him. A quiet boy, John didn't have many friends and probably spent more time alone than was good for him.

His uncle thought that it would be good for the youngster to get out a bit more.

After that first trip, Peter had been badgered for more. Soon every school holiday, John Slater and Peter were on the road. The youngster's enthusiasm for the trucking life was obvious and his mentor gladly imparted the knowledge and wisdom he had gathered over the years.

Peter himself understood that enthusiasm and hunger. Born in a little village called Scarning, just outside East Dereham in Norfolk, he spent a lot of time in his front garden just watching the trucks going past on the A47 trunk road. Leaving school at sixteen, he had become a driver's mate and began the same sort of apprenticeship he was now giving another truck mad youngster. When he was old enough, his first driving job had been in an old Bedford TK truck collecting chickens from farms and delivering them to the nearby meat factory.

Not the most exciting job but good experience. Soon the trucks got bigger and the jobs better. Eventually he was driving all over the UK, leaving on a Monday morning and arriving back at base on a Saturday morning or afternoon.

Along the way, he had met and married Elizabeth. Meeting her wasn't hard because she lived in the next village and they had been to school together. The reason for moving to Rugby wasn't clear in his memory but he had been there long enough to think of it as his home town.

As the bond between himself and the young Slater had developed, both he and Elizabeth had begun to think they had gained a new family member. When his own kids had left home, John had filled the gap in their lives. So, when his aunt and uncle decided to move to sheltered accommodation, it was an easy decision to make when John decided he wanted to stay in the area. He moved into the spare room and lived with them as family.

Of course, he wasn't there all that often once he got his truck licence. Mainly at weekends, and the occasional night, when he first started driving trucks. Then, only on weekends, after he graduated to continental work. Mainly, he had nights out in his truck.

After his aunt and uncle had died and left him a sizeable inheritance, it was possible for him to buy his own truck and trailer and become an owner operator. With the vast distances of continental work to keep him satisfied, they saw less and less of him as John Slater virtually lived in his Magnum truck.

Only now he had died in it.

Even though the body hadn't been released from post mortem yet, Peter had already begun to plan the funeral of his almost-adopted son. During the countless hours they had been together in one truck or another, they had talked about everything. Even death; an always present possibility on ever crowded roads.

So he knew exactly what John would have wished for his funeral. Planning it now kept the very reason for that funeral from Peter's mind. He and Elizabeth had both shed their tears and now the big trucker was determined to give John Slater, trucker and best friend, a suitable departure to the land of ever lasting roads, far horizons and big, fast showtrucks. It was, in fact, that last item that was currently giving him the most problems.He knew many drivers who had showtrucks. Working trucks that had all the extra chrome, paint and accessories to transform them from ducklings into elegant swans. Trucks that regularly competed against other such trucks at events like Truck Fest where the best and the hopefuls from the UK and Europe competed against each other.

Events that were held in places like Peterborough Showground, where drivers polished, cleaned, paraded and showed off their vehicles. Lines and lines of big, expensive and obsessively turned out trucks that competed to catch the eye of the judges . Events where the truck struck and the envious could overindulge on the sights and sounds of their version of Heaven. He and John had attended, and won, many such events in John's own customized Renault Magnum. That particular vehicle would win no more prizes for Best Owner Driver Truck. It, or what was left of it, was now in a compound down in Kent somewhere waiting for Peter to salvage what he could of John's possessions.

Thankfully, most of the paperwork for the Renault was still in the bedroom where John stayed on his rare weekends off. Peter had already contacted the insurance company and was waiting for the claim forms to arrive. That it was going to be a mess to sort out he already knew. It wasn't just the truck but the trailer and the goods to be claimed for as well. He had already spoken to the transport manager of Coventry Continental Transport where John had been a valued subcontractor for the last three years. Here, it wasn't the loss of the goods that concerned them but the death of their most reliable and experienced owner driver.

Now, the insurance procedures were under way and there wasn't much Peter could do until the insurance assessor did his job and got back to him.

All he had to do now was find a suitable vehicle to bring his friend's body back to Rugby and his final journey to Coventry's Canley Crematorium.

Although he knew the owners of many such vehicles, it was the timing that was the problem. Because John's body hadn't been released from post mortem, it couldn't be collected by the undertaker and be prepared. Without a definite date to work from, no definite plans could be made. In the meantime, Peter couldn't expect busy truck drivers to wait around for some future and undeclared date. John Slater wouldn't have wanted fellow owner operators to lose money because of him. But, at the same time, a vehicle would have to be booked so that the rest of the funeral arrangements could go ahead. Of course, a normal hearse would get the job done but that wasn't what Peter wanted and he knew what John would have wanted. Catch 22 or what? He decided to go down to the allotment, get some exercise and hopefully clear his head.

The Kent allotments were council owned and contained forty one plots. Of these only thirty four, due to boggy conditions, were workable. Some people had rented and worked the same plot for years. Other plots had a fast turn-around as newcomers who were initially full of enthusiasm – fuelled by gardening programmes on the telly where crops were planted, grew and were harvested with minimum work and maximum results – took over plots and, just as quickly left them as they realized the amount of effort required to grow vegetables that could be more easily and painlessly purchased at the supermarket. But, as the regular allotment holders knew, growing crops was just a bonus.

Allotments were for getting exercise, hiding from the wife in one of the various ramshackle sheds that got cobbled together, talking to other regulars or for being on your own to contemplate nature , to relax or to just think out a problem.

Peter Tiler parked up his big, black and beautiful –to his eyes – Ford pick-up truck and used his key to unlock the metal gate. His plot was five numbers down a path almost directly opposite the gates. He opened up his shed – like most of them, a home made effort of salvaged wood and corrugated iron sheets –took out his fork and began to dig. Simple exercise with little mental requirement, it kept him in reasonable shape –provided he remembered to pull in his thickening waist line – and provided definite results. And, after the last few hours, definite results were just what he needed right now.

At the end of the first turned over trench, he took a breather and looked around. Old Pete wandering about in one of his three plots. John Armstrong digging. George hoeing at the far end. Wally just coming out his garden gate directly into his plot and the new couple, Dave and Lynne. Well, not quite new as this was their third year, but still regarded as such by the Kent hierarchy. Probably another couple of years and they would be viewed as regulars by the old guard. Even an allotment had its snobbery and pecking order.

Because of his job, Peter's allotment appearances were a bit spasmodic but, over the last year, he had developed a friendship with 'the new couple'. So much so that, whenever he was there, they called him up for a coffee they brewed on a gas ring in their shed. As he was thinking it, a piercing whistle made him look up. Dave was holding up a cup and shaking it. Gratefully leaving his digging, he made his way to the top of the allotments and onto plot No 1. On the paved area between the metal shed and greenhouse were three garden chairs and a table. An empty chair and a full cup of coffee showed him where to sit and he did so gratefully.

'Morning Peter, you ok?' Lynne asked. She was a bubbly woman, recently retired and obsessed with her allotment. Her husband was also retired and they made a good team together. She was 'technical' and he was 'maintenance' meaning she planned and planted and he did the heavy digging.

'Not so good' Peter replied after a sip of coffee. Dave gave him an enquiring look and he told them what had happened.

Dave was an ex trucker who had become an owner operator with first one truck then, as business grew, adding a further two. After years of international work to the continent and Middle East – a member of the famed 'Overland to Iran' band of pioneering truckers who drove their trucks all the way to Saudi Arabia and beyond in the seventies – he had woken up in his truck one morning in Malden, Essex, and decided that was it for him.

Within a couple of weeks he had sold his business and retired at forty three. And, just like Peter, had also become bored and returned to work as a freelance transport journalist. With his trucking background, his articles had an authenticity and passion which both drivers and operators could relate to. Soon as well as writing about trucks and truckers, he was in demand for road testing and development with the truck manufacturers. Three years ago, after twenty five years of truck driving and nearly twenty of writing for truckers and helping develop safer and more comfortable trucks, he had once again retired. Now in his mid sixties, he was a quiet, confident man with a wicked sense of humour.

Peter knew he would understand and relate to just how he was feeling. 'That's really tough Peter' he said with sympathy. 'Anything I can do to help?'

'Not unless you know someone who has a showtruck available at short notice' he replied and went on to tell them of his funeral plans and the problems he was having in organizing them.

Dave surprised him with his reply 'No problem. I know just the truck and it doesn't do anything other than drive to shows and win prizes. It is even parked up in Kent. The guy owns me a few favours. I got him a lot of publicity with some articles and I reckon it's time to collect. You ever handle a left hooker Peter? No? That might be a problem because, not surprisingly, the guy won't let just anyone drive it. Tell you what though, how about if I drive it for you?'

'That would be just great. Can you really get one just like that?' Peter asked a little fearfully, afraid that it might be just talk and not develop into anything.

'Peter, I wouldn't mess you about with anything as important as this. You know what I used to do for a living' Dave told him quietly and sincerely. 'I can guarantee you the best showtruck in Europe because that's just one of the awards this truck has won. In fact, let's take it a step further and do something else on this. I'll contact some magazine editors I know and try to get some publicity for you. I might be just in time to get something out for most of next month's mags. I'll try for next week's Commercial Motor as well. I didn't know John Slater but, from what you have told me, I would have liked him. He was a trucker, a damn good one, and that's enough for me. We truckers always take care of our own. That's the code, Stu. You know that. It would be an honour and a privilege to do this for him'.

Peter finished his coffee with misty eyes.

EIGHT

When I opened my eyes, I knew instantly where I was. So, that was obviously an improvement. I also knew I had slept well because I had that slightly groggy feeling you get after a really good night's sleep. Just as I was thinking about getting up, there was a knock on the door. Jean's /Mum's hand appeared and pushed the door open. She was carrying a tray with a mug of tea and two rounds of toast and marmalade.

'Morning John love, did you sleep well?' she asked as she put the tray down.

"Yeah, great, thanks Mu…Jean' I was still a little unsure of what to call her. 'Look, would you be offended if I called you and Dad, Jean and Mike? I just can't get my head around calling two people younger than me Mum and Dad'

'It must be a bit weird. You just call us whatever comes naturally. Anyhow, have you looked in the mirror yet? Not that much difference now. Don't be too long. Remember you have a job interview at nine'.

Look in the mirror? Come to think of it, I hadn't looked in a mirror since I came here. I knew what I looked like. I had a sip of tea and started on the toast. Surprisingly, I felt full of energy and was raring to go. Wonder what sort of job I would be allocated? I finished the tea and toast and began to put on my new clothes. Everything fitted. Resplendent in my new gear, I made my way to the bathroom. Mike was just coming out.

'I'd give it a minute if I was you son' he said. 'Jean told me what you said and you just call us whatever feels the most comfortable. Like your new look by the way. Good choice'

You'd think that in Heaven you wouldn't have to crap or pee or that at least it would be odourless. Walking into the bathroom after Mike disproved both those theories. If there had been a window, I would have opened it. Holding my breath, I went into the shower cubicle and switched on. Again, the needles and pins sensation over my body and, after a couple of minutes, the machine switched off. As I walked out, I looked down and saw that the creases on my new clothes had all dropped out. I looked up and saw myself in the small mirror or rather, I saw someone who looked like me… only different.

As the image duplicated all my movements, I knew it had to be me. Of course, Aging. Oh Wow, all my thick curls back, tighter, firmer face with less wrinkles around the eyes and no sign of the small double chin I had recently begun to develop. I flexed my arms and legs. Yeah, definitely better. Pulling up my tee shirt, I sucked in my stomach and saw that I had a six pack again. Good choice Slater and, just think, this was me for the rest of my life or, to be more accurate, death and eternity. Well, I think I could live with that, thank you very much.

'Survived it did you?' Mike joked. 'You should have been here during the energy crisis of the 80s. No regular lighting and only able to red button the bog when absolutely necessary. It really did stink then. I remember I came in one morning and saw your Mum jumping up and down on the seat trying to close it. I told her we HAD to empty it occasionally. How do you like your new look by the way? Happy with your choice?'

'Yeah, great. Still look older than you two though. By the way, Mike, does the sonic shower shave you as well? I haven't shaved recently and I'm still baby smooth. I was hoping to grow my moustache again'.

'Yes, it does but how it removes facial hair for men and body hair for women without leaving you bald is beyond me. Not many beards up here except for the Disciples, Archangels and the Committee. If you want to grow anything on your face, you need to get your nanoprobes reprogrammed. Doesn't take long, I had to have it done for my sideburns'.

Just then there was a knock on the door and Jean went to answer it. She came back with young Alfred Howley-Smythe. He gave me an approving look.

'Suits yuh' he decided. 'I ave to wait until I am at least thirty before I gets to decide my Eternity age. Ere, got a joke for you, Mr Slater. God is resting on the seventh day and admiring the world he has created. He decides it need more people so he calls Adam and Eve over and tells them to start having kids.

'How do we do that Lord?' asks Adam

'First you have to kiss Eve' God explains

'What's a kiss, Lord?' God explains and Adam and Eve go into the bushes and come out some time later.

'Right, done that. It was nice. What's next Lord?'

God says he has to caress Eve and tells him how to do it. They go into the bushes and come back much later.

'Really enjoyed that, Lord. Is that it?'

'No, now you have to make love to Eve'

'How do I do that Lord?' God explains to Adam and they both go into the bushes. Adam comes out a couple of minutes later and says 'Lord, what's a headache?'

Outside on the corridor, I was still chuckling. 'How come you aren't at school?' I asked Alfie.

'Only go to school twice a week, don't I? Rest of the time, I run errands and show Newcomers where to go'

'How does my navigation thing work? What do I have to do?'

'You ave to fink where you're going and just go. It's easy peasy. Tell you what, we both set orf togevver and see who gets there first. Orl right?'

I didn't get chance to reply as he was already legging it down the corridor. I thought 'Job Allocation, Arrivals Hall' and set off after him. It was immediately apparent that losing those ten years had done wonders for my stamina. I felt like a new man. Well, actually, I felt like a new woman but that would have to wait until later.

I never did catch Alfie as he got the lift before me and I had to wait for it's return. I had forgotten about the lift but really didn't fancy walking down all those stairs either: 1,494 floors, how many stairs would that be? The lift arrived back in very short time. Short enough to make me think that maybe the stairs would be better after all.

I have never parachuted out of a plane but I now have some idea of just what it must feel like. Compared to the lift, it would be bloody slow. The moment I pressed the button, I felt that the lift floor had opened and I was dropping with about five tons strapped on my back. I kept my mouth so firmly shut that my teeth hurt. How I didn't pebble dash the lift interior with tea and toast, God knows. Well, He probably did. I could swear that my legs pushed past my ears as the lift stopped. Barry told me to depart and I did.

Whilst I waited for my heartbeat to return to normal and my legs to return to their normal size, I looked around the lobby. No sign of Alfie, no sign of anyone. Just where were all the overcrowded souls? So far, apart from the Arrival Hall, I had met exactly three people; Mike, Jean and Alfie.

It was exactly the same outside. Just rows of Astroblocks. Run down, grimy, neglected, litter everywhere. No vehicles, no bikes, no nothing except block after block after block adnauseum. I set off for Arrivals. That was easy. Without even thinking about it, I dodged between blocks, down corridors, across backyards and down alleyways. I used shortcuts that I didn't even know existed but just knew that it was quicker to go down there, cut across there and dodge in here. I was a Navigating God.

Running up the hill – yes, actually running, my toned leg muscles pumping up and down like pistons – I arrived at Arrivals. I stepped almost desperately through the doors such was my need to see people. Just inside the threshold –now that I was expecting it –I could almost see the difference in Time or maybe I just imagined it. Whatever. Just seeing crowds of people was enough and I wasn't imagining them.

People everywhere. Lost and bewildered people. People talking to each other in groups or singly. People shouting, arguing, crying. Pacing up and down looking for something, someone to reassure them. People queuing at the various desks. People of all hues in every hue of clothing imaginable. Wonderful, wonderful people everywhere.

It was a bit like the first time I went to the continent. That was in a truck and I had no proper maps, no languages and no experience. After a week of virtually not speaking and just using sign languagc and shoving bits of paper under people's noses, I was back in England. Words that I could understand and being able to interact with people again was such a wonderful experience. After a week of virtual isolation – even Radio 2 deserted me after Prague – I was amongst people again. The noise and bustle of Arrivals was a bit like that.

I spotted Celeste and waved. She obviously didn't recognize the younger, fitter and incredibly more handsome John Slater and gave me the sort of look I got after failed chat-up lines.

I spotted Work Allocation and knocked on the door just before my appointment deadline. This time I was under no illusions about what to expect décor-wise and I wasn't disappointed. Same grey walls and ceiling and standard issue desk and chairs. What did surprise me was that it was a middle-aged man at the desk. I was so used to finding gorgeous girls, yes even Molly, behind the desk that it was a surprise to find a bloke. But, as I got closer, bloke was probably not the right word. Not unless you were used to seeing blokes with black guyliner, blusher and a hint of shimmer on his lips. His dark hair was brushed forward from the back – way, way, back – and ended in a kisscurl. Somehow, I guessed he batted for the other side. Probably the bright red flared trousers, - with braces,yes, braces - yellow shirt and red bandana helped me make that deduction.

Let me say here and now, I have nothing against gays. I just didn't meet many on the road. I used to know a gay guy at Folkestone docks. He ran the Hole in the Wall snack bar and used to serve me with hot dogs and always let it be known that he would have preferred to serve me a sausage without the roll. Actually I got on all right with Dereck who was so obviously camp that it was no surprise when he asked what you wanted with a lisp and a wink.

Anyway I digress. The name badge informed me that this guy's name was Colin Burke. He was older than me, about my height –I am only four inches short of six foot two – and slim. Except, that is, for the protruding belly that made him look about seven months pregnant. Maybe he hadn't had to time to get his ageing nanoprobes yet? If this was his idea of his best looking age, I would hate to see his worst.

'Oh hello, I'm Colin' he pronounced it Co-lin and, no surprise, lisped. 'You must be John Slater. I am very pleased to meet you John' he stuck out a small hand that was decidedly limp at the wrist. I shook it gingerly and resisted the impulse to wipe my hand on my trouser leg. Yeah, I know. Just give me time, that's all. 'You're my first Grade 2. I've only been here five months and am still learning the ropes. Did you get settled in ok?'

'A bit strange, Co-lin. My parents turned out to be younger than me. And, I positively hate that lift. I have an inner ear problem and lifts that fast make me nauseous. I'll have to have a word with Celeste in Accommodation to see if I can get something on the ground floor'.

'Humph" Co-lin replied putting his hand on my arm and giving it a little squeeze. 'That might not be necessary. I have a job that will suit you perfectly and has its own living arrangements'

If he even started to hint that I move in with him, I was out of here. I lifted his hand off my arm and, in a creditable impersonation of Barry White, asked for details. Keep it subtle for the moment, I told myself.

'I see from your record that you are a truck driver' he said in a hurt little voice. 'It just so happens that I have a driving job going and' he got his own back by drawing out the moment 'you even get your own truck back. What do you think of that then?' What did I think? Was the guy mad? I could have kissed him. Gays are such wonderful, caring and sensitive people, don't you think?

Then my cynical side stepped in. Was this legit? Was he just trying to get his hands on my firm young body? I asked for more details.

'Most of the time, goods are moved around Heaven States by transporter' he saw my look. 'Yes, just like on Star Trek. Alien Heavens have had the technology for years. Where do you think we got replicators and sonic showers from? We had to do a deal with the Ferengi. Anyways, transporters are very efficient in moving small quantities of goods around the States but quite heavy on energy. Six months ago, the Committee decided that it might be more efficient and energy saving to revert to the more traditional methods. At the moment, it is going to be a three month trial. If it works , then you have a permanent job, if you want it, of course'.

Did I want it? What do you think? Of course I wanted it but there were still a few questions to be answered.

' Have you seen the roads out there? No? Maybe that's because there aren't any. I could drive between the Astroblocks just about when there are no people about but what happens when there are? And that is another question. If everyone works here, then where are they? Why is it always deserted outside?'

'Most of them work on rebuilding. This place is a permanent building site. Others work on the hydroponics areas growing vegetables. The reason you don't see anyone is because they all travel around underground. Each Astroblock connects with each other and people leave their accommodation, travel to the basements and then use the air tubes to get to where ever they need to be.'

This was getting more like sci-fi every minute. Transporters, Ferengi's, underground commuting, air tubes. What the hell were air tubes?

'Have you seen those old fashioned shops on the telly?' Co-lin explained. 'You know, the ones where the assistants are always polite? Well, have you seen how they take the money off the customer and put it into a little cylinder, pop the cylinder into a tube, pull a lever and the cylinder disappears? Well, that is the principle of the air tubes. Just on a bigger scale. Tube carriages fit exactly into vacuum tunnels, the end of the tunnel seals and the carriage is sucked to it's destination. Very similar to the Tube underground systems in big cities but using a vacuum instead of electric trains to pull the carriages. Very energy efficient at moving large numbers of people.'

Oh well, another one of Heaven's mysteries explained. But I wasn't finished yet.

'You said I would get my own truck back. Well, I'm no mechanic but, after slamming into the motorway bridge support, I reckon it would take more than a few new parts to get that truck up and running again"

'Oh yes, your truck was a total write off. You hit that support so hard that you imprinted the manufacturer's name into the concrete. However, you are still thinking in Earth terms. Once the Committee decided that it was your Time, - it's like a big Lottery draw every week – arrangements were made to make an exact copy of your truck and trailer, just before you crashed, and transport them here. We had to use The Big 'un for that. She's a huge replicator and transporter that can beam anything really big from anywhere to Heaven. We only use her very sparingly because of the huge energy drain and because she's old and there are no spare parts available for her anymore. And, before you ask, no, she can't just replicate spare parts for herself. The Ferengis have put a control node in her to prevent that. Basically, they want us to buy a new one and we can't afford it. So yes, Mr Slater, your truck and trailer are in Maintenance being checked over and modified. I suggest you go there, see for yourself and then report to Traffic for your work allocations. Any problems, come and see me anytime. Look, I'll even give you my address in case anything pops up after office hours'.

I took the piece of paper from Co-lin and put it into my back pocket. I still had the sneaky suspicion that he had other designs for my back pocket and things that popped up. Must learn to get rid of these nasty Earth thoughts and think only pure Heavenly ones. I left the Work Allocation office with relief and excitement.

Celeste still looked busy and as there was no sign of Angelica –probably still fussing over Swayze – I decided it was coffee time. I went over to Molly's office and stuck my head in the door. She was busy with a customer/client? and barely looked up. I suppose she didn't recognize me either. 'Molly, it's John Slater' I reminded her. She glanced over and, finally, gave me a beaming smile. 'Molly, is there a canteen around here? I'm gagging for a coffee and something to eat. I also have some really exciting news'.

'Canteen at the far end of the Hall' she said. 'I'm on a break in five minutes so I can meet you there. White, no sugar for me and an iced Danish.'

I left her to it and went to find the canteen. Inside, there were lots of people sitting, walking around or chatting in groups. You could tell the staff because they all looked young –well most of them. I spotted Brother Simon and he still hadn't taken his Young pill – and their clothes were nicely pressed.

The line at the replicators wasn't too bad and I had barely got what I wanted and found a couple of seats before Molly plonked herself down beside me. She drank most of her coffee in one long gulp and half the Danish swiftly followed.

'Oh, I needed that. What a morning. We have got a lot of tsunami flood victims in today and they are so confused, poor dears. Anyhow, I like the new look. I could quite fancy you myself if Celeste doesn't want you anymore. Now, what's the news?'

'Well, apparently I am getting my truck back and going driving again.'

She frowned. 'I didn't know we needed drivers up here. Where are they going to go? There are no roads of any use and what are you going to carry? Who told you this?'

I repeated everything Co-lin had told me. She still looked skeptical. 'Are you sure he's not just trying to get into your pants?'

'I'm sure he is' I held up the address he had given me. 'But, I have been told to report to Traffic so I can find out then.'

'Well, I hope it works out. Just don't get your hopes up to much. That twat has been in trouble before, promising jobs that weren't available. He only got the position because he used to work for an agency on Earth . I don't know how he made it here in the first place. Look, I have to get back' she took Co-lin's piece of paper from me and, using the pen from behind her ear, wrote something on it. 'Here's our address. Pop round after six and have something to eat and a natter. Then we can either celebrate or commiserate with you. Cel and Angel are pretty good at both.' She gave me a wink and left.

Bugger, that was a bit of a blow. Just when I had got my hopes up as well. I was finishing my drink when someone asked if it was all right to sit down. I looked up and saw Celeste beaming down at me.

'I knew it was you' she said triumphantly. 'My, don't you look good' she leaned over and gave me a quick peck on the lips. 'How do you feel now?'

The taste of her lips and the smell of her perfume was starting to wake up Little John. She must have seen something in my eyes because she grinned and ran her tongue over her lips. I thought about grabbing her and letting Big John have his way with her over the canteen table. I decided it wasn't quite appropriate.

'I'm feeling really excited' I told her. 'And, before you get any ideas, I was feeling quite excited before you came over. That Molly is really something, isn't she?' I couldn't resist it and was rewarded with a spark of jealousy in her eyes.

'Humph, well, it you don't want me here…' she began. I didn't let her finish.

'Of course, I want you here. I have been thinking of you all night' I gave the full Slater treatment. Big smile, puppy-dog eyes and reaching across for her hand.

'Well, that's all right then' she held my hand and sat down again. 'Now, apart from me and Molly, just why are you so excited?'

I told her and she got excited as well. 'Oh, I've never been in a truck before. Can I come out with you some time?'

I explained that I might have to sleep in the truck some nights if I ran out of hours. Oh come on! You really believe a simple thing like driving hours would bother me? It never bothered me on Earth and what could happen here? Some angel chasing me on a cloud with a blue light attached. Some guy in a uniform giving me a fine? I don't think so. No, in typical Slater fashion, I was testing the water, throwing out a few breadcrumbs, running an idea up the flagpole and see if she saluted it.

'Oh, I see' her face fell. An idea was suddenly born and she delivered it. 'Aren't there two bunks in sleeper cabs? I am sure someone told me there were'

There were and, no, I wasn't going to admit it just yet. 'In my truck, I specified the single, extra wide bunk and had storage fitted where the second bunk would have been'

'That's all right then. I can have the bunk and you can sleep across the seats. I suppose it has a bathroom and everything?' I suddenly had the feeling that maybe the dumb blonde act wasn't just an act.

I shook my head. 'No, there isn't and I can't sleep across the seats. I need my rest and it would be too uncomfortable.'

She considered this. 'I guess you'll just have to sleep in the bed with me then' she announced in a 'Gotcha" tone of voice and laughed out loud. 'Honestly, your face. It was a picture. Just how dumb do you think I am, Slater? I was knocking back blokes like you when you weren't even a twinkle in your dad's eye.'

I guess I was in then. Another thing I was equally sure about was what would happen to Camp Co-lin if he was messing me about. He wouldn't need a lisp. He would talk Falsetto and sing *Castrati*.

I needed to get across to Traffic just as soon as I could.

NINE

'Hi, Pete. It's Dave. How are you keeping? Oh good. Look mate, I need a favour. I need a bit of publicity'

True to his word, Dave Williams was phoning around. Peter Minnis, the publisher of Trucking International was the last on his list. Peter was himself an ex owner driver and would understand and identify with Dave's request.

When he finally put the phone down, Dave was satisfied. He had contacted the editors of the many transport publications he had freelanced for and explained what he wanted and why. Some of the magazines had already been 'put to bed' –meaning they were finished and at the printers - which meant he was too late for the next edition. Of the ones he caught in time, he had the promise of a short editorial and, more importantly, updates on each of the publications websites. With hindsight, he realized that this method of keeping the readers in touch was probably the most efficient method of getting his message across.

He rang back the editors he had contacted too late for publication and got them to agree to website updates as well. That way, as soon as Peter Tiler had any news, it could be loaded onto the website. If he knew drivers, once one had seen the John Slater story it would spread like wildfire. In his day it had been the cb radio; today it was the mobile phone that was the trucker's communication method of choice.

Mike Henshaw, the owner of the award winning Kenworth showtruck had already been contacted by Dave. Even if he didn't owe the ex journalist a massive favour, Mike would have agreed anyway. He lived not far from where the accident had happened and had heard all about it. In fact, he knew the father of one of the children that John Slater had saved.

Apart from the free publicity involved, Mike felt that it was an honour that his truck should be involved in the funeral arrangements. In fact, thinking about the funeral had given him an idea that he was currently pursuing. He decided to phone Dave Williams to sound him out.

'Dave, it's Mike. Look, I've had an idea and have been seeing if it's feasible. The father of one of the kids that John Slater saved is a friend of mine. He also runs a small specialist company just outside Faversham. Basically, he makes bespoke coffins. Yeah, I know it sounds a bit strange but there are many people out there who want something different. He is currently working on one that resembles an Orient Express railway carriage. Anyhow, he knows about my passion for trucks and, some time ago, invited me over to see a coffin that a client had ordered and he had just finished.

He keeps all these specials in a storage shed until they are needed. Sometimes the customers take them home…no, I don't know why. Perhaps they want to try them out for size or something. Anyway, this one he wanted me to see is in the shape of an American truck. Yeah, it's great. Actually, I've ordered one for myself. The thing is, if the customer is willing, he'll build him another one and use this one for John. His way of thanking the guy who saved his kid from injury or worse. Would that be ok? Yes? I thought it would be. It all depends on whether the customer will agree.

Well, no, he can't build one anyway. Apparently they take weeks to build because of the unusual shapes and the amount of painting involved. I'll get back to you. Cheers Dave'. Putting the phone down, Mike Henshaw decided he would keep his fingers crossed.

'Peter? It's Dave. Look the guy who owns the Kenworth has agreed to let us use his truck but has also come up with something else' As he updated Peter Tiler on events, both of them were thinking that this funeral procession was going to be pretty spectacular and a worthy tribute to the dead trucker.

TEN

Traffic, as I soon found out, was quite a way from the Arrivals hall. I left Celeste, with the promise of getting in touch later on, and set off. This time I made my across the Astroblocks rather than through the centre. I felt that I was heading in a westerly direction but couldn't really tell without some sort of compass. Apparently, the Navigation programme didn't rely on compass directions but some other weird method.

It was all quite strange. Normally, I found my way to a place using maps, directions from other drivers or intuitive guess work. A lot of drivers used sat-nav. I had one fitted but I preferred the tried and tested method to something that led me up narrow country lanes or bridges that weren't tall enough for a trailer. If, for example, the address is Hillmorton Rd, Rugby, then you look at the map to see if there is a place called Hillmorton, near Rugby. If there is then it's a good guess that's the road you want.

I couldn't do that in Heaven because there were no maps. The place was expanding and changing so fast that cartographers couldn't keep up. Therefore I had to put all my trust in something I couldn't see and didn't understand. For a trucker, that was weird. But, it was all I had and seemed to work ok.

Anyway, the voice, or more a feeling, I got in my head was telling me where to go. Sure enough, in a really run down part of Heaven –no I didn't think it was possible either – I located Traffic.

Traffic was situated in a mere fifty storey building that had obviously been there for some time. Maybe one of the original skyscrapers that had been replaced by the Astroblocks? I didn't know and really wasn't that bothered. I was too worried about whether I was going to be reunited with my Magnum truck or not.

The relationship between a trucker and his truck is a strange one. It becomes his work place, his home and his pride and joy. Even if it looks the same as every other truck in the fleet, he knows *his* truck straightaway. It's probably not the same for a

trucker, like Peter Tiler for instance, who has to drive whatever is available but any trucker who has the same vehicle on a regular basis becomes very possessive about it. He cleans it outside and keeps it clean inside. He knows every little squeak and rattle. He knows whether it is pulling properly or not. If his company allows it, he customizes it out of his own pocket by fitting extra foglights, a sun visor, anything that is feasible and affordable. When he is on holiday, he even worries about who is driving it and whether it is being kept clean or not. And that is just the company driver.

Being an owner driver is something entirely different. It literally is HIS truck. It is his income, his job, his home, his way of life. Consequently, when an owner driver orders his first brand new truck – after maybe a few years building up the business and bank balance with second hand vehicles –he can indulge all himself with all the extra trimmings whether for operational needs or just to stand out on the road. When I ordered the Magnum, it was my third new truck and I had the money to indulge myself.

It had a special paint job with pearlescent Candy Red paint that changed from red to orange to purple depending on the light. It had extra lights, extra chrome and extra stainless steel fittings. Inside it had the leather option interior and seats, the microwave, coffee maker, fridge, aircon, satellite tv, dvd player, a mega sound system, sat nav, reversing and side cameras and a very expensive security option with satellite tracking. Silly? A waste of money? It was little different from what people had in their homes or their vehicles. Just that, in this case, the home and vehicle were one and the same. Little wonder then that I was eager to see my truck. And, it if wasn't here, then there was going to be hell to pay.

Like most garages, there were large double doors with a smaller pedestrian entrance fitted into one of them. The small door was open and I went inside.

I have been in many workshops all over Europe and they all have the same basic requirements. An inspection pit dug into the floor or a hydraulic metal elevator that rises once the vehicle has been driven onto it. There will be a compressor for powering the air tools that snake around on long black hoses. Against one wall will be a long workbench with vices and grinders attached. There will be tool pegboards on the wall over the workbench. The shape of the tool belonging to each peg will be outlined in paint so you can see, at a glance, if any tools have not been replaced.

At various places around the workshop will be the fitter's personal toolboxes. These are large, most often red with the Snap-On Tools motif and be on wheels for easy transport. Most experienced fitters have a lot of money tied up in their tools and guard them possessively. If you want to annoy a fitter, ask if you can 'borrow' one of his spanners.

This particular workshop was no different. It had all of the above and many other pieces of equipment whose purpose I couldn't even begin to guess at. Most workshops tend to be pretty basic with little or no frills. This one was definitely the no frills type. It was basic Heaven décor: bare concrete walls, filthy floor and grimy ceilings bearing the accumulation of many years of heat, dust and moisture blended into a depressing black/grey colour with dust and cobwebs hanging thickly from the chains supporting the overhead fluorescent lights.

This workshop was different in one aspect; there were no fitters working on vehicles or equipment. The place was deserted. At the far end was an elevated section with windows and steps leading up. I guessed they would lead to an office and maybe a staff restroom.

As I made my way across the workshop towards the steps, I heard a buzz of conversation. I couldn't see anyone but did spot a small door on the far wall that was slightly open. The noise seemed to come from the other side of the door so I followed my ears. As I got nearer, the conversation got louder. I pushed open the small door –normally called a Judas door but that might not be PC here – and walked into a large walled compound.

The first thing that caught my eye was my truck. It was in the centre of the yard and it was surrounded by five guys in overalls. I barely noticed them as I feasted my eyes on my Magnum. God, it was a sight for sore eyes.

I had a definite lump in my throat as I walked towards it. Ask any trucker and he will have trouble defining just what he feels for his truck. He probably wouldn't admit to love but his wife or girlfriend wouldn't dare ask him to choose between it or her either. I didn't have a wife or girlfriend – that might change very soon though – so I could admit to loving my truck. Not just a piece of expensive, sophisticated and brilliantly engineered metal but a living, breathing machine that epitomized all my hopes, my dreams and ambitions. My workmate, my home and my work of art.

The fitters fell silent as they noticed me. They kept silent as I walked round the truck and the length of the trailer. Their eyes followed me as I did my customary checks. Checking the tyres, the suspension, looking for rips in the trailer sidecover, for new scratches or dents; for anything that compromised safety and marred the look of the Magnum and it's trailer. This, like the truck, was a custom order. It had an extra fuel tank slung up under the belly, chromed alloy wheels and stainless steel lockers built along the side. The whole outfit had cost and arm and a leg. The other leg went to pay for all the extra fittings, stainless steel and chrome accessories that combined with the whole and turned this dark and dismal yard into my version of Truckers Heaven. Apart from a light coating of road grime, it was just perfect.

Almost as if they had been waiting for my reaction, the buzz of conversation started up again. I answered question after question. I told them how fast it was and how it pulled, how much the outfit had cost. How the 500bhp Mack engine performed, how the semi-automatic gearbox worked. I listed the accessories and extras in the cab. I told them how comfortable it was. I swaggered and showed off. Just as if this was a bunch of fellow truckers and I was parked up on a truck stop somewhere on Earth.

For the first time since I arrived in Heaven, I felt completely at home. I had my truck, accommodation that didn't involve rocket lifts, a job and a crowd of truck enthusiasts to brag, boast and tell tall stories to. I *was* in Heaven.

Eventually, all the questions they had were asked and answered. Now, it was my turn. I asked who was in charge and, as one, they turned and pointed back into the workshop. We all trooped back inside and one of them went with me up the stairs and pointed to a door at the far end. I knocked. No reply. I thought I heard someone saying "OH God!" and wondered if there was a prayer meeting going on. I knocked again and waited. Finally, a voice told me to enter.

Just as I went through the door, a flustered looking girl was seating herself at a desk to the right of me. She was, you've guessed it, in her late teens to early twenties and a bit on the heavy side. To compensate for this she had a pretty face and wide brown eyes. Her brown hair was a bit untidy and her complexion was red with an 'I've been exercising recently' sheen to it. The buttons on her blouse were in the wrong holes as if she had dressed in a hurry. I presumed she hadn't come to work that way or it would have been noticed earlier. Had I arrived at the wrong time?

At the other end of the office, a man had his back turned to me and, from his stooped back and bent elbows posture, was obviously doing up his zipper. He had no coat on and his shirt was out of his trousers and heavily creased at the back. I stood and waited.

When he turned round, I could see he was in his early thirties and well built with very broad shoulders. He had a noticeable, rather than a handsome face. His nose had been broken at some time and there was a long, narrow, scar down the side of his right cheek. His eyes were those unusual Paul

Newman kind of light blue with deep crinkly laughter lines at their edges. He had gingery/blonde wavy hair that, like the girl's, was in disarray. He too had a red face and was also breathing heavily. Obviously, they had both been exercising together.

I knew he was Irish as surely as if he was painted green, dancing a jig, and shouting "Begob and Begorrah". I knew because I *did* know him.

'John Slater, as I live and breathe' he cried as he took my hand in a bone crushing grip. He pumped my arm up and down as if he was trying to draw water.

'Hi Noel' I said as I tried to get my hand back. 'I didn't expect to see you in this place. I would have thought you'd have been in the other warmer one.'

I had first met Noel Flynn in a truckstop parking area just outside of Frankfurt. He had got into a fight with a German truckdriver who, for some reason, took objection to Noel siphoning diesel from his tank into his own.

Built like a brick *scheisserhaus*, the enraged driver had delivered his own brand of punishment and left the Irishman in a heap by the wheel of his truck.

I had gone into the truckstop, called an ambulance and made sure he was ok until the efficient ambulance crew arrived. By this time, he had regained consciousness and was able to stand. The paramedics treated his cuts and bruises and suggested that he come with them to the hospital for x rays. Noel decided he was ok and told them in very fluent German, that he would get checked out at the hospital on the American Army base, just outside Frankfurt, that he was delivering a load of frozen Irish beef to.

I had continued on my journey and, two days later, whilst parked up for the night on an industrial estate on the outskirts of Stuttgart, his black Scania 142 truck had pulled up alongside mine. The intervening two days had given him some mobility but had done nothing for his face. There was a roap map of black, blue and yellowing bruises decorating his features. His broken nose was still taped up and he had a row of black stitches running down his right cheek. He moved slowly like an arthritic old man. In one hand he carried a bottle of Southern Comfort.

'This is for you' he said as he held up it to my window. 'Thanks" I said as I leant down to accept it. 'But, you didn't have to. I only gave you a hand'. I opened my door and got down.

'Well, many would have thought I got what I deserved'. He had a soft Irish brogue but with an educated tone to it. He held out his hand.

'Maybe you did' I observed as I shook it. 'Any reason you couldn't buy your own diesel?'

'Aah, but that would have eaten into my profits' he laughed. I laughed back. He was one of those Irish charmers that you meet all over the world. People often said that Ireland's greatest export was it's people and that was probably true. Whatever, with his cheeky grin, brogue and easy laugh he could probably get away with anything.

'Your business' I said. 'But, if I find your truck parked up to mine one night, the first thing I'll be checking is my fuel tank. Clear?'

'As day' he said seriously. 'You're my friend now and it'll never happen'.

We finished the bottle that night and I woke up with a monumental headache. The space next to me was empty. Fearing the worst, I got up and checked my fuel gauge. It still showed the same amount as it had the previous night.

As often happens with truckers, we saw each other spasmodically. Sometimes on opposite sides of the road. Sometimes I would be cruising on some motorway - minding my own business and probably not concentrating as well as I should have been – and a black Scania 142 would go barreling past with airhorns shrieking. Sometimes we would actually get to speak to each other.

Noel always seemed to have some sort of deal going. Though his paperwork showed he was carrying beef, you always had the impression that there was more on board than there should have been. He was always liberal with his booze and cigarettes – I smoked heavily back then – and was always entertaining. I suppose he could be likened to an Irish version of Arthur Daley or Del Boy Trotter. He was that kind of character.

Mind you, he wasn't alone in his smuggling. Most of us international drivers did it in one form or another. Back in the Duty Free days, I always used to buy a large quantity of booze and fags on the outward ferry to sell to whom ever I could. On regular runs, I had regular customers. On new journeys, I could always sell
my stuff. British cigarettes were in demand all over Europe and cut price spirits –even with my 50% mark-up – were always welcome.

With the money from the outward leg of the journey, I purchased home produced goods for the return to England. Leather coats, cb radios, locally brewed speciality liquers;

whatever looked like returning a decent profit –a tax free profit – I would bring back to England.

Did I always declare these goods? Of course I did. Is the Pope married? No, like most truckers, I had my hiding places. Most of the time I would get away with it.

The times I didn't? Well, so long as HM Customs found something every now and then, they didn't bother to look much further than an undeclared bottle or carton of cigarettes.

Like most international truckers, I carried a container of drinking water somewhere on the vehicle. In my case, it was strapped conspicuously in a custom holder at the rear of the cab. On many return legs, the water was substituted for pure vodka. Looked like water, must be water right?

The hiding places that truckers found for their contraband were legendary. One of the most talked about Customs finds involved an Irishman. This guy used the fiberglass "cap" on the top of his cab roof – a cab-width illuminated cowling that usually displayed the name of the company – to stow as many bottles as he could. He had cut a door into the rear of the cap, put his bottles in and closed the door. Up on top of the cab, it escaped all but the most rigorous inspections.

Until, the night he drove off the ferry, into the Customs inspection area and waited for the officer to ask if he had anything to declare. Getting a reply in the negative, the officer then invited the driver to get down and walk with him to the front of the vehicle. There, clearly displayed under the fiberglass cap were the illuminated bottles. Too many drinks on the ferry had caused the driver to forget to switch off his lights. It was a mistake that cost the driver a lot of years at

Her Majesty's pleasure. Not content with just the drinks, the suspicious officer called in the 'rummage' crew.

This crew's function was to unload trailers and then to go over every inch of both truck and trailer. When they lifted up the trailer's floorboards, the IRA's explosives were found.

Now, I never had any proof but there was always the niggling suspicion at the back of my mind that maybe Noel Flynn didn't always carry 'legitimate' illegitimate goods.

Noel was that sort of character. You just knew that he was up to no good but he had such charm and likeability that he could get away with it. In many ways, he proved to be a good friend to me.

I was broken down once near Osnabruck with a fractured brake pipe. Noel was driving on the other side of the road, saw me, stopped and dodged four lanes of busy autobahn traffic to see if he could help. This was before the mobile phone era and getting help could have taken hours. He took the damaged pipe with him, drove thirty odd miles to a Volvo dealer, bought the replacement pipe, returned, helped me fit it and then drove off. No charge for the new pipe. That was Noel. Once you were his friend, you were his friend for life.

For about five years we saw each other fairly regularly. Sometimes we got to chat, sometimes it was just a flash of headlights or blast from an air horn . Then, I just didn't see him again. Rumour on the trucker's grapevine had it that he had been killed in an accident in Bulgaria. It was never substantiated so I never knew what had happened to him.

Now, he was standing in front of me, pumping my arm and about to tell me just what the Hell my new job entailed.

'How are you, John?'

'I only got here....' How long had I been here? It seemed like a long time. '...three days ago. Everything is a bit strange. The strangest part is seeing you here. I would have definitely put you down for the other place.'

'Ah, sure, that's where I should have been. But there was some sort of administrative cock-up and by the time it had been sorted, they came to me with an interesting proposition"

'They?' I removed my hand and tried to get the circulation flowing again

'The Management team. The guys directly under the Boss. The Archangels, the Martyrs and Saints. Those are the guys who actually run this place. The Boss decides who comes here and They have to accommodate them, allocate housing and jobs. Well, you must have got some idea of the sort of fecking problems there are up Here. Quite honestly, Heaven is going to Hell.'

'Um, you're not supposed to say certain words up here' I reminded him.

'Oh, feck that. I can't do my job without a bit of effing and blinding. Here at transport we have a sort of dispensation, a bit of leeway. None of us here can do our jobs and be all holy as well. And, believe me, if Heaven has got to be sorted then I told them to leave us alone and let us get on with it'.

'I suppose that was some sort of prayer meeting I interrupted" I said all innocently. 'I heard someone saying "Oh, God". Was that you?'

"No, that was Imogen' he indicated the girl at the desk and leant in close. 'She gets a bit carried away when we are....'

'Praying?' I supplied helpfully.

'As good a word as any for one of the Boss's greatest gifts to mankind'

'You haven't changed a bit. Just how long have you been here and just what do you do?'

'Five months and it was just six months ago that They came up with this idea. If I was a suspicious man, I would think that my time on Earth was ended a bit prematurely. I was doing a bit of business in Bulgaria when the police suddenly
arrived. Before you know it, there were guns blazing and I was dazed and confused in this white fog. The rest you know. After two days I get called to Job Allocation and get to see this Camp Co-lin. He sent me to another office and They interviewed me and asked if I wanted the job of organizing the transportation and supply problem they had.'

'Just like that?' I asked getting suddenly suspicious myself. 'So, you suddenly think to yourself "now who would I like to drive for me? I know, John Slater." and I coincidentally become available? You bloody organized me being up here didn't you, you Irish bastard?'

'We were both brought here prematurely John. I've seen the records. I was nine months early. If I had served out my destined life, it would have ended with me getting beaten to death in the prison I had been sent to for the Bulgaria business. You also were due a messy death. To be sure, three years into the future, but killed by Turkish thugs trying to hijack your load. Given the choice, John, what would you have picked? Dying needlessly to save some pallets of bathroom fittings or as a hero saving children? You tell me John. You just tell me what you would have chosen.'

'But I lost three years of life' I shouted back angrily.

'Three years of what John? You lived in your truck, your only fixed base was Peter and Elizabeth Tiler's spare bedroom. How much longer could you have gone on? Until you were fifty –three years longer - or sixty? You tell me realistically how easy it is being an owner driver trying to make a living. When was the last time you had a rate rise? The ex Commie Bloc hauliers have cut the transport rates to the bone. And what about the driving conditions? The crowded roads, the endless repairs, the sheer aggravation of being on the roads these days. And, it's getting worse every day, week and month. Don't tell me you enjoy being on the road these days. It's not like the 70's or the 80's when it was fun and exciting and there were new destinations, diesel was cheap and the roads weren't so congested. The Golden days of trucking have gone, John, and the business will never be the same again. So, shout at me, hit me if you want, but I think I did you a favour'.

'Oh, Bugger off, you stupid thick Mick. Do me a favour? I wish I hadn't done you that favour in Germany. I should have walked away like everyone else and left you bleeding on the ground. If I had done that, we would never have become friends. So Sod you Noel, just leave me alone'. I pushed past him angrily and stormed out of the workshop and into the yard.

Almost instinctively, I headed for my truck and climbed up into the cab. Despite my anger, it was good to be behind the wheel again. I leant back in my driving seat and, grabbing a duster, began polishing the dash. An almost automatic task, it was what I did in traffic hold-ups, waiting to load or unload. Whenever I stopped, I polished my dash. It was an absentminded equivalent to stroking your dog or petting your cat. I polished and thought.

Eventually, I got down and went back to Noel's office.

'You back to talk or fight?' he asked warily as he got out of his seat and stood up holding his arms by his sides.

I slumped into the seat opposite him. 'Talk' I told him. I hadn't forgiven him but I couldn't disagree with what he had said either. He was right. Truck driving just wasn't the same anymore. Crowded roads, stagnant haulage rates, ever increasing competition from newly admitted Common Market countries whose transport operators didn't have the same strict government controls over vehicle safety and drivers hours.

Even as an owner driver I wasn't cocooned anymore. Sure the Magnum was paid for but would the next one be? My rates hadn't moved in two years yet the cost of diesel, road tax, insurance, equipment and consumables – like tyres, servicing items and the like – had been steadily increasing.

I was still making a comfortable living but at what cost? I was definitely putting in more hours and the job was definitely harder. And, at the end of it, what was it all for? To pay the taxman? To become rich? If I did make money my needs were small. No house, wife or children to maintain. No dependants or relatives to leave any money to. Basically the only people I now thought of as family was Peter and Elizabeth. They were comfortably off and didn't really need anything I could leave them. So, basically, I was working my butt off, in a job I didn't enjoy as much as I used to and for what? Three more years of the same and then get killed over something as trivial as bathroom equipment?

Maybe Noel was right. Quit at the top and go out in a blaze of glory. At least those kids and their parents would remember me. I would probably get a few flowers at the spot for an anniversary or two. Passing motorists might remember that not all truck drivers were mindless morons. Maybe truck drivers themselves would remember John Slater, how and why he died, and maybe act and drive a little more professionally themselves.

I wasn't quite ready to forgive Noel Flynn just yet. Maybe I couldn't fault his logic but it wasn't for him to decide just when somebody died.

Truthfully, I wasn't that upset about it. I had gone out of a life, that had lost it's shine, as a hero. That simple act of steering one way or the other had given me a Grade 2 distinction in Heaven. I had made friends, more than friends I hoped, with four gorgeous girls, been re-united with my parents –and a lot of long gone relatives sometime in the future – and had my best ever truck with me. I was in my prime, surrounded mainly by young fit men and women. Apparently, there were no diseases, no illness, no aches or pain. Food, clothing and accommodation were provided. The entertainment, no pun intended, was out of this world. People that I missed on Earth would, eventually, be joining me. So, after my initial reaction, I wasn't too upset. But, Noel wasn't getting off that easily. I intended to make him squirm. I sat down and faced him. Noel also sat and, opening a drawer of his desk, produced a bottle of whiskey and two glasses. He poured and handed one to me.

'I'm glad we can work together' he said. 'It's a big job and we are the best men for that job.'

'You haven't said what the job entails yet' I took a sip of the fiery spirit and grimaced as it hit the back of my throat. Irish whiskey isn't my favourite drink.

'We are going to be trucking pioneers again. At least you are. We have three months to get results. Oh, by the way, because I am not quite the bastard you think I am, I did negotiate some terms. If, after three months, for whatever reason, you are not entirely happy with your conditions up here, you can return to Earth. I have even got the Management to scrub your three year demise date. You have an Open Ticket Arrangement which means that you will die naturally when your body has had enough.'

'Oh sure, I just jump out of the cab before it hits the concrete and that's it'

'Basically, yes. Just before impact, your angle will be deflected and you will be thrown clear. You'll probably have a few broken bones and stuff but people will call it a miracle escape. And, that's just what it will be.

You won't remember anything of Heaven and will live your life out normally and naturally. You'll still be regarded as a hero and you'll carry on making the good or bad decisions and following the same impulses that affect your life just as before. Is that a fair deal or not?'

'How can I trust you?'

'You do or you don't. I could get it in writing but you'd probably think that was a forgery, wouldn't you? John, I want to work with you and we need to trust each other. Do what you normally do. Follow your gut. You have already made up your mind as to whether we can work together so just say "yes" or "no" and we can get started or not. What do you say?'

He was right. I had already made up my mind and was following my gut instinct. My gut, that peculiar and unexplainable feeling that told me which path in life to follow, which person was trustworthy and which hadn't let me down before. I held out my hand and Noel reached across and took it.

'Welcome on board. Right, to business" he stood up and walked to the far side of the room. The window overlooked the yard and he looked out at my truck. 'Have they told you about the energy and how it is obtained?' I nodded. 'Then you know that it can be spasmodic. Holy days, operations, tragedies, confessions, whatever: the reasons people pray are varied, follow no set routine and are, mostly, individual.

Collecting solar energy is just as unpredictable. Once, the open land between each Country State was a hundred miles wide. Today, it is barely fifty. Every Astroblock that goes up nibbles away at that land just a little bit more.' Noel returned to his desk and sat down. 'Every new block takes away a little less sunlight. You've been in the Blocks and you know how little sunlight there is. Soon, maybe fifty years, there will be no solar energy. And, then what?'

I figured it was a rhetorical question so I said nothing.

'Currently, the Energy Team collect all that prayer and solar energy and store it in the abundant times for later use. A bit like the electric storage heaters we used to have in the 70's and 80's. The problem is that the increasing population in Heaven uses more and more energy. Replicators, air tubes, clothing; everything that people do uses energy. Even using the most stringent energy saving measures, the gap between having and not having energy is closing. With me so far, John?' I took another sip of whiskey and waited. My parents, Mike and Jean, had already told me most of this. I still wondered where I came into the problem.

'You've seen StarTrek on Earth, right?' Noel was on his feet again. He still had that same nervous energy that meant he was seldom still. Just how he had kept himself seated behind the wheel of his truck for hours on end was a mystery.

'Yeah, sure' I had watched it now and again. Even had some Voyager dvd's in the Magnum cab. 'You're going to tell me that some alien culture has the answer to our problem?'

'The Management seem to think so. Most of the Alien Heavens use the same energy sources they used on their home planets. Their technology is far in advance of what we have. They don't have the same overcrowding problems and, so far, no energy shortfalls.'

'Why is that' I asked. Seemed like Alien favouritism to me. Maybe we ought to think about invading some of those other Heavens.

'John, I'm just a simple Irishman, ok. I don't have all the answers. The best thing I can do is arrange for you to have a chat with someone who does. In the meantime, let's stick to the short version'

The short version was that some of the Alien Heavens – the Mumbo Jumbos for all I knew – had agreed to let Earth have some of their energy. What they got in return was never mentioned. Maybe they had been ordered to or maybe it was out of the goodness of their internal recirculation organ.

This was being delivered in beams that were delivered via space conduits. Once here on Earth Heaven, this energy was compressed and stored in containers. This was where Noel and his team of fitters entered the picture. They had assembled the equipment that caught, compressed and stored, from kits that had been delivered via the Big 'Un. Keeping up so far? I must admit to having problems. Beams of energy being shot from one planet Heaven to another? I had to keep reminding myself that this wasn't Earth and that my Magnum and I weren't on a routine earthly delivery or collection.

Speaking of which, this was what I and my truck had been delivered from Earth for. Maggie –well, what else? – and I were going to be pioneers. It was going to be our job to deliver the energy containers - probably be easier to start calling them batteries – to the various States. The idea was to deliver the batteries to England State first and see how it worked out.

Once all the initial storage and delivery problems were ironed out, then more trucks would be assembled to deliver to what I would call Europe. For the other continents, the energy would be sent direct from source to the various storage depots in each of the furthest States/Continents and delivered from there.

As each battery contained the estimated equivalent of a months worth of energy and each trailer could hold six then, if it worked, it would solve Earth Heaven's energy problems. As Noel had said, it was going to be a big job. First thing on the agenda was to convert Maggie to run on the alien energy. If that wasn't possible then the whole idea would need another re-think.

Noel and I left his office and returned to the yard. It was a *one small step for a trucker but a giant leap forEarthkind* sort of moment as I uncoupled the trailer and drove Maggie into the workshop.

Once on the bay, I stowed all the loose objects in the cab, jumped down and started to raise it. I had the electric option fitted and it was just a matter of releasing the locking clamps and pushing a button. The cab was hinged on thc front and started to rise from the rear. Once it had passed the point of balance, it fell forward only to be restrained by the hydraulic dampeners. I had once seen a Ford Transcontinental cab being raised like this and fall right onto the workshop floor as the rust weakened restraints gave way. Thankfully, Maggie's restraints held and the cab stopped at what looked like an impossible angle. Basically, it was only the weight of the chassis and powertrain that was keeping her horizontal on the bay.

Noel's fitters gathered round and inspected the Mack engine's fuel pump, fuel lines and injectors. Noel grabbed my arm and pulled me away.

'Best leave them to it, John' he said as we walked towards the exit. 'They have been planning the conversion, in theory, for days now. This is the first time they have actually seen what they will be working on. It could take some time and will require a certain amount of modification to both engine and cab'.

'I will have something left to drive, won't I? And maybe have something with a little bit of power.' I looked over my shoulder as Maggie was being taken to pieces by the swarm of mechanics. It was a bit like leaving your child as the operation room doors closed.

'Go home John. Get some rest. Have a night out. Relax. Come back in the morning' Noel pushed me through the door and firmly closed it.

Wasn't as if I had a lot of choice, was it? I set off for home only I didn't think of it that way. I thought of it as Mike and Jean's place. My younger than me parents.

ELEVEN

'Mr Tiler? Oh hello, it's Sergeant Marshall from Faversham police. You are the contact for the late Mr John Slater? No, no problems. Just to let you know that the post mortem has been conducted and the body is awaiting collection. Do you have anyone in the area? Findlay and Sons? Yes, we know them. Ok, Mr Tiler, I'll contact them and arrange for the deceased to be collected. You will have to make your own arrangements from there. The results of the post mortem? They have been forwarded to the coroner. No, as far as I know, they didn't reveal anything untoward. No sign of drugs or alcohol. Unfortunately, you'll have to wait for the Inquest for the full report. We'll notify you when that is scheduled to take place. Thank you Mr Tiler'.

'Bloody Jobsworth' Peter thought as he replaced the phone. He returned to the kitchen and finished his cup of tea. Rummaging in one of the kitchen drawers, he found a note pad and biro. Seated at the kitchen table, he began a To-Do list. First thing was the undertaker. Phone him to get John's body collected and prepared. Remind him about the new coffin arrangements as well. Mr Findlay would probably not be too pleased to learn that he was not providing the coffin.

Most people, he thought, when in his situation just rang the undertaker of their choice and let them make all the arrangements. Well, John Slater was not going to be cremated with production line monotony.

However, once he had contacted Canley Crematorium he realized that he was going to have to alter his plans. When he had told the receptionist just what he had planned, he was dismayed to learn that it couldn't happen. The road leading up to the crematorium just wasn't built for what he had in mind. The receptionist also told him tactfully that a funeral director would probably be able to facilitate the arrangements more speedily. Expertise really did count in this case. Making the booking as a private individual could mean lengthy delays until a suitable date became available. Most directors, she explained, made block bookings months in advance and took the seasons into account. Winter was always busy.

Looking through the Yellow Pages, Peter was amazed at just how many funeral directors there were in the Rugby and surrounding areas. He rang the three with the biggest adverts and the best date available was nearly three weeks away. Finally, he made contact with a company that had the bare minimum of advertising space. Here he was able to get a crematorium date only nine days away. He provisionally booked it and promised to confirm either way the next day. As he put the phone down, he felt exhausted. Who would have thought that arranging a funeral could be so tiring? He made a mental note to get signed up to one of those pre-paid funeral plans that were advertised on the telly. At least, his kids would not have to go through the same thing when their parent's time came. Picking up the now warm phone again, he made a call to Dave Williams to get things organized with the various transport magazine websites. Dave picked up on the third ring.

'Hi Dave. It's Peter. I can finally begin to make the funeral arrangements. Yes, John's body has been released and I need to contact the Kent undertaker to collect him. I also need to tell him about the change of coffin.. I have booked the 25th of September provisionally and need to confirm tomorrow. Any problems with that? No, it's a Friday, I've just looked. Yeah, that should bugger up the traffic. Ok, can I leave that with you? Cheers mate, see you'.

Almost as soon as he put the phone down, it rang again.

' Mr Tiler ? Good morning Sir. It's Mr Findlay from Findlay and Sons. The police have contacted me and I am making arrangements to pick Mr Slater up this afternoon. Have you got any further on the funeral arrangements?'

'I was just about to call you. Will you be able to prepare John and keep him until the 25th ?'

'Certainly Sir. No problem. Actually, there was something else I was ringing about. A local manufacturer of …er.. unusual caskets has contacted me. He implies that one of his caskets will be used. Is that correct?'

'I'm sorry you heard about it this way, Mr Findlay' Peter apologized. 'That was one of the things I wanted to discuss with you. After we last spoke, the person who makes the coffins has contacted me. He has a personal interest in this funeral as it was one of his daughters that Mr Slater saved. She and her friends were on that school trip. He asked to be allowed to show his gratitude by donating one of his custom built coffins. I accepted, of course, but this now means that I will not be needing the one I purchased from you. Is that a problem?'

'No. Mr Tiler. I was merely confirming that it was what you wanted. Since we last spoke, I have learnt the details of Mr Slater's death and find that I too have an interest. My grandson was also a passenger on that coach. He also owes Mr Slater a great debt of gratitude. My son, the boy's father, has asked that we waive our usual fees. I have agreed. Rest assured, Mr Tiler, we here at Findlay and Son will treat Mr Slater with the utmost affection, dignity and respect. Perhaps we may speak a bit nearer the 25th to finalize arrangements? I assume you will still be providing your own transport?'

'Well, thank you Mr Findlay. I am overwhelmed. People have been so kind. Yes, we will still be picking John up in suitable transport. I will contact you around the 22nd? Fine, speak to you then. Goodbye Mr Findlay and thank you once again'.

Well, wonders will never cease, Peter thought as he put down the phone. An undertaker with a heart.

After making another cup of coffee, Peter contacted the local undertaker, confirmed the date and explained exactly what he wanted. Not surprisingly, with not much work or profit coming his way, the undertaker's fees were negotiated fiercely. Finally, both sides were satisfied.

Sighing heavily, Peter once again picked up his phone and began phoning his trucker friends. Each was told the date, time and details and asked to contact other drivers. This way, Peter reasoned, there should be a sizeable number of people involved. He knew from experience just how effective the trucker's telegraph could be at spreading information.

Finally, he declared himself finished. Apart from looking on the various publisher's websites, there wasn't much more he could do for the moment. Nearer the time, he could work out some sort of schedule and get that uploaded to the web sites as well.

He thought, briefly, about contacting the police and asking their advice but decided not to. It would be quite likely that the relevant police forces involved would veto the whole idea. Besides which, Peter reasoned, he had no idea just how big this was going to be and he didn't envisage that there would be any traffic laws broken. A bit of disruption maybe, but that might be for the good as well. It would only confirm Trucker power and highlight the congestion on the nation's highways and byways.

Reasonably satisfied with how his plans were progressing, He decided he might go down the allotment and finish his digging. Bit of fresh air, bit of exercise. Maybe put a bit of netting over the cabbage.

TWELVE

I didn't hurry back to Mike and Jean's. There would be no point as they were both at work. Maybe I could get something to eat and see Celeste or Angel. I needed to talk things through with someone who wasn't involved with this whole energy transportation project.

I made my way back to Arrivals without even thinking about it. It was still a fair old foot slog but it gave me time to think. And, I had a lot to think about.

Being in Heaven was, I decided, not such a bad thing. It wasn't of my time and choosing but I wasn't that bothered. My time alone in Maggie collecting my thoughts had helped. The prospect of continuing my trucking career in a new place was exciting. I would be doing what I loved to do without the aggravation of having to make a profit. Still my own boss but without any pay as such.

During my early days of European trucking, I had never felt more alive. Whether it was the joy of driving to completely new destinations, the five or six day trip duration or the extraordinary sense of satisfaction and achievement as I drove up to my delivery destination, I didn't know.

I did know that I craved that anticipation and excitement as I started each new trip. The feeling that I, and other adventuring truckers, were creating legends that would be remembered and discussed by other less fortunate truckers. The pride of being part of an elite bunch of consummate professionals who risked truck and limb to carve out new routes to faraway places with strange names and even stranger customs and prejudices. The satisfaction of haggling with border guards for the quantity of cigarettes that would get your paper the all important entry stamp. The satisfaction of dealing with any problems, whether caused by man or machine, by yourself and finding the solutions. The unexplainable feeling of pride, achievement and of just getting the job done. Just being a Trucker.

Now, whilst I still enjoyed being behind the wheel of a nice looking truck, the sense of adventure just wasn't there. No matter where it is, a road will eventually become just a road. The more times you travel it, the more familiar, the less exciting. I had spent years travelling to Europe and even those distances had lost their edge. Now, if I am being totally honest, the best part of being a trucker was driving my own truck and getting the admiring looks from both fellow truckers and the general public.

So, whilst I still hadn't completely forgiven Noel Flynn, I was coming round to what he had said. I was getting that old familiar tingle with the prospect of a new job, new destinations and that anticipation of the unknown.

When I finally arrived at Arrivals, I was more at peace with myself. I would see if Celeste or Angelica was free and see how they felt about it. I made my way through the crowds of bewildered, flustered and confused New Arrivals.

I couldn't see Celeste but did see Angel leaving her desk. I hurried after her and asked if she wanted a coffee. She seemed surprised but not displeased to see me.

'Look at you. If Celeste hadn't told me, I wouldn't have recognized you" she said, holding up her arm and making a turning motion. I held out my arms and duly turned round slowly. 'How are you and what have you been doing?'

'Come and have a coffee and I'll tell you. If, that is, you are not too busy with a certain movie star' I couldn't resist the little dig.

'Now, now. Don't start fighting over me. I was only doing my job. Remember how you felt when you first came here? Besides, Patrick is too confused just now. He's missing his wife Lisa. They were married for thirty four years, you know. Of course, he's glad to be rid of that Pancreatic cancer but it will take time for him to adjust.' She slipped her arm through mine and guided me over to the canteen. 'Grab a seat and I'll get them'.

As usual, the canteen was busy. Staff were having their breaks and the lost souls were, well, lost. You could see it in their faces as they wandered aimlessly about. Those who had died with people they knew were the luckiest. At least they had a friend for comfort and support. The older ones were, on the whole, just glad to be dead. It was an end to their suffering, loneliness and just trying to survive on an Earth that didn't encourage old people. Most seemed just glad that Heaven actually existed. Maybe they were looking forward to seeing their Earth partners or old friends who had passed earlier. Probably they were just glad to be here and not in the Other Place.

Angel came across the canteen with a tray holding two cups and two slices of cake. She looked good in her chosen outfit. She had that kind of beauty that turned heads and cheered peoplc up by just looking at her. She certainly cheered up both Big and Little John.

'I got us a slice of Angel cake' she smiled as she sat down. 'It's my favourite. You're looking very pleased with yourself. What's happened?'

I told her as we ate and drank. I described Noel Flynn and our previous relationship. I enthused over getting my truck back and my feeling about what Maggie and I would be doing. She seemed impressed.

'First I had heard about it' she admitted. 'But, it does make sense. The overcrowding is getting really serious now. It must be nice for you though. Getting to travel to the other States. Maybe you could pick up some perfume for your friends when you go to France State' she grinned mischievously and I felt her Doc Martins sliding not too gently up my leg. Just when she was getting to an interesting place, she stopped. 'We would be EVER so grateful

'Yeah well, we can talk about that later' I said going all shy. 'So, you think it would be a good move for me?'

'If it was me, I'd jump at the chance. I get really fed up sometimes just being in this place and listening to some of these moaners' she turned her head and indicated the New Arrivals around her.

'Well, maybe you could come with me sometime. I could always use some company. I don't want to lose contact with you and the others.'

'Oh yes, Celeste is really going to let me go with you and leave her behind.' I could see that she liked the idea though.

'Well, it's up to you' I said dismissively as if it didn't matter. 'Maybe you can both come together.'

'Ooh, you're a greedy little trucker, aren't you' she laughed'

'Can't blame a bloke for trying. Now, what are you girls doing tonight? I fancy going to see one of these shows Mike and Jean have told me about' I saw her inquiring look so explained about my parents.

'That must be so weird. I hope my parents don't do something like that'.

As she said it, her face fell, her bottom lip trembled and she started to cry. I went round and held her in my arms. Tried to comfort her, as she had comforted me. I realized that I knew nothing about her Earth life.

Was she, like Celeste, a young again Oldie or had she been young when she came here? Gradually, her tears stopped and she tried to dry her eyes on the sleeve of her tee shirt.

'Sorry about that. It just gets to me sometimes. I really miss my Mum and Dad. My Dad especially. It must have really cut him up when I ki….when I died.'

I fished a reasonably clean handkerchief out of my jeans and gently dabbed around her eyes. Suddenly, I had seen the hurting side of this outwardly confident and in control girl. I guessed there was also some darker reason she was here.

'Don't apologize Angel. You're only human after all' we both saw the absurdity of that statement and laughed together. I gave her a final hug and sat down again. 'If you ever want to talk, I'm a good listener' I told her.

'You know, you're a really nice bloke' she told me and I suddenly felt ashamed for my earlier thoughts. 'I'll tell you about it some day. Only not just now. Now, I have to get back to work. If you can, meet me here at around 5.30 and you can come back to ours and we'll decide where to go tonight' She leaned over, gave my arm a little squeeze and kissed my cheek. 'Thank you' she whispered.

I watched her as she made her way across the canteen. Watched and tried to think pure thoughts. Tried but failed miserably.

Just as I was thinking about leaving and having a wander to pass the time, I saw Brother Simon. He had a cup in his hand and was looking for somewhere to sit. We caught each other's eye and he came over.

'Mr Slater' he said formally as he sat down. 'How are you keeping? Have you been assigned a position yet?'

Somehow I got the impression that he knew exactly what kind of job I had. 'Hello Brother Simon. How are you? Actually, it is kind of lucky meeting like this. I have some questions and maybe you can answer them. You being Management and all'

'Certainly, if I can, I will' he sipped his coffee and looked across enquiringly.

I told him how confused I was about the Alien Heavens, the different States and the general state of things in Heaven.

'It's not that easy to explain but I will try. First of all the Boss decided that it would be easier for all the different cultures to live in a familiar environment. Initially, everyone mucked in together in one Heaven. It soon became plain that it wasn't going to work. The Martians, for instance, couldn't stand the Venusasians.

They all had different food requirements, were used to different technologies, everything just clashed. Whilst our Eygptians were building pyramids, the Saturnites were building spacecraft. It just wasn't working.

The Boss and the Committtee then decided that each planet had to have its own Heaven. That way, they could keep their own culture and everything else they were familiar and comfortable with and would be happier. Are you keeping up with me so far, Slater?'

I nodded. Should I be taking notes? Would I be marked at the end? It was obviously going to be another classroom lesson but I had the time and the curiosity. Brother Simon half rose as if to pace and talk but looked around and decided against it.

He went on to explain that, whilst everyone kept to their own planet Heaven, even that method didn't work. Soon the inhabitants began to group into their different races and cultures. Returning once more to the drawing board, the Boss and the Committee came up with the different States.

"Here on Earth Heaven, the inhabitants behaved much as they did on Earth. The English didn't like the French, the French wanted to build a wall to keep the Germans out and everyone hated the Americans. Hence the different country States. Every State is separated but accessible to each other if the people want to visit. Much the same as on Earth. The Boss gradually realized that people stuck to what they knew and were familiar with. Once that had been organized, each Heaven was much happier.'

'Ok, I can see that' I replied. 'It makes sense. Presumably that is why the Boss is called the Boss and not God. It is easier to have just one title rather than several like God, Allah, Manitou and all the other names that that people give to the God they worship. Stops people getting confused. Right?'

By now several of the people nearby had given up the pretence of not listening and gathered round. Brother Simon, born teacher that he was, got into his stride.

'You should have paid this much attention when you were in my class, Slater. Yes, quite right. So things were generally getting organized and people were happy. Then the populations on all the different planets began to increase and the populations of the different heavens grew as well. Some faster than others. Earth, for instance, had a high death rate because people didn't live as long as those on other planets. Average seventy years for mankind, up to two hundred years for Martiankind. Consequently, some Heavens are more overcrowded than others'

One of the Newcomers, an elderly man, put up his hand. Brother Simon graciously allowed him to speak. "But why don't the overspill population of the more crowded Heavens move to less crowded ones?'

'There is nothing to stop anyone doing that if they wish to do so. Provided the alternative Heaven agrees. But, it gets back to the same problem. People stick to what they know and are comfortable with.

Here on Earth planet, they will all know someone or will, in time, have someone they know join us. Whenever possible, Newcomers are housed with relatives, friends or acquaintances. But the basic fact remains that all the Heavens are crowded; some more so than others.'

A young man joined the argument. I guessed he was a Newcomer but couldn't say for certain. Most of the Heavenly regulars were young. This particular guy looked a bit geeky with horn rimmed glasses and side parted hair. When he spoke, it was in a high pitched nasal whine. Probably the reason he was up here, I thought rather uncharitably. If I had to listen to that whine for too long, I would probably contemplate murder.

'Why don't the authorities just recycle?'

'Recycle what?' Brother Simon was getting a little annoyed that his coffee break was becoming a general discussion. 'Rubbish?'

'No, people. Instead of just having new babies born on Earth, why don't the people in Heaven get sent back to Earth instead?' Geek Boy said triumphantly.

'We have been doing that for eons.' Brother Simon replied. 'Every generation is replaced with a generation from Heaven. If, for instance, your Earth mother has a new baby, then it is either a direct dead relative of hers or the baby's father. Sometimes, a combination of the two. The genes or DNA are always the same. They all come from the first people on Earth. That is why there are family resemblances. That is why everyone has a double somewhere; it has to happen with the same limited number of genes. It's like baking a cake. Throw all the same ingredients together and you get the same cake. Add an extra ingredient or miss one out and you get a slightly different result. Like a black person or an Oriental. But, the combinations are limited by the ingredients. Eventually, the same cake turns up time and time again. So yes, Mr Smarty Pants, we do recycle. Now, if you will excuse me, I have to get back to work. Mr Slater, will you accompany me please?'

I got up and followed him. As I did so, I couldn't help but notice his hair. It was pulled up from the nape of his neck and rearranged on the top of his head to – in his eyes - loosely resemble a full head of hair. To me, and probably most other people, it looked like it was; a full blown comb– up and over. Strange that someone so seemingly relaxed about his appearance that he had chosen to remain this age for eternity, bothered about not having hair. In his shoes, I would have gone back to an age when I at least had some hair on top. He must have used some sort of super glue to keep it in place or perhaps it was a sort of trade off. 'I keep this age if you agree that my hair never falls down' kind of deal. The other thing I wondered about was his cassock.

As I followed him, his hem swept the floor. If there had been any rubbish lying about it would have disappeared under his cassock and, presumably, built up until it tripped him up. And, did he wear anything underneath it? These and other irrelevant thoughts kept me occupied until we entered his office.

By now I was used to seeing the same bare concrete walls, tatty furniture and lack of any aesthetic appeal in his and the other offices I had visited. Brother Simon sat at his desk and indicated that I should take the other chair.

'I can't stand that man' he said crossly as I sat down opposite him.

'Who?' I asked. 'The old guy or the young geeky one?'

'Young Mr Standish. He is always stirring up trouble with the Newcomers. He used to be in Green Peace but I think even they threw him out. He asks the most stupid questions and has the most improbable solutions to Heaven's problems. Unfortunately, his stupidity does not take away the fact that there is indeed a crisis here.' He got up and began pacing.

'Is it true about sending people back to begin a new life" I asked

'Of course it is. You can't keep on making new people and keeping the old ones. The Earth's population is growing fast enough as it is. Nearly every soul that comes here is replaced on Earth by a Volunteer'

'I didn't realize you had to volunteer to go back. Surely people would be glad to go back?'

'Some are but not everyone. If you have a comfortable enough life up Here and you have your loved ones around you, what incentive is there to return? And return to what? The Volunteers have no idea what sort of conditions they are going back to. It could be abject poverty, deformity, suffering, oppression or it could be just the opposite. If Volunteers could pick and choose, there would be only rich, pampered people living on Earth.'

This was getting intriguing. 'Do the Volunteers remember their previous existence? How many times can they go back?'

My old teacher sighed and sat down. 'No, they don't remember. They can go back as many times as they like but they can't remember any previous existence. Or rather, they shouldn't be able to'.

'I guess that sometimes the system screws up?' I ventured hoping it wouldn't be a dumb question and set him off again.

He looked around as if there were other people in the room. 'This is highly confidential' He said as he leant across his desk. His voice dropped low enough that I had to strain to hear. 'Before returning, the Volunteers are processed. Their memories are wiped clean and they are supposed to start each new existence with no knowledge of any previous life. I don't know how it is done; I suppose it is a bit like wiping a computer memory clean.

But, just lately – in the last five hundred years or so – more and more Volunteers are starting a new existence with more or less complete memories of previous ones. The Boss has got technicians working on the problem but there is a definite glitch somewhere and it is interfering with the memory cleaning.'

I recalled seeing a television programme about people who claimed to have lived before. It was pretty convincing. Some people showed the tv crew where they remembered living before and under what name, how they had died and all sorts of details they couldn't have found out ordinarily. I told Brother Simon about it.

'It was probably true' he admitted. 'There is no doubt that it is happening. At first just the odd one or two but now it is getting more frequent. At present, they only remember past lives and not their time here in Heaven. If that situation should change and they can remember what life Here is like then it could be ruinous. Once people on earth find out that Heaven not only exists but that the conditions are not like what they expected then the whole concept of leading a good life on earth to be rewarded by the promise of eternity in Heaven goes out the window.'

I could see his point. During my early school days I was constantly told about the glories of Heaven. How there were green pastures and running streams. How cherubim, angels and the saints were your constant companions and how you would want for nothing. And, all you had to do was be good, keep your nose clean and all this would be yours. I also had the disjointed thought about how the suicide bombers who had been promised young virgins and a land of milk and honey felt about it. Been promised Paradise and, instead, been given a crock of Sh.. you know what. Not that they would arrive in Heaven but they couldn't have been best pleased where ever they turned up.

I pointed this out to my old teacher; the one who had told me most of that stuff.

He took it on the chin and even smiled a little sheepishly. 'I only preached what I believed were the facts. And, as I have mentioned before, I was pretty annoyed when I got Here. But, you are missing the main point. If people stop believing in Heaven then they will also stop believing in the Boss and stop praying. No prayers, no energy. It's a vicious circle. That is why the replacement energy programme is so important.

Frankly, when I was told about it and who would be involved, I was appalled. I had previously sourced your life records. They made interesting reading. Two reprobates would be running what is probably the most important new source of energy we have.

But, on reflection, and after meeting with both you and Noel Flynn, I have changed

my mind. The two of you will work well together. You are both used to cutting corners and thinking on your feet to achieve your aims. And, I have no doubt, one of you at least will profit personally.'

'I should protest that last statement' I replied. 'Unfortunately, I believe you are correct. Noel always has his eye on the main chance but I do think he will get the programme up and running to everyone's satisfaction. Including his own. For my part, I am just relieved to have my truck and home back and to have the chance to continue doing a job I love.'

'Well, I am glad I ran into you in the canteen. Before you leave, is there anything else you would like to ask?'

I decided to ask the question. 'Why are you keeping your age so old" I almost blurted out. I had intended to ask about the hair also but lacked the necessary courage. Besides which, I quite liked the old codger.

'Because when I was young, I was almost a carbon copy of young Mr Standish. I annoyed people without meaning to. As I got older, I gained wisdom and stature in people's eyes. Therefore I stayed the age I felt the most comfortable with. I hope that answers your question and..'He gave me a stern look '..don't even think about asking your other question' He held out his hand. I shook it and left. As I said, I liked him.

Back in Arrivals, the crowds seemed the same. Celeste had told me that the New Arrivals figures stayed almost constant 24/7. It was hard to envisage that so many people were dying worldwide. Normally you only hear about large numbers of deaths after disasters. In your own area, you hear that old Mr Jones has popped his clogs or that so and so had died in an accident but it never really hits home just how many people do die every day. Until, that is, you come to Arrivals and see for yourself. But, of course, you are just another statistic yourself at that point. The organization machine behind the scenes must be huge to deal with those numbers. No wonder things were reaching crisis point.

I saw both Celeste and Angel on the way out. They both waved when they saw me but were too busy to stop and chat. I mouthed "5.30" and pointed to my watch to make sure they got the message. Now I only had a few hours to kill.

I contemplated going back to Mike and Jean's but there didn't seem much point. They would both be at work. I really wanted to see what was happening to my truck but didn't quite have the nerve to see Maggie with her innards all over the shop. I decided to have a look around and familiarize myself with the area.

I suppose what I really wanted to see was where all the people outside of the Arrivals Hall went during the day. Mike had told me that they worked in the basements of the Astroblocks and that every block inter-linked. I decided to go back to Archangel Gabriel house and try to find this underground world. If nothing else, it would pass the time.

Finding the Astroblock was no problem thanks to my Navigation node. I used whatever shortcut I thought of and arrived back at my parent's home. In the foyer, lobby or whatever it was called, nothing had changed. The decorating fairies hadn't been but by now I was worried that if I saw a splash of colour on a building I would go blind or something. One does get so acclimatized, doesn't One?

There seemed to be no other door available other than the lift. I did have a quick hike down the corridors that stretched off on either side but couldn't find any door other than that to someone's apartment. Back to base and I summoned up my courage and approached the lift. God, I hated this thing already. I pressed the door button, they opened and I entered. They closed. I pressed the Down button gingerly as if a light touch would make it go slower. Did it? Did it buggery. The thing descended as it the rope had been cut. I didn't count floors. It would have been a bit hard through tightly shut eyelids. I concentrated on keeping my stomach in its designated place and my mouth shut. Funny how I was just thinking about a splash of colour on a wall wasn't it?

The ride from Hell stopped hard. Either the floor or my legs bounced up and down. Barry invited me to leave. I did. Left the lift and walked into another world. A world of colour and people and noise.

There was a high arched ceiling, maybe 100 foot high. There were banks of bright lights festooning down and illuminating the area. The ceiling was a brilliant white and the walls were a cheerful yellow. The floor was tiled in different coloured patterns and there was light pop muzak struggling to be heard over the noise of hundreds of people. The scene was so at odds with the stark outside, upside world that I experienced a moment's panic. I leant against the wall and allowed my heart rate to slow down, my breathing to return to normal and my senses to take it all in.

There was a long central walkway between the banks of what?..fish tanks, waterways, containers that lined either side of the central walkway. Whatever the structures were, they contained water and machinery and plants. Lettuce, cucumbers, tomatoes, sweetcorn, whatever you could wish for in a salad was there. Growing out of the water which seemed to be flowing slowly. No soil, no raised beds, just a sea of vegetables shimmering in a kaleidoscope of colour.

I dimly remember Mike telling me that Mum worked in Hydroponics growing vegetables. This must be Hydroponica or whatever it was called.

Either side of the structures there were people. Walking up and down, pulling vegetables out and packing them into containers. People in white coats with nets over their hair. Young people mainly but a few grayheads here and there. These older looking people tended to have clipboards and have a supervisory role as they stopped and checked produce and noted in their clipboards. The immediate and lasting impression was of a large factory floor and workers enjoying their work. Calling across to each other, laughing, chatting to each other as they pulled, trimmed and packed whatever they grabbed. Whenever a packing container was full, it was stacked with others on a waiting pallet. I looked around for a forklift truck but couldn't see one. One pallet seemed to be fully loaded because a young man came over and began to wrap it in clingfilm. Walking round and round the pallet, he cocooned it in a shiny transparent film. When he had finished, he pulled a lever alongside the pallet and it began to travel slowly down the length of the hall. I followed its progress and noted that it was running on a moving road set into the floor. I watched its progress until it was out of sight but still couldn't see to the far end of the gigantic area.

Above the noise and bustle, I heard my name being called. Or, rather, I heard someone shouting "John, John". I looked around trying to find the source of the voice. A waving hand helped pinpoint it. A young girl with a hair net and white coat was waving vigorously. I made my way in her direction and, belatedly, realized it was Mum/Jean. Believe me, it still felt odd to have someone younger than me as my Mum. I threaded my way through the laughing, smiling workers in her direction. I was very aware that I was the only person there not wearing something white.

'Hi John' Jean hugged me and gave me a quick kiss. 'Glad you found your way. What do you think of it, then?'

'I can't believe it' I replied conscious that I hadn't called her anything. Married men friends tell me that they have the same problem with their mothers in law. Can't call her Mum because it feel funny and can't say their Christian name because that doesn't feel right either, Eventually, they don't call her anything. Blokes and father in laws don't seem to have the same problem. It's either Mr or Mike or whatever their first name is. Anyhow, strange as it was, this was my Mum standing before me and I was going to have to call her something.

'Call me Jean, if it's easier" she obviously realized my problem and gave me a way out. 'Come over here. I've got some people I want you to meet.'

She grabbed my hand and pulled me towards the group of people she had been working with. A twenty something bloke held out his hand. 'Hello John. It's good to see you again'. There was something familiar about the way he moved and his facial expression. Other than that, I had never met him before in my life. As I shook his hand, he realized my confusion. 'Sorry' he grinned and became even more familiar. 'I keep forgetting this ageing thing. I don't suppose you have ever seen me this young, have you? I'm William, your dad's dad, your grandfather'. Suddenly I did know him. It was like looking at my dad when he was young. It was, I suddenly realized, like looking in a mirror and seeing my smile, seeing the familiar crinkles around my eyes, seeing myself slightly distorted. He was right. I remembered him as an old man with grey hair, whiskers and stooped over a walking stick. An old guy I spent a lot of time with when I was young and loved dearly. Now here he was; walking tall, young and proud. I got a lump in my throat and my vision blurred. I hugged him tightly and couldn't speak. He patted my back and rumpled my hair just like he used to when I was six years old.

What followed next was pretty much the same. I was enveloped in a sea of white coats. Young people hugging me, crying with me, reminiscing. Laughing and obviously delighted to see me. People from my past recognizing me. Me not recognizing any of them. A weird, wonderful, confusing and comforting experience. My favourite Aunt, giggling and blushing, now a nineteen year old beauty. An irritable uncle, smiling and joking now that he was free from the excruciating pain he had lived with for so long.

Old relatives, old neighbours, old friends and people I just used to speak to in the street. People like Trevor from up the road, now young, standing straight and free from his cancer. Many, many people that I knew and yet didn't know. Names I remembered, faces I didn't. People I loved, liked and plain just couldn't stand. Time passed and blurred. Faces came into and out of focus sometimes sharpening into a picture of an older person for a fleeting moment. It was a humbling, exhilarating experience that will stay with me forever. One that I would look back on and savor always. I felt as if I had finally come home. I felt as if I had finally broken free from Earth' ties and was now a part of Heaven. I felt as if I finally belonged, was loved and wanted. It felt like ….it felt just right.

Once all the excitement of meeting and greeting had died away, people began drifting back to work. Jean stayed with me and acted as my guide as we walked down the walkway between the hydroponic tanks. She tried to explain the process by which plants and vegetables could be grown without soil but I gave up trying to understand. I was still hyper after finding this place and my relatives.

I still couldn't quite get my head round the colours, bright lights and cheerful peole. The contrast between Topside, as it was called, and Work was poles apart. Drab, dreary, lacking definition and dying, Topside was a depressing place. Work was a happy place. It would be where I wanted to be. Like a light bulb going off in my head, I suddenly had the thought that the contrast was deliberate. Maybe Management kept Topside colourless not only to save money and energy on paint but to make it so miserable that people wouldn't want to stay there for any length of time. I had only seen my parents accommodation but that was Earth normal. It was bright and cheerful and reflected their individuality. It was a nice place to be after work.

Leaving such a haven of normality would be such a wrench that people would naturally want to be at work with its comforting colours and chatter. Work would actually be preferable to wandering aimlessly around Topside. Happy workers were productive workers. I asked Jean if I was right.

'Yes, I suppose you are' she said thoughtfully. 'I have never looked at it in quite those terms before but there is certainly no incentive to be anywhere other than at home or down here. All the entertainment venues are down here as well.'

As we walked, she pointed out the various growing processes and where the produce ended up. This was in a storage facility that branched off from both sides of the central roadway and had those clear plastic strips hanging down from the large doorways. As I watched, a loaded pallet slid noiselessly alongside, followed it's tracking left and through the hanging plastic barrier strips. I couldn't see much inside but there didn't seem to be the same sort of activity as in the growing area. I asked Jean what went on in there.

'I don't know the whole technical process' she explained as we continued walking. 'I have never been in there. Not many of us have. Mainly it's just maintenance teams or technical guys who work in there. From what I have been told, some of the produce is scanned and sort of melted down into its chemical components. Those components are then converted into pure energy and stored for the replicators. Whatever people order is then converted back from that energy into a solid form. Because everything is made up of chemical components, all the replicators do is convert chemical formulas into the product ordered. It's a bit like baking a cake' she finished lamely

I really didn't understand what she had just said but determined to find out what did happen. Obviously the replicating process was more involved than just approaching one and ordering a "Tea. Earl Grey. Hot" in Captain Picard mode.

We had been walking for about twenty minutes and still I couldn't see the far end of the giant underground area. Jean said she had never walked far enough to reach the end though she had tried to when she and Mike had first come here.

At various positions, there were smaller buildings. I asked what these were for. Jean explained that they were the Airway tunnels that inter-connected everywhere and ferried the worked about.

"Can I have a go" I asked. I nearly said 'Please Mum, can I? Can I?' but that would have been silly. I was a 36 year old with a teenage Mum. 'Sure, you just enter, study the schematic map and press the button to where you want to go. It's dead easy. A bit like being on the Tube back on Earth but faster and more comfortable. If you go to Zone 35, you can have a look at where all the entertainment takes place. That is really impressive. There are the large stadiums for football and other sports. There are the venues for all the different kinds of entertainment. You can see an opera, a rock concert, a classical recital, films, virtually every kind of entertainment you had on Earth in one place. Go and have a look. I have to get back to work anyway or old Jobsworth will be docking me credits. Go on, you can't get lost and it will pass the time for you. See you later at Home?'

I told her I had to meet someone and wouldn't be back until later. Maybe much later if I get lucky, I thought but didn't tell her that, She was my Mum after all. I gave her a chaste kiss on her forehead and watched as she walked back. It was so weird. I was actually starting to fancy my Mum. At that moment, it was a toss up as to whether I continued my exploration of the Hydroponics area or got even more adventurous and tried the Airway. Truth be told, I was a bit wary of entering another enclosed space and being transported at high speed. At least the Airway journey would be horizontal, wouldn't it?

Firmly telling myself I was a man and not a rodent, I figuratively girdled my loins and walked towards the small building. There was no door but I could see a brightly lit walkway so I entered. I must have walked for about ten yards when I saw some sort of clear carriage ahead of me. As I got closer, I saw that it was about seven foot high, round and tapered to a cone at either end. The sharp end of each cone was just inside of a clear tube made of a plastic-like material. There were no seats inside the carriage which was, I guess, about thirty feet long.

I realized that the carriage was actually inside the clear tube and that a section, the length of the carriage, was cutaway and hinged upwards. A bit like cutting a flap in a drain pipe, hinging the flap and holding it open to expose the interior of the pipe. Judging on what I had been told, I guessed that the flap came down and sealed the carriage inside the tube.

On the walls of the walkway were schematic diagrams like the route maps on the London underground. Each destination was allocated a number and a table alongside the schematic gave each number a location. Zone 35, as Jean had said, was labeled Entertainment. I noticed that there were other numbers, that included Hydroponics, Arable, Engineering, Transporation –my department – Planning, Maintenance, Energy and Accommodation. The last list carried over onto another table as it listed each Astroblock with a name and a number. Interestingly, there was a sub division for Accomodation –Grade 1 and Higher.

Obviously the Posh End of Heaven. As a Russian once said "everyone is equal but some are more equal than others".

I was torn between Entertainment and Transportation. I choose Entertainment because I wanted to see what options I had tonight when I, hopefully, took the girls out. I got inside the carriage, although I was already thinking of it as the tube, and pushed buttons 3 and 5. As I reached up for the hanging grabstrap, the outer hinged section closed. There was a momentary delay and then my ears popped slightly and I could feel the carriage start to move. Unlike the lift, it kept at a reasonable speed and I started to relax enough to open my eyes and release my death grip on the grabstrap.

Apart from a slight rushing sound, there was no noise. As each location sped past, I could sometimes get a glimpse of people or brightly lit interiors. I was even beginning to enjoy the sensation when the carriage stopped with a hiss and the outer section of the pipe opened . I left the carriage and entered the walkway. I must have had the subconscious thought that I would exit onto a street lined with theaters, cinemas, clubs, strip joints –I wish – or something like Blackpool on a good day. I was wrong.

There was no one else about that I could see. And, it wasn't a street as such. It was more like a collection of aircraft hangers lined up either side of a paved walkway. It was also back to Heavenly Drab. Unpainted and unloved concrete walls and dilapidated facades. After the riot of colour and people in Hydraponics, it was a disappointment.

Outside each building was a sign that showed what if offered and when. I walked up the left hand side and saw Football –Busby Babes V Football Legends – Basketball – Harlem Heaven Trotters V the W.A.S.Ps – Wrestling –Big Daddy V Giant Haystacks; the list was endless. Even I, who wasn't that interested in sport, recognized many of the names. There were sports that I knew and many that I couldn't even begin to imagine. Welly Whanging, Bog Snorkeling, Sheep racing, Nipple Tweaking –that sounded interesting – and Pig Poking were some of the more far right sports on offer.

The other side of the street proved more interesting and traditional. A theatre advertised Shakespeare's new play – The Banker of Birmingham. There was Opera, Gilbert and Sullivan, Pop, Country –that was one I was definitely going to as it featured Red Sovine – classical, Indi, garage; what ever your musical taste, it was there.

I saw many famous singers featured. Frank Sinatra, Elvis Presley, Billy Fury, Judy Garland, Jimmi Hendrix, Marc Bolan, Buddy Holly: think of an Earth dead singer/entertainer and they would probably turn up on this street.

The cinemas had a good selection of films. Heaven Can Wait was the one that made me smile. There were bowling alleys, disco clubs, casinos, dance halls, funfairs. Las Vegas, Blackpool, Hamburg's Reeperbahn and Rugby's Church Street all rolled into one. Actually I put the last one in as a Rugby in-joke. But, there was no doubt that entertaining the masses in Heaven was serious business. Dead Serious. No sign of entertainment being a Dying Business up here. Oh come on, they weren't that bad. Made me smile. And that was exactly what I had on my face when I had finally walked up and down green zone 35. There might not be any telly on Heaven but with that sort of guest list and facilities, you certainly wouldn't lack for entertainment.

I made my way back to the Tube with a spring in my step and high hopes for a good night night out. And, best of all, it wouldn't cost me a penny. I had to wait for a tube. After about five minute, one coasted to a stop, the outer flap hinged up and this time I confidently walked on board. There was one other passenger inside.

'Allo Mr Slater. Ow you doing?' Alfred Hawley-Smythe chirped. Alfie seemed to get everywhere.

'Hallo Alfie. What are you doing here? No school again?'

'Naw, I bunked off. What's the point of getting any smarter? Me Mum says I'm too smart by 'alf. I can read, write and do 'rithmetic. Don't need much more up 'ere, do I?. Naw, I'm just running an errand for a mate of yours. Noel Flynn in Transport. 'E's a card, in't he?'

'Yeah, well, just watch he doesn't get you into trouble' I warned as we set off. Alfie for Transport, me for Arrivals. He didn't seem to be carrying anything so I was curious as to just what sort of errand Noel had him involved in.

'Naw, Noel's orl right. Good mucker to me. 'ere, Mr Slater, I've gotta joke for you. St Peter decides to stand in for the regular gatekeeper to the gates of Heaven. The regular isn't feeling too well and fink's he's coming down with summat. Holyitis, probably. Anyway, he tells St Peter to direct the new arrivals to their designated rooms but warns them to keep quiet as they pass Room 8. St Peter welcomes the first bunch, finds out they are Jews, looks at his list and directs them to Room 15. Tells them to be very quiet as they pass Room 8.

The next bunch are Muslims and St Peter tells them the same fing, different room. Same with the Protestants and all the rest. Be quiet when you go past Room 8, 'e tells 'em. There's a group of Mormons on the end and, after St Peter has delivered his instructions, one of them asks what's so special about Room 8 and why they 'ave to keep stum? "Room 8 is for the Catholics" St Peter tells 'em. "And, you 'ave to keep quiet because they fink they're the only ones up 'ere".

I struggled to keep a straight face. "I happen to be a Catholic' I told him sternly. 'And, I don't find that very funny at all'

'Course you do' Alfie said with a cheeky grin. 'Everyone know that you have a sense of humour. They can tell by the way you dress' . Cheeky little bugger. I pressed the appropriate buttons and the tube moved smoothly away from Entertainment and gathered speed. After the horrors of the lift, I found this mode of transport quite relaxing and would definitely use it more often.

Arrivals arrived first and I got off. Alfie pressed his face up against the glass as the tube moved off and gurned goodbye.

I still experienced the slight dizziness as I entered the Arrivals hall. Celeste assured me that it would go away in time but it was still a bit disconcerting. You stepped from normal time into an area where time had slowed down. If you hovered just between the time zones, you got the illusion of people blurring as they moved. Like when you fast forward a dvd or video. That sort of effect. But, by now, the abnormal was getting to be routine everyday normal.

I still had a bit of time before the girls shift ended. I was hungry and thirsty so made my way to the canteen. The girls had told me that many people, when they weren't working, came here and celebrity spotted. If you sat at the far end, you could look directly at the door where the New Arrivals got out of the Ascension Lift. I wasn't that bothered about spotting a celebrity but, like all truckers, I had got into the habit of observing people. I made my way to a seat in the far corner and made a start on my meal of spaghetti bolognaise. With chips, of course.

The doors to the lift never seemed to stop opening and closing. People stepped out of it and just stopped and reacted to the scene before them. Some recovered quickly and joined queues as if it was the most natural thing in the world. I guessed that the majority of them were English. No other nation enjoys a good queue as much as we Brits do.

Others looked back at the closing doors of the lift and just stood there dazed and confused. The one I noticed the most was half naked and black. I would have called him a pygmy but in this PC era that would have probably not been correct. Maybe Vertically Challenged or Person of Short Stature? Whatever he would be called, he was very small, very confused and very frightened.

'Poor little sod' said a voice in my ear. The geeky Mr Standish was standing beside me and looking at the New Arrival. 'Imagine being plucked from a jungle and into this madhouse. He probably hasn't seen this many people together in his whole life.'

He may have been a geek and Brother Simon's least favourite person but there was genuine sympathy in his voice. We both watched the little guy cowering in a corner. 'What's going to happen to him?' I asked with concern.

'The same as with all the people like him. The one's who have never experienced our so called civilization. Guys like him are living a hunter gatherer life style and are not equipped mentally to live in our world. There are many like him all over the world. The Pygmys, the Australian Bushman, the Forest People of the Amazon and other remote jungles. People untouched by progress and unprepared for it. Can you imagine just how he must be feeling?'

'Probably not' I sympathized. 'I know how confusing it was for me. This must be a thousand times worse for him. Where do people like him actually go? Are they expected to survive and adapt to an alien environment? What is the alternative? Is there one?'

'Look, it is already being arranged' Standish pointed out a similarly dressed little guy approaching the New Arrival and greeting him. The relief on the newbie's face was obvious. 'The guy greeting him is probably from the same area, if not the same tribe. The Boss makes special exceptions for cases like this.

You must remember that it is not only modern day isolated groups that are in Heaven. Have you ever thought about the people from before civilization? The people from the Bronze Age or earlier. The earliest descendants of man. In their own way, they all worshipped something. It might have been just a stone but they still believed in it and prayed to it.

All of those people have a right to Heaven. But just where do you put them?' Standish was just like Brother Simon in that he couldn't keep still as he warmed to his theme. 'What the Boss has done is set aside large tracts of Heaven and created a similar environment to what they were used to. It would have been cruel to just drop them in modern day Heaven and expect them to fit in, right? So now, that newbie is being escorted to a Heaven that he is used to. One that he will feel right at home in. So everything is ok now, isn't it?'

I suspected that it was a rhetorical question so I kept quiet. I was aware that many people were standing around and listening in.

'But,it isn't ok, is it?' Standish asked to no one in particular. He was obviously in his element. I got the feeling that, if it wasn't for the hassle involved, he would always carry a soapbox around with him so he could stand on as he preached. 'What is happening, *has* happened, on Earth is starting to happen here on Heaven. The land set aside for the indigenous tribes, the pre-historics and the like is being slowly encroached by Astroblocks.

Granted, we are not at crisis point yet because the land is not being populated as quickly as it would be on Earth. The less there are of a people on Earth, the less there will be up Here. But, in a few thousand years or so, there will be a problem.'
People were already starting to move away and Standish realized that he was losing his audience. 'If something is not done now to prepare for then the future of these minority people will be in danger…….'
He tailed off as he saw that he had already lost all but one of his audience. I drained my cup and prepared to leave. I saw the dismay on his face and felt sorry for him
'I gather that this is what you did on Earth?' I asked.
'I was proud to be in Green Peace' he confirmed.
'Look, I've not been here too long but I get the feeling that things will work out just right. The Boss has muddled along for a few years now and I expect he has already put plans in place to deal with it. Whilst I can't agree with some of your views, I do respect the sincerity with which you pursue them. It is just that preaching to Newbies is never going to be very productive. They are all feeling very frightened, lost and confused right now. You can't expect them to worry unduly about something that may or may not happen. They are too concerned with *right now* to worry about the long term future. Maybe you should think about preparing a long term plan and submit it to the proper people?'
'That's a good idea' he said visibly brightening. 'In fact, I think I will make a start on it right away. Thanks for your imput'. He held out his hand and I shook it. As he walked away, I had a bright idea. 'Why don't you go and discuss it

with Brother Simon in Counselling? He was telling me that he enjoys talking with you very much'.

I watched as Mr Standish made his way to Counseling. Yeah, I know I said I liked the old bugger but I still hadn't forgiven him entirely for all the detentions and warm hands he gave me.

It must be nearly knocking off time for the girls, I thought as I made my way through the New Arrivals to see if I was right or not. I wasn't. I had to wait another thirty minutes before the girl's shift replacements eventually arrived.

Finally, we were all walking out of the Arrivals Hall and heading in the direction of Downtown Grunge. By now, it didn't have the same depressing effect as it had earlier. I had seen the Light, Halleluja and the Light was a bright and interesting place. I told the girls about my afternoon as we walked along arm in arm.

'I don't think I could work in Hydraponics' Angelica said as we made our way to their apartment. 'I find my present job interesting, most of the time. Helping people and all that.'

'Presumably that is why you moan about it all the time' Celeste teased her.

'Yeah, well, some of the Newbies expect too much. I had one rich bitch today telling me she wanted a lakeside apartment with hot and cold running servants. I put her in one of the older Astro's for the time being. That should give her something to think about. Remember when we lived in that grotty block until our new one was built, Cel? No modern replicators, the vacuum bog always blowing instead of sucking and that sonic shower. Like being rubbed down with a hedgehog' Angel shivered at the memory.

I had a question. 'Why are there no animals or birds in Heaven?'

'Because they have no Souls, silly' Celeste laughed.

'Yeah, but it would be nice though to have a dog or a cat'

'Heaven is grotty enough without having dog crap all over the pavements as well.' Angel pointed out. 'Besides, where would you draw the line? What if someone wanted something different. Like a snake or a tarantula. I quite like living in a place that has no creepy crawlies. No spiders in the shower. No, having no pets is all right. Besides, we have got you now, haven't we, if we want something to pet'.

I quite looked forward to being petted and petting back. I grinned at the thought and we all burst out laughing. For no accountable reason, other than it seemed right, we began to do that silly "follow the yellow brick road" kind of linked arms dance. Celeste was nearly in hysterics by the time we arrived at Sister Theresa of Calcutta House.. " Stop it, stop it" she pleaded. 'I'm going to wet myself soon'

'How come you girls don't use the Tube? I asked

'Our place isn't really far enough away to warrant it' Angel explained. 'Besides, we need the fresh air every now and then. Then, of course, there are all the gropers. Everyone packed in, the tube moves off and then you start to feel hands wandering over your bottom.'

'But, this is Heaven' I protested. 'Surely you don't get gropers here?'

'Humph' she snorted. 'Men are men. They are all the same. Even here. Honestly, they must have really lowered the bar, some of the blokes you have to talk to. You wouldn't believe all the disgusting suggestions I get all day long. I have a good mind to tell the Boss about it.'

'Oh come on' I said anxious to defend myself and most of mankind. 'We are not all like that. I haven't had a really decent grope for ages.'

'Oh, you're all right' Angel said a little less angrily. 'you're a nice sort of bloke. But there are some really nasty ones here and I don't think they should be.'

By now, the moment I had dreaded had arrived. My grip on Celeste's hand tightened and I sort of dragged my feet. She must have felt it because she gave me a look that clearly said 'what's wrong?'

'I can't stand these lifts' I confessed a little shamefully. 'They make me nauseous and frightened. I have this Inner Ear problem and these lifts just aggravate it'

'Ok, not a problem' Celeste laughed. 'You could always walk instead of using the lift.'

'Oh yeah, walk up a few hundred flights of stairs. I'd be knackered before I got a quarter of the way there.'

'What do you want to go up for anyway?' Angel asked.

'Well, I was hoping to see your place, have a shower and sort of plan what we are doing tonight. We are still going out?'

Celeste and Angel continued walking right past the lift door and down the corridor. 'Aren't you coming then?' Angel laughed over her shoulder. I followed them down and waited while she opened the fifth door down. "Voila' she said triumphantly as she pushed the door open and they both entered.

'You might have told me before I made a complete fool of myself'. I followed them down a short hallway and into what turned out to be the living room. It was about the same size as Mike and Jean's. But, whilst my parent's place was done out in bright colours, this décor was nearly all white. The far wall had a stunning mural of horses galloping across a meadow. My first reaction was that it was a French window that opened on to a meadow and the horses were real. It was only when I got closer that I realized it was a very skillfully executed painting. 'That's one of Astra's' Celeste said. 'She studied art at college and she was, is, very good'

I looked round the rest of the room. There wasn't much furniture. Just a sideboard, settee and a couple of easy chairs. A shiny wooden floor completed the minimalist effect they had achieved. It wasn't really my cup of tea but then, it wasn't my place.

The real surprise was how tidy it was. I had expected the place where four girls lived to be more untidy. 'We had a good tidy round last night' Molly said as she came into the room. 'We don't get many guests and we wanted to make a good impression. How do you like the painting?'

'I think it's stunning' I said with genuine admiration. 'I wouldn't mind getting Astra to paint something on Maggie. Maggie is the name I give my Renault Magnum truck' I explained after seeing a flurry of "Who's Maggie?" looks pass between them.

Molly came over. 'I wouldn't ask her that, if I were you" she said quietly. 'Astra isn't inclined to like truckers and trucks'.

'I can understand that but, referring to my previous statement, we aren't all like that.' I felt that I had well and truly blown the atmosphere so asked for a guided tour.

Molly volunteered whilst the other two went off to titivate, as they called it.

As with Mike and Jean's place, there wasn't all that much to see. Two bedrooms, one with a shut door as the girls were inside, and the other one had two beds in it. 'Both bedrooms are pretty much the same.' Molly explained. 'This is the one Astra and I use. We did think of decorating with some really wild colour schemes but decided we liked something calm and soothing to come home to.'

Molly's bedroom was white with one wall in a dove grey. There was a nice carpet on the floor, two built-in wardrobes and two dressing tables/chests of drawers. There was a full length mirror behind the door. Angel's and Celeste's was similarly equipped but the contrasting wall was primrose yellow. The kitchen was adequate when you remember that it only had to house a replicator and a waste disposal unit. The bathroom had the standard equipment of vacuum toilet, sonic shower and a mirror.. Everything was amazingly clean and tidy. I mean, not being sexist, but I have visited girls flats before and they were all untidy with clothes strewn everywhere and wet towels all over the bathroom. The one common feature seemed to be that the kitchens were all tidy and clean and, I suspected, never used.

Bloke's places weren't any better, I hasten to add, but I sort of expect women to be neater. I mean, they certainly dress neater and tidier. Speaking for myself and my OCD – Obsessive Compulsion Disorder – I can't stand things not being in order, in place and logically arranged. There, that's my secret out. I am *not* perfect. But, it did mean that I could instantly relax in the girl's place without having my OCD kick in and start me tidying, dusting and arranging things in straight lines. I told Molly about my slight imperfection and she laughed.

'Nothing wrong with a bit of OCD. I suffer from it myself but I try not to let get out of control. You and me have got a lot in common, Slater. Better watch yourself or I might just try to steal you away from the other two' Molly laughed heartily at this suggestion and I joined in, fascinated. When Molly laughed it was like shaking jelly on a mould. Everything moved.

'Decided where you are taking us all tonight yet?' she asked innocently. Oh-oh, I thought I was just taking Angel and Celeste out.

'Perhaps we could discuss it together?' I said playing for time while I brainstormed frantically.

'Got you" she declared. 'You really think that Astra and I would be playing gooseberry on your first night out in Heaven?

Just then the bedroom door opened and two angels stepped out.

'Hello' I said in my best Lesley Philips lech voice. 'Where did you two beauties spring from? What have you done with Celeste and Angelica?'

I would have already rated both of them as gorgeous and that was in their work clothes. In night out on the town finery, they were super stunning. Celeste had on a light blue trouser suit that really highlighted her blonde hair and pale complexion.

Her feet were in white cowboy style boots with blue fringing. She had put some blue eye shadow that made her blue eyes seem even bigger. At work, she usually wore a red lipstick but now she had pale pink lips that shimmered with some combination of glitter and moisture. Her white/blonde hair was loose on her shoulders.

Angel's workaday tomboy look was replaced by an elegance that made the contrast even more ethereal. A light green skirt replaced the usual jeans and she had green sequined high heel shoes replacing her Doc Martins. A white blouse with a generously low neckline empathized just what a big girl she was. Her hair was centre parted and cascaded down in red waves. Like Celeste, her green eyes seemed even bigger due to skillfully applied emerald eye shadow. Without their workday red, her Scarlet Johansson lips seemed even fuller in a light scarlet shade of lipstick.

Apart, they looked incredible; together they were awesome. I felt really proud and humbled that they were going out with me.

Together, they came over and kissed me on the cheek. They trailed some exotic perfume behind them. I got all misty eyed and had to swallow hard before I trusted myself to speak. 'Oh' I managed. 'Not going to be a dress up do, then?'

They both froze and looked at each other and then back at me. 'Just joking' I assured them. 'You both look absolutely jaw dropping and drooling gorgeous. I just hope that I survive the night. I'll be fighting off so many men, it'll be a massacre. I just hope that I can come even close to looking like I deserve to be with you both'

I was going to go back to Mike and Jean's to get my new going out clothes but the girls unanimously decided they liked me as I was. Obviously I am a well dressed little trucker. I decided to have a shower and freshen up both myself and my clothes. Sonic showers are brilliant at doing both at the same time. I wondered if it was possible to have one fitted in Maggie. I would have to ask Noel when I saw him tomorrow.

I exited the bathroom feeling suitably cleansed in body and clothes and saw that Astra had returned home whilst I abluted. 'Hi Astra' I greeted her. 'How are you? What are your plans for tonight?'

'Hello John' she said a little.. what? Reservedly? Guardedly? something in her voice told me that I wasn't altogether welcome here. On reflection, not surprisingly perhaps. Here I was, a type of man she had good reason to hate, in the one place she probably felt to be both safe and secure. Sometimes, I just feel ashamed to be a man.

I walked over and stood a reasonable distance from her. I looked her squarely in the eye. 'Astra' I said in a low enough voice that only she could hear. 'I apologise for being here. The girls invited me in and I just didn't think. If it will make you feel happier then, in future, I won't come here again.'

She just looked at me with her sad eyes and her bottom lip trembled a little. I felt that I had to try and reassure her. 'Look Astra, I realize just why you don't like men, and truckers in particular, but we are not all like that. I genuinely feel ashamed sometimes when I read about what some man has done to a woman. What goes on in some men's minds I don't know and I am just glad that I don't. But, I can promise you that you will never have to be afraid of me….for any reason. I have never hurt or forced myself on a woman in my life and cannot ever see myself doing so. Most of the blokes I know feel the same way. You just happened to meet one of the really evil ones.

But, please don't think we are all the same. I hate to see that look of fear, however fleeting, in your eyes when you see me. I just wish I could make you believe me when I say that you need never be afraid of me'

I turned round to join the others but, before I could do so, I felt her hand on my arm. I turned back to face her and saw the tears running down her cheeks. My first instinct was to take her in my arms and just hold her. My second was to do no such thing. She moved her hand up to my cheek and clumsily and haltingly caressed it. She never said a word but just gave a slight nod and went into the bedroom she shared with Molly.

Celeste came over and hugged me. 'Give her time John. Just give her time' she whispered into my ear. I just held her tight.

I won't pretend that what just happened didn't take the edge off the excitement I was feeling. Taking two beautiful girls out to see an artist I had always wanted to see but never thought I would.

I first heard Red Sovine over the radio just outside of Berlin in 1997. I was driving from Berlin to Frankfurt and had just got into my stride when Terry Woebegone announced Teddy Bear by Red Sovine. It wasn't a song as such but a narrative with music. Red Sovine had a rich Deep South kind of accent and he told the story about a little crippled boy who used to go out with his trucker dad. He was talking from his home on the cb and telling anyone who was listening that his dad had died in a crash and how he never got out in a truck anymore. I got so involved in the story that I pulled into the nearest layby and stopped the truck to listen properly. As the boy told his tale about how he never got out of the house anymore and his mother had to work all hours to support them, he said that his greatest wish was to go out in a truck once more. If there were any truckers out there who could give him a ride, he would much appreciate it and gave his address out over the cb airwaves. Red Sovine was playing the part of the trucker and, without further ado, he turned his truck around and made his way to the address. When he got there, he found he was in a queue of about thirty trucks. As each trucker returned from giving Teddy Bear - the boy's cb handle or name – another one would take him out again.

When the trucker finally got back on the road, he picked up a cb message from Moma Bear who thanked all the truckers for the joy they had given her son and wished them all a safe journey. When the track had finished, I had tears streaming down my face and a big lump in my throat. It wasn't so much the story but the way Red had interlaced it with music and the emotion he put into it. In fact, as soon as I got back to Dover, I went into the town whilst awaiting Customs clearance and bought the cd with that particular track on it. I liked all the other songs as well because they were all trucker orientated but with a country music background. I subsequently bought every Red Sovine album he had ever released. It wasn't until a long time afterwards that I learnt that he was dead.

I was telling the girls the reason why I wanted to go and see him and about Teddy Bear . 'Wow, I would really like to hear that one myself' Celeste said as we left the apartment..

'I have them all in my truck' I said as we walked to the nearest tube tunnel. 'You can come with me one day and I'll play it for you.'

‘Ooh, you truckers’ she said giving me a dig in the ribs. ‘You’ll do anything to get a poor innocent girl in your cab, won’t you?’ Suddenly she realized what she had just said and how it sounded after what had taken place between Astra and I. ‘Oh, John’ she said contritely. ‘I am so sorry. I didn’t mean it like that. We both know you aren’t like that. What a stupid thing to say.’

‘It’s all right, love. Don’t worry about it. I know you didn’t mean anything by it.’ I gave her a little squeeze to show her that there was no harm done.

The tube entrance, as it turned out, was only about five minutes away. With a stunning girl holding each hand and Red Sovine to look forward to, I was really looking forward to my first night out in Heaven.

THIRTEEN

Dave Williams was just about to hang up when the phone was answered.

'Mike Henshaw.'

'Hi Mike. It's Dave Williams. I just need to touch base with you on a couple of things. First of all, is the turntable still off the chassis and the stainless steel cover in place?'

'Sure is. With no turntable in place, I can drive on an ordinary licence. Road tax and insurance are cheaper too. Why, is it a problem?'

'No, that's great. It means that we can place the coffin on the cover and strap it down securely. Secondly, how many other show truck owners do you know in the South of England?"

Mike Henshaw thought about it for a moment. Though the other truck owners were competitors and rivals, there was no real problem. Showtruck owners liked to show off their trucks whether there was a prize involved or not. 'I can contact quite a few. Why? What did you have in mind?'

'I just thought that a few flash trucks might create an even bigger buzz. You would still be lead truck but a few others behind you would look great. You'd better warn them though that I'm not entirely sure that what we are planning is strictly legal. And, quite honestly, I'm afraid to ask'

'I can't see any problem myself. So long as we are all road legal, what law are we breaking? We are just driving on the motorway, aren't we? So long as we drive at a reasonable speed and not inconvenience any other road users, there shouldn't be any problem.'

'Yeah, I know but I just don't want it getting out of hand, you know? Once we hit the motorway, it gets beyond our

control. I don't want any cowboy grandstanding and causing a nuisance and a bad impression for other road users.'
'I don't think anyone is going to do anything to ruin the day. John Slater had a lot of friends from what you tell me. I am sure those friends will come down hard on anyone who tries to spoil things. I think it is just going to be one of those play it by ear things'
'Probably. Ok, thanks Mike. See who you can rustle up and I'll get details to you as soon as. So far, we are still on target for the 25th. Oh, remind everyone that this is a freebie, will you? They will have to sort out their own fuel costs on this one. I'll be in touch later. Thanks Mike'.

As he replaced the phone, Dave's head was still buzzing with the number of things he had to organize. He had tried to phone Peter earlier but got no reply. Maybe he was down the allotment. Thinking about the allotment made him decide to go down there himself. If Peter wasn't there then at least he could get a few things done. Something positive to do might just clear his head.

Grabbing his coat, he told his wife where he was going. Lynne had been married to him long enough to know when he wanted to be alone. Walking down the road he soon felt better. Though he pretended not to, he was glad they had an allotment. When Lynne had first mentioned getting one, he had tried to talk her out of it. It was like talking to a brick wall. Nothing was going to stop her. Once she had made the decision, things had happened very quickly.

An allotment had become available just weeks after applying for one. Once they had been down to inspect it, it was soon clear why. It hadn't been worked for at least two years and the only thing growing on it were weeds. What he saw as hopeless, Lynne had seen as a challenge. It had taken him days of back breaking, unaccustomed labour, to get the plot cleared of weeds. Sixty one barrowloads of weeds, roots and assorted debris later, he was left with a bare earth plot.

Now, as he looked around, he felt a pride in what they had achieved since. Raised beds contained a variety of vegetables and there were paved areas between the his and her sheds. He had constructed a large enclosed area with scaffolding poles and netting that kept the runner beans, cabbage, brussel sprouts and sweet peas safe from butterflies and birds. There was a line of raspberry and blackcurrant bushes that were still doing well despite the lateness of the season. Even the potatoes that were dug up last month had produced enough to keep them going all winter.

He had barely opened up his shed and taken his coat off when Peter's familiar figure walked up the path. Normally a happy person, his face showed the extent of his grieving. Like Dave, Peter had come down to his allotment to get away from his problems.

'You look like you need a coffee'

'Yes, please" The big trucker said as he hauled a chair from the shed and sat down. He watched as Dave filled a saucepan and put it on the gas ring to boil.

'Problem, Stu?'

'No, not really. Just things getting on top of me I suppose. Beth and I really miss John. He was like one of our own kids. I can't believe it is only four days since he died. It's another week until his funeral and there is still so much to organize.'

'I reckon that we are going to do him proud, Peter.' Dave made two cups of coffee and handed one over. He grabbed another chair and sat down. “I have got things sorted with Mike. He is trying to get a few more showtruck owners involved. The only thing I am worried about is how big this is going to get.’

‘That thought had struck me as well. I have updated the magazine websites and the word should be getting out very soon.’ Peter sipped his coffee and reflected on what had been done and what was still to do. He was just glad that he hadn’t had to organize it alone. He realized that, without the assistance of his older companion,

John’s funeral wouldn’t be quite the same. But, like Dave, he too worried about things getting out of control. Still, too many was better than too few. Besides, they still had a week to fine tune the event and get things organized. Until then, it was nice to just sit and think about all the things he had to do now he was here. The plot could do with a bit of a tidy. Get all the weeds up and down to the skip. A bit more digging. Slowly, he began to relax.

FOURTEEN

In Transport, there were still five mechanics working on Maggie. Three were modifying the trailer to take the energy cells. The vinyl sidecover had been stripped off completely and the side support struts removed. The rear doors were open to allow unrestricted access to the floor of the trailer. Two of the mechanics were busy removing floorboards whilst a third welded steel brackets to the chassis to support extra strengthening steel strips.

The cab of the Magnum still hung down in it's raised position. The remaining two mechanics were bolting the modification to the fuel system into place. Instead of it's usual diesel, the Mack engine was now going to run on Radnum. A member of the hyper sonic series of power, Radnum was more commonly referred to as Dilithium. As Dilithium was the energy source being transported from the alien planet Arcturus and stored in the energy cells or batteries, it was the logical choice to fuel the truck. A mixture of Dilithium and water was fed from the energy cell that had replaced the diesel tank and into the engine's fuel injection system. Once in the combustion chamber and ignited by the pistons, it behaved in a similar manner to diesel but produced much more power for far less fuel.

The problem for the mechanics had been to find the right ratio of energy to water. Too much water in the mix and the fuel wouldn't ignite under combustion. Too much Dilithium and the pistons would melt with the increased temperature as the powerful fuel ignited. As well as the fuel modifications, there had been extensive remapping of the engine fuel management system's computer chip. With the last bolt properly tightened, it was time to see if the engine performed as well in the real world as it had in the computer simulation.

Positioning a step ladder adjacent to the open window on the cab, a mechanic reached in and turned the ignition key. For a moment, nothing happened as the fuel
pump turned over and filled the empty fuel lines. Suddenly, the engine gave a cough, fired up briefly and then stopped. The mechanic turned the key again and this time the engine caught immediately and began to run slightly erratically. After a few minutes, whilst the air was being purged from the system, the engine settled down into a regular rhythm. One of the other mechanics stepped closer to the engine and operated the throttle linkage. The engine bellowed on full power and then died to a whisper as the linkage was released. Twice more the throttle was opened and released. On each occasion, the engine ran at full power immediately and then died to a low rumble as it returned to idle.

Noel Flynn was standing on the walkway outside his office. A big grin lit up his face and he descended the stairs to join the jubilant mechanics. He stood in front of the engine and gestured for the throttle to be operated again. He listened critically as the revs rose and then held. He walked around to the other side of the engine and operated the linkage himself.

'Great job, lads' he enthused. 'Watch the exhaust stacks whilst I blip it again'. As the powerful engine ran at full throttle, they all looked at the stainless steel exhaust pipes behind the engine. Pointing straight upward and supported by their own support struts, they flared and bent slightly at the ends. With the engine's normal fuel, it was expected that there would be a modicum of black smoke from a cold engine. With the diluted Dilithium, there was absolutely nothing but a deep throated roar coming from the shiny pipes.

'Clean as a nun's conscience' Noel said to the self satisfied men gathered around him. 'What is the projected fuel consumption?' he asked Sean the foreman.

'About five hundred mpg and over twice the power' was the reply.

'By all that's holy, I could have used this system on earth. Just think, I would never have to siphon a tank again. Never have the taste of diesel in my mouth again. How volatile is it?'

'As combustible as diesel. You could throw a lighted match into the tank and it would just go out. It is only once it is compressed that the mix becomes flammable. Even then, it is nowhere near as dangerous as petrol.'

'Thanks lads. Great job. It is only six o'clock. Knock off early for a change. I'll go and deliver the glad tidings to the Committee and then go and find John Slater. Put his mind at ease. He looks after this truck like a baby.'

Whilst the mechanics cleared up their equipment, Noel Flynn returned to his office. Imogen, his secretary, was still working at her desk. 'Get me the Committee on the phone will you, dearest girl?'

Whilst he waited for his call to come through, he opened his desk draw and lifted out a bottle of Jameson Irish whisky. Pouring himself a generous slug, he returned the bottle just as the phone buzzed. 'Just to let you know that my lads have worked miracles' he said as he took a sip of the fiery liquid. 'The truck is ready and the trailer should be completed tomorrow evening. Everything will be ready for a full road test the following day. I don't expect any other problems at all. Ok Sir, I will keep you updated' With a satisfied smile, he downed the rest of the whisky and looked across at Imogen. 'Do you fancy a little prayer' he asked with a quizzical expression on his face. She smiled and, unbuttoning her blouse, came over. Kissing him lightly, she pulled his shirt out and ran her fingers over his chest. He removed her blouse completely and reached round to undo her bra. He nuzzled between her pert breasts and unzipped her skirt. It fell down and he ran his thumbs under the waistline of the scanty panties and gently eased them down over her hips. In the meantime, her fingers were busy at the zip of his trousers. Sliding it all the way down, she reached in and pulled him out. Sinking to her knees, she groaned 'Oh God' as she enveloped the hardening shaft with her lips and began to "pray". Noel arched his back, grabbed her hair and groaned softly 'For what we are about to receive, may we be truly thankful' Speaking around stretched lips, Imogen mumbled 'Amen'.

***

Molly walked into the room she shared with Astra and found her on her bed. Sitting down beside her, she reached out a hand and the distraught girl reached out and held it. 'I'm sorry Molly' she whispered. 'It's just that it was such a shock. Coming in and finding him here. Am I just being stupid?'

'No love, you're not. It is understandable that you are scared of men and particularly truckers. How you do your job all day, speaking to strange men and not freaking out is a mystery to me. But, you have to remember that the bad ones don't get in. And, as for John Slater, I reckon he is one of the better ones. The other girls like him and they are good judges of character.'

'It's not that I dislike him, Molly. It's just that I don't really want to get close to any man just yet. Celeste and Angel say that he is a real gent and that it will probably be them that seduce him. I know that I am going to have to change and start to trust again but it is hard for me'.

'Take your time gal, take your time. But, for what it's worth, I had my mate in records check his life history and even his most secret thoughts aren't that bad. Well, for a bloke that is. The odd lech now and then but that's in their dna. They can't help it. If ever you are going to start trusting men again, then I reckon John is a good place to start. Think it over. I don't reckon he would ever do anything a girl didn't want him to. Even then, he is going to be pretty gentle. He's that sort of bloke.'

'Thanks Molly. You've given me something to think about. I think I'll have a nap now. It's been a pretty tiring sort of day.'

***

When we arrived at the tube, the station was empty. Obviously we had just missed one. 'When's the next one?' I asked the girls.

'When you press the call button' Astra replied reaching over and pressing the red button marked "call". Then it takes around three minutes.' As she leaned over, I breathed in her scent. It was a heady mix of musk, sharp lemon and light blossom. It was intoxicating and I put my arms around her and pulled her close. I put my lips to her ear and whispered 'I love your perfume. What is it?'

She looked into my eyes and smiled 'Woman, Slater, woman'.

I suddenly remembered that there were three of us. I broke away guiltily and looked over at Celeste expecting to see a little anger or jealousy. Instead she came over and put her arms around us both. 'Ooh, I am looking forward to this' she said as she hugged us both. She said it with such passion that Little John heard her and began to stretch. Which promptly popped the question into my mind 'looking forward to the show or later?' Down, boy.

When the tube arrived, there was no one else on board. The section lifted and we walked inside. Celeste pressed the button for Green Zone 35, the outside section closed and we were off. Again, there were periods of dark and light but we were travelling too fast to see much of what was happening in the lit areas. Just a blur of light, colours and a few people.

'Is there going to be a lot of people about tonight?' I asked more to make conversation than anything else. I was feeling just slightly confused. I was going out with two gorgeous women and I was attracted to both equally. And, equally confusing, there didn't seem to be any jealousy between them. Weird or what?

'It depends on which venue we go to' Celeste said. 'I have never seen any one place packed to the rafters. There is so much choice that everyone goes where they want and see who they want.'

'Where would you normally go?' I asked bracing myself as the tube slowed slightly and then resumed it's journey.

'Well, I don't think we have ever been to a country and western concert before'. Angel replied for them both. 'Normally we like rock or swing. Every now and then we go all classical and go and see an opera or Gilbert and Sullivan. Celeste likes the ballet because she took ballet lessons when she was a girl. You know, back in the Dark Ages. Ouch' she exclaimed as Celeste elbowed her in the ribs.

'Better than taking art lessons from Da Vinci himself' the blonde girl replied with a laugh. 'Angel fancies herself as a bit of an artist. That is, until Astra moved in with us and did the wall mural. She sort of lost interest after that'

'Can you blame me' Angel asked. 'That girl is brilliant. Such talent. Imagine what she could have gone on to be but for what that bastard Sutcliffe did .....' she broke off and looked over at me. 'Sorry John. I keep forgetting'

Sensing that the mood of the evening was beginning to get darker, I put my arm around her and then reached out to Celeste. Both snuggled close. 'Don't keep apologizing. I feel the same way but let's close the subject for now and concentrate on enjoying ourselves. You sure you don't mind Country?'

I still had my arms around them as the tube reached Green Zone 35. I moved my arms and grabbed a hand from each of them and we made our way to the exit. Even though I had been there earlier, I still wasn't sure what to expect. Earlier there had been no people but now, judging from the sound that grew louder as we approached the exit, all that had changed.

We went from the half light of the tube station to the bright lights of the Green Zone. And, I do mean bright. Think of Disney World, Alton Towers and Blackpool promenade on a busy night and then double it. There were bright street lights, flashing neon signs, strobe lighting coming from the nearest venues and the multitude of colours from the arcades. And people.

People everywhere. Inside the venues, coming out, waiting outside the entertainment of choice or just walking. People of all colours and in all hue and styles of clothing. Fashion from decades ago right up to a few days ago. Suits, evening gowns, jeans, casual, skirts; the whole gamut of design, decade and desire. I stopped dead and tried to take it all in. The girls just stood there and humored me. I had seen the people working underground in the Hydroponic areas but this was totally different. At work they had dressed uniformly in uniforms. Here they dressed in clothes of choice; so much choice, so many people. I felt overwhelmed again.

They must have sensed my apprehension because they slowly pulled me forward. From darkness to light. From relative silence to happy sounds. I relaxed and let them lead me. They led me to the venue I had seen earlier. The one advertising “Red Sovine and Various Artistes”; the one that promised an unforgettable night. We swam through a sea of people. Young, old, men, women, girls and boys. Somehow, I had expected a predominantly young crowd but I was wrong. I spotted some old guys who must have been at least sixty. Imagine being able to choose the perfect age to be and deciding that sixty was it. I said as such to Angel. She pointed out that the older people were probably new arrivals who hadn’t taken their Nanoprobe pill yet. I hadn’t thought of that. I remembered my first night in Heaven and how confused and upset I had been. Going out was the last thing on my mind. But, different strokes and all that.

When we reached our venue, it looked different. Bigger, brighter, brasher. I half expected to see a cashier desk and a couple of bouncers but we just went straight in and sat down. It was about a third full so we found good seats four rows back from the stage. The show didn't start for another half hour so we just sat and chatted whilst I looked around.

It wasn't the plushest of places but it was comfortable. A bit like your local cimema. A bit seedy but comfortable and welcoming. The wall lights were half dimmed so I couldn't really tell what colour the walls were. They looked like cream but could have been white. There was that air of expectancy and chatter that you find at places like this. I found myself willing the time forward. You have to imagine just what it meant to me. One of my favourite artists was going to perform on this stage in just a short time. Something that could never have happened on Earth.

I was already mentally running through the list of who I would like to see next. Elvis, of course. Then Billy Fury, Dusty Springfield, Jim Reeves, Jimmi Hendrix. Think dead stars and then think who you would like to see. It wasn't a Wish List as much as a Must See list. I told the girls what I was thinking.

'Yes, it's like being a kid in a sweet shop' said Angel.

'I saw Buddy Holly last week' Celeste chipped in. That started them off on the list of stars they had seen. I half listened and half watched the clock. With five minutes to go and not many more people inside, Celeste got up and walked off. 'She's looking for the little girl's room' Angel explained.

She came back about ten minutes later and sat down again. I noticed a little look pass between her and Angel but thought nothing of it. Just then the lights dimmed further and a familiar figure walked onto the stage. People started clapping and whistling. I looked behind me. There still weren't that many people in but they made up in volume what they lacked in numbers. And, they were dressed ordinary. You half expect country lovers to wear Stetsons, cowboy boots and fringed waistcoats. But, I remembered, with only two sets of clothes to last eternity, there probably wasn't much choice. The lone figure reached the microphone in the centre of the stage and paused. The lights went brighter and there he was.

'Howdy folks. I'm Red Sovine and I'd like to thank you all for coming. My first song is Phantom 309' and, just like that, he strummed his guitar and started narrating the tale of the hitch-hiker and the ghostly truck. I just sat there in shock. Red Sovine. On the bloody stage. Right in front of me and looking just like I had pictured him from his album covers. No body else on stage. No other sound but that deep rich voice and the gentle guitar. I looked at the girls. They were concentrating on Red and his words. I looked behind and around and saw nothing but rapt attention. I just settled back and enjoyed. I was in Heaven, literally and locally. Red finished to a wall of applause and waved to his audience.

'Thank you folks. It's nice to see some old faces here tonight. I see a lot of new ones as well. And, I have a message and request for one of you from a very pretty little lady who came to see me backstage. Will John Slater stand up please?'

I heard my name but it didn't register. I heard Celeste and Angel laughing and they pushed me up. I looked at them and up onto the stage in a state of confusion. I just stood there in that sort of embarrassed and pleased stage where you know something is going to happen but you are not sure if you are going to like it. At the back of my mind was the hope that I wasn't going to be asked to sing.

'Howdy John. Pleased to see you. Folks, John is a Newbie. A Grade 2 Newbie at that. I'm told that he is also a trucker and, as you know, I am particularly partial to truckdrivers. Back in the day, they used to be my main audience. Anyhow, John was driving out of Berlin, Germany, when he heard one of my songs. It moved him so much that he went out and bought all my albums. Pity he couldn't have done it while I was still alive but better late than never, I suppose.' There was sustained laughter and clapping at this point and I got more embarrassed than ever. I looked down at the girls and they were laughing and cheering as much as anyone. 'I'll get you for this' I warned them.

Once the audience had calmed down Red continued. 'Now, one of his pretty companions has just told me that John starts an important job here in the next few days. He is going to be the truckdriver that will deliver the new energy supplies and it is a big job; an important job. And, John, if you ever want a passenger, I would be honoured if you let me come with you now and again. Now, at the request of Angelica and Celeste, I would like to sing the song that he first heard that day in Germany – Teddy Bear. Thank you folks, enjoy'

I didn't realize I was still standing until the girls pulled me down. As the story unfolded up on the stage, there wasn't a sound except for Red and his guitar. He must have sang this song thousands of times but he still put all his feelings and emotions into the words. I got a lump in my throat and had to wipe my eyes. I looked around, a little ashamed of my emotion but saw tears streaming down the girls faces too. When he got to the part where the trucker had turned round and found a queue of trucks waiting at the little cripple boys house, they - and most of the audience – lost it and cried/laughed/cheered together as the song finally finished. They mightn't have liked Red Sovine before but the girls certainly liked him now. They liked him even more as he talked and sang some of his and the audience's favorites. Daddy's Girl, Little Rosa and Giddyup Go came and went and still the fans cried for more. After another thirty minutes, Red finished and held up his hands for quiet.

'Thank you, folks. Nice to be appreciated. Now, I'd like you to show your appreciation for my next guest. This little lady doesn't need any introduction so just sit back guys and enjoy. By the way, John Slater, don't forget my truck ride.' As he waved again and went off stage, a blonde haired young woman came on and took his place. The audience erupted and the girls looked at me as if to say 'who's that?'. I waved towards the stage and made 'sit back and listen' gestures.

When the audience went quiet, the girl strummed her guitar and started to sing Sting's "Fields of Gold". Her voice was warm honey and full of the same emotion as the last singer. It was hard to see her face with the bright lights and the way her hair fell down but you just knew she was beautiful. The girls just looked at each other with open mouths and then settled back with rapt expressions on their faces. After she had finished that, she immediately launched into Songbird to be followed seamlessly by Over the Rainbow, You take my Breath Away, Early Morning Rain. That little girl just stood there and sang her heart out. The purity of her voice and the way she interpreted the songs were breathtaking, joyful and heart achingly beautiful. When she launched into Danny Boy there wasn't another sound in the hall. I have often heard the old Irish song but never this way. Her voice dropped to a whisper, her eyes were closed and she was totally lost in the lyrics. Her voice rose and fell hauntingly and the words dripped with emotion. The audience just sat and listened with tears on their cheeks and a shine in their eyes. They didn't clap between songs, they didn't make a sound, they just hungered for more and more.

Finally, she sang her last song and, with a shy little wave, she left as quietly as she came. It took a few moments for the audience to return from where she had taken them. When they did, they erupted with clapping, cheering and cries for more. The girls grabbed me and practically shouted in my ear 'Who was that?'

I swallowed hard and told them in a husky little voice 'That was Eva Cassidy'.

Eva Cassidy who had departed aged thirty three. Who had only truly become known to the world after her death in 1996 from cancer. A relatively undiscovered star who struggled with shyness and was determined to sing every song in her own way. Fortunately, she had made many demo tapes and, when these were discovered after her death, the songs were recorded and became instant worldwide hits. Now she was here. In Heaven where her talent truly shone for eternity.

As I told the girls about Eva, they wept. 'You know, John' Celeste said as she snuggled close. 'I only came to this venue to please you. Same with Angel. We both thought it was going to be all "yeeha and dosiedo' and all that hillbilly stuff. I think we both got into Red Sovine. I loved his voice and the way he told his stories. That mix of talking and singing. But Eva.....wow, she just blew us away. I have never heard anyone sing "Over the Rainbow or Danny Boy" like that'

'I'm glad you appreciated it' I smiled. As if I had known she would be here. It would have been enough just to hear Red but, with Eva thrown in as well, it was another dimension. 'I'm glad you liked both of them because I have all their work on cd in Maggie. But, I keep forgetting, you can hear them here anytime you want to. Live and for free.'

Angel looked up and her eyes were still moist. 'Would you mind if we left now?' she asked. 'I don't know about you two but I feel as if I have been through an emotional spin dryer. I don't think I could cope with any more for now. Can we just have a walk outside?'

As no one else had come onto the stage, it looked like that the entertainment in this particular venue was finished for the night. I suddenly realized that we had been here nearly three hours. Three hours! It had gone in an instant. Everyone else in the audience was slowly emerging from wherever they had been and were leaving. We followed them out into the still busy street.

We just wandered aimlessly up and down. Looking at this poster or picture of the artist appearing at that particular venue. People were coming and going, in and out, all the time, wherever we went. There was laughter, carefree talk, bright lights and that wonderful atmosphere of people just having a good time. The slot machines in the casinos were jingling and the passengers in the fairground rides were screaming. There were little groups of people waiting in line for a hot dog or beef burger. We heard snatches of where they had been, who they had seen or were going to see as we passed. In one particularly busy area, I felt something pulling my sleeve. I looked down.

'Allo, Mr Slater' said Alfie. 'How you doing? I like your birds. They're real smashers. Allo, Miss Celeste, Miss Angel. Ere, I've got a joke for you. Two old geezers are in hospital. They 'ave been lifelong friends but one of them is dying and the other is visiting. The one visiting is talking about what good mates they've been and how he's going to miss him. "Once you get to 'eaven, you gotta get in touch and tell me if they play football up there." The other bloke agrees and shortly after, he dies. The one left is in bed one night, a few days later, when he 'ears his name being called. "You awake Bert? It's Sid. I'm in 'eaven and just keeping my promise to get in touch. But, there's good news and bad news. What do you want first?" The bloke in bed goes for the good news. "Right Bert. The good news is that they do play football in 'eaven. The bad news is that you're the goalie in tomorrow night's match" That's a good un, innit Mr Slater? See yuh'. Celeste whispered something in his ear. He grinned and ran off.

'That Alfie' Angel said shaking her head. 'He gets worse. Got a heart of gold, though. And, he knows his way around better than anyone else I know. I'm just worried that he is getting a bit wild. I don't like him hanging around with that Noel Flynn either. Always off running errands for him'

'Noel's all right' I reassured her. 'He's a bit dodgy but he wouldn't see Alfie come to any harm. I imagine that Alfie gets something out of it as well. Two peas in a pod, those two. Right, where are going next?'

The girls looked at each other and some sort of secret girl message got passed along. 'Um, I think we ought to head back now. Both Angel and I have to be up early for work tomorrow. Apparently it's going to be busier than usual. You don't mind, do you?'

'No. I am glad you said it. I didn't want to disappoint you two but I am tired. It's been a busy day and a wonderful night but I'm having a job keeping up with you two youngsters.'

I got an elbow dig in each side and saw the secret look passing between them again. Damn, all the languages I speak and I still can't understand women. They lined up beside me and each slipped an arm through mine. Three tired but very happy people were calling it a night.

On the ride home, the tube was busier than when we came. Not exactly packed but we ended up wedged into a corner. It wasn't totally necessary but I wasn't going to complain. I had Celeste in front and Angel behind. I felt like the filling in an angel cake. Every time the tube rolled or lurched, I could feel a pair of breasts and thighs pressing into me. It was a good feeling. Still flooded with adrenalin, emotion or both, I was on a high.

Little John was feeling the effects as well. I did that sort of bent over thing that men do when they are trying to hide an erection but, with the girls pressing in front and back, it was difficult. It didn't take Celeste long to feel the difference. Her eyes widened and I felt her hand patting me gently. 'Ooh...' was all she said. Of course it didn't take long for Angel to realize that something was up and her hand snaked around from behind and patted the something as well. I felt her lips nibbling my ear and, not to be outdone, Celeste started on the other one.

It didn't take long for that tingly, itching feeling to become a full blown embarrassment. In my defense, I should say that it had been a long time between missions for Little John. It wasn't long before the girls realized what had happened because they started laughing at my discomfiture. It wasn't a nasty sort of laughing, more of a "Mission Accomplished" self satisfied chuckle. Well, it had happened. I couldn't deny it or do anything about it. I had to laugh as well. 'Now, I'm going to have to take another shower when I get back'.

'Don't worry about it, John. You didn't stand a chance, did you?' I looked into Celeste's brilliant blue eyes and thought I detected more than humour in them.

I put my arms around her, pulled her in close and kissed her full on the lips. Long, loving and lingering. 'Oi, what about me? Don't I get one too?' I released Celeste and grabbed Angel. Did the same thing. I'm a good kisser, I've been told. And, when I put everything into it, as I just did, the effects were gratifying. Angel's legs sort of buckled and I had to hold her up against me. It wasn't a hardship. One up for me, I think.

Far from spoiling the mood of the evening, the incident had made it better. We had got that first embarrassing moment done and dusted. We had laughed about it and everything was fine. Actually, it had probably improved things. That first pent up moment of first-time passion had passed and we were now all at ease with each other. If there was going to be more action tonight, I would now be a marathon man now and not a sprinter.

But, frankly, that anticipation was beginning to worry me. Both girls had shown no jealousy about me being with them both. In fact, I was fast getting the impression that they were a team and I was their newest member. When I was younger, the prospect would have had me panting at the leash. It is probably most young men's dream and ambition to have two young, willing and adventurous women at the same time.

At that time of your life, it is all about action not affection. Affection, and being with someone because you have feelings for them, comes along later in life. You have to do the first to enjoy the last. Personally, I had felt, and proved, that thirty five is probably the best age for a meaningful relationship. The fact that mine hadn't survived my job didn't detract from the fond memories I had of her. Anyway, I digress. I was now right back in my thirty five year old *experienced but looking for more* age slot and, best of all, in it permanently. And, frankly, I wanted more than sex with these two gorgeous and sexy women. I wanted to make love to them and, there is a difference. But, I couldn't achieve that with both at the same time. I needed to be alone with each of them to give that particular lady my undivided attention without the distraction of the other. But, and here was my problem, how did I manage that without giving my second choice offence? Probably more important right now, which one would be my first choice? It would be difficult because I already loved them – oops, that one slipped out effortlessly didn't it? – equally.

Celeste, my blonde haired angel. Slightly dippy but gorgeous with it. A wonderful, caring and affectionate lady. Angelica, the fiery redhead with her 'don't mess with me' attitude and the vulnerability that she had shown me without realizing it. Who would give her heart hesitantly but with the unspoken warning that it must not be messed with. I had the feeling that I would be faced with the problem and choice sooner than I would have liked. Without me realizing it, we had reached our destination. Whether the tube had stopped to allow other people on or off, I couldn't say. There were still passengers staring out at us as we made our way out of the station.

All too soon, we arrived back at Mother Theresa of Calcutta house. I followed the girls in and Molly greeted us. Whilst the other two told her all about our night out, Red and Eva but not, I hope, the tube incident, I walked across to admire Astra's mural. I nearly said 'Muriel' but that would have shown that I watched too much Coronation Street, wouldn't it? I don't know what Hilda Ogden would have made of it but I felt that it was superb. The brush work was so fine that you couldn't see the lines and you would swear that the horses moved the instant you turned your back.

'Wonderful, isn't it?' Molly said coming up beside me. 'Such talent. I've been trying to get her to put on an exhibition at our local gallery. You should see her canvasses. They are wonderful.' She turned towards me and I looked into her eyes. They were sympathetic, caring eyes. 'I've had a word with her about earlier. It'll take time but I think you and she will be ok.'

I leaned over and kissed her cheek. 'Thanks Molly.' She giggled and waved me away but I could tell she was pleased. 'Drink?' I told her a coffee would be fine and she went away to get it. I went over to the girls who were on the sofa. 'I think I might grab a shower, if that's ok?' I told them with a smile. 'I feel a little grubby after all that *travelling*'.

'Yeah, we did warn you about the tube, didn't we?' Angel teased. 'All that groping. Never know where it might lead'

Both giggled as I went into the bathroom. I didn't care. I was past the embarrassment stage.

When I came out, I felt much better....and fresher. Wonderful things these sonic showers. Body and clothes cleaned and freshened together.

I joined the others and drank my coffee. It had been a good day and a memorable night. The others were quiet, each thinking their own thoughts. It seemed that Celeste and Angel were avoiding looking at me. I decided to test the waters. I yawned mightily and then again. I used to do that at parties. There is something about someone yawning that sets everyone off. I gave another yawn and was rewarded by Molly doing the same. Within a minute, everyone was yawning, each set off by the other. You should try it yourself sometime. It always works.

'Well, sorry about that ladies'. I said stretching. 'It's starting to catch up with me. I must be making a move.' I already had but they just hadn't realized it.

Between yawns, the others looked at each other and Molly spoke first. 'Why don't you stay the night? We can easily make up the sofa and it would save you the bother of travelling to your parent's.'

I pretended to consider the offer. 'I should probably go. I won't be able to contact Mike and Jean and they will probably worry that I'm ok'. Actually, the thought of two teenagers worrying that their thirty five year old son hadn't come home was ludicrous.

' Oh, that's ok. I told Alfie to drop by on his way home and tell them you might be staying here' Celeste said. She couldn't look me in the eye but I now knew what the whispering in Alfie's ear had been about. They had got it all planned, hadn't they?

'Well' I said very reluctantly. 'If you're sure it won't be any bother?'

It obviously wasn't because that sofa was made up with sheets and blankets in the blink of an eye. We all did another yawning, arm stretching and "I'm ready for my bed" pretence round and I kissed them all goodnight. Molly backed off. The other two gave as good as they got. I stripped off to my whitey tightys –now a bit more tighty than normal – and got into my bed for the night. The lights went off and I waited to see what would happen……if anything.

I must have dropped off because I started up with that "What?" feeling you get when you doze off and something wakes you. As my eyes adjusted to the dark, I could see the *something* standing in front of me. I knew it was one of the girls but couldn't tell which one. She was wearing some sort of white, nearly but not quite, transparent night gown which shimmered around her. It sort of revealed her body but I wasn't quite sure whether it was my overheated imagination or not.

She moved closer and whispered my name. I held open my covers in invitation but she hung back. I suddenly realized that it wasn't Angel or Celeste. I didn't think it would be Molly so that left only one other option.

Astra just stood there and I could she was shaking. I didn't move. I just lay there with the covers held open whilst she stared at me. 'Can you just hold me without doing anything else?' she whispered in a little girl voice. 'I just need to be held'

I raised the covers slightly and she made up her mind. Still shaking violently, she crossed the deep void between us and slipped in beside me. Her head rested on my left arm. Still lying on my back, I dropped the covers and slowly let my right arm down across to my side. She lay there shivering. I couldn't even begin to imagine what courage it had taken her to get to this point. Gradually, she started to get warmer as our combined heat built up. Her shaking subsided and I could feel her body relaxing against mine.

She turned her back to me and I could feel her breath on my arm. She hesitantly pressed her back against my side. I lay there hardly daring to breathe in case I disturbed the wonderment of what was happening. I felt her breathing getting deeper and more regular and knew she was finally starting to trust again. I could feel the heat of her body all down my side. I had to fight my, or any man's, natural reaction and not move. My arm was trapped under her neck and was starting to cramp. I tried to ignore it.

After a few more minutes, she reached across me with her free arm and felt for my hand. She laced her fingers into mine and gently pulled. I followed her arm and turned onto my side. I found myself spooned against her. My chest against her back. My groin against her bottom. The heat from our bodies fused us together and I felt every inch of her pressing into me. By now, she had stopped shivering and I could hear her breathing getting deeper and slower as she drifted off. I thought she was asleep and was thinking about trying to release my trapped arm when she disentangled our laced fingers and moved my hand down to her breast and pressed it gently. Hesitantly, hoping that I was reading her intentions correctly, I cupped her breast lightly in my hand

and left it there. I could feel her nipple hardening against my palm. Her hand was still on the back of my hand and she pushed it firmly against mine. I tightened my grip and, with a contented little sigh, she relaxed totally and drifted off. I held her breast gently and pressed my body more firmly against her. I just held her all night long and let her damaged body and mind heal whilst she slept.

When I awoke in the morning, she was gone. Had I dreamt it?

Molly came bustling in with a tray in her hands. She was dressed ready for work and had a big smile on her face. 'There you are, Slater' she beamed as she put the tray down. "There you are" was a full English with a cup of tea on the side. I sat up.

'This is nice' I thanked her as I plumped my pillows and reached for the tray. She

reached out and rumpled my hair. 'You deserve it. That was a wonderful thing you did last night. I was awake when Astra came back to our room this morning. I have never seen her so content and relaxed. She told me what happened and just to say "thank you" when you were awake. We all pooled our replicator rations to give you this as our way of saying thank you'

I looked at her as I took my first sip of tea. 'Thank you. And not just for the breakfast. I felt honored and humbled that you three decided that I could help her. I just hope that I have made up in some way for what that man did too her. Showed her that we are not all animals'

'She still has a long way to go. She might trust you but that doesn't mean she trusts all men. But, last night was a start. Her first step on a long journey.'

'You know Molly, I had already worked out that I was being set up for something. Celeste and Angel are a good team. They have told you about the tube incident?' She nodded. 'I guess that was a safety precaution. Letting off the steam in case I couldn't control myself? You know, if you had asked me directly, I would have tried to help gladly'.

'Actually Celeste said you would. It was my idea to keep you out of the loop. If I have offended you, then I apologize but, where Astra is concerned, I don't like to take any chances. Even with, as you put it, the steam released, there was still a chance that you would react on instinct. But, sometimes you have to go with your gut and mine told me that, essentially, you are a good, decent guy. And, believe me, I am a good judge of men'

'Oh? Had many then" I asked as I started on the food.

'I guess you could say that I have had more men than you have had hot breakfasts' Molly said, looking directly into my eyes. 'On Earth, I was a prostitute, street walker, call girl or whatever you like to call me. And then, when I got too old and ugly, I ran my own brothel. So, yes, I guess you could say that I have had a lot of men'.

Looking at Molly, big, motherly Molly, I half expected she was joking. She read my mind.

'Yes, even we big girls can be on the game. There are a lot of men like big girls –chubby chasers is what they are called – usually because we are so grateful' she laughed.. 'I was young, I liked having sex and men liked me, gave me presents. It wasn't long before I was given money and it seemed such an easy way to earn a living. I wasn't much good at any other job I tried. Getting paid to do something you liked seemed a very good deal to me.' Molly looked at

me defensively as if expecting some sort of horrified response.
'I am not going to judge you Molly. It was your life and, if it suited you and nobody got hurt, then I can't see any problem. Certainly, it is not a problem to me' I had never used a prostitute myself but had seen plenty on my travels. It was just a bit of a shock that this jolly woman had not only been one but had obviously enjoyed it.

'When I got too fat, I decided to open up my own place. I specialized in big girls at first but then went more conservative to cater for the bigger market. I felt that I was giving a service. Men wanted women, were willing to pay and girls were willing to take their money. I ran a good clean establishment, vetted my customers and really looked after my girls. I always felt that my girls were safer working for me than being on the streets. I must have done a good job otherwise I wouldn't be here, would I?'

'Still, it's a bit of a change to what you do now, isn't it?'

'Not really, I'm still performing a service, giving people what they need and I am good at what I do. I've still got my girls to look after……'

'Celeste and Angel…they weren't…….?' I blurted out.

'Good Heaven's, no. And, what if they were? Would it have made a difference.? They are still lovely girls. No, up here, everyone gets to start over with a clean slate. No, I meant that I look out for them, sort of a Mother Hen'
I looked up from my food. 'Do you know what they were on Earth? They haven't said much and I didn't like to pry. Angel let slip something yesterday and I guess that she has something she keeps to herself.'

'Can't keep much to yourself up here, John. Everyone's Earth life is public record. But, yes, I do know what they were in their previous life. They also said that I could tell you if you asked. Celeste's life was nothing out of the ordinary. She was born rich and lived most of her life rich. She never married or had kids, never did much at all but have fun. But, in spite of everything, she lived a good life and died old.' Molly took away my empty plate and cup and returned with another cup of tea.

'Angelica is slightly different. She got involved with a married man, fell out with her family and ended up living rough after the bastard deserted her. She got into drugs, overdosed accidentally and was rushed to hospital. A nurse found her parent's phone number in a pocket and contacted them. They had a big reconciliation and, after she was discharged, went back home. Everything was good for a couple of months until she found out she was pregnant. She had no idea who the father was but guessed that some bloke had taken advantage when she was high on drugs. She didn't want her parents – her dad particularly – to find out so she had an abortion, was sent home and then started bleeding. She was too ashamed to call out to her parents and basically just bled out.'

'So, she didn't mean to kill herself?' I asked. 'Only, I got the impression she thought she had killed herself.'

'Well, yes, she did kill herself but not intentionally. She is coming to terms with herself now but it has taken a long time. You're the first bloke she has been out with since she got here. And, I'm not giving away any secrets here but you are also the first one she is going to sleep with'.

'Then, as we are clearing the air, can I ask you something Molly? I fancy both of them rotten, maybe love them but don't know what's going on. I know they are both keen on me but… but, there is no jealousy between them. Do they intend to share me or what? I can't choose between them and don't know what to do. If I go with Celeste first will Angel get the hump? Or vice-versa. What do you think I should do, Molly?'

'You are still thinking in earth terms John. It is different up here. There are no sexual diseases. No female gets pregnant. Sex is a completely different experience. If it feels right, then it is right. The girls aren't going to fall out over which one gets you first. Nor are they proposing a threesome. Celeste is already head over heels in love with you and Angel not far behind. You go out with either separately or together. When you are ready for something more, then talk it over with them. They don't expect you to be a Superstud or anything. If you make one happy then you make them all happy. Spread yourself around. And don't get all hung up on Earth principles. And, I get the feeling that you will also have to consider that you are going to have three girlfriends to look after. Astra has needs too. But, one word of caution, take it slowly with her. Anytime you want to sleep on the couch is ok. In fact, I think we will agree to think of the couch as neutral ground. Who knows' Molly said with a big smile and a chuckle 'Maybe we had better draw up some sort of rota system. All I can suggest is that you eat properly and build your strength up. Now, you lucky Stud, I have to get to work.' Still chuckling, Molly grabbed her bag and left. Left me with a lot of thinking to do.

I wasn't due at Maintenance right away so there was no hurry. I finished my tea, had a digestive transit – such a polite term, don't you think? - and took another shower. Sat down and thought about what Molly had said.

On the road, I had seen many prostitutes. Had been propositioned many times. On the European roads there were many motorway service areas and many trucks parked up at night. A lot of girls, or their pimps, drove to the rest areas and plyed their trade. Many drivers took advantage of the service offered but I never had. It never seemed right to me. Probably embarrassment came into it as well. Plus the old macho "I never pay for it". And, strangely, I always felt sorry for the girls as well. As if they were being forced to sell their bodies to whoever had the price.

Probably, the majority were working as a means to an end or in fear of their pimps. It had never crossed my mind that some might actually enjoy their work. Looking at Molly now, who would guess what she had been in her Earth life? She wasn't ashamed of it, had obviously enjoyed it and, when she took the step to management, had created the safe environment for her girls that was far better than working the streets. Probably better for the customer as well. So, a win win situation all round.

Molly and her past wasn't a problem for me. I could never see her as other than what she was: an affectionate and caring lady who loved life and who looked after those who needed help. My problem was still Celeste and Angelica. And, if what Molly had said was true, Astra as well. Despite Molly's advice, the whole situation wasn't a comfortable one for me. I suppose I should have been happy to have two ladies after me. You know, the whole

Jack the Lad macho bullshit but I wasn't. I couldn't envisage a situation where I had to choose between them and not worry about how they felt about it. And, even if they were happy sharing, could I be? The thought of hopping from one bed to the other, whilst most bloke's dream situation, was unsettling for me. As if I was being unfaithful to the one not with me. Maybe it was just me who needed to lighten up and accept things as they were. Maybe it was different here than on Earth. And then there was Astra.

Of course, I felt something for her. I felt that I needed to protect her, show her that things could be different. That not all men were the same. Last night, I never even considered trying to take it any further than she was happy with. Even Little John had behaved himself. I felt proud of myself. Happy and honored that she had trusted me enough to try to face her fears. I felt proud of her. I felt that, maybe, she would be ok. I felt, I felt……just confused about the whole situation.

With these thoughts just going round and round in my head, I decided to go and see how Noel's blokes were getting on with Maggie.

*****

When I went through the workshop entrance, the first thing I saw was my Magnum. My pride and joy. Filthy and covered in grease, dust and whatever other debris had accumulated on her since I had last seen her. Other than that, I didn't detect much difference. There were no fitters working on her so I presumed she was finished. I climbed the stairs to Noel's office to find out. Remembering my last visit to his office, I made plenty of noise as I approached and knocked on the door to give more warning…if it was needed.

I needn't have worried. Imogen was working at her desk and gave me a cheeky grin as I walked through the door. I could see what Noel saw in her but not what she saw in him. He was at his desk, tapping away on his keyboard.

'You've made a right mess of my truck" I said by way of greeting. 'She's absolutely filthy.'

'Get away with yourself.' Noel looked up and waved me into the chair opposite. 'Bit of a wash and she'll be as good as new. In fact, she is now even better than new. She has twice the power, runs smoother, has more torque and sips fuel like a nun sips whiskey'.

'If that is true Noel, then we are talking a thousand bhp. What have you done to her?'

'Modified her to run on Dilithium and water. The mix creates a gas and this is fed into the modified injector system and bingo, power like you have never experienced before. You could say it's like no other truck in Heaven. But, then of course, it is the only articulated truck in Heaven. Now, do you want me to get my big clodhopping guys to clean her or are you going to do it yourself?'

He accompanied me downstairs, out into the yard and showed me where the pressure washer and cleaning gear was stowed. My trailer was in a far corner with mechanics working on it. We returned to the workshop and he handed over my keys. I climbed aboard and sat down behind the wheel. I hadn't realized until that moment, just how I missed being in that cab. Talk about feeling at home. I was home. I gingerly turned the key in the ignition. The

Mack engine caught first time and I listened with a critical ear. One thing a truck driver gets to know is whether his truck's engine is performing properly or not. It's a combination of sound, experience and a plain old seat of the pants feeling. In the first few moments, I knew that Maggie had never sang so sweetly before. Just a tickle on the throttle and she responded instantly and smoothly. Definitely much better than before. I selected reverse and carefully drove her out of the workshop and into the yard. I switched off and just sat there, enjoying the moment. I looked around the cab and made sure everything was in it's accustomed place. My OCD kicked in enough to make me run a duster around and polish my dash. Finally, reluctantly, I climbed down and set about making her sparkle again.

Some two hours later I was finished. I had washed her, dried her off with a microfibre towel – much better than a leather – polished her multi hued skin and buffed her stainless steel. I had a prize winning showtruck again.

I locked her up, force of habit and maybe redundant here, but you never know. Not all the villains were in Hell. Noel wasn't, was he?

My trailer modifications weren't due to be finished until the next day. I walked over to see what they were doing. Two of the guys were busy replacing floorboards. I could see where the deck had beens strengthened with extra steel supports and tie-down rings were now placed at regular intervals. Other than that, there was nothing major. I saw that I would also be washing the trailer tomorrow when it was finished. I hated driving a dirty truck and trailer. OCD rules ok.

By now, it was mid-morning and I was hungry. If I knew Noel, there would be food available. I did the whole noise making, loud knocking thing again before entering the office. Noel was sitting on the edge of Imogen's desk and talking. I asked about something to eat and drink.
'No problem. Let's go down to the workshop and get some proper food. Sausage sandwich ok?'.
It sounded better than ok. I followed him back down and over to the replicator. This was only my fourth day here but already I loved the replicator. 'How about putting one of these in my cab" I asked more in hope than anything.
Noel handed over a hot sausage sandwich with plenty of brown sauce. Talk about Trucking Heaven. He waited for his to appear and we walked over to the fitter's mess room. It was well named.
'Sean, how big a job would it be to fit a replicator and shower in the truck?' he asked a young guy sitting at the table.
'Need about two hours. And, I would have to run a feed from the fusebox. Not a big job. I could put one of the compact units in the wardrobe. You won't be keeping many clothes in that now, will you' Sean decided. 'I would have to run the shower pipe work up the back of the cab and through the roof for the height. I have enough copper pipe but stainless or chromed will need a day or two to obtain.'
'Chromed would look nice' Noel decided for me. 'And make it neat and tidy will you? Mr Obsessive here likes things just so'.
Obsessive? Moi? I arranged to bring the truck back later that day.

'Going somewhere?' Noel asked with a grin. As a trucker himself, he knew I was itching to have a drive. 'Come on, let's give her a road test'.

We climbed in and I fired her up. 'Where are we going?.

'I have just the place' Noel grinned.

Following his directions, I eased out of the compound and turned right. There were still many Astroblocks about and road room was a bit tight in places. Tighter still with a trailer behind. But, today, we were solo. And, solo in a truck designed to pull a trailer and a lot of weight is like driving a racing car. Acceleration is phenomenal because you can put it in top gear, rev the engine, pop the clutch and let her rip. I watched a solo Scania truck out accelerate and beat a Porsche on Top Gear once. No surprise for any truck driver but it left Clarkson's lantern jaw hanging. With more than double the horsepower of that particular truck, I was driving very gingerly, trying to get the feel of what was now a very different vehicle indeed.

After about five miles, the road widened and the Astroblocks were replaced by more traditional housing. Noel explained that this was one of the oldest parts of Heaven. 'Eventually, even this place will be as bad as everywhere else. New blocks are going up at an incredible speed and still there is overcrowding. Right, about a mile further on is the Divide. You've been told about the Divide right? The area set aside for the souls who are not used to civilization. The pre-historics and the like.'

'Yes, I have been told about it briefly but didn't realize it was so close to where we lived.'

'You have to think of this road as a ring road. On one side is relatively untouched areas where specific environments are set up. It is for those people who came here before what we call civilization began. There are desert, jungle, stone age, iron age and other specialist areas set aside for eternity. Most of them have a stable population except for the jungle area where the last undiscovered tribes and those currently living in jungles end up. The Boss felt that the inhabitants of these environments wouldn't be able to cope with our so called civilization. Basically, they live their live the same as they did on Earth. Frozen in a time warp if you like. They build their own habitations, have their own cultures and eat the animals and crops that they rear and grow. In many ways, they have a much better Heaven than we do.'

Whilst he was talking I noticed that the road was indeed getting wider. On one side I could see where we had come from. On the other there was nothing as far as I could see. Before I could ask, Noel told me that the emptiness stretched for about fifty miles and was the barrier between the two Heavens.

I stopped Maggie and we looked at the road ahead. It wasn't a dead straight line but more a meandering concrete stream. When the first stretch of the M1 was built, it was dead straight. It didn't take long for the road builders to realize that drivers needed hills and bends to occupy their minds. Dead straight roads were dead boring; the emphasis being on the dead. Drivers just switched off and ran into the back of other vehicles, overtook without checking mirrors and many other stupid things. Once bends and gradients were introduced the accident and mortality rate dropped dramatically. Obviously the Heavenly road builders had learnt from our early Earthly motorway experiences.

I engaged top gear, left my foot on the clutch and blipped the throttle. I looked across at my passenger and grinned. It was a real Thelma and Loise/John and Noel moment. He laughed out loud and shouted 'Do it!'

I took my left foot off and floored the right. With a squeal of tyres, Maggie took off. She flew down that deserted stretch of road like a fighter jet. I kept my right foot hard down and held on. I watched the speedo climb to 80, 90 and then stick at the end of the gauge. Things began to blur and the steering wheel began to shake violently. It was obvious that, whilst the engine could carry on, the rest of the truck wasn't built for this kind of speed. I gradually bled the speed off until the speedo returned to 80mph. It felt like we were crawling.

I drove on at different speeds and in various gears. Maggie performed faultlessly. Better than before and with a new defiant note escaping from the twin stacks. I couldn't wait to get hitched to a trailer and see how she did with a load behind her. Being back in the cab made me realise just how much I wanted to head up the road again. The old Siren Song of the Road was playing it's sweet music in my ears and the faraway horizon beckoned. I looked across at Noel and saw the same yearning in his eyes. I lifted off and hit the middle pedal. Slowly, reluctantly, I brought Maggie to a halt and engaged the hand brake. We both climbed down and stood there on wobbly legs, fired up with adrenalin and the need to drive. Noel turned to me. 'Wooo! I needed that. Can I drive back?'

He drove cautiously, getting a feel for Maggie. We did one more speed burst but his heart wasn't really in it. He was like me; just driving a truck was enough of a rush. The speed was just a bonus. He stopped at road's end and we swopped places. I drove back more relaxed and settled than I had been for the last three days. Into the yard, and back to the workshop.

The fitters were waiting and surrounded us as we stepped down. As eager for a progress report as we had been to road test the theory. Noel gave a thumbs up and they were delighted. Sean raised the front grille and plugged a hand held scanner into the diagnostic point. He downloaded the results and took them to his computer. As the achieved speed figures came up on his monitor, he whistled disbelievingly.

'You know your maximum recorded speed was 183mph?' he told us. 'Was that it or did you have problems?'

'No problems, as such' I assured him. 'I had no idea what the speed was once the speedo reached the end of the dial. 183mph? Damn, that's fast. The problem was that the truck started vibrating and the steering wheel was wobbling so much, it was difficult to control. As far as the engine is concerned, it was nowhere near maximum revs. There was no power surge or turbo lag, the speed just built up. If the truck was altered to take the strain, I have a feeling that we could have gone twice as fast. Good job, men. I really appreciate it.'

Sean unhooked his equipment. 'You know, I used to be chief mechanic for Scania GB when they were into truck racing. We used to struggle to get 150mp and that was using racing slicks, high ratio back axles and modified gear box linkages. We even rigged up a system of spraying cold water directly onto the brake discs to keep them cool. With this fuel, we could have lapped everything'.

Still shaking his head, Sean walked back to my trailer to supervise it's completion. I accompanied Noel to his office for a much needed coffee. Maybe something stronger. As he ordered our drinks from the replicator, I had a sudden thought. Or, rather one that kept popping up.

'How do I pay for all this stuff I am getting from the replicator?' I asked Noel as he passed my cup over. 'How does it know who is ordering and who keeps score of what's ordered'

'Easy enough. That nanoprobe pill you swallowed gives out a continuous signal. Anything that needs Credits to operate –replicator, entertainment, canteen and such – picks up that signal and automatically debits or credits your account. If you are near to being overdrawn, the machine you are using lets you know. First week or two, everything is free whilst you settle in. Once you start working, a rate for your job is already agreed upon and you get that. Sort of like union rates.'

'But what happens if you don't like your job? Are you stuck with it for eternity or what?'

'People generally get to work in Hydroponics, Housing, Supply –basically whatever they feel like doing. If they want a change, they get it. Most people like to do jobs similar to what they did on Earth. And, let's face it , the work isn't exactly hard. You've probably worked out by now that Topside is kept deliberately grotty to encourage people to get jobs rather than roam the streets.. Wouldn't you rather spend time with happy cheerful friends and relatives in a bright cheerful environment than wandering around the Astro's and the dirty dark streets?'

'So, what's the rate for an owner driver in Heaven? Mileage or set rates?' I was keen to know just what I was deemed to be worth.

'There is no rate for you. There is no rate for those lads out there in the workshop. I don't get paid. This is a totally new set up. For this unit, everything is free. Anything you want is on the Boss. There has never been a need, or set rate, for mechanics, workshops and hgv's. There are a few pretty basic electric vehicles for local deliveries, refuse etc but they just get recycled and replicated rather than repaired. This is a specialist unit. All those lads, you, me, we are all hand picked by the Committee. All brought here before our allotted time just to do this job. You should be proud John'.

'I've got over my initial anger about that. But, how do the guys out there' I gestured towards the workshop 'feel about it?'

'They were all due to die within the next five years. Like you. Sean, for instance, is a brilliant truck mechanic. He has an estranged wife, no kids, no other close relatives, was heavily in debt with his gambling problem and nothing going for him other than his love of trucks. He admits he loves it up here. The other lads are the same. They weren't just plucked from loving families or long term relationships. Their Earth life had lost it's meaning. They were just drifting through life like you…' I opened my mouth to protest but he waved me silent.

'Don't let's go into that again. You know it's true. You love it here already. Why wouldn't you? Three gorgeous women gagging for you. Once you get back on the road, you'll be in Heaven'. He laughed at his own joke and slapped me on the back. 'Take your truck John. Go and show Maggie to your women. Get laid. Come back tomorrow and get your replicator and shower fitted in the cab. Your trailer will be ready and we can do a test run the day after.'

I couldn't say much to that. It was all true.

I was much more relaxed driving Maggie this time. I threaded my way through the narrow streets. The throb of the twin stacks boomed and echoed off the buildings. My left hand itched and I didn't resist the temptation. I pulled the cord for my twin airhorns and a deep foghorn like bellow ricocheted from building to building and signaled that John Slater was coming. Damn, it felt good to be back where I belonged.

I parked up outside Arrivals and entered the now familiar building. I saw all the usual mixture of Newbies; lost, confused and queuing. Always queuing. I saw Celeste and Angel busily working and decided to get a coffee whilst I waited for them to knock off for the day. I popped into Molly's office enroute to the canteen. She was with a client and waved five minutes. I sat down and watched her at work.

The woman she was with was about thirty, heavily made up and dark. Whether it was her natural colour or just the wrong mix of tanning paint was hard to judge. She was wearing obvious designer clothes and lots of bling jewellery. Some of the stones might even have been real. Her long red nails clattered on the counter and she was obviously having a hissy fit.

‘What do you mean? Only two sets of clothes. I can’t possibly exist on just two sets of clothes. Where is your superior? I demand to see your superior’

I’m terribly sorry, Madam’ Molly said in a bored shop assistant tone. ‘My superior is not here at the moment. Might I suggest that you return when she is. In the meantime, perhaps you would like to take these with you? Once your accommodation is settled, we can plan more accordingly.’

‘And that’s another thing. I don’t want just anywhere. I want somewhere select. Somewhere with others of my class.’

‘Leave it to me Madam. I’ll have a word with one of my colleagues in Accommodation and see if we can’t sort you a pent house suite somewhere. I’ll just pop these into a bag for you, Madam. You’ll find Accommodation two doors down’

Molly packed the two sets of clothes into a Heavenly Designs bag and handed it over. The disgruntled woman snatched it off her and stomped off in that peculiar stiff legged walk that women use when they are angry.

I grinned at Molly and she glared at the departing woman. I smiled even more broadly, her lips twitched and then she was smiling. ‘See what I have to put with?’ she asked. ‘Now, what can I do for my favourite little trucker?’

‘Hi Molly. How are you? Having a good day?’ I asked sarcastically. ‘No, don’t answer that. Look, I just popped in to see Angel and Celeste but they are busy. Can you use your internal phone and tell them to meet me outside after work. I’ll give them a ride home’.

'Just bragging or have you got your truck?' She asked with a twinkle in her eye.

I waved at her as I opened the door and admitted a young guy dressed only in a pair of brief leather shorts and with a dog's collar round his neck. His back, I noticed as he went to the desk, was covered in red, angry looking weals. I was in the wrong job. Thank goodness.

In the canteen, I picked my now familiar Newbie watching place and sipped my tea. Did this place never stop? Every time I came to Arrivals, it was full of confused, crying and complaining Newbies. Suddenly, my vision blurred and my eyes were blocked by a pair of hands snaking round from behind. 'Brother Simon' I exclaimed. 'For the last time, I don't want to go out with you.'

I had expected Celeste or Angel. When I pulled the hands away and turned my head, it was Astra. A very different and vibrant Astra. She looked as beautiful as always in her work clothes but her face had a glow that hadn't been there before. She dropped her arms and looked at me shyly. I indicated the empty chair next to me. She hesitated briefly and then sat. I could see that she was struggling so I helped her out.

'If it is about last night, don't say anything. I just glad that you decided you could trust me. I told you I would never do anything to hurt you and I meant it. Any time you feel the need for a hug, that's all that will happen, I promise.'

Her eyes misted over and she reached across with her hand. I held it gently and she gripped hard. We just sat like that for a few minutes then she disengaged and stood up. 'Thank you, John' she said throatily. 'Would you like to come round again? I think, no I am sure, it would help.

If you don't mind that is?' She stood up and walked confidently away. I even thought that I detected an extra swing to her hips. Did I mind? Was she kidding? I would have been content to just hold her for eternity.

That little episode brought out the whole dilemma of the girls to the surface again. Could I care for all three equally? Could I care for more? Without conscience or the feeling that I was cheating or misleading any of them? I was starting to believe that I could.

I mulled over the problem and watched the lost souls outside the canteen window. From where I sat, I could just see Angel's desk. She was still busy but then I spotted another girl coming over to her. The newcomer waited at her side until Angel had finished with her current Newbie and then replaced her at the desk. Shift change already? I hadn't realized how quickly the time had gone. I would have to be quick. I got up and walked rapidly towards the exit.

By the time Angel and Celeste walked out of the doors, I had driven Maggie right up to the exit and stood proudly alongside her. They saw her instantly –they could hardly miss her – and, talking excitedly, walked over. They ignored me and walked slowly around Maggie. They pointed to the chrome and stainless steel. They marveled at the mural of a female Viking emerging on the back of the cab and they ooh'ed and aah'ed over the ever changing colours.

Finally, they stood in front of me and Celeste jumped excitedly up and down like a little girl. 'Can we have a look inside, John, please?' I reached up and opened the door. The Magnum has a very high cab. There are steps set into the bottom of the cab to help get into it. Even so, it wasn't easy until you knew how. You had to start the steps with the correct foot otherwise you ended up trying to change step before entering. Angel was first to try and, whether by luck or instinct, made it up and in on the first try. Celeste got stuck and I moved forward to support her whilst she got her feet sorted. I looked up to point out the handle to grab when her skirt blew up and over my head. The light coming through the thin white material showed a pair of shapely legs, divided at the apex of her thighs by a pair of flimsy white panties. Not Victoria's Secrets but Angel's.

'Oi, keep your eyes to yourself' Celeste screamed. 'Bleeding pervert'

I disentangled her skirt from my head and looked up at her. I just grinned and grinned. I now knew what Angels, one at least, wore under their skirts.

I climbed up into the cab and found Angel looking through my wardrobe space. There wasn't much to see. A couple of tee shirts, spare underwear and socks and a warm outdoor coat. Celeste was bending over the passenger seat, her skirt riding up dangerously high. 'Ooh, I love the smell of leather seats. This reminds me of my Roller. I do miss my car and driver. You'll have to do in future, I suppose' she grinned at me.

I let them rummage through my dvd and cd collection. 'Can you put this on John, please?' Angel handed over a cd and, without looking at it, I put it into the overhead cd player. Eva Cassidy's voice flooded out of the multi-speaker system. I had spent a lot of money on my in-cab entertainment and had never regretted it. As she sang

Fields of Gold, I looked at Angel. She was stretched out on the bottom bunk, boots off, eyes closed and listening. Celeste, sat down on the passenger seat, hands linked behind her neck and long legs stretched up on the dash, also had her eyes closed. The sound system picked up every emotion in Eva's voice. Her live performance was superb. Maggie's expensive sound system raised it to another level. As the last note died away Angel roused herself and, in a very throaty voice, asked if I could play track 10 next. I pushed the button already knowing what it would be. It was. "Somewhere over the rainbow" leaked out of the speakers like warm honey on a summer's day. As the crystal notes rose and fell, I happened to look out of the open window. Outside, in little groups, people had gathered outside Arrivals to listen.

I saw a scene once in a film, the Shankshaw Redemption I think it was, where a crowd of convicts stopped and listened to an operatic record being played over the loudspeaker system. Those hardened criminals just stood there whilst the song was played. Some had tears in their eyes as the notes rose and fell. I was experiencing a similar scene outside Heaven's Arrivals Hall.

Once the track had finished, there was a pause until people started to drift away. I wound up the window and looked across at Celeste. She still had her eyes closed, almost in a trance. Angel was still in the same position.

She opened her eyes and saw me looking at her. Her cheeks were wet and her breathing shallow. She held my gaze and said one word "Celeste?" then reached out her hand for mine. Out of the corner of my eye, I saw Celeste leaving the cab. I heard the cab door shut. My eyes still locked on Angel's, I obeyed her insistent tugs and joined her on the bottom bunk. She wrapped her arms and legs around me and locked her lips greedily on mine. Our lips melted into one and our breathing synchronized. I felt her hands on my belt and moved to give her access. I tugged her tee shirt out and pushed it up. Her red bra was flimsy and offered no resistance to my insistent hands. Her breasts sprang free, dark nipples standing erect. I closed my mouth over the nearest and felt her body shudder. I sucked and teased with my mouth whilst my hands pulled down her jeans and eased them over her feet. I felt my own jeans following hers and Little John springing free. Her hands found him and pulled insistently. With my mouth still at her breast, I broke body contact and my hands found the waistline of her panties and pulled them off. I barely had time to register that she was a natural redhead before, with greedy need and short, sharp breaths, Angel guided my redhead into her warm, moist launch bay and we locked together. Without moving, we lay there together and then her body started to tremble in mounting waves of desire and she lifted her legs and locked them around me. The trembling became more and more insistent. Suddenly, she arched her back and spasmed violently, her mouth open and screaming soundlessly. Her nails dug into my back again and again. I could hold on no longer . I let go and joined her in a mutual orgasm that took us both to the heights of ecstasy and beyond. Slowly, soundlessly, we subsided into reality and the confines of Maggie's cab. Still locked in each other's arms, I opened my eyes and gazed into hers. Her luminous green eyes had a sheen to them that I hadn't noticed beforc. She reached up and stroked the side of my face. Gently, she drew my head down onto her waiting lips. She kissed me with a fervor that made my toes tingle. 'Oh, you wonderful man' she whispered in my ear. 'Thank you, thank you so much.'

I didn't say anything. There was no need. I rolled over onto my side and held her tight. Her body relaxed in my arms and, almost instantly, she drifted off. I reached behind me, pulled down my duvet and covered us both.

When I opened my eyes, she was still in my arms. She must have sensed the moment because she turned and pressed herself against me. Without any words or urgency, we made long, slow love in the confines of the bottom bunk. We took our time and explored the delights of each other's body with gentle hands, warm mouths and teasing lips. Molly was right. It was different. Better, longer lasting. Later, much later, Angel sighed and nuzzled her head into my shoulder. Without looking directly at me, she whispered 'I'm glad it was you, my first time in Heaven. Somehow, the moment I saw you, I knew it would be you.

I like you a lot, John. Maybe more than like. Celeste does too. Does it bother you? Having two of us after you'.

I raised her head and looked into her eyes. 'Yes, Angel. It does.' I saw her enquiring look and tried to explain. 'I think too much of both of you to be content with just a quick roll in the cab' She giggled at that. 'Seriously, I have given the matter a lot of thought. I guessed, no, I knew that you both fancied me. Does that make me big-headed?' She shook her head. 'I have never met two girls like you. When I first saw both of you, I couldn't believe that I stood a chance with either of you. When we hit it off, it was obvious that it would be one of you. I worried whether the other would jealous or offended. Molly said it wouldn't happen. Was she right?'

'Celeste and I have discussed it. Obviously, in our job, we meet many eligible men. We get asked out all the time. You had that extra sparkle and decency that we wanted. You could have taken advantage of us in that caravan but you didn't. You came across as what you are, a caring, brave and honourable man. But you weren't afraid to cry either. Something that we hadn't experienced before. Neither of us could believe how quickly you became part of our lives.' Angel raised her head and brushed her lips against mine. 'We agreed that, when the moment was right for one of us, we would take it to the next level. No discussion, no arguments, no jealousy and no recrimination. I just happened to need you first. Celeste understood that and she understood why. She will be happy for both of us. It won't change how she thinks about you or me. I feel the same about you and her. Does that answer your question?'

Resting my chin on her red locks, I held her even tighter. 'I guess it does. I was told that things were different up here. I believe it now. Can I ask another question?' I felt her tense slightly almost as if she knew what was coming.

'You can ask me anything. But you don't have to ask.' Her voice dropped to a whisper and I had to strain to hear. 'When I was young, my Dad used to sing "Somewhere over the Rainbow" as he tucked me up at night. He was a big Judy Garland fan. When I grew up, we grew apart. I messed around with drugs and the wrong men. I started an affair with a married man and my parents couldn't handle me any more. I left home and moved into this guy's London flat. He stayed there during the week and headed home each week-end. I wanted more and he wouldn't give it. He was a local MP and didn't want a scandal. He threw me out and I had nowhere to go. I couldn't go back home and lived rough on the streets. I developed a drug habit and drifted into crime and, and…..'

I kissed the top of her head 'You don't have to tell me anymore' I reassured her.

'…and went with men for money to feed my habit. I overdosed and was found and rushed to hospital. They telephoned my parents –my diary was in my bag with their number – and they visited every day until I was well enough to come home. Dad and I grew close again and then I discovered I was pregnant. I didn't know who the father was and I couldn't saddle them with that.' She broke off with a sob, stroked my arm and then continued. 'I had an abortion but it went wrong. I started bleeding heavily. I was too ashamed to call my parents and I just lost consciousness. I didn't mean to kill myself and Molly said that the Boss understood that or I wouldn't be here. Hearing Eva sing that song at the Venue brought back memories of my dad and how much I miss him. Today, it hurt even more and I just needed you to take away the pain. So, now you know. Do you still like me?' she asked in a small voice and tensed in my arms.

'Oh Angel, you have no idea how much' I said with tears streaming down my cheeks. She lifted her head and I saw that she was crying too. We held each other tight. I held her until the hurting had gone away. I hoped that I could keep her from hurting again. That I could heal my damaged Angel.

We didn't go back to her flat that night. I got down from the cab and held out my arms. Without any hesitation, she jumped into my arms and I lowered her gently to the ground. In Arrivals, we got a drink and hot meal. A quick visit to the facilities for a shower and back to Maggie. I started her up and drove her to the ring road. .About a mile up the road and away from everything, I pulled up. Dusk was just surrendering to darkness. Just like I had done a thousand times, I parked up for the night. Sometimes with company, most times not.

The Magnum is a tall cab and I could stand up straight in it. I raised the top bunk and fastened it in position against the bulkhead. I pushed the two seats back as far as they would go. I pulled the curtains round and we were in our own little world.

I lowered the window. There was no sound outside. I could see strange stars in the night sky. In the distance, the night glow of the thousands of lights in the thousands of building that made up Heaven. I would much rather have been here alone with a beautiful girl in our own version of Heaven.

I pulled down the dvd screen and Angel rummaged through my dvd collection. She tut-tutted over a couple of blue titles then handed over her choice. 'I love this one. I would have preferred Ghost or Dirty Dancing but this is great. I guess you like it too or it wouldn't be here, would it? Or, has it been left by some other lady?'

'Angel, of course I have had other girl friends. I lived with one for a couple of years. But, the way I see it, this is a No Questions Asked new start for everyone. If you really want to know, I will tell you. But....not tonight ok?

Tonight is about you and me.' I pressed Play and "Love Actually" started. And, yes, it was mine. I loved that film and don't care who knows it.

After about twenty minutes, Angel asked me to Pause. She got up and went to the bunk and sat on it with her back to the bulkhead. She patted the mattress and I joined her. Putting my arm around her shoulders, I pressed Play on the remote and we watched the whole film from there.

When it was finished, I got up and brewed us a mug of tea using my supplies and gas ring. I told Angel that I would be getting a replicator and sonic shower fitted in Maggie tomorrow and thought it was a great idea. 'No toilet?' she asked. I explained the problems involved and she shrugged. 'I guess I will have to pop outside for a moment then. Got any tissues?' I rummaged in a locker and found a box. I reached into the door pocket and grabbed a torch. I helped her down and warned her not to go too far off. Noel had said that this No-man's strip of land was deserted but why take chances? I watched the torch beam searching, stop and then bob up and down as she attended to her business. I went to my usual spot behind the cab wheelarch.

As I waited for her to return, I looked up at the night sky. There was no familiar moon or star clusters but several larger objects could be seen. I presumed that they were the Alien Heavens but didn't know. They were glowing in a similar fashion to our Earth moon but were strung out like pearls on a necklace. With just a little imagination, I could believe that I was on a saucer floating in space. Early men believed that the world was flat. Maybe this world was. I heard Angel coming back. She saw me looking up and came to stand next to me. She slipped her arm around my waist and looked up as well.

'Is it always this pretty?' I asked with an encompassing wave of my hand.

'Dunno. I've never seen the night sky, or much of the day sky, for that matter. You know how dark it is outside because of the buildings? Well, we just stop looking up. Most of our traveling is underground on the Tube or between the Astro's. It's nice though. What is this place?'

I told her what I had learnt from Noel, Brother Simon and Mr Green Peace Standish. She seemed skeptical at first but gradually agreed that it could be true. 'Anyway,' she declared 'Can we go inside now? I'm getting a little chilly'.

Inside, she fussed about getting the bunk ready. She found an extra blanket in the wardrobe and threw that on the bed as well. I flicked the remote locking button and heard the door locks click shut. Probably not necessary but old habits die hard. I turned round in my seat and Angel was stripping off. 'Come on Slater' she said slipping off her jeans and standing there in her red underwear. 'I'm getting cold'. She saw the way I was staring at her. She removed the last items then held up her arms and pirouetted slowly round in front of me. I instantly thought of Exodus 3.2. She had a gorgeous body. Firm, fit and fantastic. 'You like?' she asked softly.

'You know, you are the first bloke I am comfortable with seeing me naked. Normally, I am quite shy.'

Holding her eyes, I stripped off . I have one of those metabolisms that keeps me slim whatever I eat. At my Earth age of 46, I was in good shape. Here, at 36, I was in peak condition. I had good muscle tone, a reasonable six pack and, I felt, was reasonably good looking. No wait, no false modesty, I *was* good looking. I got down to my underpants and awaited her survey results. She shook her head. With an exaggerated sigh, I pulled them down over Le Grande Bulge. She held her arm up and made a twirling motion. Feeling slightly stupid, I complied. She gave me a thumbs up and patted the mattress beside her.

Once beneath the covers, we warmed up. We stretched out together. Angel in front, in my arms and me spooned into her back. Little John let her know that he wanted to play. Without turning round, she said in a low voice 'Can I ask you something?'

'So long as it's not too kinky' I said enjoying the pleasure of her warm body and my questing sex machine.

'Would you mind if we didn't? At least, not tonight.'

What, blowing hot and cold already? No, I didn't think so. I asked why.

'Well, it's just that I'm a bit sore. It's been a long time and you're a big bloke and……well, I'm a bit uncomfortable. Would you mind? I know it's a lot to ask and..' her voice dropped to a mumble.. 'I could help you, you know, to…'

I laughed out loud. She flinched as if I had hit her. She sat up '…you're just like all the other's aren't you, only after…...' I put my fingers on her mouth to silence her and then drew her head down to my lips. She squirmed but I persisted and kissed her gently. 'No, Angel. I'm not like all the others. I was laughing because you were embarrassed. You're not in the mood, that's it. I'm content to just have you here in my arms.' She looked at me. 'Really. Sex is lovely but holding you is just as nice and just as meaningful.'

She looked down at me and a single teardrop rolled down her cheek. 'Oh, I love you, John Slater. And I didn't mean it about the others. I know you're not like the others..........'she raised her head and spoke to the ceiling '........and, and, shit, I've just told you that I love you, haven't I?'. She buried her head in my shoulder to avoid looking at me. I raised her head and looked into her wondrous green eyes.

'I love you too Angelica' I said as I kissed her. And, in that moment, I knew it was true.

We spent the night locked in each other's arms. Safe and secure. Content and confident. In love and loved.

In the morning when she woke, I kissed her and told her again that I loved her. Strangely, the journey back to Arrivals was made without either of us saying another word. I pulled up outside, killed the engine and applied the parking brake. I climbed down, opened the passenger door and held out my arms. You know the scene in Dirty dancing when the girl in the white dress flies into Swayzee's arms and he holds her aloft? Well, it wasn't like that. Angel turned on the second step, jumped and I caught her. Tripped, and we went down. We were both laughing as I helped her up. 'Pinch me, Slater' she asked. I looked around, saw no one watching and tweaked her nipple gently. She placed her hand over mine and smiled her million watt smile. 'Just wanted to be sure I wasn't dreaming.' She said as she kissed me goodbye and made her way to work. Just before she entered, she turned. 'See you tonight?' she asked, waved and entered thc doors. Just before she entered completely, I could have sworn that I saw her body shimmer. Must have been the Time/Space thing I thought as I opened Maggie's door.

A familiar voice called me before I got in. Alfie came running up. Still in his school uniform, cocky smile and hair falling over his eyes. 'Cor, I like your truck, Mr Slater. Can I 'ave a look inside?' Without waiting for an answer, he scrambled up into the driving seat and grabbed the steering wheel. He wrestled with it, trying to move it but gave up. The power steering only works when the engine's running. He left the seat and walked round the cab. He opened the wardrobe, fridge, lockers, had a quick look through my dvd and cd collection and gave his verdict.

'Bloody nice, innit? 'ere, before I go, I gotta joke for you.'

I groaned.

'Naw' he said. 'It's a good 'un. These three geezers die and, after going threw the Cleansing Mist and the Plain of Enlightenment, they arrived at the Tower of Ascension and get talking.

'Why are you 'ere" one of them asks an elderly gent. He replied 'Had a heart attack. I was feeling a bit dicky so I finished work early and went home. My wife was meant to be at work so I was surprised to hear voices coming from upstairs. I rushed up stairs, opened the bedroom door and there she was. Not a stitch on and this naked bloke hanging over the balcony rail with his fingertips. I saw red, rushed over to the balcony and started hitting him on the fingers. He let go, fell five stories and landed on his back in some bushes. He started to get up so I rushed back into the flat, picked up the fridge and threw it over the balcony at him. I remember it hitting him fair and square before I had a heart attack from all the exertion and excitement and ended up here.'

'Oh, that's bad luck. Bit similar to my own story.' the other replied. I was naked and doing my exercises on my six story balcony when I heard a funny noise from the flat below. I leant over the balcony to see what was going on and lost my balance. As I was falling I managed to grab the balcony rail of the flat below. I was hanging there when someone comes up and starts banging on my hands. I let go and fall to the ground below and land in some bushes. "Bloody hell" I think "That's lucky". I'm trying to get up and the next thing I see this fridge coming down straight at me. It must have hit me because I landed up here.' The geezer then turns to the last bloke to arrive and asks what his story is.

The last bloke looks at the other two and says 'Picture the scene. I'm naked in this fridge..............' Alfie looks over. 'That's a good 'un innit Mr Slater?'

I laughed and have to agree.

'Ere' he said. 'Are you going to Mr Noel's place? Can you give us a lift?'

I couldn't see any harm in it so I climbed in and sat down. I made Alfie sit down and put on his seat belt before pulling away. He looked at me and pumped his arm up and down. Just to amuse him and because it was that sort of a moment, I pulled down hard on the air horn cord. The howl of the lonesome truck echoed between the canyon walls of the City of Souls. We laughed together.

Looking over at young Alfie in the passenger seat, beaming with excitement, I remembered myself at that age and my first trip with my mate Peter Tiler? I wondered what he and Beth were doing now?

FIFTEEN

Peter Tiler was down at the allotment. It was mid-afternoon and he and Dave Williams were the only ones there. Over coffee they had been finalizing the plans for John Slater's funeral the following day.

Despite the short notice and all the other problems involved, things had finally come together. Mike Henshaw, the showtruck owner, had phoned Dave on his mobile and said that everything was ready his end. He had the definite promise of another three showtrucks.

Mr Findlay, the undertaker in Faversham, had answered Peter's e-mail and confirmed that all was in order and he expected to see them at around 9am. The crematorium was booked for 3.30pm and, although the schedule was a bit tight, John Slater should arrive on time. The local funeral director had confirmed that his hearse would be there for the final part of the trucker's last journey.

Peter and Dave would be driving down to Mike Henshaw's place that evening and staying the night. The schedule was too tight to chance driving down first thing tomorrow morning. It had been agreed that Peter's big black Ford pick-up would be the best vehicle for the journey south.

'I reckon we should set off about seven' Peter decided. 'Miss the rush and still get down there in plenty of time to go over the arrangements again. I must admit that I am looking forward to seeing Mike's Kenworth'.

'Yes, I just wish it was in different circumstances. Look mate, I'm going to go now. I have a few jobs to do before we set off. Can you pick me up about quarter to?'

Just after seven pm, the pair were on the road. As predicted, the traffic was moving freely on the M1. For Peter, it was almost like being back at work. The Ford Ranger was big but nowhere near as big as the truck he normally drove south each night. Usually he drove with the radio on or a cd playing. Tonight he wasn't in the mood. At first, he and Dave had swopped road stories but had eventually fallen into a companionable silence.

At the South Minns services on the M25, they pulled in. Both were tired, pent-up and excited at the same time. Tomorrow would be the culmination of days of e-mailing, telephoning and planning. Peter ordered coffee whilst his companion found a seat. There were plenty of customers sitting around, evidence that the motorway never stopped.

Back on the road, Dave told of his driving days pre-M25 and before much else either. 'The M1 ended at Crick when I first started driving. A Leyland Super Comet and I thought it was the bee's knees. It was my first driving job and you didn't need any special licence back then. You could have passed your test in a car in the morning and legally drive an artic on the road in the afternoon. Crazy or what?'

'Weren't so many vehicles back then so there was more room. It must have been difficult though, driving through London every time you had to get to Dover for the ferry?' Peter asked.

'Tell me about it. It used to take four hours from Rugby to Dover. I could do the journey from Oostende to Dusseldorf in the same time but that was twice the distance. Mind you, I used to love taking a smart outfit right through London. It was a real adrenalin rush. Not just the people admiring the truck but the level of skill and concentration required to make good time and not hit anything. Some of those junctions definitely weren't made for trucks. You had to swing out so wide that you were practically on the other side of the road. Most of the time you had to bully your way through because Londoners don't like giving way to anything. At times, I used to dream of the M25. Now, I reckon I could still get a truck to Dover quicker by driving through London rather than use the motorway. If I could afford the Congestion Charge that is.'

'Do you miss it? Driving, I mean' Peter checked his mirrors before pulling out to overtake a truck. By force of habit, he still stuck to around 60mph, a truck's legal motorway speed limit, rather than increase his speed to 70mph.

'Every day' Dave said wistfully. 'Except of course, when I actually drive on the roads and then I think I am well out of it. Couldn't sleep for weeks when I first came off the road. Had to get a Cummins 350 engine to put under the bed at home before I felt really comfortable'.

'Yeah, I know that feeling. I sometimes think the only good night's sleep I ever got was in my sleeper cab. I used to take my shoes off, roll into the bunk and I was off in seconds.'

'I hear that you still manage to get a few hours kip at night' Dave looked over at his companion with a sly smile.

'Sometimes, if I get my collections or deliveries finished early, I pull over and have a kip' Peter agreed. 'Purely in the interests of road safety, of course.'

'Of course' his companion agreed.

As if by mutual consent, the conversation dropped off and each returned to his own thoughts. Almost before they realised it, the motorway exit they wanted came up. Leaving the motorway, Peter followed his companion's directions until they pulled up beside an imposing detached house. The drive way gates rolled back on oiled tracks and the outside security light came on to illuminate the driveway. Almost before the Ford's engine noise had died away, the front door opened and Mike Henshaw came over with outstretched hand to welcome his guests. He went to Dave Williams first as the pair were old friends. After welcoming the older man, Mike then turned to Peter. 'Peter, welcome. Nice to meet you. I'm just sorry it had to be under these circumstances.'

In his mid-thirties, Mike was about average. Average height, average build and, with his almost completely bald head and black framed glasses, not what Peter had expected the owner of a prize winning Showtruck to look like.

'Hello Mike. Nice to meet you too. Dave has told me a lot about you. I am grateful for all you are doing. It means a lot to me and Elizabeth, my wife'. Following their host into his house, Peter was instantly aware of how the "other half" lived. Opulence didn't quite do it justice. Dave had told Peter that Mike Henshaw was well off but it was obvious that it was quite a bit better than that. It wasn't that he flaunted his wealth, more that he had spent it on quality. That much was apparent as they entered the sitting room. You only had to look at the leather chairs and sofas to know that they would be supremely comfortable and that the leather was kid glove soft.

There were several paintings hanging on the walls. Not huge in your face monstrosities but small and tastefully arranged portraits and landscapes. A large oak sideboard was against the far wall and a cheerful fire was lit and flickering in the fireplace. Waving his guests to sit down, Mike went over to the sideboard and opened one of the bottom doors to reveal an assortment of bottles and cans. 'Can I get you guys anything?' he asked getting out a can of lager for himself.
'Same again for both of us please' Dave replied after getting an affirmative nod from Peter.
Sat down and drinking appreciatively, Peter looked around the room. 'Your wife do all the decorating?' he asked as he relaxed on the sofa.
Mike raised his eyebrows and looked across at Dave. 'You haven't told him?' he asked.
'Told him, what?' Dave Williams looked puzzled. 'Oh, about you being gay? Sorry, I didn't even think about it?'
'Well, that's something, I suppose. Some sort of progress, you old Neanderthal' Mike laughed. He turned to Peter and explained. 'When Dave first interviewed me and I told him I was gay, he didn't quite know what to make of me. Here I was, owning and driving this huge truck and quite fancying him.'
'Yes, well, I could understand him fancying me. I just couldn't get my head around why an investment banker – a seriously rich one – should want to drive a big truck' Dave turned to Peter. He decided to keep quiet.
'Well, really' Mike lisped and camped it up. 'However else would I get to meet so many butch truckers. The truck shows are quite heady with the essence of testosterone'

Mike took a drink and turned to Peter. 'Sorry Peter. I don't mean to be disrespectful. Let me tell you the full story. I am married to Dereck, - in every respect but the law - who has been my companion for many years now. Dereck used to run The Hole in the Wall café down at Folkestone docks and I used to go down there to help him sometimes. Meeting all those truck drivers was part of the attraction but wandering around and looking at their trucks became my main interest.' Mike remembered.

'I became particularly interested in a Kenworth truck that a Swiss driver had. Apparently Kenworth had an agency in Basel and I got the details off the internet. I didn't do any more about it until I went to the States on business and, in Florida, went to a truck show and saw what a Kenworth could look like with a bit of money and imagination.' Mike finished his drink and looked around to see if anyone else wanted another. Opening one for himself, he continued.

'That particular year I made a good bonus and decided to go the whole hog and get myself a customised Kenworth. I looked at what the Swiss dealer could offer but, frankly, it was cheaper to order in the States and ship one over. That's what I did. I went on holiday to Texas and dropped in to a dealership. I was in that salesman's for five hours. I started with a basic truck and chassis and went on from there. Anything that was big or shiny got added to the list' he remembered with a fond chuckle.

'Anyhow, I left a sizeable deposit and waited. Whilst I was waiting, I took lessons and got my Class 1 driving licence. Passed first time too. I was really chuffed about that' Mike laughed as he took another sip of his drink.

'About seven months later, I got the call that it was ready. The Double Eagle sleeper cab and the paint job was what took the time. The dealer arranged shipping for me. I paid him in full, sat back and waited for my new toy to arrive. I had it collected from Southampton docks, taken to a specialist and got it registered for the UK. There wasn't a turntable fitted so I had a stainless steel cover made for the top of the chassis. I also added a few extra lights and other gizmos and the big day for collection arrived. I had contacted Trucking |International to tell them about it and they sent Dave down to do the story. I had intended to drive it home myself but bottled out. It was so different from the little ERF truck I took my test on. Dave did the driving home and then spent a lot of time getting me confident enough to take it out myself. And, that is basically it. That's how Dave and I met and that's how I got my beautiful truck'

'I reckon that you and I are also connected' Peter said as the small man sat down. Seeing the enquiring look, he explained. 'You said that Dereck ran the Hole in the Wall down in Folkestone Docks? Well, every time we came into Folkestone, John and I used to have a sausage sandwich there. If it is the same Dereck, he is tall, slim and looks a little like that guy from Only Fools and Horses…..uuh, Trigger, that's it. That's the name. John always used to say that the guy who ran the caff fancied him'. Suddenly Peter remembered where he was and who he was talking to. 'Sorry Mike, it's probably not the same Dereck, after all.'

Mike Henshaw laughed at the big trucker. 'That sounds exactly like my Dereck. I used to keep telling him that he could look all he wanted to but he had better not touch.

Well, well. Strange how it all links up isn't it? Anyhow, he will be here soon and we shall find out. Changing the subject, what sort of a guy was John Slater, Peter?'
Peter considered his reply. 'He was one of the best truck drivers you could meet. He drove professionally and tried to upgrade the public image and perception of the trucker. He was an owner driver who spent most of his time on the continent. He was happy with his job. It's all he ever wanted for as long as I knew him.'
Peter Tiler spent the next fifteen minutes telling Mike Henshaw about how he met John Slater, how close the two had become and the antics they used to get up to when they travelled together. 'I doubt you will ever find anyone who had a bad word for him. He was that type of guy. He did his job and got on with everyone. The wife and I miss him a lot'.

'Sounds like the type of person I would have liked' Mike said sincerely. Just as he was thinking of something else to say that would lighten the atmosphere, the glow of lights swept across the window. Dimly, they heard a vehicle door slam and the front door open. A tall bronzed and distinctively dressed man entered the room. In his early fifties, he wore a pink shirt, flowered waistcoat and blue flared jeans. A Paisley pattern scarf was tied around his throat.

'Oh, hello' he greeted everyone as he entered the room. 'I'm Dereck.' He came over to Dave Williams and extended his hand. 'You must be Dave? Mike has told me about you'. He turned to Peter, was half way to shaking his hand when he froze. 'I *know* you' he exclaimed. His brow furrowed as he tried to remember. 'Wait, don't tell me' he

said dramatically, his hand on his brow. 'Ooh, I know, YOU were with that dishy young driver at my place in Folkestone. That was some time ago now. He was called.....it's on the tip of my tongue....he was called...John' he said triumphantly. 'Am I right?' He saw the looks on everyone's face. 'What?' he asked in a puzzled voice.
'Yes, Dereck' Peter told him. 'You are right. You obviously have a good memory for faces. Yes, it was John. John Slater. He is the reason we are here. It is John we are cremating tomorrow.'
'OhMiGod' Dereck said sitting down quickly. 'I am SO sorry. I didn't know. Oh, he was such a lovely guy'

Peter walked over to him, and put his hand on his shoulder. 'It's ok' he said in his soft Norfolk burr. 'How could you have known? It was a long time ago. You were right about one thing, though. He was a lovely guy'

'Right, what's the plan for tomorrow?' Mike asked in an attempt to change the subject. 'Peter and I are going to pick up John tomorrow morning in the pick-up. We'll bring him back here and get him strapped securely in place on the Kenworth and set off about 10.30." "What did you arrange with the other Showtruck owners, Mike?'

'I asked them to meet up at Junction 7 and we could go past Junction 6 and give an airhorn salute as we did so. I just have to phone them to tell them the time. I can do that in the morning. Is that ok?'

'That sound great Mike' Dave replied. 'You sure you don't mind me driving your truck?'

'Of course not. You drove it before me, didn't you? Why should I mind? I have had another thought though. If Peter trusts me with his pick-up, Dereck and I could follow in that and, that way, we could attend the service as well. It also means that you don't have to come back here to pick it up. Would that be ok?' he turned to Peter.

'That sounds like a good idea to me'

' Right, then might I suggest that we get off to bed? It's going to be a busy day tomorrow. I've put you and Peter on the top floor in the two guest rooms. You've slept there before, Dave, so you know where they are.'

After the round of good-nights, Dave and Peter left and went to their respective rooms. Peter didn't expect to get much sleep that night. Mike was right, tomorrow was going to be a busy day and a sad one as well. One he hadn't expected, but one that he was going to do all in his power to get right. He got into bed and turned out the light.

SIXTEEN

It still felt really strange. I was driving Maggie as usual but there was no traffic, no pedestrians, no traffic lights, no....well, no nothing. The road, such as it was, was bumpy, narrow and almost dark due to the towering Astro's. By the dashboard clock, it was around nine in the morning but, I had the almost stupid thought, was that Earth or Heaven time? Was time the same up here? I knew that it was different in Arrivals. I had never worn a wristwatch because most of the time I had to keep taking it off and putting it in my pocket to avoid it getting damaged during loading or unloading. Mainly, I knew the time by listening to the radio or looking at my tachograph.

That last instrument, if you don't already know, is a lawful requirement in trucks to record the driver's time at the wheel, his rest breaks, his sleep time and the speed the truck was travelling at. Police and Traffic officials have the right to see the engraved paper disc it produces at any time. It is meant to make sure that drivers keep to speed limits and have enough rest. Like most such devices, it doesn't deter drivers. The fine for not having such a record is less than being caught driving over hours. Many drivers, pulled in for a check and knowing that the little white disc will show speeding or hours offences, will destroy it first. On the other hand, if you haven't been naughty, that little piece of paper will also confirm it.

I took some comfort that, when my last tacho' disc was pulled from the mangled remains of Maggie 1, it would show that John Slater (deceased) had not been speeding and was not over hours. Had in fact, been driving professionally and was blameless in the accident. Whether the tv or papers choose to report that fact was something else. There have been many headlines of truckers killing innocent people; a trucker saving innocent people probably wouldn't have the same impact. However, since 2006, drivers are now having digital tachographs fitted into their cabs. Accessed only by Smart card, the device has proved pretty fool-proof. But, as with all things electronic, it will only be a matter of time before the Smartcard gets outsmarted.

Right, having got that off my chest, back to wondering about time. Knowing that this was my time and place for eternity, time, somehow, didn't seem so important. I remember reading in a book that someone asked how long eternity was. The reply was to look at eternity as the highest mountain peak in the world. Every thousand years, a little bird would come along – probably not the same one - and rub his little beak against the top of the mountain five times. Once the mountain had been reduced to nothing by this action, then eternity might begin. Sobering thought eh? And, what would happen if that little bird didn't show up every thousand years? Would I still be stuck in this place, still hauling batteries around? Thankfully, we arrived at Maintenance before I got too depressed.

'Thanks for the lift, Mr John. Smashing motor. Can I come out wiv you again, sometime? 'ere, before I go, gotta little joke for you. It's a bit naughty. A young boy's pet chicken dies and 'e's telling his Dad about it. "What was the chicken doing when you farnd it?' his Dad asked.
'It was lying orn it's back wif it's legs straight up in the air'
'That means it's gorn to 'eaven' his Dad says.

A couple of days later, the Dad gets 'ome from werk and the little boy comes rushing over. 'Dad, Dad' he shouts. 'Mum nearly died today and went to 'eaven'.

'Why, what 'appened?' his Dad asks.

'Well, I come 'ome from school and I 'ear Mum upstairs and she is on the bed wif 'er legs straight up in the air and screaming 'Oh God, Oh Jesus, I'm coming'. If it wasn't for Uncle Fred lying on top of 'er and holding 'er down, we'd have lost 'er. See yuh, Mr John'.

Little Alfie obviously knew his way around because he was out of the cab and legging it to Noel's office. I still had the nagging feeling that Noel had another agenda. But, for the time being, I would have to go along with the current plan. Truth be told, I couldn't wait to start pulling a loaded trailer and getting back to work.

Nothing had changed in Maintenance. My trailer was still in the yard and being worked on. I saw Sean and asked how long my cab conversions and additions were going to take.

'I reckon that, if you come back this time tomorrow, everything should be ready for you. Trailer's about done and fitting the replicator and shower in the cab isn't going to take too long. The stainless steel pipework came this morning so that should look good. G…Boss knows where Noel got it from. I reckon it's one of those 'best not to ask' things with Noel. You know what he's like.' Sean smiled knowingly.

I did indeed know what Noel was like.

'Oh, by the way, I'm going to fix up a communications module in the cab. Sort of like a cb radio. Might be handy for keeping in touch. Also, a tracker devicc and a dash mounted sat nav module. I don't know about you, but I am happier having something to look at for directions rather than having to rely on something in my head. If you think of anything else, let me know. We can always fit at a later date. Hopefully, we can get a trail load up and running sometime tomorrow. See if the theory works in practice'.

I thanked Sean and set off for Noel's office.

As usual, I made unnecessary noise walking down the hallway before knocking briskly on the door. I walked in and there was Imogen at her desk. She gave me a nice smile and I returned it. I wondered briefly what her story was. Was she also here before her allotted time? Or, was she just the person that got the job? Maybe, working for Noel was her punishment for something she did on Earth? Whatever, she seemed like a nice girl and too good for this place. I gave her the irresistible John Slater smile and wink when she asked if I wanted a coffee. Surprisingly, she seemed to resist it quite well. Probably because she was sitting down when she went weak at the knees.

'Save your charm, boyo, for your own women' Noel greeted me. Waving me down to the seat opposite, he turned to young Alfie and said something in a low voice. Alfie nodded vigorously and turned to go. 'Fore I go Mr Noel, I gotta joke for you.' Noel and I groaned simultaneously. Alfie pretended not to hear.

'A banker goes to Heaven and finds St Peter waiting for 'im. Saint Peter tells him that, because he cheated on his Income tax, he has to be tied to this really ugly woman for five years. The banker finks it's not so bad particularly when St Peter tells im he can have sex wif ' er whenever he wants.

Later on, this gezzer sees his old mate and he is also tied to a really ugly woman. They get talking and his friend tells him he has got to be with his woman for seven years because of Income tax fiddles.

A bit later on and they both see another mate of theirs but he is tied to a really gorgeous bird. They get talking and the third guy tells them that he has to be with this girl for nine years. "It's bloody marvellous" he tells them " except for one thing. Every time we have sex, which is great by the way, she turns over and moans about bleeding Income tax." That's a good 'un innit? See yuh.'

As Alfie heads off down the corridor, we look at each other and shake our heads. 'I don't know where he gets them from, the little bugger' Noel said affectionately.

'I hope you're not leading him astray'

'No, I like little Alfie. He's a good kid. I give him little errands to run. It keeps him busy, earns him a few credits and I've told him that he can have a job in Maintenance when he's a bit bigger. It must be lonely being a kid here. All the little ones are in the nurseries. When they are big enough, they get sent to school to learn the basics …'

I interrupted him 'Why do they have to go to school?'

'Well, they don't really. They could just as easily take a Nano pill and learn everything that way. Being at school gives them an interest, discipline and companionship'.

'Is there a reason why Alfie doesn't go to school very often? Apart from running errands for you?'

'He's told you how he got here, right?' I nodded. 'Well, do you wonder that he's a bit wary of school?'

'No, I suppose not. Tell me something else now that you have mentioned babies. Presumably the babies here are

ones that have died? Only I've been told that no babies get born naturally here?'
'Isn't this place overcrowded enough? The Boss can't allow unnecessary new souls here. What happens is this….if a couple decide that they want to be together, like a proper married couple, they apply to foster a baby or an older kid. A lot of babies die on Earth every day so there is always plenty for couples to choose from. That way, the babies get raised in a natural environment - if being raised in Heaven can be called natural – with family support and all the things they need. With older kids, it's more of a fostering until their natural parents arrive here and take care of them again.'
'How come you're such an expert on Heaven?' I asked. 'You haven't been here much that longer than me yet you seem to know all the answers. How is that?'
Noel finished his coffee and considered his answer. He reached into one of the desk drawers and pulled out a blue booklet. He tossed it over to me. 'I'm surprised they didn't give You one of these.' I looked at the book which was titled " Heaven: Everything you wanted to know. Frequently Asked Questions" The penny dropped. If all else fails, read the manual.
'Of course. I was given one of these but it's in a drawer in my room at Mike and Jean's.' I saw his enquiring look. 'My parents. I'd forgotten all about it.'
'More likely you haven't been home since that first night. You know, I could have sworn I heard a souped up truck go past here late last night. You randy sod.'

'You can talk. You and Imogen are always "praying" so I'm told.. Anyway, what were you doing here that late? Do you live here?'

'The whole Maintenance team live here. It's one of the perks of the job. We have the whole building to ourselves. No overcrowding here. The only thing we are missing is a tube link to town. The nearest station to Maintenance is about a mile away. And, even that is being rebuilt to accommodate the rising population. Another six to eight months and we can go out on the town by tube instead of walking or taking a Maintenance vehicle. I tried to talk the Management into providing a company car but they wouldn't even think about it. They haven't got company vehicles so they certainly aren't going to give one to a jumped up Mick, are they?'

'You really love it here, don't you?' I finished my drink and put the empty cup on his desk.

'Don't tell me you don't. Sure I love it. It's interesting work. The food and all the other stuff we get provided with is great. The Entertainment is superb....Did you enjoy Red Sovine the other night, by the way?'

'You keeping tabs on me?' I asked suspiciously. I wouldn't have put it past him.

'You're not the only one who enjoys a bit of Country' he said with a knowing smirk. 'But, unlike you, I only went with one lady, not two. I have to hand it to you. They are certainly beautiful girls. I tried to pull them on my first day. I struck out on both Celeste and Angelica. It knocked me back so much that I didn't even think about trying with the other one… what's her name?'

'Astra' I told him. I also told him about Astra's problem with men in general and truckers in particular. And, no, I didn't tell him about how I was trying to help her. That was strictly between Astra and me. And Molly. And Celeste and Angel. Astra has enough problems without adding Noel Flynn to them. Mind you, I was chuffed that the other girls had knocked him back.

'Yes, I have got to admit, I did enjoy the concert the other night. I'm hoping to go and see Elvis soon. Anyway, what's happening on the energy front? Sean tells me that everything should be up and running tomorrow.'

'That's right. They have done a great job, my lads. The day after, provided everything is ok, I reckon we can load up the energy cells and do a trial run. Go out on the ring road for a few miles and see if anything drops off or shakes loose.' Noel got up from his desk and walked over to the door. 'Right, I've got work to do and you have to walk back. See you tomorrow morning, bright and early-ish. Say at around ten?'

Noel doesn't mince his words, does he? I took the hint and, trying another Slater wink at Imogen, went down stairs to the yard. I told Sean what I had just been told and then set off for the walk back to downtown Heaven.

I didn't have much planned for the day so there didn't seem much point in hurrying. The weather was, well, it just was. Apparently it never changes, never rains or snows, just gets light or goes dark. At least the temperature was pleasant. A bit of sun and it could have been somewhere on the Costa Packeta. As I went along, it was possible to see the older side of Heaven. The bit when it wasn't so overcrowded and the habitation wasn't so tall.

The bit where you could see some blue sky. If what Noel said was correct, then this area would soon look like the rest of the overcrowded and over tall section that most of the inhabitants knew and presumably loved.

As soon as the first Astro block came into view, I decided to get the Tube and go and see Mike and Jean in Hydroponics'. They were my parents after all and they must have been worried where their older and only child was spending his time.

By now I had grown to like the Tube as a means of transport. Given that the alternative was the dreaded Lift, it was no contest. I waited for the transparent bullet to arrive and, once the side section had lifted, got in. I had it all to myself again. I punched in the buttons for Hydroponics and, after it had sealed itself, moved off. As with my other journeys, there wasn't much to see. Brief glimpses into lighted areas intermingled with darkness. Within a very short time, I had arrived at my destination and got off. Walking up the entrance/exit tunnel, I could see the light getting much brighter and the noise increasing. Even now, I still was unprepared to see so many people in one place. Topside there was nothing and no-one. Here there were thousands of people working, chattering and generally seeming to enjoy themselves. Vegetables were being picked, packed and palleted. The automatic delivery trollies were moving up and down on their guide rails and. apart from the size of the place, it looked like a normal working environment.

And, it was the sheer size of the place that gave me my first problem. How on Heaven was I going to find Mike and Jean amongst all these people? In their white coats and headgear, everyone looked the same. I decide to just walk up and down until, hopefully, someone who knew me, would show me where to find my teenage parents. In my workclothes, I must have stuck out like a sore thumb because it wasn't long before a young man came over.

'Hi John. Nice to see you again'. I recognised my granddad mainly because it was like looking at a younger me. 'Looking for your Mum and Dad?' he asked.

'Hi Grandad, how are you?' I said feeling just a little stupid. It was going to take some time to get used to this ageing thing. 'Yes, have you seen them?'

He nodded. 'Best if I take you to them' he replied. 'They're both here as your dad is helping out this morning. If you don't know your way about, you could soon get lost in this place. Hear you have got yourself a couple of girlfriends?'

Were there any secrets in this place I wondered as I followed him down the main aisle and then down a side path between the water tanks where the vegetables were growing. It was strange seeing lettuce and other salad stuff floating on the surface of the rippling water with their roots dangling below. However strange it looked, the results confirmed that this method worked. Grandad reached over the side of one tank, pulled out a carrot and tossed it to me.

'There you go. That'll help keep your strength up' he laughed.

I caught it and looked at it. Yep, it looked like a carrot and, as I bit into it, it sure tasted and crunched like a carrot. I'm not a carrot connoisseur but it tasted better than any earth carrot I had ever eaten. Maybe it was growing in Holy water?

'There they are' my young granddad pointed out my parents at the far end of one of the tanks. 'See you around, John. Look after those girls of yours' he waved and gave me a very ungrandadly man to man wink and grin.

'Hello Son' Mike looked up from packing lettuce. 'Nice to see you. Where have you been? Your Mum was getting quite worried.'

'Hi Mike, sorry, I should have contacted you. I sent a message with Alfie. Did you get it?'

'Yeah, the morning after. He forgot to pass it on that night. Never mind, you're a big boy now. Should be able to look after yourself, eh? Still, I did hear that you weren't lonely'

Was there nothing sacred in this place? First my Grandad and now my Dad getting onto me. He must have seen something of what I was thinking on my face because he came over.

'Nothing to get upset about' he said. 'Young Alfie said you were staying with a couple of smashers. There aren't many secrets in this place. You enjoy yourself. Mind, don't tell your Mum I said that'

Mum/Jean came rushing over and kissed me. Reaching up on tiptoes, she ruffled my hair like she used to. Taking my hand, she led me off down the aisle. I looked over my shoulder and saw Mike grinning and shaking his head. In a quiet corner, Jean stopped and turned to face me.

'Right, what's this I hear about you and two girls?' she said in a stern voice that was belied by the twinkle in her eyes.

I told her all about Celeste, Angelica, Astra and Molly. Well, not all of it. Just the bits a thirty five year old bloke should tell his eighteen year old Mum about. She seemed pleased.

'I'm glad that you have met some nice girls. Mind you, they're all nice girls up here. Now, when are Dad and I going to see this truck of yours? Everyone is talking about it and what you are going to be doing with it.'

'What am I going to be doing with it?' I asked because I wasn't sure how much I should be telling her.

'Well, young Alfie says you are going to be loaded up with some new sort of energy from one of the Alien Heavens and then you will be delivering it around our Heaven. Is that right?'

Humph, so much for it being a big secret. I just hoped that everything was going to work now that the secret was common knowledge. 'Well, that's the idea. Tomorrow I shall be having my first trial with a loaded trailer and then, if everything goes ok, I start delivering. Just England State at first and then into the European States. Not much different from my old job back on Earth'

'Sounds exciting. Maybe your dad and me can come on a trip one day? Or, will there be too many girls waiting their turn as well?' she teased me.

'Maybe one or two' I smiled. 'Tell you what though, if you can come round to Arrivals this evening about five-ish, you can come and see my truck.'

'Ooh, I bet you say that to all the girls' she dimpled and acted coy. This was my MUM, acting like a teenage girl. Well, she was actually a teenage girl so perhaps not surprising. 'I'll tell your Da...Mike' she finished lamely. 'He's been going on about your truck since it arrived. He's telling everyone who'll listen that it belongs to HIS son.

He's so proud of you....we both are. I take it you're not coming back home this evening?'

'No, sorry Jean. Nothing personal but I just can't take those turbo lifts. I'll sleep in my truck tonight. I feel more comfortable there. After all, I've slept in one truck or another most of my adult life. It must be the gypsy blood in me. Are you ok with that?'

'Whatever suits you best, love. Just pop in to see us from time to time and we'll be happy. Anyhow, gotta go before old Miseryguts starts complaining again. See you this evening. Take care love'. She gave me a quick kiss on the cheek and I hugged her back.

The problem with not having or rather not starting, a job was the amount of time on your hands. As I watched Jean rejoining her workmates and being enveloped in the friendly banter and enjoyment of being with workmates, I was envious.

Trucking can be the most lonely job in the world. You are stuck in a cab each and every day isolated from the world around you. Mainly you get glimpses into the real world as you drive through it; a woman hanging out clothes, two neighbours gossiping over a garden fence, people going to work, children coming home from school. All the snapshots of life glimpsed from your cab as you drive along a crowded road.

The nights can be the most lonely, when you feel cut off from the human race. Driving through the night you saw people through their windows and sometimes envied them their settled existence. Or, parked up in some layby, reading a book or eating a solitary meal, talking back at an annoying radio or tv presenter, a trucker really feels the isolation of his chosen profession. Those are the negative points of truck driving. Then there are the good points. Never being in one place long enough to get bored with it. Never quite knowing what each new day and each new trip would bring. The feeling that every thing you did was your decision and not that of some authority figure. The thrill of each new horizon and each new mini adventure.

Sometimes I had envied my married trucker friends. Their family was their goal in life and something to look forward to at the end of each trip. But, I also felt that a life on the road wasn't fair on wives and children. I had seen a lot of my truckers friends get divorced and that was particularly hard to see. The hurt, the recriminations and the sheer overwhelming stress and disbelief.

So, no, I hadn't ever really regretted my decision to stay single. I had lived with a couple of girls for a time but it hadn't worked out. I didn't blame them. It must have been hard coping with my absence and continuous changing of plans because I had missed a ferry or had been held up somewhere. So, maybe selfishly, I had chosen to continue my nomadic existence and put a stable relationship and, ultimately, family and family life on hold. Now, it was on permanent hold.

Perhaps, not surprisingly, I needed to get away from Hydroponics and get my head sorted out. I needed to talk to one of the girls and feel something other than the loneliness I was feeling at the moment. I headed for Arrivals.

As usual, Arrivals was busy. It was one of those 24/7 busy places that never stopped. Celeste and Angel were both at their desks and barely had time for a quick smile before getting on with their jobs. The good thing was that I detected no change in Celeste's attitude and Angel's smile was certainly a lot more intimate. Molly and Astra's doors were both closed so I presumed they were busy as well. I wasn't having much luck. Maybe a coffee was in order and I could people watch at the same time.

I choose my regular seat by the window. I say regular, as if I had been coming for years instead of just days. Exactly how many days? Try as I might, I couldn't seem to remember. I told you that time was weird and irrelevant in Heaven. When the weather and temperature never change you can't mark the seasons. I could only tell the difference between day and night because it was either light or dark. Here in Arrivals, the time was also different to that outside. You just gave up trying to measure the passage of time in Earth terms and just accepted that time.........well, time just was. It really had no meaning up here. Eternity was Eternity. End of.

I was drinking my coffee when a lady wandered over. She was, I suppose, in her mid forties, scantily dressed and extremely attractive. She had a slight figure, was about my height and had short black hair cut close to her head. Whilst giving her a slightly butch look, it actually suited her. She had a small face with upturned nose and wide brown eyes. She was wearing what looked like a hospital gown. 'Hallo,' she smiled. It was a killer smile and she knew it. It lit up her face and made the recipient feel the most important person alive. It worked for me. 'Are you a regular here or just arrived?'

'I guess you could say I am a regular but haven't been here too long' I replied and threw back my own killer and make them weak at the knees smile. She didn't catch it. Instead she sat down and crossed her long legs.

'I've only just arrived. Talk about confusing. It's nothing like I expected. I wonder if I could talk to you about it? I'm Ludi, by the way' She held out a dainty hand across the table and I enveloped it in my great paw and shook it gently.

'John, John Slater' I held her hand until she sort of squirmed it out of mine. ''I don't know all the answers but I can try. Counselling is the place you need to be'

'Been there, done that.' She laughed. It was a polite upper class sound. 'I met this weird guy in a cassock and a hairdo that looked like a cat asleep on his head. I was so busy trying to see how he had done his hair that I missed most of what he said'

'Brother Simon?' I asked. She nodded affirmation.

'Funnily enough, he used to be my teacher. He's a bit strange but is not a bad old bloke. I got on all right with him on Earth and still do here. It's a question of time. He has too many people to see and can just give the basics. I take it you have been to Accommodation and Supply?'

She shook her head. 'I have to go there in about an hour to get sorted. Apparently they are overwhelmed today. There has been some sort of earthquake in China. The bloke in Counselling suggested I get a cup of something in the canteen and look for a person looking exactly like you to ask my questions. Is that ok?'

Bloody Heaven, was I that predictable or was there some sort of monitoring system in place? 'Yes, sure. What do you want to drink? Tea or coffee?'

‘ I could do with something stronger but tea would be fine. Can I come with you and see how that dispenser thing works? I’ve watched people going up and talking to it and then getting their drinks but didn’t like to try it myself.’

‘No problem. I’ll show you how it’s done. But, can I just do something first? Can you turn round?’ She looked up puzzled and just a bit warily as if they were all nutters up here. She turned round and I was presented with a nice view of her back and the cleavage of her buttocks just showing above paper panties. I pulled both ends of her gown together and tied all the tags tightly. She jumped when I did the first one and then must have realised what I was doing. As I did up the other two I watched her porcelain skin turn a deep red. When I finished, I patted her shoulder and she turned round. Her face glowed and she couldn’t meet my eyes.

‘Open all the way?’ she asked and looked up.

I nodded. ‘No wonder I was getting strange looks. I just didn’t notice. Oh well, now that I have been properly introduced, I shall have to get over it.’ She grinned mischievously and, taking my hand, we walked over to the replicator. I showed her how easy it was and she ordered a scone to go with her Darjeeling tea.

‘I shall be glad to get some proper clothes’ she said as we sat down at the table again. ‘I hate wearing this bloody gown. Why can’t they make them attractive?’

‘Looked all right to me. Why are you wearing it anyway?’ I looked over and was rewarded with a mini blush.

‘Well, I have been in hospital for the last week. I’ve had bowel cancer hence the short hair.’ She patted her hair.

'We thought the chemo had beaten it but it came back. I was due to be operated on today. I remember having my anaesthetic and drifting off. I woke up in this mist and......well...I guess you know the rest. Obviously, there were complications during the operation.'

Her eyes brimmed up and her face fell. Moving quickly I got up and held out my arms. She stood up and hugged me tightly and I could feel her shaking as she quietly cried against me. Gradually the sobbing subsided and she released me. I helped her down to her chair and sat back in mine.

'Sorry about that' She said as she dabbed at her eyes with the short sleeve of her gown.

'It happens to all of us' I told her how I had broken down with Celeste and Angel. She gave me a misty eyed smile and patted my hand by way of thanks.

'So, what is it like up here? It's not like I imagined. How did you get here?' She put her hand over her mouth and shook her head. 'Sorry, perhaps you don't want to talk about it.'

'No, it's ok' I reassured her. 'Not much to tell. I'm a trucker and there was an accident. I had to make a quick choice and that was that. Curtains for John Slater.'

'Now I remember.' She exclaimed excitedly. 'I thought your name sounded familiar. It was only when you mentioned you were a truckdriver that it gelled. You're the guy who saved all those school kids aren't you? It was in the papers and on the tv. They said you were a hero. It is you isn't it?'

'I don't know about being a hero' I said as modestly as I could. 'It all happened too quickly to make any rational

decision. I acted on pure instinct. It could have gone either way. Then the same paper and tv reporters would have called me a motorway monster and not a hero.'
'Never the less, you saved lives. At least your ending had some meaning. Mine was just another hospital statistic.'
Her eyes brimmed again and I tried to distract her.
'You'll like it here. Have they told you about Ageing?'
She shook her head and gave me an inquiring look.
I told her all about Ageing, Accomodation, the conditions and the housing, the bad news and the good news. Meeting departed family, relatives and friends. Meeting loved ones left behind at some future date. I painted a somewhat rosier picture than I might have when I was a Newcomer.
Ludi listened intently and smiled when I told her about all the entertainment. She clapped her hands excitedly.
'Does that mean I get to see Michael Jackson perform?' she asked. 'I had tickets for his last tour but gave them to my friend because I wasn't well enough to go. Then he died. Now, I'll get my wish to see him live?' she looked at me as if fearing a leg pull.
'That's assuming he is up here. No reason why he shouldn't be.' I didn't add that she might not recognise him after Ageing. What age would he think was his best, I wondered. I wasn't a fan so wasn't really bothered whether he chose to be black or white.
'Tell me about Ageing' Ludi begged. 'You're not making that up are you? I can really choose what age I want? Go back to when I was young and pretty and had a full head of hair and no pain. I would settle for no pain.'
'You're still very pretty' I told her and she was. 'And, are you feeling any pain?'

She looked at me and sort of flexed herself. A look of wonderment came over her face as she realised she was pain-free. 'Oh, that's wonderful. I have lived with it for so long that I had forgotten what it was like for it not to be there. I can't believe I didn't notice it myself. And this is permanent?'

'So they tell me. You never get any pain here. Not even a headache or hangover.'

'Oh, that sounds heavenly' she suddenly realised what she had said and burst out laughing. I joined in and realised that I liked talking to her. I didn't fancy her....yet. Whether I did when she had Aged was another thing. I felt sure she would choose to be young and, judging by how she looked now, she would be a stunner.

'Oh, I have to go' Ludi jumped up, nearly knocking the table over in the process. I should be in Accommodation and Supply. It's been really nice talking to you John. Maybe we can meet again?'

'Sure. One thing though' she raised an enquiring sculptured eyebrow 'you'll have to tell me who you are. I might not recognise you with proper clothes on and looking different'.

She laughed and held out her hand, then thought better of it and gave me a warm hug. I was very conscious that she had nothing much on under the thin gown. She released me, gave me a knowing grin –women always know these things don't they? – and waved her hand as she walked away.

I had come to Arrivals feeling lonely and a bit down but was now ok. Talking to Ludi had helped me as well as her. I hoped I bumped into her again one day. I finished my drink and left the canteen to see if either Celeste or Angel was free for a few minutes.

I was lucky. Celeste had just finished her shift and was tidying her desk. This consisted of sweeping everything off the desk and into a drawer. She smiled broadly when she saw me, walked over and gave me a hug. I hugged her back and held her at arm's length.

'I guess you know about Angel and me?' I asked her. She nodded and leant over to kiss me on the lips. 'And, you are ok with it?'

'Why wouldn't I be' she said simply. 'She's my best friend and you are the bloke we both love. She just happened to be first. It could have easily been me. Why did you think there would be a problem?'

'I don't know' I stammered. 'If it had happened on earth, I imagine there would be fireworks. The other way round, you with two blokes, I would have probably got jealous.'

'You're still thinking in Earth terms' Celeste reminded me. 'Here in Heaven, it's different. I don't know why but it just is. There is no jealousy, no squabbling no catfights over men or brawls over women. A bloke can have just one girl or as many as he wants. The same for us girls. Nobody minds. Although, I must say, for myself, that it would be nice if you could limit yourself to Angel, myself and Astra - if she decides to take it any further with you. But, even if you don't, it won't stop us being your friends or going out with you. Don't worry about it, John. I am pleased for you but I would like to have a ride in your truck as well. In every sense of the word'. She winked and smiled mischievously.

'I promise and, truth be told, I thought it would be you first'. I held her hand as we walked over to Angel. Angel seemed pleased to see us. We waited whilst she finished up and then we left Arrivals together. Outside, I told them that I was going to see if Maggie was ready and then show her to my parents. We agreed to meet up at their flat later and have a night out. I desperately wanted see Elvis perform and the girls humoured me by agreeing.

By now, I was used to walking to Maintenance. In fact, I quite liked going there if only to see something different Topside. More than anything though, I wanted to get into my truck, hitch up to a loaded trailer and just go. The old Call of the Road was whispering in my ears and I was ready for the Road Music and chorus to begin.

Less than an hour later, I was walking though the now familiar workshop door. I made my way to Sean's hideaway and found him rolling up some paper and putting it into a filing cabinet drawer.

'Hi John' he greeted me. 'Just putting the wiring details on your truck away for future reference. Noel guessed you would be back this evening. He said you couldn't wait. You timed it well. We've not long finished. Come and see what we've done. You're going to like it.'

Maggie was out in the yard and we climbed in. I sat behind the wheel and looked around. There were two new monitors on the dash and a few more switches. The top bunk was still raised and the door to the wardrobe was now in two halves. I could just about see where extra hinges had been added. Sean opened the door and I could see a small replicator in the bottom half of the now empty wardrobe. He undid a latch on the side and pulled a handle

on the bottom of the replicator. The whole unit came forward and, once clear, swung out on hinges to rest against the back of the driving seat.
'I'm quite pleased with that' Sean explained. 'You can now use the sonic shower whilst standing inside the wardrobe. You can see the head of the shower in the roof lining there'. He pointed out the small metal rosette at the top of the wardrobe. He must have gone to a lot of trouble to hide all the pipework and wiring in the wall and headlining because nothing else showed. 'Nice, neat job eh? Noel said you were a bit cabproud so I made sure the lads did a good job. Once you've had a shower, the replicator slides back in and operates as normal. The menu is a bit limited because of the size but you should be ok so long as you don't order anything too exotic'.
'Wow, that's great' I said and meant it. 'Not quite the kitchen sink but probably better. All it needs now is a toilet and I needn't leave the cab at all' I joked.
Sean looked at me and grinned. Shutting the wardrobe door, he raised up a section in the bottom bunk and, with a magician's flourish, revealed a small vacuum toilet. My own mini- version. 'It also acts as a waste disposal for rubbish' Sean explained. 'It works on a similar principle to a domestic one but everything goes through and gets cut into extremely small pieces by spinning blades in the outlet pipe and gets dumped in a container on the chassis. You just empty the container every now and then. Oh, and don't put your fingers or anything similar down it.' He lowered the bunk section and returned to the front of the cab.
'These two monitors are for Sat Nav and the extra cameras we've installed. The smaller one is for Sat Nav and works

like any other system except you don't have to programme it manually. You just think where you are going, like you do now, and the monitor shows you the way. The larger one splits into four sections for the four cameras or you can have just one camera view up at a time'. Sean flicked one of the new switches and the larger monitor lit up. It showed split screen views of the rear, either side and in front. 'Once you have hitched on, the rear camera shows the view from the back of the trailer. You can adjust the angle of all the cameras separately with this joystick but I have set them as I think you would want them'

I had a little play but had to agree. They were set up perfectly. I asked about the front camera and why I would need it.

'Because it is an infra red camera and will help you to see far better in the dark than with your conventional headlights. We played with it outside last night before we fitted it in the truck. It gives you a very clear picture for about a quarter of a mile. Run into fog or heavy mist and you'll appreciate. I don't suppose you'll do much night driving but you never know. Mercedes Benz put a similar system in its S Class limos but your system is superior. The communications unit' he indicated a small unit fitted under the header rail 'works like a cb radio. You'll be in constant contact with us and the tracking module we fitted means we know where you are. That's about it. Any questions?' Sean looked across at me. I shook my head.

'Not for now. You've done a brilliant job Sean, I really appreciate it.' I held out my hand and we shook. 'Now, can I take it away tonight? I promised my young Mum and Dad that I would show it to them'.

'Yes, I've finished with it. Be back first thing in the morning though. Noel is anxious to get the trailer loaded and to do a test run. I'll just get the doors open for you.' Sean climbed down and went to open the workshop doors. I fired up and drove slowly through them and back to Arrivals. I was looking forward to showing Maggie off to my parents.

Getting back to Arrivals took no time. No hold ups, grid lock or anything. I was going to like driving up here. I wondered how long it would be before I started thinking about motorway hold-ups and all the other Earth driving problems with affection and nostalgia?

As I pulled up outside Arrivals, I was met by a crowd of people. There was Mike and Jean, Grandad, Aunty Winnie and UncleWag –who had been my adopted parents when Mum and Dad died – and several other assorted relatives, friends and old neighbours. I had a lump in my throat when I saw them all lined up to see me. Apart from Peter and Beth, I had no one really close and then, suddenly, I had all these people loving and looking out for me.

I climbed down and let Mike and Jean into the cab and showed them around. Mike was really impressed and asked a lot of mechanical and technical questions which I answered as best I could. Jean was more concerned about whether I would be warm enough and whether she could replicate some nicer curtains for Maggie. I drove them around for a bit and then let Mike drive the short distance back. Considering he hadn't driven in years and nothing this size, he didn't do too badly but decided he wouldn't like to do it full time.

Next up was Wag and Winnie. I had seen them the first time in Hydraponics but hadn't recognised them. I know that sounds bad but I had never really seen them as young people. Jean had pointed them out to me earlier in the day and, if she hadn't, I probably still wouldn't have known them. Now, instead of the serious middle-aged couple who had been saddled with a youngster, they were both in their mid-twenties, full of fun and smiling. I took great pleasure in telling them that it was their inheritance that had allowed me to buy my first truck. In a way, I suppose, Maggie was theirs as well.

'You make sure you look after my truck' Wag joked as he climbed down. 'I'll be making sure you keep it clean and tidy' He wasn't joking. His OCD was worse than mine.

I suppose it took another hour before everyone had Oo'd and Aa'd about the interior and exterior of my truck. That was one of the things I liked about having a nice truck. People admiring it was as good a buzz as actually driving it.

Finally, everyone had gone and Maggie and I were alone. I had made arrangements with Jean for Alfie to bring my few belongings over to the girls place and I could then get them stowed away. In the meantime, time was getting on and I had to get over to meet the girls for our night out. I pulled the curtains, swivelled the replicator out and had my first trucking shower. It worked as well in the cab as it had in the apartment. Suitably refreshed and pressed, I started up the engine and drove over to the girl's apartment.

Driving amongst the Astro's was a challenge. Clearance without any other vehicles on the streets was just about ok but was going to be infinitely more difficult with a loaded trailer. Hopefully, Noel's statement that the delivery destinations were more accessible was true. For now though, driving was do-able and I did. I pulled up outside the girls block and parked up. I even clicked the remote central locking button as I walked away. Well, better safe than sorry, eh? You never knew who was about and I couldn't just forget the ingrained habit of locking up every time I left my vehicle. Hopefully, Maggie would still be here when I returned. If she wasn't, then Heaven was in a sorrier state than everyone imagined.

I knocked on the door and Astra answered it. I was pleased to see a smile on her face instead of a wary look. She was wearing what looked like a paint smeared plastic bag over her clothes. Seeing my look, she explained. 'I'm working on my mural. I use this old bin liner to keep paint off my clothes. Come and see what I've done.' She held out her hand with no hesitation whatsoever and I held it as she pulled me into the living room. Standing before the mural, she turned round and looked at me expectantly.

The horses were still galloping round the pasture but now there had been a road added to the background. And, there in all her finery, was a miniature Maggie roaring up the road with a hint of smoke coming from her twin stacks. It was beautifully done. I said as much to Astra.

'Well, I hope I got it right. I only had a brief glimpse myself and had to rely on the other girl's description. You don't mind do you?'

Mind? I was chuffed to bits. Not because it was done so well but because of what it represented. I held out my arms and she came into them. I hugged her hard and, lifting up her face, kissed her. For a brief moment, she hesitated then

kissed me back. I looked over her shoulder and saw Molly smiling and wiping a tear away.
'Cup of tea, John?' Molly asked as Astra returned to her painting.
'Never say no to a cup of tea Molly'
As she placed the cup on the table in front of me, Molly leant over and whispered 'She's been working on it all afternoon'
Just then the bedroom door opened and Celeste and Angel emerged trailing a tantalising perfume behind them. They were dressed pretty much the same as the last time we went out. They still looked just as gorgeous. Funnily enough, wearing the same clothes was kind of reassuring. You knew what you were getting and that was fine with me.
I had asked Celeste how she felt about it and she was ok with it now. At first, she thought it was limiting and missed changing clothes. She also realised that it was mainly competition with other women that created the need in the first place. Now, with just two outfits, everyone was the same and, ultimately, happier at not having to compete. Of course, most room-mates mix and matched each other's clothes and accessories for those little changes in Eternity wear.
For myself, I was happy wearing what I had on. Sure, I had my nice dress up and go out outfit but I was saving that. Basically, like most blokes I suppose, I was a bit of a slob and fashion dinosaur. Clean and tidy but striving for the utilitarian look rather than the latest up to the minute style. Hell, I even bought my underpants from M&S. Once a

year, I bought twelve new pairs. One for every month. Keep it simple.

'Hi girls, you both look fantastic' I told them as they presented their cheeks for a kiss. I duly obliged. I still had a niggling feeling about this no-jealousy thing but, if they were happy about it, then I was more than happy to have these two stunners on my arms. I never had it this good on Earth.

By now, travelling on the tube had become as routine as it had been on Earth. This time of the evening, there were a lot of passengers going to the Entertainment areas. I ended up in a corner with the girls and managed a quiet grope with Angel then felt bad about it and groped Celeste as well. They both giggled and then started discussing my groping technique. Huumph, can't even have a decent grope in Heaven these days without it being discussed between all and sundry. I put my hands in my pocket and kept them there. That'll teach them.

The nearer we got to Entertainments, the more heightened the anticipation I was feeling. No, not the groping but, the bizarre thought that I would soon be seeing Elvis live on stage. It was almost worth crashing into a concrete pillar just for that.

As we got off the tube and walked up the passage, the noise got louder and the lights got brighter. There was that sort of excitement you get just before a cup final or a rock concert. I sort of hoped that they weren't all going to see Elvis. I wanted my first in a Deathtime experience to be up close and as personal as I could get. I had the feeling I wasn't going to get my wish as we joined the longest queue there was.

As we stood in line, it was easy to get distracted by the sights and sounds all around. The penny arcades were full of people pulling levers, piling pennies, shooting ducks and all the other silly and totally absorbing games you got in seaside pier establishments. A little further up, there was a line of people waiting to get into a football match. There were boxing and wrestling booths, swimming areas, archery and rifle shooting ranges, you think of a sport or an entertainment and there were people waiting in line. Suddenly, our line started moving and we tried to keep with the rush of people entering the building. Inside, it was pretty much a free for all as people claimed their seats. The first two rows of seats were blocked off but the ones behind those were soon filled. At this rate, the girls and I were going to be at the back and standing. And, I had the uncharitable thought, what was with the reserved seats? Who were they for? I thought everyone was sort of equal up here?

'Come on John. Keep up' Celeste pulled at my arm and I followed both girls down to the front. As we reached the reserved seats, a big bloke stepped in front of us. And, believe me, he was BIG. He stood about head and shoulders above everyone else. His suit was stretched tight front and back and the sleeves ended below his elbows. He wasn't smiling and he wasn't saying anything either. He held up his hand and sort of scowled at us. He didn't frighten me. Well, he did actually but I wasn't going to whimp out in front of the girls.

I was just debating whether to go for his feet or to head-butt him in the knees when his face cracked slightly and, in a very soft voice that was completely at odds with his size, he

whispered 'Hi Celeste, Hi Angel. I kept them free just like you asked. Is this John Slater?'
' Thanks Tiny. Yes, this is John. John, Tiny. Tiny, John' Angel made the introductions as I gingerly shook the giant's hand. He was obviously used to shaking hands with midgets because it didn't hurt. It probably would once the feeling came back, though. Tiny let us through into the reserved area and we sat down. I looked across questioningly at Angel. She winked back. 'I told Tiny you were a Grade 2 and that you wanted a good seat for tonight's Elvis concert. I hope these are ok?'
Ok? They were bloody perfect. All my former thoughts about reserved seats had conveniently vanished.
'Yes, great. Thanks Angel. But, two rows? Wasn't that a bit greedy?' I asked.
'Don't worry about it, Boyo' a familiar voice said from behind me. I looked around and there was Noel, his girlfriend/secretary Imogen, and the rest of the transport crew. Most of these had their own female company as well. More or less in the blink of an eye the two rows of seat were full and everybody was settling in. Noel and Imogen were on Angel's side, I was in the middle of the two girls and Sean and his friend were on Celeste's side. I looked across with a 'What are you doing here?' sort of look at Noel. He winked back and held a finger up to his lips as the lights dimmed and the curtains opened. A familiar figure walked onto the stage and stood in front of the microphone. He was a big guy as well. He was dressed in a rumpled suit and had a very distinctive hat on his wavy hair.

‘Two truckers get out of their cab and walk into a caff. You’d think at least one of them would have seen it.’ The audience erupted. It was a stupid gag but told by one of the funniest men alive or dead. Tommy Cooper stood there with his trademark fez on his head and beamed down at us. ‘I had a trucker friend who drowned in a bowl of muesli. A strong currant pulled him in.’

‘A truck driver went to a seafood disco last week. He pulled a mussel’

Tommy looked directly at me and winked. I had the distinct feeling I had been set up. ‘Sorry about all the trucker jokes’ He said. ‘They are in honour of a trucker friend of mine. Ladies and gentlemen, John Slater.’ Me, a friend of Tommy Cooper? Everyone was applauding and the girls sort of pushed me to my feet. I stood there looking and feeling stupid as the clapping continued. ‘You’ll be thanking that little trucker once he starts delivering your energy’ Tommy joked.

I sat down feeling embarrassed. Noel and the rest of his crew were still clapping and enjoying my discomfort.

‘And, don’t forget the rest of the people who made it possible. The Maintenance people who got John’s truck ready and set everything up. Let’s have a big hand for them as well’ Now it was Noel and his guys who looked embarrassed.

‘I went into a butchers the other day and bet him fifty quid he couldn’t reach the meat on the top shelf. He said ‘No, the steaks are too high’.

A man goes to the doctors with a strawberry growing out of his head. The doctor says ‘I’ll get you some cream for that’

I was getting into my car and a woman comes across and says 'Can you give me a lift?' I tell her she looks great, the world is her oyster and she should go for it.'
It was insane. Some of the audience were actually rolling on the floor with laughter. The jokes were so stupid that if anyone else had told them, they would get booed off the stage. Tommy's delivery was so good that even the simplest statement created howls of laughter. It was hard to imagine that he had been up here since April 15th 1984 and was still proving that he was one of the funniest men around.
'Doc, I can't stop singing The Green, Green Grass of Home. The doc says 'That sounds like Tom Jones Syndrome.' Is it common? 'It's not unusual'
A man takes his Rottweiller to the vet. 'My dog is cross-eyed. Is there anything you can do for him?' 'Well,' says the vet 'I'm going to have to examine him'. So he picks the dog up and examines his eyes, then he checks it's teeth. Finally he says 'I'm going to have to put him down'
'What, because he's cross-eyed?'
'No, because he's really heavy'
'Two aerials meet on a roof – fall in love- get married. The ceremony was rubbish but the reception was brilliant'
I was laughing so much it hurt. I looked at the girls. They looked like pandas with their mascara running down their cheeks. Noel and his crew were holding their sides and howling. It must have been a wonderful feeling to make everyone so happy. But, as all good things must, Tommy's act came to an end. To thunderous applause, he left the stage. On Earth he had died doing his act, right

there on the stage. Here he was still doing what he did and loved doing best; making people happy.
Then, even before we had time to settle down, a voice boomed out “Ladies and Gentlemen, Elvis is in the building”. A loud guitar competed with the rapturous applause and that oh so familiar voice followed the guitar into Jailhouse Rock. I looked up and there he was. The King. Gyrating and singing as only he could do. A young Elvis. Elvis in his prime. Elvis as he should have been remembered. The slim, quiffe’d and glorious Elvis and not the sad fat person people always think of.
The next two hours flowed away in a sea of music, forgotten youth and memories. A trucker friend told me he was going through the Kennedy Tunnel just outside of Antwerp when the radio announced that Elvis had died. August the 16th 1977. He thought he had misheard and then lost reception in the tunnel. He suddenly saw brake lights ahead and slowed down. It was only when he drove into daylight again that he knew the news was true. Virtually every vehicle he could see had stopped. Some on the hard shoulder but most, right there on the expressway. Everywhere he looked there were people crying and holding each other. The grief was palatable. You could feel it, taste it, he said. It continued for almost five minutes before everyone sort of shook themselves off, climbed into their vehicles and drove off. Continuing with their life but with a life that would never be the same again. The only time I had seen a similar universal grief since then was when Diana had died.
Now, all that was forgotten. It had always been my dream to see him in concert. I had always wanted to go

Graceland to pay homage. I had never been able to achieve either. But now, here I was, in front row seats, seeing the legend. I was truly in Heaven.

For the next two hours, Elvis had everyone enthralled. He sang Young Elvis, Middle-aged and Large Elvis. He sang songs he had performed and songs that hadn't been written when he departed. He laughed, he joked and he had his audience begging for more. Finally though, as they must, all the good things came to an end. Elvis left the stage. The audience sat stunned, erupted into clapping and then became reflective as people thought about leaving.

I looked around as I stood up. People in groups discussing the performance. It was easy to forget that many of the people in this audience had seen Elvis perform before. Probably many times. It was equally obvious that his audience never tired of hearing him sing. As Elvis himself had once remarked 'The body has let me down but the Voice never has'

I looked at the girls to see if they were ready. They were still sitting down. Just as I was going to say something, I felt a tap on my shoulder. I turned round and there were Mike and Jean.

'What did you think of that then, John?' Mike asked me. Jean looked at the girls and then at me. I took my cue and introduced them. Jean hugged each of them and they looked pleased. Moment over . In-laws met and accepted. I had just finished when Tiny lumbered over. Not sure whether he was going to chuck me out or not, I looked him straight in the kneecaps and prepared to stand my ground. He went to Celeste instead and stooped over to whisper in her ear. She nodded excitedly and turned round to me.

'Come on then' she said as she grabbed my hand and pulled. Noel and his crowd got up to follow her. She suddenly stopped and turned to my parents. 'Come on, Mike, Jean, you're invited as well'.

Invited? Invited where? I soon found out as we followed Tiny through a door, down a dimly lit corridor and through another door into a room. There were a few chairs and a table and a sofa at the far end. Tiny told us to sit and we sat. I looked at Celeste questioningly and she pretended not to see me. Suddenly the door opened again and in came........in came Elvis Presley himself.

'Hi, everyone. Thank you for coming. Hello Celeste, how are you?' He came round and stood in front of me holding out his hand. 'I guess you must be John, huh? Pleased to meet you, Sir. Celeste has told me so much about you I feel that I know you already'

Elvis calling me "Sir"? Well, they said he was polite but calling me "Sir". He was older than me for Ch...Goodness sake.

I looked over at Celeste and she gave a little satisfied grin. 'Well, you said you wanted to meet him'. I was torn between kissing her or shaking Elvis' hand. I kissed her quickly and then shook his hand.

Celeste introduced Mike and Jean. Mike didn't say a word. He just stood there shaking hands in a dazed fashion. Jean was worse. She actually dropped into a curtsey and went bright red. Elvis couldn't have been nicer. He helped her up. 'I guess you must be proud of John huh?' Jean just nodded.

Noel and his crew were all introduced and were suitably starstruck. I guessed that would be the end of it but no,

Elvis insisted on hearing all about Maggie, the conversion work and everything else. 'My pop Vernon was a truck driver, you know. I drove supply trucks in the army and, I guess, I kinda miss driving. I certainly miss my Caddies, that's for sure'.
'Oh, I didn't know you played golf, Elvis' Celeste said. 'Where would you go? 'Sorry Celeste, I was talking about my cars, you know, my Cadillacs. I really had a thing for Caddies. I used to give them for presents. I'd have sure given you one, honey' Elvis joked with a suggestive wink. Celeste went pink, then realised he was talking about cars. Whilst she was working out whether to be hurt or disappointed Elvis turned to me and asked if it would be possible to come out in my truck sometime? I told him I'd think about it. Yeah right.
Tiny came back into the room with a tray engulfed between his giant hands. He laid it on the table at the end of the room then left. He reappeared again with a larger tray. Elvis turned round and invited us to have a drink and a bite. The small tray contained bottles of Coke and the larger had hotdogs. Everybody suddenly realised they were hungry and the trays emptied quicker than a Scottish church when the collection plate came round.
Elvis left the room and returned with a guitar. He strummed a few chords and the noise ceased. Looking over at Jean, he started to sing Wooden Heart, the old German folk tune. I had already told him it was her favourite. When he got to the bit where he sang in German, he looked over at Noel and me. 'Come on guys, help me out'.
My voice is rubbish but, in that company it didn't sound too bad. Noel's was a revelation. Deep and husky, it

blended in and, truth be told, enhanced both of our voices. Wooden Heart was followed by His Latest Flame and I stepped down and left Elvis and Noel to it.

The rest of the room was singing along and it turned into a real jam session. Noel borrowed the guitar and broke into Guitar Boogie, Foot Tapper and several other solos. Elvis danced with Celeste, Angel, Jean and most of the other girls in turn. I smooched with Angel and Celeste when Elvis sang some slow numbers.

Finally, some three hours later, it came to an end. We left in a trance. Outside the Venue, everybody started to talk at once. No doubt about it, it was one of the best nights of our lives/deaths.

Noel and his crowd left with instructions for me to be early the next morning. Mike and Jean were still buzzing and sort of wandered off engrossed in each other. I looked at Celeste and held out my arms. She came into them and I hugged her and kissed her as thanks for a great night. Angel looked at me as I hugged her friend and smiled. 'Come on, you two. Wait until you get home'.

Was that a suggestion I wondered? It was still hard to keep up with the idea of having two women at the same time and both in agreement with the situation.

When the tube arrived, there was nobody else on it. Probably everyone else had gone to bed and the night shift was already on duty. That was something else that took some getting used to as well. The fact that Heaven was run like a factory. There were three shifts and everyone took turn and turn about. The work never seemed to stop either. The food growing, the building, the maintenance; everything struggled to keep up with the ever growing population. Even on December 25th, the Boss's birthday, the work ground relentlessly on. If it wasn't for that, Heaven would be a helluva place to live.

The ride back to the apartment didn't take long. By now, we were all flagging and looking forward to bed. Which, of course, posed more problems. Did I go to Maggie alone or take one of the girls back with me? Did I stay at the apartment and, if so, where would I sleep and with whom? I decided to worry about it at the time.

Back at the apartment, we had to keep the noise down as Molly and Astra were asleep. Celeste solved the problem of where I was sleeping by putting a pillow and a blanket on the settee. On reflection, that was the sensible solution. The girls only had single beds anyway and why should one of them have to sleep on the couch? I didn't have to pretend to be tired. I was shattered. It had been quite a day. The girls were obviously feeling the same way. They both kissed me goodnight and went into their room.

I stripped to my Y fronts and stretched out on the settee. I half expected a door to open and get some company. I shut my eyes and snuggled down as I waited.

*****

'Come on John. It's seven thirty. Time you were getting ready for work'. Molly beamed down at me as she put a cup of tea and some toast within reach. 'Did you have a good time, last night? I didn't hear you come in. Was Elvis as good as you expected?'

Without waiting for an answer, Molly went back to the kitchen area. I struggled to wake up properly. I must have went out like a light. I felt better for a good sleep though.

I reached for the tea and had the thought ‘Today is going to be a good day’.

SEVENTEEN

'Today is going to be a good day' Peter Tiler said as he sipped his tea. 'It will be a sad day but we are going to do John proud'

Dave Williams paused with a fork halfway to his mouth. Both were in the kitchen and tucking into a full English breakfast. 'We will certainly try' he agreed.

Both men continued eating and reflected on the day ahead. Mike Henshaw was outside getting his truck prepared with a final polish. His partner Dereck was washing up at the sink after cooking breakfast for them all. All of them had been in a sombre mood as they went over the day's schedule.

'Do you know, I haven't even seen Mike's truck yet' Peter remembered. 'What's it like?'

Getting up from the table, his companion took his empty plate to the sink and passed it over. 'Thanks Dereck, That was great' he turned back to Peter. 'The easiest way is to show you. It's outside in the yard by now and, if I know Mike, it'll be gleaming. Good job the weather is going to be dry all day. Mike doesn't like getting his KW out if there is a chance of it getting wet. Hell, he even built a heated garage just for the truck. That's why you didn't see it last night. It was all tucked up when we arrived. Come on, finish up and take a look. See for yourself'. Waiting whilst Peter took his plate to Dereck, Dave then beckoned Peter through the back door. As Peter followed him through, Dave stood to one side and let his friend continue round the side of the house. As he expected he would,

Peter suddenly stopped dead in his tracks. 'Bloody hell' he said with awe in his voice 'What a monster'
Mike was up a stepladder busy polishing the top of the Kenworth. Even though the sun was barely up, the truck gleamed with reflected light. It stood 10 feet high at the top of the Double Eagle custom built sleeper pod at the back of the cab. It was 30 feet long from burnished radiator to the rear of the stainless steel clad chassis. The gap between the two chassis rails lacked the usual fifth wheel assembly for hitching to a trailer. Instead there was a custom made chromed cover that covered the entire framework. The two diesel tanks were polished alloy as were the wheels. The bonnet seemed to go on forever but, in reality, was only six feet long.
Nestled between the bonnet and the sleeper pod was the relatively small driving cabin. By the standards of the trucks Peter normally drove, the cab was tiny. Opening the door, he peeped inside. Two richly upholstered leather seats, leather linings and what looked like an aircraft dash behind the large steering wheel. Peter had often heard that American truck's dashboards looked "like the gauges had been fired from a shotgun" and he now understood the expression. Instead of the organised array of logically placed gauges and dials he was used to, the dash was crammed with a myriad of large and small dials. Massive rocker switches seemed to grow from the wood effect surface and there were three extra large push switches in the middle.
Peter shook his head in wonderment and dismay. Once again, he thanked the wisdom that had led him to his friend Dave Williams. Peter was a good driver but coping with

this overly complex vehicle whilst sitting on the wrong side of the cab? His mind reeled from the thought. He stepped back shaking his head.

Almost instantly, he saw his own reflection in the deep, almost black blue surface that lightened almost imperceptibly until the top of the vehicle was transformed into a light sky blue. Looking closely, his attention was drawn to the surface of the paint where rainbow flecks of metal were embedded. He realised that the metal flakes would give a similar pearlescent ever-changing appearance as that used on John Slater's Magnum.

Still shaking his head in disbelief, he walked round the truck and took in even more detail. Apart from being almost entirely chrome, stainless steel or burnished alloy, the outline of the vehicle was determined by rows of tiny led lights. He started counting the lights but gave up at a hundred. 'Bloody hell' he said to no one in particular 'this must look like Blackpool illuminations at night.'

'Over two hundred lights in total' Mike said proudly. 'I had a separate wiring system and heavy-duty alternator installed just for the lights alone. I don't have to have them all lit' he said, almost defensively, then he grinned 'But I always do. Got to be seen at night haven't you?' He swiped at a non- existent spot on the paintwork and then stepped down from the ladder. 'I think that will do' he said proudly.

'Show Peter the engine, Mike' Dave was still grinning at the bemused expression on his mate's face. Mike reached into the cab and pulled a lever. The bonnet popped open and then, as a switch was flicked, began to rise up electrically. Underneath the bonnet was a gleaming

600bhp Cummins engine. The rocker box covers had been heavily chromed, all the pipe work was polished copper or braided armoured sleeving. Even the manifold and exhaust were gleaming stainless steel. The interior of the engine space was the same deep blue as the bottom of the vehicle and even the most fastidious person would have had no qualms about eating his food off any exposed surface. Mike grinned proudly as he flicked the switch again and the bonnet started it's majestic descent.
'I like to keep it clean' he explained as he shut the door. Peter had already guessed that Mike Henshaw was obsessed with the same sort of cleanliness bug that John Slater had suffered from.
'Come and look inside.' Peter followed him round to the side entrance of the large sleeper pod. When Mike opened the door and stepped inside, he followed. Then stopped short. He swivelled his eyes upwards to the roof, around the interior and out through the interior entrance to the cab beyond. The inside of the pod was leather lined in the same colour as the cab. There was a single bed opposite and a large full length storage unit beside it. At the back of the cab partition was a small cooking area with microwave and gas oven. A small table had two chairs nestled under it. Food storage units were under the worktop with two extra on the wall. A plasma tv was fixed to the rear wall of the pod along with a dvd unit and cd/ radio. A smaller monitor showed split screen views of both sides, front and rear of the vehicle.
Peter took it all in and finally spoke 'I didn't realise that the Yanks had to rough it quite so badly' he announced with a solemn expression belied by the twinkle in his eyes.

'You like it then?' Mike asked.
'Like it? I bloody love it' Peter assured him. Stepping down, he walked round the vehicle yet again. He faced Mike and Dave and, with misty eyes and a wobble in his voice, gave his verdict.
'Thank you guys. It is absolutely, just exactly, what John would have picked if he could have chosen for himself.'
'Oh, I'm so pleased' Mike said busy with a tissue at his eyes. He came over and gave the big trucker a hug. Peter hesitated for a fraction then returned it.
'Right, come on then, It's time to get busy' Dave Williams reminded the pair. 'Peter, let's go to the undertakers and get John. Once we get him back here we can secure the coffin to the chassis bed. Mike? Can you ring the undertaker and let him know we are on our way.'
Peter started up his pickup and, following the directions his companion read from the map Mike had given him, soon arrived at the premises of Findlay and Son, Funeral Directors. Entering, they were met by a tall, elderly man in a black suit. Having introduced themselves, they followed him to a side room. Mr Findlay opened the door and stood aside as the pair entered. 'I'll give you a few moments' he said quietly. He indicated a bell push set in the door frame. 'Ring that when you are ready and my staff will come and help you carry Mr Slater to your vehicle'
As the door closed, Peter and Dave looked at the coffin lying on two cloth covered supports. It was an accurate representation of an articulated truck with a trailer behind. It had been beautifully crafted and expertly painted. The pair walked round it and nodded approvingly. Peter laid his hand on the smooth surface and patted it gently. 'Hi

John' he said softly. Tears flowed down his cheeks. 'We've come to bring you home. This is Dave Williams. You haven't met him but he's a trucker as well. He helped me organise all this and I couldn't have done it without him. Remember all the times we joked about our funerals? How you wanted a big American truck to take you to Canley and what you wanted afterwards. Well John, we've got the best truck you ever saw. You'll be so proud riding up that motorway for the last time. Everyone will notice and know that it's John Slater having his final ride home. Enjoy it mate, you deserve it'.

Peter gave the coffin one last pat and, looking across, nodded. Dave pushed the button. Shortly afterwards, four solemn looking men entered and, after getting a confirming nod, picked up the coffin and slowly carried it outside to where Peter's pick-up waited with its tailgate lowered. With a quiet dignity, the four men loaded the coffin and fastened the tailgate. One stayed behind as the others walked back towards the building.

He came over and stood in front of Peter. 'Mr Tiler?' he asked. 'I'm Gordon Findlay and my daughter was on that coach. I can't tell you how sorry I am about your friend but, if it's any consolation, I feel that he saved a lot of young lives that day. I do hope that thought brings some consolation. Now, if you don't mind, my daughter has some flowers she would like you to have' At her father's beckoning, a young girl walked over carrying a bouquet of white lilies. She was very pretty in a white dress and looked to be about ten or eleven years old. She came and stood next to her father. He indicated Peter and she handed the bunch over and, suddenly overcome, ran back into the

building. 'All the children on the coach contributed to the flowers and many, many, masses have been said in your friend's name since then. As you go to the Junction 7 motorway entry, you will get some idea of just how many people owe Mr Slater a debt that can now never be repaid. But, rest assured Mr Tiler, he will never be forgotten by us, our children and our children's children. I do hope that thought brings some solace and comfort to you.' Shaking both men's hands, Mr Findlay walked quietly away.
Peter looked over then tossed the keys to Dave. 'Can you drive back mate?' He asked. 'I'm a bit too choked up just now. That little girl did it for me.'
Both men were silent on the journey back to Mike Henshaw's. Driving through the gates, Dave carried on to the rear of the building where the Kenworth was waiting. Pulling up alongside, he stopped the engine and looked over. 'Ok mate? Up to this?'
Peter nodded and both men walked to the back of the pick-up. Mike and Dereck stood silently together and watched as the tailgate was lowered and the coffin was revealed. Mike nodded approvingly and Dereck put his hand up to his mouth as his eyes misted over. 'Come on, guys. We need a hand here' Dave reminded them. Working as a unit, they retrieved the coffin from the pick-up's loading bed and carried it around to the rear of the truck. Silently, they slid it up along the shiny surface until it came to a rest a foot away from the rear of the cab. The truck part of the coffin faced forwards and, after some slight adjustment, was judged to be just right. Peter returned to his pick-up and returned with some brand new orange tie-down straps with ratchets. Not trusting the coffin handles, he placed the first

strap over the coffin near the front. Using the chassis frame underneath as anchoring points, he placed one hook and then, walking round, hooked the other to the lip of the chassis. Threading the longer end through the ratchet mechanism, he pulled the surplus strap taut and then began operating the ratchet to get the final tightness. He did the same for the rear of the coffin and then tested his handiwork. Satisfied, he turned to the three men and shook each one's hand in turn.

'Thank you guys. You have all been brilliant. Now' he looked at his watch, 'we have to make tracks. It's a Friday and the motorway traffic might be a bit iffy.' He handed his keys to Mike, who promised to catch up with them after locking up, and turned to Dave. He nodded and then climbed up into the cab.

Dave sat behind the steering wheel and turned the key. The big Cummins rumbled to life and, after checking the gauges, he selected a gear, released the hand brake and the truck moved majestically forward.

As he grew more confident with the Kenworth, Dave Williams relaxed. It had been some time since he had driven anything so large and with left hand drive. It took him a while to get his perspective worked out and to accommodate for the vehicle's large bonnet and poor turning circle. Peter remained silent, lost in his own thoughts. Thinking of the night the accident happened and how, without knowing it, he had been so near to the scene of his friend's fatal crash.The short journey to the M2 passed without incident and then, as the approach to the motorway junction appeared, Dave almost stopped on the road. First checking his mirrors for traffic behind, he slowed right down in disbelief.

The first thing he saw were the three trucks parked on the side of the road. No ordinary trucks, they were obviously the vehicles belonging to Mike's friends and fellow showtruck competitors. As soon as they saw the Kenworth, the drivers blasted their airhorns in a mournful dirge. But, beyond the trucks, was a large crowd of people. Adults and children, they lined the road and began clapping.

'Bloody hell, Peter. I'm guessing these are the parents and their children that Gordon Findlay told us about. It looks like the whole school had turned out. What do I do?'

'Nothing much you can do mate' Peter decided. 'It's not safe to stop and that's not what John would have wanted. It's nice that these people have turned out to show their respect but we have to keep going'. His companion looked over and nodded. As they drove past the people lining the road, both men were visibly moved. Several children threw the flowers they were holding in front of the truck. Many parents mouthed a silent "thank you" as the truck and its sad load drove slowly past. As the Kenworth passed the last of the waiting trucks, the other drivers pulled in behind and followed.

Joining the M2, the four vehicles picked up speed and settled at 55mph. Trucks passing on the other side blew their horns and flashed their lights in a show of respect. Clearly the news of John Slater's final journey had spread. As they passed the accident scene, Dave pulled the air horn cord and blasted a final salute. Even as the Kenworth's deep bass note died away it was replaced by many more until the whole motorway seemed to reverberate. Looking

in his rear view mirrors, Dave turned and told Peter to look in his.
Looking beyond the three showtrucks, Peter was astonished to see a long line of trucks keeping pace behind them.
'Bloody hell' he breathed. 'How many of them are there? The police aren't going to like this'
'Not a lot we can do, is there? It's just a busy Friday on the motorway. If the other trucks don't want to pass us then there is nothing we can do. The other two lanes are clear for anything that wants to pass.'
However, that wasn't strictly true. Many vans and cars slowed down as they passed the funeral convoy. Whether out of respect or just curiosity, it was hard to tell. Things started to get out of hand once the Kenworth joined the M25 and drove down to the barriers at the Dartford Tunnel. There, to the astonishment of the two friends, there were a battery of photographers and television cameras waiting. As the Kenworth came to a halt at the pay booth and Peter handed over the toll fee, the media swarmed forwards.'
'What do we do, mate?' Peter asked as he hastily powered up his side window. The pay booth barrier rose and, in answer, the truck drove past and down the incline to the tunnel.'
'We keep going' Dave replied. 'If we stop, then we are causing an obstruction. I didn't expect this sort of attention.'
Even though it wasn't that dark in the tunnel, he almost automatically switched on the Kenworth's lights. Suddenly, the whole tunnel, it seemed, glowed in the reflections from the vehicle's lights. Looking in the mirrors both men saw the other showtrucks behind them lit

up like Christmas trees. Overtaking motorists looked and grinned as they motored past. Many cars had children in them who pressed their faces to the glass in wonderment. 'Nothing like keeping a low-profile' Peter grinned as they exited the tunnel and switched off the lights. 'Bloody hell, look at that' he exclaimed as an mpv drove slowly past. The side door was open and a cameraman leant perilously out as he swivelled his shoulder held camera towards them. The logo "BBC Outside Broadcast" was clearly visible on the side of the vehicle.

Several other vehicles drove slowly past and each seemed to have either a still or video photographer standing up through the skylight or poking a lens through either the side door or a side window. Concentrating on keeping a safe distance from the vehicles at the side or in front of his vehicle, Dave drove on as fast as the conditions allowed. Eventually, the media seemed to have enough material and ordinary traffic started to drive past in a near normal fashion. The inside lane was still nose to tail with a convoy of assorted trucks as they respectfully escorted a fellow trucker on his last motorway journey. The nearer they got to the M1, the more the bridges over the motorway seemed full of waving and clapping people. People had obviously heard about the convoy, whether by radio or tv, and had come to either gawp or applaud as the long conga of trucks travelled towards and then under them. A few flowers floated down and ended up on the motorway or stuck to one of the trucks.

Even as trucks left the motorway to continue to their destination, others joined the cortege as it made its way relentlessly north. The few police patrol cars that sped past

them seemed to give an unauthorised approval to the longest continuous line of heavy goods vehicles the M1 had ever seen or would see again.
Passing motorists, who earlier had waved or peeped their horns as they passed, seemed caught up in the solemnity of the moment and maintained a respectful silence as they overtook the lead truck.
Neither men in that lead vehicle would know, until later when they had seen the aerial news footage, that the line of trucks behind them stretched for nearly five miles. Police spokesmen who were questioned about the unauthorised convoy praised the truck drivers for their orderly conduct. Apart from monopolising the inside lane, the convoy had not obstructed motorway traffic in any way.
As the Kenworth ate up the miles, the two men had little to say to each other. There was nothing to say. They were simply finalising the plan that had grown from a chance remark at a Rugby allotment. That it was working out more successfully than either had dreamt was simply a bonus. Almost before they realised it, the sign for the Watford Gap Services appeared and, just past it, their exit onto the M45 then the A45 to Canley. As the Kenworth drove onto the lightly trafficked motorway , the other showtrucks and Peter's Ford ranger pick-up behind them, the remainder of the convoy carried on. For a few minutes, the M1 seemed to reverberate with the mournful cacophony of air horns as the truckers paid a last tribute to one of their own.
At the end of the short motorway, there was a roundabout connecting the A45 to the M45. On the other side of the roundabout heading towards Coventry, there was a small

crowd of silent people at the side of the road. As they drove past, both men recognised people from their allotment and Peter saw his next door neighbours. 'That was nice of them' he said. 'Turning up like that. Makes you feel that people care'.

'People do care, Peter. At least about the important things. It's just that we don't know until something like this happens. I tell you what, if I get half the send-off that John has, I'll be more than happy'.

'Yes, I can't believe just how well it has all gone. Or how so many people have put themselves out for someone they have never met. Like those guys behind us. Mike and Dereck. The other showtruck owners. All those people on the bridges. All those truck drivers lined up behind us. It is very humbling'.

Dave glanced over and saw that his companion was only just holding it all together. He kept silent and concentrated on his driving. As he passed the long closed Bob's transport cafe, Peter remarked how busy it used to be.

'Yeah, the sleeper cab killed off many of those old time cafes' Dave negotiated the nearby roundabout and continued along the A45. 'Mind you, some of them were right dumps. Even Bob's when you think about it. It was rough and ready back then. Drivers used to overnight there. Just mattresses on the floor and a really greasy fry up to send them on their way. I don't know about you but I preferred sleeping in the cab across the seats than one of the old transport cafes. What do you remember?'

'No, you're right. It's just memory playing tricks again. Everything seemed better than it actually was. I also slept in the cab. I thought I was in Heaven when I got my first sleeper cab. But, the old style caffs played their part in the driver's life. Even if it was just as a break for a cuppa. You would always meet someone you knew whatever place you stopped at.' Peter suddenly pointed across the cab. 'Look at that. Did you ever think you would ever see that?'

Both men looked at the pile of bricks and rubble that was the only reminder of the Peugeot factory that had once employed thousands of people within its walls.

At the busy London Road roundabout, they had to wait at the traffic lights. A truck driver who had pulled up alongside them looked over and, catching Peter's eye, took off his cap in a respectful salute. Peter mouthed a "Thank you" as the Kenworth pulled away. Almost before they realised it, the roundabout and turning for the Crematorium was ahead. Taking the left hand exit, the truck made its way along a street practically nose to tail with parked trucks. Many had foreign number plates. The drivers were all congregating at the entrance to the drive leading to the crematorium. An empty hearse was parked up nearby. The driver was busy polishing the already spotless and gleaming bodywork. There were also several still photographers and two tv news teams recording the event.

'I guess that's for us' Peter said as they pulled up behind it. He got out and walked over. Dave also got out and stretched as he suddenly realised how stiff and tired he was. It had been a long drive and looked to be an even longer day. The pick-up and three trucks pulled up behind him and the drivers approached. Mike introduced Dave to the showtruck owners and drivers: Ben Golding, Trevor Thompson and Bruce Uttingley. Shaking their hands, he thanked them for their support, time and expense.

'I don't think any of us would have missed it for the world.' Ben Golding told him. 'I had no idea it would get so big. I think I speak for all of us when I say we were proud to have taken part'. As the others nodded their confirmation Peter returned and said simply 'It's time, Guys'
The others helped him take off the restraining straps and load the coffin into the hearse. As the vehicle began its slow drive to the final destination, Peter, Dave and the rest were joined by the waiting truckers and followed in its wake. As it drove almost silently up the tree lined avenue, the black vehicle underlined the solemnity of the moment. Many funeral processions had followed many hearses up this avenue on a daily basis but few had as many press photographers and news teams to witness one man's departure. Even the Press recognised the mood of the assembly and remained silent and almost respectful as they captured the moment. As they moved into the building , the Panpipes version of ‘Long and Winding Road’ played softly from the speakers. At the far end, they placed the coffin on the stand and took their seats. It was a large room but it was filled. Peter's wife Beth was at the front and he sat down beside her.
'You ok, love?' she asked as she saw how tired and upset her husband looked. 'I saw you on the news before leaving. I've never seen anything like it. You must be so proud'
Peter just nodded and squeezed her hand. Looking around, he saw many familiar faces. Others he didn't recognise but guessed that they were the drivers of the trucks lined up on the road outside. They were all in ordinary work clothes as if - and indeed many had - just left work and popped in to

say their goodbye to a colleague. A minister stepped up to the lectern and tapped the microphone as he adjusted his notes. Putting on glasses he looked at the waiting assembly until the music died away.
'Thank you all for coming. We are gathered here today to celebrate the life of John Slater. I didn't know John personally but, from what I have been told, he was a good man. He was a young man who lived a full life............'

*****

As he continued, Peter tuned out the sound of his voice. How could he possibly know the real John Slater from the few scraps of information he had been given by Beth? What could he know of the truck mad teenager he had shared so many miles and experiences with? As he sat there, almost in a trance, he had flashbacks of some of those moments. John grinning as he sat in the passenger seat, laughing as he got his licence and progressed over to the driver's seat. Bits of long ago conversation about anything and everything. The pride when he pulled up outside the house with the first of his own trucks. The pride in his profession and the integrity he bought to it.........and so, I would like to leave it to Peter Tiler to tell us about the man he knew and who was like a son to him'.

*****

As the man stepped down, Beth tugged at her husband's arm and told him it was time. Peter rose and walked over to the lectern. As he passed the coffin, he paused, patted it and then stood looking at everyone. For almost a minute, he remained motionless gathering himself for his last duty. Finally he walked to the lectern and halted behind it.
'Today has been a sad day but it has been an uplifting one'.

He told them in his soft Norfolk accent. 'John was like a son to Beth and me and we will miss him. But, he died doing the job he loved and almost certainly saved many young lives. John always knew what he wanted to be and he was proud to be a trucker. That might not mean much to those of you who aren't but all these fellow truckers here will know exactly what I mean.'

He indicated the massed truckers and got many confirming nods. 'Truckers used to be called the Knights of the Road and that title was well earned. Today, with changing road conditions and traffic laws, truckers are looked upon less kindly. I have to say that truckers are not the same as they once were. There is too much pressure on their time and on the roads. But, many truck drivers still try to stick to those old principles and see their job as some sort of crusade to maintain the same high standards.

John was one of those. Sure, he broke the traffic laws on occasion. But, he always tried to act and drive professionally. He looked after his truck, his load and always looked out for other drivers whatever they drove. He always tried to deliver on time and usually did. I doubt you will find another truck driver who will say a bad word about him.

John wasn't religious. He didn't believe in Heaven or Hell. To him there was no afterlife. This was it. He lived each day as if it was his last and to the full. When we were on the road together, we talked about things like this. Life, death and the ever present possibility of a road accident. Heck, we even planned each other's funeral, not knowing when that would occur but wanting to have it the way we wanted. Well, thanks to a lot of help from my friends

Dave, Mike, Dereck and many others who all contributed, John arrived here in the way he wanted.
Neither of us thought about a truck-coffin but here it is. That same coffin arrived here on the back of another truck. The kind of big and beautiful truck he said he would like. But, before we joined the motorway down in Kent, we drove past a large group of children and their parents. Many of those children were on the coach that lost its wheel in front of John's truck. We will never know how many of those young lives he saved when he took the decision to hit a motorway support pillar rather than a coach full of kids going on holiday. But, whatever the number, he saved some of them. This beautiful coffin you see was donated by the parents of one of those kiddies. The undertaker's daughter was another on the coach and he wouldn't accept a fee. In one school and in many people's hearts, John Slater's memory will live on.
Many of you truck drivers here will have stories of how John helped you and vice-versa. He was that sort of guy. A good friend, always willing to put himself out for others. He always knew, as all we truck drivers do, that there was a good chance he would die on the road. Sadly, that was the case but, if it had to happen, what better way of going? One life for many. I can live with that but I am going to find living without John very hard. Now, I am not going to say much else. I have said what I wanted, needed, to say. John Slater will not be forgotten. But, I would like to leave you with the one thing that he always had in his truck. He first saw it in a trucking magazine and cut it out. It was a prayer and, though he didn't believe in God, he did like the humour and sentiments it contained . Strangely, and I

didn't know this until recently, it was written by an extrucker, turned truck journalist. That person is Dave Williams who is with us today and to whom I owe a big thank you. It goes like this:

My Trucking Prayer by Dave Williams

"Lord above, if you are
there
Help me drive with
proper care.
whether the load be feather-light
or heavy steel,
guide my hands upon the wheel.

Be my eyes as I sit up high.
Protect me, as other drivers speed
on by.
Help me read the road ahead
and avoid the accident that I
dread.

Protect my load, my truck too.
Watch my back, I ask of you
Do not let anyone stray
under my wheels today.

Put your strength into my hand
as I travel on your land.
Help me find where I have to go,
in sun, rain or snow.

Protect me and others too.

Lord, this I beg of you.
Keep me safe on land or sea
Keep your presence strong in me.

Sometimes I don't pray enough
when life gets too tough.
But, it doesn't mean that I don't
care,
I know you are always there.

Help me to be a better man,
always to do the best I can.
Keep the police and Ministry
away,
so that I can get on with my day.

Lord, I know it's a lot to ask
because it's not an easy task.
Make road safety your priority
for the others but mainly me.

Let the collections and deliveries
be both hassle and stress free.
Make the road signs big and
clean,
low bridge warnings, easily seen.

Thank you Lord, for all of this.
Be my eyes so I do not miss
the speed gun and yellow Gatso.
Please make sure I am going slow.

Lord, take me into your care
it's good to know that you are there.
Protect me and the idiots too
Thank you Lord, for all you do".

Peter's voice began to break and his eyes were bright with unshed tears but he put down the poem and looked up. 'As I said, John didn't believe but you don't have to believe in God to be a good man. John was a good man and I am proud to have known him. Now, we have to send him on his final trip. The song is his choice and I think it says it all. Goodbye mate. Good roads and far horizons.' Then with tears running down his cheeks, he walked over to the coffin and gave it one final pat before returning to his seat. Many of the truck drivers silently applauded him and many more in the assembly dabbed at their eyes also.

Then, as the voice of Katherine Jenkins began to sing Con te Partiro, better known as Time to Say Goodbye, the curtains in front of the coffin opened and the truck and it's trucker moved slowly away. The congregation stood and watched until the curtains softly closed and the mortal remains of John Slater vanished from view.

Slowly, people began to leave their seats and walk outside. Peter and Beth stayed behind both lost in their own thoughts and memories. Then, they too stood up and joined the others outside. The truckers stood in a group on one side. Peter went over to them and began to thank them for coming. He shook their hands and listened to their personal memories of John Slater. Many were on their way to deliver loads but had left their trailers and travelled solo to get to the ceremony. Some had called in favours or juggled their timetables to make it. Most had to get back to their jobs and on the road again. Each man was aware that it could be them or any one of the group that was next. Each hoped that they merited a similar send-off when their time came.

When the last truck had left, Peter turned to the remaining mourners and invited them back to the Jolly Abbot pub in Rugby where they could get a drink and something to eat. Mike, Dereck and the three showtruck drivers followed the big Kenworth.

'How do you think that went, mate?' Dave Williams asked his passenger. 'As you wanted?'

'Pretty much' Peter agreed. 'But, there is one last thing we have to do before it's all over. John asked that his ashes be scattered on the M1 because that's where he started and ended his journeys. He said that he spent so much of his life on the road that he would rather be there than stuck up on a mantelpiece somewhere. So, as soon as we get his ashes, Beth and I will be doing just that. One night, when traffic is light, we'll carry out his last wishes.'

'Sounds like a plan' Dave smiled. 'Something I always said as well. Either that or at sea. Either way, if the relatives want to dance on my grave, they are welcome.'

The Jolly Abbot pub is situated on the Lower Hillmorton Road just up the road from the allotments at the Kent. A medium sized building, it is in an “L” shape design. The car park was full of mourner’s cars. Fortunately, it is on a quiet stretch of dual carriageway and the five vehicles parked as tidily and considerately as they could on the road outside. Inside, the atmosphere was subdued as the funeral attendees gathered in small groups and discussed the service. Peter led the others up to the bar and got their orders in. When each had a drink in his hand, he raised his glass. 'John Slater' he said. 'Good roads and far horizons, mate.' The toast was repeated around the pub.

Shortly afterwards, Mike, Dereck and the other three truck drivers said their goodbyes and returned to their vehicles. With the Kenworth in the lead, each driver gave one last salute on his air horn and drove off. Heading for the M1 and home. Each saddened by the need but proud to have taken part.

Peter gave one final wave and suddenly realised that it was over. The planning, the execution and the final act. Done and dusted. Just as John Slater had wished.

Before returning to his wife and the others, he stood quietly and reflectively. 'I'll miss you mate. But I am so proud of you'. He drained his glass and held it aloft one last time. 'John Slater. Good roads and far horizons, mate'.

EIGHTEEN

'John Slater! If you don't stop daydreaming and get up this minute, you are going to be late.' Molly's smiling face belied the tone of her voice as she bustled into the living room. I had a swig of tea and reached for my toast. Obviously the novelty of having a Grade 2 overnighting had worn off. The last time I was woken up with a full English. Oh well.

Just as I was finishing off the last round of toast, Celeste and Angel came out of their room. 'Come on John' Celeste said as she came over and gave me a Good Morning kiss. 'You're going to be late. Busy day and all that'

Angel gave me another kiss and accidentally let her hand fall into my groin. Obviously Little John was more awake than I was because he raised himself up to see who was disturbing him. 'Whoops, sorry' Angel giggled as they both wiggled suggestively out of the room. 'See you tonight?'

If she played her cards right, she might. Just as I was deciding to put my not so little friend back, Molly returned. If she saw that my duvet had mysteriously turned into a tent, she didn't say anything. She took my cup and plate into the kitchen area and gave me the chance to dismantle the tentpole and sit up. 'Right, I'm leaving' she said as she returned. 'Can you pull the door closed as you go out?'

I assured her I would, got a quick peck on my cheek and suddenly had the apartment to myself. Or thought I did. Just as I had got off the settee and preparing to put my jeans on, Astra walked out of her bedroom. I stood there with one leg in and balancing on the other when my little friend made another break for freedom. Hopping on one leg, I tried to turn round and promptly fell over.

Astra came rushing over, all concerned and tried to help me up. 'Are you ok?' she asked as I tried desperately to cover up. Suddenly, she must have seen the problem because she let go and just stood there. I finally managed to my jeans on, got up and zipped up. Damn, just what I didn't want to happen. Just when I was making a bit of headway, she must have thought I was just another sex crazed trucker. She was certainly looking at me a bit oddly. Her face was flushed and she was panting. Oh no, I thought, don't have a panic attack and scream the place down.

She just stood there and I made no move either. We looked at each other and I saw her mouth opening and shutting and her eyes were wide. I held up my hands to show her I meant no harm. 'I'm sorry' I said softly. 'It happens to blokes in the morning. It doesn't mean anything. I told you I wouldn't do anything to hurt you and I meant it.'

I picked up the rest of my clothes and made as if to go to the bathroom. I did everything slowly and deliberately so as not to alarm her. As I backed away, I could see her relax slightly. Then, just as I reached the bathroom door, she called my name and suddenly rushed over to me and hugged me tightly.

'I'm sorry, ok?' she said into my shoulder. 'I know you don't mean me any harm. It was just a shock coming out and seeing you like that. I'm just being silly' She lifted her head up and looked into my eyes. Slowly, she raised up her mouth and kissed me tentatively on the lips. I kissed her back just as gently and dropped my hands to her waist. I tried to keep my groin away from hers but, she just kept pushing back. Her arms tightened around me and she kissed me harder. I felt her mouth open and then her tongue was trying to get past my teeth. She began to moan softly and squirm against me.

What was going on? I mean, I knew what was going on, I just wasn't sure what to do. Carry on? Let her make the running? Stop now? Suddenly she broke away and breathed harshly into my ear. 'Yes, yes John. I want you to. Just please be gentle, ok?'

I held her at arms length and looked into her eyes. I wasn't sure what I saw in them but it wasn't fear. I gathered her into my arms and made for her bedroom. She clung on tightly and moaned into my ear. Laying her down on the bed, I raised her skirt and removed her underwear. She made urgent thrusting motions and half raised herself off the bed. I lay gently over her and kissed her hard. She kissed back harder and more urgently and pressed the length of her body into mine. She locked her hands behind my neck and started to shudder violently. As each tremor came more and more quickly, I moved my hand down and began to massage her gently but insistently. Suddenly, with a sharp intake of breath, she thrashed and then became rigid under me. As she climaxed violently, I held on as gently as possible and then, suddenly, it was over and she sighed and relaxed.

I waited until her harsh breathing became normal and looked into those wonderful brown eyes. I may have imagined it but I thought I finally saw peace and contentment in them. She looked back and I kissed her gently. 'Ok?' I whispered. She nodded.

'But, what about you?' she asked throatily. 'Did you......?'

'It doesn't matter' I assured her. 'This was about you, ok?'

She looked back and, suddenly, her eyes filled with tears. I held her as she broke down and sobbed away her hurt, pain and memories.

Sometime later, she stopped and I wiped her eyes and nose with a reasonably clean handkerchief. She suddenly became shy and I looked away as she got dressed. She went into the bathroom and then returned a few minutes later. During that time, she had composed herself, re-applied her make-up and was beautiful again. Not that she had ever been ugly but she was totally different to how she looked before. Then she had been living behind a mask of fear and doubt. Now, her skin glowed, her eyes shone and her whole demeanour had changed. She was confident and relaxed. She was finally at peace with herself.

She stood before me and looked up. 'Thank you John. I am so lucky to have met you. You have given me my life back' We both realized what she had just said at the same moment. I began to laugh and, a moment later, she joined in. That laughter was the best possible thing that could have happened. It got us both over that awkward post-coital moment and we were both relaxed with each other again. It felt good. It was good. I suddenly had another thought.

'Now that you have got that hurdle out of the way, how about getting rid of the last one?'

She looked at me quizzically and I carried blindly on.

Nor knowing if it was right but guided by the instinct that it was.

'My truck is parked outside. How about I give you a lift to work?'. Once again that alarm flared up in her eyes. But then I saw from the expression on her face that she was considering it. I could almost hear her thoughts: *what harm would it do? I trust him. He's not going to harm me.*

She made her decision. She held out her hand and I took it. Making sure everything was on, in place and zipped away, I led her out the door. Pulling it firmly shut behind me, we exited the building. Outside I was relieved to see that Maggie was still there, not up on blocks and looking almost as beautiful as the girl holding firmly onto my hand.

Feeling the slight hesitation, I looked at Astra. She was looking at Maggie with wide eyes and a scared expression. I stopped and told her not to worry. 'It isn't important' I said. 'You don't have to. Another time?'

'No' she said gripping my hand tightly. 'I think I do. After all, it isn't as if a truck has ever done anything to me. If I do get in, it will be the first time I have ever been in one'.

I took her on the tour round Maggie pointing out the mural and the shiny bits. The ever changing paint colour seemed to fascinate her. When we reached the passenger door, I stopped, clicked the remote and opened it wide. She hesitantly looked inside. To help her, I showed her how to get on board and, once inside, I held out my hand. She reached up and grasped it. Suddenly she was shaking her head 'I can't do it'

'Don't worry about it. Maybe some other time'

'No, you don't understand. I want to but I just can't'

I jumped down again and put a hand on her shoulder. She must have seen the concern in my face because she suddenly laughed. 'I can't get up there in this tight skirt' she explained. I put my hands around her waist and lifted her up onto the top step.

'No problem' I told her. I followed her inside and showed her round. I don't know what thoughts were running around her head as she looked around. I didn't see any fear or worry though. More like a woman's curiosity as she examined my living quarters. She peeped into the cupboards, the fridge and finally the wardrobe cum shower/replicator.

'Wow, it's like a little caravan, isn't it'. She sat down in the driver's seat and, like a little kid, pretended to drive.

'Thank you John' she smiled at me and reached out her hand. I took it and raised it to my lips. 'Molly was right about you. You are a nice bloke'

I had never thought of myself like that before but she was probably right. I had always been brought up to respect women by both Mike and Jean and my adoptive parents, Wag and Winnie. It was second nature to me to want to protect them and look after them. Probably the main reason I wasn't married either. I wasn't as predatory as some of my mates. I always wanted a girl as a friend first and then sex came later.

Most of my single men friends used to plan their conquests with almost military precision. Make this move and this would happen. Do this and she would respond by doing that. Maybe I was wrong but I couldn't change my nature.

The funny thing was that I never had anything like the

success with ladies on Earth as I was having in Heaven. Three gorgeous girls so far and I hadn't even had to try very hard. Celeste was right when she told me that things were different up here. More intense but more relaxed as well. My biggest success so far though was looking right at me. Astra pulled me towards her and gave me a long slow kiss. I responded. She responded right back and, almost without conscious thought, we were on the bunk and making love.

This time there was no hesitation, no fears, no doubts. Later, she smiled at me and traced the outline of my face with her fingertips.

'I never thought I would be doing this today' she smiled. A little self satisfied smile. She was proud of herself. I was proud of her.

Before I drove her to work, she had a shower. I put everything back in place and once more threaded Maggie through the almost deserted streets. I say almost deserted because this time I did see another vehicle. One I hadn't expected to see and the very one I should have seen. A stretched Lada limo crossed an intersection in front of me. It was a bit battered and trailing a cloud of smoke behind it.

'Look at that. When Celeste told me that I was supposed to be picked up by a stretched Lada, I thought it was a leg-pull. Mind you, I thought she was joking when she told me I was in Heaven as well. I wonder who is getting picked up today?'

'I'll have a look when I get to work.' Astra turned round to face me. 'How do you feel about being here now that you've been here a while?'

I considered the question. I didn't have to consider it long. 'Truthfully? I hated the place when I first saw it. Now, I love it. What about you?'

'It took some getting used to. I was happy on Earth, had plenty of friends and was doing an art course that I loved. My first reaction was how unfair it was. I hadn't done anything wrong yet it felt like I was being punished. I was lucky that I was allocated to share with Molly. She took me under her wing, helped me through some bad times and, gradually, I grew to understand and like being here. Celeste and Angel are great and now you have helped me to truly find peace.'

'Glad to have been of service Ma'am.' I drawled in my best John Wayne impression. She giggled. 'You can tell me one thing though' She raised an enquiring eyebrow. 'As you know, I saw Elvis the other night and Red Sovine. Eva Cassidy was on the show with him as well. The thing that struck me was " what were they doing here?". I mean they are Americans and this is UK Heaven. Why are they here?'

'Because they travel to all the Earth States' she told me. 'All the entertainers travel. They do a few weeks in each State and give all the Newcomers and the ones who haven't had chance to see them the opportunity to do so.'

As she explained, we arrived at Arrivals. I jumped down and went round to open the passenger door. I held out my arms and, with just the slightest hesitation, Astra jumped into them. I swung her round and lowered her gently onto the pavement. She reached up, put her arms around my neck and pulled my lips down to meet hers. After a quick kiss, she put her mouth up to my ear, whispered "I think I love you, John Slater" broke contact and walked quickly away before I could reply. I watched her entering the double doors and disappear. From my position, I thought I saw her shimmer slightly as she entered the different time zone but didn't know for sure. It didn't matter anyway. I had more important things on my mind. Like the fact that she had just told me she was falling in love with me.

As if I didn't have enough emotional issue with Celeste and Angel. Now I had just added Astra to the list. I climbed up into Maggie, shut the door and got out my duster. As I dusted and polished, I thought long and hard about how I felt.

I suppose, like most blokes, I was flattered to have three gorgeous women in love with me. It had never, would never, have happened on Earth. Here, it seemed ok. But it still posed the same problem, or what I perceived as the same problem. How did I feel about it?

Separately, I could have been happy with any of them but three at the same time? The old Earth guilt feeling surged forward again. As I chased non-existent dust around the dash, I realised that I had done nothing wrong. My three girls knew each other and had no problems with it. Therefore, why should I?

My old Jesuit upbringing still insisted it wasn't right. It was almost as if I was taking advantage of them. Of the three, Celeste was the only one I wasn't too worried about. Nothing had happened between us. It was just a matter of time, of course. She had already indicated that. But Celeste had brought no emotional baggage into our relationship. Angelica and now, Astra, had.

Both, for different reasons, had been wary of men. The

fact that I had breached that mistrust was down more to my personality than any physical attraction they might have had for me. Basically, they felt safe with me. The same way one old girlfriend had told me that she felt safe with gay blokes. I obviously sent out signals that I was no threat to them and they had relaxed enough to get to know me rather than be frightened or put up any mental barriers. Obviously, they now knew that I wasn't gay but the first advances had been theirs. I hadn't gained their trust to use them or abuse them. But, would they have felt the same way about another man who had the same patience and understanding that I had? Had they, in fact, both fallen in love with the first man to show them any kind of genuine feelings and respect? Was I a token or did they really love me?

Call me old fashioned but I feel that there has to be mutual attraction for any sort of relationship to develop into something other than a basic need for sex. For that mutual attraction to extend to three girls at the same time was, I knew, at the core of my problem.

I realised that I was going to have to get all three together and talk about how I felt before coming to any kind of resolution that I felt comfortable with. I put away my duster, turned the ignition and drove away to pick up my trailer and start my new job.

Driving here was different. There was no traffic for a start but the closeness and claustrophobic of the building meant you couldn't relax. I was also aware that there was at least one other vehicle being driven here. The stretch Lada. It wouldn't do to have a collision with the only other vehicle I knew about. Consequently, having now seen it, I was being more cautious than previously.

As I left the Astro belt of buildings and into the less threatening area of high-rise, I felt, rather than heard, a series of bangs. I thought that these had been transmitted from the ground through my steering wheel. My immediate thought was a flat tyre. That would have been fun. Short of calling out Noel's blokes, I would have had to change it myself. I stopped the truck and climbed down. A quick walk-round revealed nothing. All the tyres were up and there was nothing else hanging off that would have caused the bangs I had felt.

Just as I was climbing back into the cab, I heard more bangs. A series of short, sharp explosions of noise coming from roughly where I was headed. I switched on the newly installed cb radio and keyed the mike. 'Anyone listening?' I enquired. Nothing but static. So much for being in instant communication. Curiosity got the better of me and I drove slowly forward. Ahead, I could see a darkening of the sky and, as I got nearer, I saw that it seemed to be a dust cloud hanging in the air. Strange. An accident or something else?

If you can imagine a series of buildings rising skywards until they are out of sight then slowly descending in a series of graduated lines then you would see what I saw. The latest Heaven slowly going back through time, from the latest Astro block, to ancient single storey buildings. As the buildings grew shorter, the road became wider. The dwellings on either side became more the size I was used to and I could see farther ahead. I could even see blue sky in this old section and that was something I realised that I missed. There were no further bangs and the dust cloud seemed to be slowly dispersing.

Still driving cautiously, I came round a corner and brought Maggie to a quick halt. Ahead of me I saw more vehicles. This was weird. I had gone from thinking I was the only truck in Heaven to being confronted by several tipper trucks. Furthermore, those trucks were being loaded by JCB's and then driving off in a cloud of dust away from me. What the Hel..Heaven was going on?.

I drove slowly forward and then I saw what was happening. It was a demolition team. There were gaps in the buildings where there had once been buildings of twenty floors or more. The JCB's were loading up the remnants of these old building into the tipper trucks. The bangs I felt must have been explosions. I remember Noel telling me that the Tube was being extended and that he would soon have an easier way of getting into Town. Was this the start of that development?

As I passed the site, I could see everyone looking at me. One guy detached himself from a group of bystanders and came over with his arm upraised. I stopped and climbed down. He was dressed in a Hi-vis yellow coat and had a white hard hat on.

'Where are you going?' he asked a bit sharply.

'Well, I was going to Maintenance to pick up my trailer. Is that a problem?'

'No, but you might have to wait a while. We have to get this lot cleared before letting you go any further. Health and Safety, you know'

I looked around. There were about 10 people standing around, two JCB's and four trucks waiting to get loaded. Health and Safety?

'Your trucks are driving off' I pointed out to him. 'I'm only going up the road. I'll be careful'.

He looked at me to see if I was joking. Considered and then made his decision. 'No'

Arguing with him was clearly going to be a waste of time. I got back into the cab and reached for the CB mike. Leaving the door open so he could see, I keyed the button and spoke. 'This is John Slater calling Maintenance. If you can hear me, can you put me straight through to Noel Flynn please.' I released the button and looked down at him. He began to fidget and looked around.

'Morning John' Noel's voice boomed out of the speakers. 'I was expecting you some time ago. What's the problem?'

'Hi, Noel. I'm being held up by the demolition crew's Job'sworth. He won't let me through even though his trucks are coming and going. Anything you can do?'

The hardhat looked up at me and wet his lips with his tongue. He removed his white hat and wiped a grubby handkerchief around his nearly bald head. 'Tell Mr Flynn that I am letting you through. Against my wishes and at your own risk.'

I informed Noel, hung up the mike and drove cautiously forward. Not because I could see any immediate danger but because I didn't want to pick anything up in my tyres. I could almost feel Mr Hardhat's eyes burning into my back. Turning out to be quite a morning.

Everything seemed normal at Maintenance and I drove round the back to where my trailer was parked up. I didn't back up to it but stopped in front of it and went into the building to see if it was good to go.

Instead of going straight up to Noel's office I popped into

Sean's little cubicle at the back of the workshop. He was busy tapping on his keyboard but finished up when I came through.

'Morning John, here to pick up your trailer?'

'Yes but I had a bit of trouble getting through the demolition work just down the road. What's going on? New building or something?'

Sean laughed. 'Just a normal day in Heaven. Knocking down the smaller buildings to build even bigger ones. You know, at this rate there won't be a bit of original Heaven still standing. One of the reasons we like it out here. We can see sky and no body bothers us. The rate the building work is progressing, we will have to move further out soon.'

'Noel mentioned there would be a Tube station built around here. You must be looking forward to that surely?'

'I suppose it will be handy for going into town but it is no great hardship to walk. Actually, I quite miss walking. Back on Earth, I used to backpack quite a lot. I was even drawing up plans for the Land's End to John o' Groats walk. Apart from the Ring road, there is no where here to go that isn't overcrowded and congested. I actually quite envy you and the trips you'll be doing'.

I wish I hadn't asked now. One aspect that I hadn't thought of. There weren't many places to go where you could be alone within easy travelling distance. It was the first time I had seen Sean in a bad mood. Normally he was a genial easy-going type of bloke. I asked if the trailer was ready for its trial.

'Yes, ready and waiting. If you hitch up, I'll get the forklift round and we can load up.'

Hitching up didn't take long and it was good to be doing such a familiar task again. I was actually getting quite excited about hitting the road once more. Obviously, a far different road than I was used to, but one that would take me over the far horizon. It had only been a few days - don't ask me how many because I didn't have a clue – in one place but I was getting the wander itch again. I just didn't like to be tied down to one location and have set routines. Hey, I was a born and bred trucker, now born again, and I just wanted to truck. Diesel was in my blood and distant places were calling me to them.

I pulled the trailer up outside the garage loading doors and switched off. I had just started to release the cover from the side of the trailer when Noel came over and gave me a hand. Undoing the tension locking bars, I pulled the locking bar out of it's socket and we both pulled the curtain back to give access to the length of the trailer.

'Damn, I miss this' Noel grinned ruefully. 'How about you take over the workshop and I do the deliveries in your place?'

'How about you get your butt back on the office seat where it belongs and leave real truckers to get on with their jobs' I countered back.

'Hey, just you remember who got you this job in the first place'.

'I'm hardly likely to forget that, Noel' I told him a bit angrily.

'Calm down boyo. Remember out agreement? If you don't like it you can go back. But, would you really want to go back? You get to meet a far classier kind of woman up here. That Astra would be out of your league back on

Earth'. he grinned slyly.

Are there no secrets up here or was he just guessing? I decided to sound him out on the problem I was having such turmoil over. Once I started, leaving out the intimate details of course, he became serious and heard me out. When I had finished he just shook his head.

'Only you would worry about having too many women in love with you. I keep trying to tell you, things are different here. Earth bound morals don't count. Here, if it feels good and right, then it is. You just have to accept that. If it wasn't allowed, the Boss would have done something about it before now. From what you tell me and from what I know, you have helped Angelica and Astra to come to terms with themselves and found peace. Why is that such a bad thing?'

'I don't know, Noel. It just doesn't feel right.'

'So, you would rather be on your own and miserable, is that it?'

'No, of course not' I told him. 'I just can't get over the feeling that it's wrong. I admit that the girls seem happy enough with the situation'.

'Then, that's all that matter isn't it? In the religions that allow a man to have more than one wife, the wives appear to get along just fine. Just think of yourself as a Sheik and the girls as your lawful wives. Of course, as you'll be away a lot, the answer might be quite simple. Once you have got the wrinkles ironed out, why not take one with you every week? It'll be nice for them, give you a chance to find how they really feel and maybe you'll feel differently then. At least, you won't be lonely. If they are happy, just accept it as a reward for a good and pious life on Earth'. Noel slapped me on the back and laughed. 'Hey, remember that Helga? I wonder if she'll ever get up here?'

Helga was an Austrian truck driver. She was more than just a truck driver though; she was a legend amongst truckers. She was a blond, blue-eyed Aphrodite. To say she was gorgeous and oversexed was like saying the Pope was a bit catholic. Whenever she parked up at night, the news would travel up and down the road like wildfire. Her favourite overnight halt was at a motorway service area. She would have a meal, get a shower and return to her cab. The curtains would close and that was the last most of us would see of her.

The reason she was legend was because in the small hours she would leave her cab, knock on the door of her chosen truck and then proceed to give the lucky occupant the night of his life. In the morning she would be gone and the battered and bruised truck driver would be the envy of the truck stop. I remember parking up one night when she was there and hardly slept a wink hoping my fancy truck would catch her eye. It didn't but that never stopped any of us from hoping that one night she would knock on our door.

'Don't tell me Helga got into your old black Scania?' I asked enviously.

'Gentlemen don't tell but I can tell you that she was a natural blonde' Noel replied with even more of a twinkle in his eye than normal.

'Did she say why she choose you?'

'I asked and she revealed her system' The date of the month and the number they added up to. She would

search out a truck with those numbers in their registration and that was the target for the night. She said it was a bit like Russian Roulette and that gave it the extra spice she wanted.
Sometimes she got lucky and sometimes.......'
'She got you' I finished for him.
'Yeah, well, she had no complaints. Now, are we going to load this trailer or not?.
'Ok, but one last question. What happened if the driver was female? How did the system work then? Was there a back up plan?'
'Helga really didn't care. She knocked on a few lady truckers doors and only got turned down once. Now....the trailer....?'
I shut up and looked at the trailer loading bay. I could see where Sean and his team had strengthened the floorboards and supports. I noticed that the air suspension bellows had been modified as well. Obviously this trailer was designed for a bit of weight. Well, there wasn't much chance of a Ministry of transport weighbridge here so a bit of overloading didn't matter. Truth to tell, it wouldn't be the first time that either Noel or I had been overloaded. Loads had to be shipped and if they didn't exactly fit the legal weights then the driver had the choice of saying “No” and seeing the load go to someone else or just get on with the job.
Noel went into the garage and returned after a few minutes. Behind him came a large forklift truck carrying one of the Dilithium containers or batteries as we had taken to calling them. This was a rectangular steel box with cut-outs in the base for the fork truck to slide its two

steel forks into. Once this was done, the forks were raised hydraulically and the battery raised from the ground and driven over to the waiting trailer.

The battery didn't seem overlarge but, judging by the way the forklift truck was struggling, they were heavy. This was soon confirmed as the first one was slid gently into the trailer and placed against the headboard and just inside the trailer. The trailer dipped sharply as the battery was lowered onto the floor boards and the fork truck withdrew. The next one was loaded on the opposite side and so on down the length of the trailer. The number of batteries loaded was six and the trailer floor was considerably nearer to the top of the wheels when the forklift truck finished. Noel and I got up into the trailer and set about lashing the batteries to the supporting rings placed on the trailer floor.

'Anything lethal or catching from this lot?' I asked half jokingly as we secured the ratchet tie downs from the rings, over the batteries and to the rings on the other side.

'No, I don't think so. You'll probably glow green in the dark and you'll never have kids but, other than that, you should be all right'

I looked up startled and saw him grinning at me from the other side of the battery. 'Caught you. Do you really think I would be up here if there was any risk? I'd have sent Sean and his grease monkeys in to do the job'

We strapped down the last one and climbed out of the trailer. Slid the curtain-side back into place and secured it with its ratchet ties.

'How strong are those batteries?' I still didn't trust Noel entirely.

'We have pressure tested them way beyond anything they

are expected to be subjected to. We have had them underwater testing for leaks. I even had Martin - that demolition Job'sworth you met this morning – try to blow them up. He failed. And, Martin is one of the best in the business, or was, until he made one tiny mistake and ended up here.'

'Are you trying to convince me or scare me? What was the mistake?'

'He was doing a Health and Safety sweep and failed to notice that a dog had entered the building he was about to blow up. Just as he had pushed the switch with a four minute delay, he saw it in one of the doorways. The mistake he made was ignoring his own advice and training and trying to rescue it before the charges went off. He didn't make it. Probably one of the reasons he is so anal about Health and Safety up here.' Noel looked across at me and I had the grace to feel a little ashamed of myself.

'So, in answer to your question....Yes, the batteries, trailer and truck are as safe as they can ever be. If you don't believe me then I am quite happy to take the loads out myself.'

'Like Hel...heck you will. You are far too eager to get away from this place. What's up, getting the trucking itch?'

Noel's face went suddenly serious and he nodded. 'What do you think? I am going up the walls sometimes. Oh to feel a truck under me and eating up the miles to somewhere new. You know what that is like so you can understand how I feel'

I placed my hand on his shoulder and squeezed. He was right. I did know how it felt. It was like a deep hunger eating away at your insides. It was what it was....an addiction. I suddenly felt sorry for him. Not sorry enough to swop places but I did understand.

'Come on you silly, sad little trucker. You can get behind the wheel and we'll give this rig a good testing. See what shakes loose, eh?'

I tossed over the keys and he caught them. I climbed into the passenger seat and looked over at him. He had a big grin on his face as he turned the key and the big Mack engine roared into life. He selected a low gear, released the park brake and Maggie moved slowly forward. Even from where I sat in the passenger seat, I could feel the weight.

'How much do those batteries weigh?' I asked across the cab.

'Twelve tons each' he replied straight-faced.

I did the maths six batteries at twelve tons each. That was... 'Bloody hell Noel, that's seventy two tons. Plus the weight of the trailer and unit. That's got to be nudging ninety tons. On these roads?'

'Why do you think you got the extra power and had the trailer and suspension beefed up?'

I shut up. And thought about it. I didn't trust Noel as much as I trusted Sean and his fitters. I felt I knew enough about Sean to know that he wouldn't send something out of his workshop if there was a problem or potential problem. As Noel gained speed, I sat back and analyzed how Maggie was coping. It was a pure seat of the pants feel. If I was in the driver's seat, I could have felt everything instantly. Noel appeared relaxed and I began to relax as well. There were no obvious sounds of distress.

As we left the built up area of Heaven and got on to the

ring-road, I could feel the instant improvement in the surface of the road. I looked across at Noel and, feeling my eyes boring into him, he turned. 'Relax' he smiled. 'It's handling really well. Time to get some speed up and see what this baby can do'. He patted Maggie's steering wheel affectionately and I felt instantly jealous. I was already regretting my spontaneous decision to let Noel do the driving. Well, he wasn't going to drive back. That was certain. I looked out the window at the uninhabited area that stretched as far as I could see to the left.

There were expanses of flat land then random stands of trees. The grass was long and moving in the wind. I could catch glimpses of water reflecting in the sun. Ahead the two lane road stretched far away into the horizon. Noel upshifted smartly and began to pile on the speed. He did it sensibly in increments of ten miles an hour. He would stay in each segment for a mile or two as he felt and listened for any problems.

After about fifteen minutes, he was holding steady at seventy and relaxing. The tyres hummed on the concrete and the engine note was a steady purr. The trailer was swaying slightly but that was to be expected. All that was missing was other traffic and a change of scenery. The road itself was missing the usual scenery of road signs, dividing lanes, crash barriers or even a hard shoulder. With the amount of traffic it carried, what was the point? It was basically a one way system for one vehicle going one way.

Either side of the concrete ribbon, the countryside was as monotonous and as unchanging as a Cliff Richard Christmas single. Occasionally, there would be a stretch of thick woodland which would then thin out to a flat deserted landscape. No house or buildings of any sort. No animals, no hippy communes, no sign of life at all. Just two guys and a big truck eating up the miles. I didn't know whether to be happy or sad.

After a few more miles, Noel bled off the speed gently and, gradually, came to a standstill. 'Time to have a walk-round' he explained as he got out of the cab. I followed suit then walked down my side of the truck and trailer whilst he did the same on his side.

A walk-round is what a good truckdriver does almost automatically. Whenever he starts or stops he walks round the outfit looking for any problems. Broken suspension, bits hanging off, tyres not up to pressure or damaged. It only takes a few minutes but differentiates between a professional and an uncaring driver.

With the amount of weight and the speed Maggie had been travelling at, Noel's decision was a wise one. Wise, but not necessary. Neither of us could find any problems other than slightly overheated tyres. Even that was to be expected. Well used concrete roads have the surface pounded smooth by the constant tyre contact of the vehicles upon it. The road we were on had little or no traffic and the ridges in the concrete surface were still as pronounced as the day it was laid. 'Looking good' I said as we made our way back to the front of the cab. 'I'll have to keep an eye out for tyre heat though. Wouldn't want to have a blow-out or change a tyre out here by myself. Not with that weight to jack up'

'You won't get a puncture. The tyres are filled with a sealing compound that will plug any holes. The heating, as you say, will need to be monitored. I'll have a word with Sean when I get back and see if he can come up with any sort of a monitoring system'

Noel made a half hearted attempt to get back into the driving seat but I quickly grabbed his belt and pulled him back. 'Not a chance, you over-eager Mick. Time to let a real driver behind the wheel'

'Now where do you think we are going to find one of those out here?' he grinned as I climbed up. As soon as he was seated, I was about to drive off when I realised that there was a problem I hadn't thought of. Where was I going to turn round to drive back to Maintenance?

'What's up, Real Driver? Forgotten how to drive?'

'I was just wondering about turning round. Or, am I expected to drive the complete length of the Ring road to get back? What's that? A few thousand miles?'

It was obvious by the expression on his face that he hadn't thought about it either. We were both so used to getting off a motorway at the next junction to turn round or using a roundabout or side road that the lack of those facilities was a problem.

'We'll just have to spin her round on the road and hope we don't pop a tyre.' Noel decided. I didn't like it but couldn't think of an alternative.

Unlike a rigid truck, an articulated vehicle can more or less spin round in its own length. With an empty or lightly loaded vehicle, provided it is done slowly, there isn't much of a risk. The driver puts full lock on and the trailer spins round on the inner tyres until the turn has been completed. It puts extra pressure on the inner tyres and, if done too quickly or with too much weight, can damage them or even pop them off the rims. I didn't like doing it empty much less with seventy two tons on board. But, there wasn't a choice. Before starting, I automatically checked my mirrors. Even as I did it, I felt foolish. I mean, what traffic was I checking for? But, can't break the habits of a driving lifetime. Noel saw me checking and didn't comment. He knew he would have done exactly the same. It was as natural as breathing.

I selected a low gear and slowly drove forward turning the wheel as fast as I could. The unit came round and then slowly dragged the trailer with it. The side of the trailer looked to be coming through the side window but, in reality, there was plenty of room. As the outer wheels turned, the inner set remained stationary. As the turn was completed, the locked tyres, pinned by the weight above, left a thick smear of rubber on the road. With a sigh of relief I straightened up and stopped. A quick check revealed that there was no obvious damage other than a slight loss of rubber on the contact area. Not a manoeuvre to make very often though.

Once rolling again, I built up the speed as gradually as Noel had done. Seated behind the wheel, I could feel every bump and vibration transmitted through to my hands. It felt normal, it felt good. Even when I upped the speed to eighty, I felt nothing untoward. The tyres hummed, the engine accompanied them with a bass note and the wind passing around the trailer provided the trebles. The music of the road, The trucker's siren song. Damn, it felt great.

All too soon, Heavenisation began to appear on the horizon. I could make out the bases of the Astro towers and the thick dark shadows they generated. I felt like turning round again and just driving away. I looked across at Noel and saw him obviously thinking the same thing. I began to slow down and the euphoric mood the test drive had generated dissipated as rapidly as the falling speedometer pointer. Even Maggie seemed reluctant to end the test trip. But, we were soon entering the deserted Maintenance yard and parking up.

Sean and a few of the fitters were waiting our arrival and began asking questions almost before the last beat of the engine had died away. We assured them that everything was ok and then pulled back the curtain side to check whether the batteries had moved or not. They hadn't. One test trip successfully terminated.

Noel began sounding Sean out about tyre pressure monitoring. As always, he came up with a solution quickly and returned to his workshop to begin preparations. He didn't need Maggie so I unhitched, had a cup of coffee with Noel and drove back to what I was privately thinking of as Heaven hell. I passed the demolition squad on the way and was impressed with the speed and efficiency with which they were demolishing and levelling Heaven's past. As Sean had predicted, there wouldn't be any old Heaven left before long. That meant more overcrowding, more food production, more energy drain. Well, at least I could do something about the latter but, as for the rest, only the Boss knew.

I pulled up outside Arrivals, checked for Parking Wardens and entered the now familiar building. Business as usual. Long queues of recently departeds, lost souls moving aimlessly about. Both Angel and Celeste appeared swamped and, after a quick word with both, I arranged to meet them in the Canteen in their break. That meant I had nearly half an hour to kill so I grabbed a meal and a drink from the replicators and sat down in my usual seat. Began eating, began people watching.

One thing about the replicators, they produced excellent food. I had ordered a nice steak, well done, chips, onions and peas. One mug of Blue Mountain coffee. One satisfied trucker.

As I ate, I looked around. The Canteen seemed to be permanently busy, 24/7. The staff ate here, of course but the main customers seemed to be the Newly Arriveds. It was easy to spot them. They were different ages, wore a varied assortment of clothes. Whatever they had on at The Moment. The regulars were mainly young, had clean clothes and didn't have that shell-shocked, ‘where the hell am I?’ look.

I spotted one guy in swimming trunks with most of his left arm missing. I wondered what his story was. The way he was handling his drink, I guessed he was left handed. Bet he couldn't wait to get his Ageing sorted out and get his arm back. And that was the one nice thing you could tell the Newbies: no matter what state you arrived in, it could only get better. Missing bits were replaced, illnesses cured, hair restored, freedom of age and re-uniting of memories.

As I have mentioned before, truckers tend to look out on the world and people watch. I finished my meal and sat back to enjoy my coffee. Everything was free. Well, to Grade 2's that is. The Common People had to earn credits to pay and that meant work. But, even that didn't seem too arduous. Without work to occupy the mind and fill the hours, Eternity would go on forever. Literally. All in all, it wasn't a bad deal at all. Once you got over the overcrowding, the Topside squalor and the lowering of your Heavenly expectations.

I realised that I liked being here. Ok, I didn't have a choice in the matter - unless I believed what Noel had told me about being able to go back – but I had a much better deal here than on Earth. Starting a great new job tomorrow, my own truck, three wonderful ladies in my life and most of my relatives around. As Noel had said during our heated argument, what did I have to go back to? Far less than I had here.

As I pondered on my life, the swimming trunks guy sat down at the next table. He had his drink in his one remaining hand so he had to put that on the table first and then pull out his chair. Just as he sat down, a young woman placed a tray in front of him and also sat down. She chatted to him as she cut up his food and helped him feed. I wasn't eavesdropping but I heard her explaining how things worked and how he would soon have his arm back. Almost predictably, his face dropped and he broke down and started crying. She got up and put her arms around him until he had composed himself and started eating again. You could see the relief and gratitude on his face as she talked softly about Ageing, Accommodation, Clothing and all the other Facts of Death. She was doing a great job.

I kept staring at her because she was somehow familiar. She was a bit shorter than me and extremely attractive. I guessed she was about late teens- early twenties. She had a slight figure and a small face with an upturned nose, wide set brown eyes and black hair falling onto her shoulders. Not just black hair but that deep shade that reflects almost blue as the light hits it. She must have sensed me looking at her because she turned and gave me a mega watt smile. I gave her a tentative one back and then realised she was coming over.

She was wearing jeans and a frilly blue blouse with some sort of waistcoat over it. She looked great. Her skin shone and she had that eagerness that showed she was enjoying life. I stood up as she approached and wondered what she wanted. Obviously she wanted me. She put her arms around me and gave me one of the best hugs I'd had in a long time. Then she pulled my head down and planted a kiss firmly on my lips. It didn't last long but I wanted it too.

'Hi, John. It's so nice to see you again. That was just to thank you for what you did for me on my first day.' I recognised the eyes first. Those were the only things that hadn't changed too much. Well, she certainly looked different from when I had last seen her. 'Ludi?'

She nodded pleased that I had recognised her. I put my arm up and made a twirling motion. She smiled and turned round in front of me then laughed. Suddenly, for no reason, I had tears in my eyes and a lump in my throat. What a change from the middle-aged lady in a hospital gown who had wandered about with it undone.

'Wow, look at you. You look fantastic. How are you? Happy? Settled?'

'Yes, to all three. I love it up here. I have a great job, I live with my grandparents -who are about my age and that's still confusing – and I love being twenty one again.

Best of all, I love not being in pain. But, enough about me, how are you? Everywhere I go I hear about John Slater, the Energy Man.'

'Starting to haul energy tomorrow. I'm looking forward to it. My truck is outside if you want to see it.' I suddenly realised I was babbling. Ludi was having that effect on me. Was I coming on to her? Show her my truck, indeed. How juvenile was that?

She laughed showing off her perfect white teeth. 'I can't right now.' She looked across at the swimmer. 'I have to get Ross sorted out with his meal and then take him to Angelica to get his accommodation sorted'.

She knew Angelica? I guessed her new job was some sort of Meet and Greet. Therefore she would know Angel, probably Celeste, Astra and Molly as well. I asked the question.

'Yes, I help the New Arrivals who are a bit handicapped. Like Ross. I have to take him to see Angel once he has come to terms with what happened. Then, as you know, on to Astra and Molly. Molly is great, isn't she? I love her. And' she gave a mischievous grin 'I really like the other girls as well. They obviously like you. They never stop talking about you.'

Just as she finished, I looked up and there was Celeste and Angel coming towards me. Oh-oh. I must have looked guilty because they stopped in front of me and glared. I was just about to explain when they both giggled and sat down.

'The look on your face.' Celeste said as she leant over and kissed me. Angel kissed the other cheek and they both turned to Ludi. 'Hi Ludi.' they said in unison.

Ludi got up. 'Hi, Girls. Just saying hello to John.' she turned to face me and smiled. 'Lovely seeing you again, John. I'd love to see your truck, sometime' She gave me a little knowing grin and then returned to the next table to help her swimmer.

'Can't leave you alone for a minute, can we?' Angel said sternly. 'Women coming on to you from all directions. What are we going to do with him, Celeste?'

'I know what I'd like to do with him' Celeste purred and gave me a very suggestive look. 'So, you fancy Ludi, do you?'

'I think she's very nice' I stammered. 'But, there's nothing going on. I helped her on her first day and this is the first time I've seen her since.'

'Nice? She's gorgeous. What bloke wouldn't fancy her? Oh, come on John, we're only joking. We told you, it's different up here. If you want to see her again, that's fine. After what you have done for Astra, we both love you even more. She's like a different person.'

'Not just Astra either' Angel joined in. 'You have a way of helping ladies in distress. The hurt and the damaged ones. You certainly repaired me. We can share you out. We don't mind'.

'Speaking of damaged' Celeste purred. 'My finger hurts. Can you help make it feel better? I'd be EVER so grateful'

I just looked from one to the other. Confused didn't even start to cover how I felt. They saw how baffled I was.

'John' Angel said. 'We don't have time to talk now but, obviously, we need to. Can you come round this evening?'

I just nodded. They finished their drinks, got up, did a tandem cheek kiss and walked back to their desks. I sat and pondered.

Ludi came back over without Ross, the swimsuit guy in tow. She stopped at the table and then sat down.

'I'm sorry if I upset the girls.' she began.

'I don't think you did' I replied. 'That's the problem'

She raised an enquiring eyebrow. 'Problems are best shared'

'I don't know where to begin......Look, when you were on Earth, did you have relationships?'

Stupid question but I was feeling pretty stupid. Of course she had relationships. They must have been queuing up around the block. She was very fanciable when she arrived here. As she was now, she was drop dead gorgeous.

'Yes, I had relationships. Some serious, some of the wild oats variety. Why?' She asked with a puzzled expression

'Well, if you were in a relationship and your bloke started fancying other women or even going out with them, would you be jealous?'

She didn't even consider the question. 'Of course, I would have been. Is this what it is all about?'

I started, very slowly, to tell her the problem. Then, it all came rushing out. The way I felt, my confusion, my conscience, my guilt. Was I being a love rat, using the girls, what?

She listened. When I had finished, she reached across and put her hand over mine. 'Have you talked to the girls about this?'

I nodded. 'And? What did they say?'

'They said it didn't matter. It was all different up Here' I mumbled.

'Well, so what's the problem? If they are happy with the

situation, why can't you be? I have heard how Angle and Celeste, heck, even Molly and Astra, talk about you. They all say what a nice, decent bloke you are. Apparently you have helped Angel and Astra with some personal problems. I don't know the details and I don't want to know. What I do know is that they all think the world of you. It is not as if you are going behind their backs. They know the situation and they accept it. Why can't you?'

'I don't know. It just feels wrong somehow' . I looked directly at her. 'They also said that if I fancied you, then that was all right too'.

She looked directly back. 'And, do you? Fancy me, I mean?'

I nodded. Her smile lit up her face. 'Good, because I fancy you something rotten'

I squeezed her hand. 'The question is, what are you going to do about it? If you keep having these hang-ups, then you are punishing not only yourself but all of us too'.

'You are really willing to share me with three other girls?'.

'Would you be willing to share us with other blokes?' she countered.

I thought about it. Here, it didn't bother me. On earth, my answer would have been a definite “No”. I told her my conclusion.

'Then, it is not a problem. Accept it.' She smiled mischievously. 'You said something about showing me your truck?'

I just nodded and, without a word, pulled her up. Hand in hand, we walked out to Maggie. I opened the door and helped her up. Shut the door and sat down. She looked around and then, came over, leant over and kissed me softly yet insistently on the lips.

With her lips on mine, I stood up, wrapped my arms around her and held her tightly. Her tongue darted between my lips and she squirmed against me. Without any conscious thought, we ended up on the bunk. We were still kissing urgently. Her lips were soft and tasted of honey. Her body was firm and pressing down on mine. Our arms were around each other and holding tightly. We kissed until we had to come up for air. We broke away and looked at each other. I pulled her head close and kissed her gently on the forehead. 'Can we leave it at that for the moment?' I asked as I looked into her eyes.

She nodded and pressed against me again. 'How do you feel now?'

I thought about it. I wanted to go on but didn't feel bad about it. I just held her. She nestled into my neck and began to nibble at my ear. I squirmed at the sensation. She laughed and looked up. 'I've got to say; you are a great kisser. I also like the fact that you are content to just kiss. I can't help but notice that you are ready to go further.' She snaked her hand down and patted my bulging trousers. 'Makes me feel wanted for being me and not just a quickie on the side'.

'I don't do quickies on the side. I like to get to know a girl first and then go to the next level. If that makes me old fashioned and boring then that's what I am. Can't change. Don't want to change.'

'Don't change. That's what makes women like you. I can see what the girls love about you. Now, do you want to go back or' she slowly unzipped me 'carry on with what you started?'

I thought about it. For a full second. I undid her zip. Heaven moved.

NINETEEN

Peter Tiler looked across at the package on the table. He had just come home from another night shift and he was tired. He didn't want to open the package. He knew what it contained.

His wife Elizabeth came down the stairs. She saw where his gaze was directed and understood his silence. She had picked up the package from Canley Crematorium yesterday afternoon whilst her husband slept. She knew he had deliberately avoided dealing with it before he went to work last night. Now, he was deciding whether to open it or not.

'No rush, Stu.' She told him as she went into the kitchen to get his morning cup of tea and some breakfast.

'Can't put if off forever, Beth. It's not as if we don't know what it is.' Peter knew that it contained the ashes of his friend and almost-son, John Slater. It had only been a few days since he had been at the crematorium to see his friend off on his final journey. Now, his mortal remains were back in the house where he had been so happy. One final task and his obligations were finished. John Slater might have gone but his memory would live on. He made up his mind and strode purposefully over to the table. He picked up the package and slowly, reverently, took off the plain paper wrapping to disclose a small wooden box. Such a small box to contain such a big man. He picked it up and returned it to the table.

Over breakfast, he thought about his last obligations to his friend. Over many miles and many discussions, John Slater had made his wishes known. Peter knew what he had to do. Knew but was reluctant to do. One last step to severing any physical contact with the boy, then the man, who had lived with them. He decided to put off any decision until he had been down the allotment. Beth knew that the allotment was where her husband went to relax and think things over. She wasn't surprised when he told her where he was going.

'Ok love' she smiled. 'See you later'

There was no-one about when he unlocked the ramshackle collection of wood and metal sheeting he affectionately called his "shed". There wasn't much inside. Just a few digging tools and other odds and ends. He grabbed a fork and started to dig over a patch of rough ground he was slowly reclaiming from Nature. Within a few minutes, he had a good sweat going and the simple rhythm of digging and forking over had its usual calming effect. It was one of those jobs he could do automatically and just let his mind drift. He sensed movement on the periphery of his vision and looked up, momentarily startled.

'Morning Stu. Didn't expect to see you this early'

His friend Dave Williams was standing on the communal pathway.

'Just come down for a think. John's ashes came back yesterday and I'm trying to decide what to do with them. No, that's not right. I know what I have to do with them. I am just reluctant to finalize things.'

'I can understand that. But, isn't it what John wanted that you should be considering? I know you told me he wanted his ashes scattered on the M1. I know you probably think you are getting rid of the last thing linking you to John, but that isn't true is it?'

'It's the last physical link with him'

Dave pointed to Peter's head. 'You've always got him up there, mate. And, every time you travel on the motorway, you'll remember him. His ashes will scatter all over. Just as he wanted'

Peter looked up. He made up his mind. Putting his fork back in the shed, he locked up and turned to his friend. 'You're right. I'm going to do it right now. Do you want to come?'No. I appreciate you asking but this is something for you and Beth to do alone. I'll be thinking of you though.'

Back at the house, Peter collected the box and he and Beth drove to Junction 18 of the M1 at Crick. Accelerating up the slip road, he joined the motorway and was relieved to find traffic relatively light. The rush hour had come and gone. He stayed in the inside lane and looked in his mirrors. Nothing immediately behind him. Before he could change his mind, he had opened the box and held it out the window. The contents were instantly sucked out in a mist of fine dust. For a brief moment, they were visible and then the slipstream dispersed them. He placed the box back on the seat and reached for his wife's hand. He gripped it tightly and, in a thick voice said a last farewell.

'Goodbye John. Sleep well. We'll miss you. God bless'

At the A45 junction to Northampton, he left the motorway and returned to Rugby on the A5 trunk road.

He felt relieved that it was finally over. His friend had returned to his natural environment. Good roads and far horizons. Last trip just started and lasting for as long as the winds blew.

TWENTY

It was the weirdest feeling.

One minute I am helping Ludi down from Maggie, the next I am staggering and trying to stay upright. I grabbed the door tightly and held on as my world seemed to fade. One moment it was there, the next it almost vanished as though the lights had been suddenly dimmed. My head reeled and I could feel my grip on the door loosening. Suddenly, I am being supported and Ludi is screaming into my ear.

'John, John. Are you all right? What's happening? Lie down.' I sense her helping me down and then my back was against the uneven road surface. I catch a glimpse of her ashen face and then it blurs. My mind seems to be snapping in and out of my immediate surroundings. One second I can see Arrivals, Ludi and Astroblocks, the next....nothing. I feel a rushing in my ears and the grey fog I have slipped into seems to pulsate with a mind of its own. Then I am back again and struggling to sit up. Ludi supports me as best she can and I begin to calm down and then, suddenly, a white hot wave of sadness, despair or loneliness that I can feel but not identify engulfs me and I begin to slip away again.

The next time I open my eyes, I am on my back again and I can see Ludi and Brother Simon kneeling at my side. She is crying and he is awkwardly trying to comfort and reassure her. When she sees my eyes open, she pulls away from his arm and cradles my head.

'What happened?' I ask. 'I had a funny turn and felt faint. Then, just before I passed out, I felt incredibly sad and depressed.'

'You went white and passed out. I screamed out for help and Brother Simon came rushing over. He took one look at you and told me not to worry. It would soon be over and you would be back to normal. I didn't believe him until you opened your eyes a minute ago. How do you feel now?' She leant back and looked into my eyes anxiously. I considered how I felt. A bit stupid for passing out but, apart from being a bit lightheaded, ok. I sat up and took a few deep breaths. The lightheaded feeling passed and I could feel the strength returning to my limbs. 'I reckon I'm ok now. Give me a hand up and we'll see how I feel when I'm standing.' They both helped me up and I stood there. Still a little dizzy but that was passing. Strangely, the thought popped into my head that I needed a cigarette. I gave up smoking almost sixteen years ago. Weird.

'Yep. I'm fine.' I turned to Brother Simon and saw a worried little smile on his lips. 'Ok, what happened? You told Ludi not to worry, that it would pass, so obviously you have seen something similar before. Right?

He looked at me and darted a nervous little glance at Ludi. 'I think you can tell me in front of her' I told him.

'No, it's all right. I can go. I don't mind' Ludi made as if to walk away but I reached out for her hand.

'Come on Brother Simon, what's the big secret?' He looked from me to Ludi and seemed to be struggling with a decision. His mouth was working but no sound was coming out. I could see his Adam's apple bobbing up and down. His eyes darted furtively to mine and then away. He was starting to worry me.

'Please, tell me' I held out my hand and gripped his arm. My touch seemed to give him the strength he needed. He sighed and, almost in a whisper, said one word 'Severing.' Severing? Severing what. I'd sever the breath from his body if he didn't tell me soon. He must have determined the expression on my face and decided that enough was enough.

He removed his arm from my grip and, almost defiantly, gathered himself up. It didn't take him long. There wasn't much to gather. Could I really have been scared witless by this man back in school?

'Severing doesn't happen that often and is what it means. It means that the last link with your old life has been severed. Most people pass seamlessly from their mortal life to their immortal live. Occasionally, what has just happened to you occurs.' He stopped and assembled his thoughts. 'It's as though an invisible band is stretched from one existence to the other. What causes this band to break or sever is something that is final.'

'Can't be anything more final than death' I told him. He started pacing. Short nervous steps, up and down. Just like in the classroom.

'I don't know the whole reason' he confessed. 'I can give you a couple of examples that I know of but there is nothing definitive. The reason seems to be individual to the person concerned. Say, for instance that you are in a near-death situation. You could live or die depending on what happens to you in an operating room. Many people have been brought back to life by the skill of a surgeon. Many of those people talk of hovering over the operating table looking down. They seem to be between the two worlds. Tied to a particular place but ready to go back to their old life or on to their new one. Whether they live or die, they have to be in one place. If the surgeon saves them then it is almost as if they are pulled back to their old body by an invisible band. If they die then the band is severed and they enter the Cleansing Mists and, eventually, arrive here. With me so far?'

Both Ludi and I nodded in unison.

'Occasionally, people arrive here with that band intact. Almost as if it hasn't been decided whether they are staying or not.' He looked directly at me. 'Have you been given any reason to believe that you are one of those?'

I thought instantly of the deal that Noel said he had arranged for me. Three months, he had said. Time to decide whether it was working out or not. But, it couldn't have been three months already, could it?

'There was mention of a time period that gave me the choice of deciding to stay or return.' I told him quietly. I was worried that I was giving away something that I shouldn't. But, Noel hadn't said it was a secret had he? He looked relieved. Obviously he was worried about his secrets as well. 'That's ok then' he decided. 'Then that was the other example I was going to give. People arrive here with a period of Grace authorised by the Boss. A Get out of Heaven Free pass, if you like. You are obviously one of those.'

'Yes, but that doesn't explain what just happened to me, does it? 'Yes, it does. Your band has been severed. The decision has been made that you are staying. The Severing usually comes about at the moment of your earthly body's release from the ties of Earth. If I was to guess, I would say that your body has been buried or, if it was cremated, your ashes scattered or placed somewhere.'

'But, don't I get a say in the matter?' Had Noel done the dirty on me again?

' I imagine so. You or the Boss must decide whether you are staying or not. But, because of what just happened, I can only say that your time on earth has just been finalized –by something that happened to your remains – and you are now here permanently. Has anything been said? How do you feel about it?'

How did I feel about it? Actually, I felt ok. I had already made up my mind that I liked it here. I really didn't have anything better in my old life to look forward to. Who looks forward to getting old with its aches, pain and problems? True, my life here was getting more and more complicated romance-wise but I could live with that. Better too much than too little.

No, what annoyed me was that I hadn't been asked what my decision about staying was going to be. I had made up my mind in my head but hadn't told anyone else. I explained this to Brother Simon.

'I feel that, by just thinking that you were staying, the Boss decided to go ahead and finalize for you. You had made up your mind, why wait? I can try and find out for you but it will take time. The one thing I can say is that, if you have made up your mind, what just happened to you will not happen again.' Ludi was still listening and appeared relieved by what she had just heard. She turned to me and, with a sly little smile on her face asked me why I didn't discuss my other problem with Brother Simon whilst he was here?

‘Other problem? What other problem?’ he queried turning from her to me.
‘John has a problem with too many women falling in love with him and getting a guilty feeling about the situation.’ Ludi told him‘Huh, if that is all you have to worry about then don’t worry’ he told me rather primly. ‘If it was wrong then you wouldn’t be allowed to do it. Frankly, I can’t see why any sane woman would want you but, if one or many do, then that’s ok. Sexual freedom here isn’t frowned upon quite the same way as it is on Earth. Not that I know anything about that’ he hastened to add.
‘See, I told you it was ok. Now it’s official. John Slater, you can have as many girl friends as you want and, so long as everyone is happy with that, then it’s ok. Now, give me a kiss and let me get back to work. Luring a poor unsuspecting female into your truck indeed.’ Ludi put her arms round me and gave me a long, very sexy and disturbing kiss and walked off swaying her hips like a pendulum. Brother Simon stood there, a bright shade of red and his mouth hanging open. He suddenly realized that I was watching him watching her. ‘John Slater, you really are the most vexing person’ he told me before he too walked away. Not quite as sexily I might add.
I returned to Maggie with a big smile and a light heart. It was as if a large weight had been removed and I was suddenly free. I determined there and then to get rid of my earthly hang-ups and embrace my new life wholeheartedly. Heck, I didn’t even dust around the dash before starting Maggie up and returning to Maintenance.

The road was clear again and the demolition crew had gone. The proof that they had been there was a very large gap in the buildings and a rubble floor. Two men in hard hats were using surveying instruments and calling out numbers to each other. As my Dad said, there was plenty of work here for good builders. How long before another bigger, taller building was built and occupied? How long before the bigger, taller building was replaced by an even bigger, even taller building?

Thankfully, Maintenance was still standing and I parked up and went to Sean's little office. He saw me coming and poured a coffee. He seemed in a better mood now and had obviously got over the morning's depression. Handing over the cup, he indicated the chair opposite and sat down. As well as everything else, he made good coffee. The old fashioned way with a kettle and milk. 'Can't stand that replicated muck' he confessed.

'So what, you just replicated a kettle, coffee, some milk and made your own?' I asked with a straight face.

'That's about it' he laughed. 'Now, about your tyre heating problem. I have fitted heat monitors to the chassis between each axle. These have a wide angle beam and will make sure the tyre temperature remains within acceptable limits. I have wired the monitors into the electrical loom and, once you connect your electrical susie, they will show the temperature on your sat-nav monitor. Anything over normal and a buzzer will sound. How does that sound?'

'Great. Did you use to do this sort of thing on Earth?'

‘ A lot of similar things but I didn’t have the same technology. Some of the Alien Heavens have stuff that will blow your mind. They have Holographic suites that you can programme to do anything you want. Walk along Hadrian’s wall, surf in Hawai, take part in a truck race or be with anyone you desire. Imagine walking across the Yorkshire moors with Demi Moore or whoever else you fancy. Just a hologram but indistinguishable from the real thing. If I could get my hands on that technology, I would have died and gone to Heaven’ he said seriously.
‘Couldn’t Noel get his hands on it for you? He seems to be able to get anything else.’
‘Yeah, Heaven’s answer to Arthur O’Daly’ Sean grinned back. ‘I imagine he could but he has his hands full right now with other stuff. How did you first meet Noel?’
‘I first met Noel after he was beaten up by a very irate German truck driver for siphoning his diesel. After that it went from bad to worse. I like him but don’t really trust him’
Sean looked at me to see if I was joking. He saw that I wasn’t and relaxed. ‘I feel exactly the same’ He explained. ‘It’s good working with him but I don’t want to get involved with his other activities. He hasn’t asked me yet and I hope he never does. Just watch out, that’s all’.Noel and I were going to have a long serious talk about his “other activities”. I still didn’t know how he had conned his way into Heaven but imagined there was a reason. Noel was one of those people who always had a deal going. Normally a shade to the right of legitimate but a good bloke to know if you wanted something yourself. To

date, I hadn't asked him for anything but who knows? I decided not to pursue the subject of Noel's business activities.

'Have you known him long?' I asked.

'I knew of him for a long time. The mysterious fixer who could get everything you wanted for a price. I have only known him since I've been up here. Even now, I still think he had something to do with that. All we fitters do. But, in reality, no-one minds too much. We all had pretty much rubbish lives back on Earth and things are much better here. Interesting work, not too much of it, better accommodation and a great entertainment package. Only thing I really miss are my long walks. Still, can't have everything, at least until I get my Holographic Suite' he laughed.

He took me out to show me the tyre temperature monitoring system he had installed on the trailer. As was usual with Sean's work, it was neatly installed, unobtrusive and, I was sure, worked well.

'What time are you getting here in the morning?' he asked as I started to walk back to Maggie.

'I have one load of batteries to deliver to the south end of England State, I don't really have a clue what sort of time is involved so I will make an early start and see how it goes. About seven thirty, I reckon. Is that ok for you?'

'I'll have the trailer loaded by then. You can do your own securing and side sheeting. Save you having to check my work.'

How well he was starting to know me. I climbed up into Maggie and drove to the girl's flat. I was a bit apprehensive about the 'meeting' but not as badly as I felt earlier. My Severing experience, along with the chat with Brother Simon, had made up my mind for me. I was here to stay and, as long as the girls weren't bothered about sharing, then I wasn't either.

As I had mentioned I had OCD. I preferred to live a tidy and orderly life. And, I was starting to get twitchy about Topside Heaven. It really was a depressing place. Dark, dismal and derelict. The roads were barely wide enough to drive a truck through and I seemed to need my lights on all the time. The building exteriors all seemed badly neglected and lacking in even the most basic maintenance. I was really fighting the urge to get a shovel and broom and start clearing up around the girls flat.

I sort of understood the principle behind it. Make the Topside so unattractive that the bright lights, music and chatter of the Hydrophonics areas seemed the best place to be. Light work, a chance to meet your mates and relatives and a way to fill in the long days of eternity. I was deeply grateful and privileged to be able to have my truck, interesting work and faraway places to see. And, here I was guessing, a different female companion to accompany me. What if the girls didn't want to come with me? Naw, who could resist the chance to spend some quality time with Maggie and me?

I parked up and decided to have shower before seeing the girls. I pulled the curtains and got my sonic shower ready. I still hadn't got used to the needle-like pulsating feeling that cleaned me and my clothes. It was an excellent method of getting clean and would have been universally accepted on Earth. Just another of the perks that were seducing me into staying. Speaking of seducing, I had a meeting to attend. Actually, I was a bit apprehensive about what was going to be said. I sort of knew but would feel happier when it was over. I hoped.

I entered the building, went down the corridor and knocked on the door. Molly opened it and gave me her customary big, bright smile. I followed her into the living room and they were all there. Molly, Celeste, Angelica, Astra and Ludi. Ludi? What was she doing here?

Celeste must have read my mind. More likely she saw the confusion on my face. 'I invited Ludi along' she informed me. 'Might as well have all your harem here, eh?'

'Harem? I don't have a harem' I blustered.

'Well, it certainly looks like you have one now' Angel informed me with a grin. I looked at the others and saw nods. Even Molly.

'Girls? What's going on?'

'We decided it was time to put an end to these silly ideas you have been getting' Astra smiled. The new Astra. The one with the glow, cheeky grin and sparkling eyes.

Molly stepped forward and led me to the sofa. The others arranged themselves into a circle around me once I had sat down.

'The girls have elected me spokeswoman' Molly elaborated. 'We have all been talking about you and your problem for the last hour. John' she told me sternly. I half expected to get a finger wagging as well. 'Get the silly idea out of your head that what you are doing is wrong. None of us mind the idea of sharing you. Well, apart from me' Molly laughed. 'I want no part of it. No offence John but I am quite happy living without a man in my life. But the others have decided they want you in their lives and that's that. Accept the situation and move on. Ok? No more hang-ups, no more guilt trips. You're a lucky man and they are lucky to have someone like you. But, it works both ways, you know. If they fancy someone else, well, you have to share also. Ok?'

I nodded. And, it was ok. I stood up, held out my arms, and my "harem" gathered round for hugs and sloppy kisses.

'Right, thank goodness that's settled' Molly beamed. 'I'll go and get the kettle on.

Just as she disappeared into the kitchen, the doorbell rang. Angel got up to answer it and came back with a familiar figure.

'Allo, Mr John' Alfie grinned. I hadn't seen him for a couple of days but I could have sworn he had got bigger. 'Got a message for you from Mr Noel. He says can you come round about 8.30 instead of 7.30 tomorrow?'

'Why, what's wrong'

'I dunno. 'E didn't say. Just arsked me to give you the message and come back with your answer' I didn't like it when plans got changed suddenly. But, it was only an hour and there could be any number of reasons for the delay. I told Alfie it would be ok.

'Righti-o, Mr Slater. 'Ere, got a joke for you.' A collection of groans went round the room. Just then Molly came back with the tea and cups on a tray. She saw Alfie and beamed at him. 'Hi Alfie, want a piece of cake?'

'Oh yes please, Miss Molly. Is it Angel cake? Did you make it?' Molly nodded obviously pleased. 'Anyway' Alfie persisted. 'A couple of geezers go to 'eaven and St

Pete meets them. “Sorry gents” ‘e tells ‘em. There’s a bit of a housing problem and your villas aren’t ready yet”.
A series of derisory comments come from the room. Alfie grins. ‘Anyways, St Pete tells the geezers that they can go back to Earth until their ‘ouses are ready. And, he tells them, they can go back as anything they want. One tells him that he wants to go back as an eagle soaring over the mountains with lovely views. The
, mixed other that he wants to be a really cool stud.
Finally their ‘omes are ready and Pete tells an angel to go and get them. “But, ‘ow will I know where to find ‘em?” the angel arskes.
“That’s easy” St Pete tells the angel. “One of them is an eagle flying high over the Scottish highlands. The other is on a winter tyre attached to a lorry with a snow plough.”
Alfie laughs uproariously at his own joke. ‘That’s a good ‘un, isn’t it, Mr Slater?’
I struggle to stifle a smile. The girls are having the same problem. ‘It’s not bad, Alfie. I’ve heard better’
His face falls. Then it lights up again. ‘Ere, I’ve got another one. A bloke comes into Arrivals and ends up on Miss Celeste’s desk. He fills in his forms and then wants to know if he can arske some questions. Miss Celeste says it will be ok.
“Why did God make women so different from us” he arskes.
“So that you will be attracted to them” Miss Celeste replies. I look over and Celeste is beaming at Alfie.
“Then why did God make women so beautiful?’
“So that you will love them”

"Yeah, but why then did he make so many airheads?"
"Oh, that's easy. It's so that they will like you." Miss Celeste tells 'im'
Suddenly all the girls are laughing and nodding in agreement. Molly pats Alfie on the head, gives him his cake and sees him out. 'He gets worse' she laughed as she returns and begins to hand out cups and plates.

'So John, where are you taking us tonight?' Astra asks me just as I fill my mouth with Angel cake.

I swallow hastily and nearly choke. That prompts Angel to come over and begin pounding my back. 'Enough, enough' I tell her. 'Look, let's just go over to Entertainment and see who's on, shall we?'
Surprisingly, in a room full of girls, this suggestion meets with approval. 'Right, that's settled then. Finish our tea and then let's get ready.' I tell my official harem.
It didn't take long for them to emerge from the two bedrooms. Not having to decide what clothes to wear certainly speeds things up a bit. But, I saw, they had swopped clothesand matched and, freshly made up and smelling heavenly, they lined up for inspection.
"Perfic" I nodded in my best Pop Larkin impersonation as I walked front and back as if inspecting an honour guard. And, in a way, it was an honour guard and I was the one being honoured. "You'll do but try to do better next time" I said as I made for the door. The sounds of items hitting the door as I waited safely on the other side brought an even wider grin to my face.

"Are we going in your truck?" Ludi asked innocently. I saw the exchange of glances between Angel and Astra.
"No, I think we'll walk. Do us good" I replied as I walked towards the Tube entrance.
"I should bloody well think so" Celeste said as she looked at the others. "The next person going in John's truck is me. And, you lot won't be coming with me." She warned.
"No, she'll probably want to *come* alone" Angel said with a grin. Ludi and Astra joined in her laughter.
"Now, now, girls. Play nicely" I said in my Master of the Harem authorative voice. I sneaked a glance at Celeste. She hadn't got it yet.
Surprisingly, the tube was nearly empty but the girls crowded closely anyway. I stretched my arms around them as far as they would go and kissed each one fondly. Go back to Earth? What on Earth for? I was indeed in Heaven. The religious place and the one I used to dream about.
Entertainment was the same. Packed with people intent on a good time. Ok, I know there wasn't any other choice about where to come in the evening but who would want to come anywhere else? Whatever rocked your boat was there. Dances, films, bars, football matches, cricket and all the other outdoor sports. Bingo, slots, cards. If you couldn't find something you liked then there was no hope for you. You might as well be dead.
The girls felt like dancing but I wanted to see Billy Fury and Buddy Holly. We went dancing. Inside the dance hall, there were different choices. Ballroom, modern, ballet, western, hip hop. Everybody was catered for. The

girls opted for the hall that was full of noise and people dancing to whatever their feet told them to do. A band was on the stage and I could have sworn it was being conducted by Glen Miller. Whoever was waving the white stick, the musicians were great.

If you have seen those old movies from the 50's and 60's you would recognize the dance hall. An acre of dance floor, couples lining up on either side, a slowly turning mirrored ball reflecting light onto the couples dancing. We danced rock, slow smoochy numbers, frantic line dances. I tried to share my time equally but the girls danced with each other or who ever asked them. And, no, I didn't feel jealous. Finally, I staggered to the sideline with Celeste and we grabbed a seat and sat and watched.

"What music do you like John?" Celeste as we enjoyed the scene in front of us.

"I like *both* kinds" I told her. "Country and Western".

A rock number started and a couple in front of us started to give it all they had. The guy had a quiff, Elvis sideburns, a fancy Teddy Boy suit and authentic brothel creeper suede shoes. His partner had a low cut blouse and a frothy skirt. I watched appreciatively as the girl's skirt swirled up revealing layers of petticoats, stockings, white flesh and suspenders. Celeste saw where I where looking and poked an elbow into my ribs. "Brazen hussy" she muttered. "I haven't seen suspenders in a long time"

"Me neither" I grinned at her. "We used to call them gigglers".

"Gigglers?" she frowned. "Why?"

"Because if you got that far, you were laughing" I told her with a straight face. This time the elbow really hurt. The couple were still gyrating furiously and, as I watched them, I suddenly thought that they seemed familiar. I looked closer and realized I was looking at my parents. It was a bit like being at a wedding or something and your parents start doing their Saturday Night Fever routine. Only this time, my parents were younger than me and were really good. I had never seen them as young or carefree as this before. You always seem to remember your parents as old and grouchy. Raising a family ages people prematurely as the responsibility of caring and nurturing takes its toll.

Yet, here they were, young, happy and enjoying themselves. And, I noticed as the dance ended and they hugged and kissed, still caring for each other. Jean was looking round and suddenly saw me. She waved and dragged Mike over. I watched my Mum and Dad coming towards me and began to tear up. I suddenly realized just how much I had missed them.

"Hi Mum, Dad" I said as I got up to meet them. I saw Mum glance at Dad before she hugged me. I had just unconsciously solved something that had bothered me. Before I had called them Mike and Jean or nothing at all. Now, they had just become Mum and Dad again.

"Hello John, Celeste. How are you?" Mum said as she embraced Celeste. "Enjoying yourselves? Where are the other girls?"

"Yeah, son" Dad said with a little half smile. "Where is your harem?"

Are there no secrets here? I decided not to debate the issue and waved the other girls over. Mum and Dad had met everyone except Ludi and I quickly introduced her. " I just

hope you lot know what you're getting into" Dad said with just a hint of jealousy in his voice.
"How's the Energy Truck coming along?" Mum asked quickly changing the subject.
"I've got my first run tomorrow" I told her proudly. "Got to be there early. If everything goes ok on this first run, then I'm going to be busy"
"Yes and I'm going with him" Celeste informed her. She was? Just when had this been decided? I looked at her with a raised eyebrow.
"Oh, I thought we talked about it" she said innocently.
"I've got two days booked off, there is a packed lunch for the cab fridge and I need a break"
Mum, Dad and the others looked at each other and laughed. "Come on Celeste" Dad said as he grabbed her hand. "Let's show these youngsters what proper dancing looks like." Proper dancing looked a lot like the rock and roll gyrations he and Mum had done earlier. Actually, they weren't bad. Dad did the floor stomping bit and Celeste did the actual turns and swings. Mum looked on with a smile on her face. "He's still got the moves, hasn't he? We met on the dance floor. Did I ever tell you that? He was so smooth in those days. I just hope he doesn't start wanting more women. Like his greedy son."
"I didn't start out wanting this many girl friends" I protested. "It just sort of happened. The girls are ok with it. How do you feel?"
"Mike and I love them all. It's just like having four daughters in law. Just relax John. Enjoy death"
Dad took turns with the other girls and I looked on. I toyed with the idea of asking Mum for a dance but it didn't

feel quite right. I remembered watching her dancing earlier with her swirling skirt and quite fancying her. Eventually everyone had enough and we started to drift off. Mum and Dad carried on with their frantic dancing. I got tired just looking at them. Just where did these young folks get all their energy?

Ludi came and sat beside me. She was hot and sweaty but looked and smelt good. She looked at me and smiled in a mysterious way. "What?" I asked

"Oh, I was just thinking about things. Like how much I dreaded dying and what, if anything, came after. This is absolutely great. I feel great, got a great bloke, great job…."

"Everything is great then?" I laughed

She slipped her arm around mine and nestled her head on my shoulder. We just sat and watched everyone enjoying themselves. "That's the only thing that takes a bit of getting used to" she said into my ear. "Everyone, well, nearly everyone, is young and good looking"

"Yeah, no Fugleys allowed"

"Fugleys? What are Fugleys?"

I grinned. "Fugleys are Effing Ugly people." She looked blank for a minute and then laughed. Her elbow jab hit the same spot as Celeste's. Just then the other girls came over, all laughing and eyes shining. The band started to play Mull of Kintyre. Celeste was on the point of sitting down when she changed her mind, grabbed my arm and headed back to the dance floor. Gosh, some of these older women could be really pushy.

"I love this song" Celeste said as she came into my arms and we began to dance closely.

"I collected a load there once" I breathed into her ear and gave it a gentle nibble at the same time.
"Oy, later" she smiled. "Where?"
"Where what?" I said absentmindedly, thinking about later. She looked at me with a fond smile on her lips. "Where did you collect a load? Keep up John"
"Oh, at the Mull of Kintyre. I picked up from the factory there."
"I thought it was a beauty spot. I didn't realize there were factories there. What did you load?"
"Tyres, of course." She looked puzzled. "What? Haven't you heard of Mullican Tyres?"
It took about two minutes. Bloody the Other Place, I'm going to have a massive bruise on my ribs in the morning. I spent the rest of the evening dancing and talking to the girls. I remembered the dances of my youth and the desperation to find a dance partner and maybe more later. None of that here. There was no urgency, no trying to impress. Just the five of us, enjoying each other's company.
Later, on the Tube home, everyone was quiet. None of the other passengers seemed to feel the need to talk. We had our own little group amongst them. Astra and Angel were discussing their favourite groups. Celeste and Ludi were standing close to me and Celeste was absentmindedly stroking my leg. She needn't have bothered. Little John was wide awake and stretching.
Back at the flat, Molly was already in bed so we kept the noise down. The girls went into a huddle and Celeste came sashaying over. "That's decided then" she informed me. "Ludi's staying here and I'm staying at your place.

Come on, grab your coat Slater, you've pulled. Ok?" She got absolutely no argument from me.

Almost before I knew it, we had said our goodbyes and goodnights and making our way over to Maggie. I helped Celeste in and joined her. She sat in the passenger seat and looked over. "Can we go somewhere quiet?" she asked somewhat shyly.

"I know just the place" I said. Starting up, I drove slowly away from the High Risers and down the now familiar road to the garage. I kept the noise down as I tried to sneak past and get out onto the Ring road. Knowing Noel, he probably had security cameras and all sorts of devices to keep tabs on people. Well, let him. This was between Celeste and me.

She didn't say much as we left the subdued lights of the buildings behind and the headlights illuminated the road ahead and not much else. "I didn't even realize that this much empty space existed" she remarked as she peered out of the side window. "It's a bit scary after spending so much time amongst the High Risers. How far does it stretch?"

I carried on driving as I explained the reasoning and wherefores about the empty landscape. After a couple of miles, I stopped and switched off. I hit the switches and lowered the side windows. "Hear that?" I asked.

"What?" she queried as she moved her head from side to side. "I can't hear anything at all".

"Precisley." I raised the windows and turned round in my seat to face her. "So, here we are. What do you fancy? A bit of music, a dvd, cup of tea?"

”Nothing, at the moment. Can we just sit?” she whispered. I moved out of the seat and knelt at her side. I reached up and moved a stray lock of hair from her face. She put her hand over mine and I could feel it trembling.
“What’s up, Celeste?”
She moved my hand and kissed my palm. “Nothing.” She looked away. “Well, if you must know, I’m a little bit frightened.”
I reached back and pressed the remote door lock button. “The doors are locked but we can go back if that’s what you want”.
“I’m not frightened of being here. I’m frightened of being here with you” she mumbled as she looked straight ahead. I gently moved my hand and turned her face towards me. “You don’t have to be frightened of me” I assured her. “I would never hurt you. You know that, don’t you?”
Her eyes widened. “ I’m not frightened of you, John” she whispered. “I’m frightened of making love with you”.
What on Heaven had happened to my self assured Celeste? I had never seen her like this before. “We don’t have to do anything you don’t want” I reassured her. “We can just talk, we can cuddle, listen to music or just turn round and go back.”
“No. I want to be her with you. It’s all I have dreamt about for weeks. I’m just worried that I will disappoint you. I haven’t had as much practice as I pretend. Here or on Earth”
I stood up and pulled her up and against me. I hugged her tight and then, as she looked up at me, I kissed her gently. “You could never disappoint me” I whispered as she slowly returned my kiss. We stayed like that for a long

while. Arms around each other and kissing slowly, longingly and then with more and more urgency. Celeste suddenly moaned and pulled away. “I can’t wait” she gasped as she sank to her knees and then onto the bunk.
I lay down beside her and pressed into her. Her hands flew to my belt and undid it. I removed my hands from her breasts and pulled my jeans down. She got more urgent. She grabbed Little John and guided him into place as she frantically pulled her panties to one side. I began to move slowly and smoothly but she couldn’t wait. She reached round and pulled me even deeper into her as she began to writhe under me. She began to moan louder as her actions got more and more frantic. Then, with a long drawn out scream, she climaxed again and again. I came just as quickly and then held on as best I could whilst she trembled and undulated beneath me. Finally she subsided and, almost instantly, went to sleep. I stood up and covered her with one of my blankets. I checked her breathing, just in case, but she was out for the count. Sometime later, I lay down beside her and closed my eyes as well.
Sunlight streamed through the cab window as I reached over and silenced the alarm. I turned my head and saw Celeste on her side and looking at me. “Good morning” she breathed with her Morning breath. Why does sleep breath seem more intense than normal breath? She kissed me briefly.
“Hi, how are you?” I asked the question but already knew the answer. Gone was the frightened, shy Celeste of last night and in her place was the usual confident person I normally saw. I turned to face her and put my arms around

her. Hugged her tightly. She pressed herself against me but I put a finger on her lips and then waved it in front of her.
“I would love to Celeste, but today is my first day on the job and I don’t want to be late. Besides, we have the whole day together, don’t we?”
She pouted a bit but reluctantly started to get up. She still had most of her clothes on so her first priority was a shower. I pulled it out and then reached for the door handle. “Give you a bit of privacy” I told her as I climbed down.
“Not much point now, is there?” she said as she got into the cubicle. “You’ve already seen everything, haven’t you?”
“Enough to know that the carpet matches the curtains” I agreed. I left her working that one out as I went to the gents situated behind the front mudguard. Looking round at the green landscape, dotted with myriad trees and shrubs, I searched in vain for any sign of a dwelling, a human shape or anything other than a large truck. No birds, no noise just a green desert. Creepy and weird at the same time. But a landscape I would be seeing a lot of in the future.
Thinking of the future reminded me that I was supposed to be somewhere. I knocked on the door and heard a startled yelp from Celeste. She peered out of the window and then relaxed. I opened the door and climbed into the cab.
“Who were you expecting?” I smiled.
“I just wasn’t expecting you to knock” she returned my effort with her own mega watt beam.

"Always the gentleman." I sat down and reached for my duster. Began to polish

"Yes, you are" she replied thoughtfully. "In both senses of the word. That's what we all love about you. You look after us and make us feel important and cherished."

"What, you discuss me with the other girls? Everything?"

"Everything. We're females; that's what we do".

I had to ask. "How did I compare?"

She looked at me and thought about it. "On a rating of 1 to 10, I reckon about 12." She reached over and put her hand on my shoulder. "Sorry if I got a bit weird last night. I didn't want to disappoint you but it had been a long time between sessions. You're my first here and there was about a twenty year gap in the other place. So, now you know"

"Like I said last night Celeste, you could never disappoint me. And" I reached up and held her hand "last night was just Heavenly"

"Thanks John, Now can you get me back to Heavenisation so I can get a drink and something to eat while you do whatever it is you have to do?"

I started Maggie up, checked my gauges and, for some reason, my mirrors before turning round and heading back to Maintenance .

Celeste was quiet as we headed back to the buildings that rose into the sky and blotted out any further view. She looked out the windows at the deserted expanses of green meadows, copses and woods. Then she looked directly ahead at the massed buildings and seemed to be comparing the views.

“What are you thinking?” I asked as I kept up a steady speed. With no other traffic and not much else to look at, driving didn’t require the total concentration it had on Earth.

“I was just thinking that Heaven must have been a nice place at the start. All this emptiness scares me a bit but I have just realized how much I have missed seeing a tree or a bit of green grass.” She looked over at me. “How long before all this is taken up by all that?” she asked as she pointed out the side window and then the front.

“I don’t know Celeste. A long time but, probably not for eternity. Same problem as we had on Earth. Too many people; not enough space.”

She continued to compare views but, as the massed habitation got nearer and nearer, she looked out of the side window the most. Back among the High Risers everything seemed to take on a sense of the inevitable, the normal. Almost as soon as we entered the first section, the light got dimmer and dimmer. The buildings got higher and closer and more oppressive. Celeste actually shivered as we entered the cool, concrete canyons. And, as I pointed out to her, these first building were the older, smaller versions of the modern replacements.

I pulled into the yard and backed up and under the waiting trailer. I coupled up, made my checks then opened the passenger door and helped Celeste down. A couple of mechanics whistled appreciatively from the open doorway as she climbed down the steps. I didn’t blame them. She was gorgeous.

“Where can I find a toilet, a hot drink and something to eat?” she asked as she looked around. I pointed her in the direction of Imogen, Noel's secretary and girlfriend. She turned towards me with a mischievous glint in her eye, planted her hands either side of my face and planted a real knee trembler of a kiss on my lips. "That'll show them just what they are missing." She smiled as she did a full hip swivelling walk calculated to make the mechanics drool.

I shook my head as I returned to the trailer. True to his word, Sean had loaded the trailer and I clambered up to ratchet the tie-downs securely over each battery. Closing the side sheeting and ratcheting the side ties tight took less than ten minutes and the load was ready.

Going over to Sean's little office, I found him seated at his desk. "Any problems?"

"No, everything went smoothly and quickly" he replied as he shut down the computer in front of him. "Right, this is where the batteries are going." He handed over a printout. " It's right down to the south of England State. They are expecting you around mid-day and are all geared up to unload you and connect the batteries into the power grids. Might be worth your while to watch and see how that is done for future reference. It's a relatively easy procedure but worth knowing."

Sean reached into a desk drawer and pulled out a small, tightly secured, box. He passed it over.

"What's this?" It was fairly heavy for its size and had nothing on the box to indicate its contents.

"Don't know, don't want to know" he grimaced. "Noel gave it to me to give to you. You give it to a bloke called Michael Sweeney at the drop site. He's expecting it. And, before you ask, Noel isn't here today. I've given it to you with his instructions. What you do with it is up to you".

“I’ll take it and think about it on the way.” I didn’t know what was in the box but just knew that it had to be dodgy. Noel was the kind of Arthur Daley type who made you want to count your fingers after shaking his hand. If the contents of the box were legit, he would have told either me or Sean. He was exactly the same on Earth. Always ducking and diving. Always scamming people. I left the office and put the box in Maggie before I went to find Celeste.

She was in Noel’s office talking to Imogen. I caught a snatch of their conversation as I walked towards the door.

“……and he has this trick that he does with his tongue when he….” Imogen was telling a wide eyed Celeste who had a hand in front of her mouth. She broke off as she saw me, blushed a deep crimson, looked at Celeste and then giggled. I had to use a ladies toilet once –the gent’s was out of action before you ask – and couldn’t believe the graffiti the fairer sex had scribbled on the walls. Or the graphic designs. Some of them weren’t even anatomically possible. Sugar and spice and all things nice? Only in nursery rhymes.

“Imogen was telling me about Noel’s party trick” Celeste explained trying to keep a straight face. “I’ll tell you about it later.”

“What’s in the box, Imogen?” I asked watching her face for a reaction.

“Box, what box?” she had a puzzled expression on her face. I guessed she didn’t know anything about it. I smiled at her and shrugged my shoulders.

“Just something Noel left for me. I thought he might have told you about it”

“No. Do you want a coffee before you go? Are you excited?’
“About what? Getting a cup of coffee. No, I’ve had coffee before.”
“No” she laughed. She had a nice laugh. Sort of deep and throaty. She was pretty as well. I hadn’t really noticed it before but she had a quiet understated beauty about her. The sort a man would probably appreciate the more time he spent with her. I wondered again about Noel and Imogen.
“Oh, you mean leaving Concrete Heaven and travelling to new and exciting places? Well, I’ve always wanted to see what was over the next hill. Always had a wander lust but I don’t think it will be quite the same here. Has Celeste told you about the empty space either side of the road?”
“I don’t think she was that impressed. It seems a bit lonely and depressing”
“Actually I think it is a bit like the desert that I had to travel on when I drove to Saudi Arabia. After a while you stop thinking of it as monotonous and it takes on a quiet sort of beauty and becomes quite peaceful and calming”
“You’re a strange bloke. Noel says things like that too. I see him sometimes looking out the window and I wonder what he’s seeing that I don’t. Truckers eh, Celeste? What can you do with them?”
I drank my coffee. What was in the box? I decided to leave it in the cab and make my mind up once I got to the drop point. Thinking about the drop point made me anxious to get off. The old Road Siren was calling to me again. Come and find me she seemed to say. Leave Boring Junction and travel to New and Exciting city. I

guess that some people are content to stay in one place and others aren't. Like those medieval peasants who travelled no farther than the next village all their lives and were probably content with that. In that context and transversely, I would probably be a Viking raider or an explorer. Always itching to see beyond the next turn of the road or the next landfall.

"You ready, Celeste?" I drained my cup and put it down. I looked over and received a big smile.

"I'm always ready John" she replied. "You know that"

"Come on then, let's hit the road"

"Ooh, you make it sound so exciting. Bye Imogen"

In the yard, I helped her into Maggie and climbed up. I looked at the print out that Sean had given me and instantly knew where I was going. Ring road clockwise to about half past the hour and then turn right and straight ahead for about two miles. Everybody should have one of these personal sat-navs. Then again, everyone did.

I started up and eased cautiously out of the yard. I still wasn't completely used to all the extra power that the Dilithium fuel had produced. Plus the trailer was loaded much more heavily than I was used to. Even though Sean and his fitters had beefed everything up, the trailer still creaked and groaned as I made the tight right hand turn out of Maintenance and towards the ring road. I glanced over at Celeste. She was sitting with her legs up on the dash, sorting through my cd collection. Having made her selection, she reached up and inserted the cd into the player. I was expecting something loud and beaty but was surprised to hear the mellow tones of Acker Bilk and Stranger on the Shore.

"Here I stand, all alone and blue….." she sang along in a surprisingly good voice. Mellow and smoky. Well, well. Celeste was full of surprises.

On the ring road, I changed progressively upwards and had soon settled down to a nice steady 55 mph. Even with all that power, old habits die hard. Anyway, no rush and take things steady and let everything settle down. Bugger, it felt good to be driving a great truck down a good road with a beautiful woman on the passenger seat. I glanced over and saw her looking at me. "What?"

"Nothing." she said. I looked again. "Well, all right then. I was just thinking how good you look driving. Natural and in command. You obviously enjoy it, don't you?"

"What I born to do. I can't explain the feeling. It's like being a part of the truck. As if we belong together. I think and Maggie responds. You'll have to try it for yourself".

"Me" she scoffed. "I couldn't drive anything this big. Could I?"

"Once we drop the load off and start back, we'll find out. Look around Celeste. What are you going to hit? So long as you drive in a reasonably straight line, you'll be fine."

"Ok, if you say so. I much prefer being driven around though. I miss my Roller and driver!"

The conversation tailed off for a little while. I was used to being on my own for long periods without speaking but Celeste lasted about five minutes.

"Right, tell me about all your women" she demanded.

"All what women?"

"Oh come on, someone like you must have had lots of women buzzing around you. Any one serious?"

"I've had casual girl friends and I did live with a couple of them but it didn't work out"
"What happened? Was it because you were always away?"
"Partly but there were other reasons as well"
"This is like drawing teeth. Come on Slater, give"
"Well, Anne was great but liked to go out. I wasn't always there so she used to go out anyway. She found someone who had a regular job and regular hours. Then there was Kate. I was with her for nearly two years and we were getting along really well. Then her young sister, Jill, told her that I had sexually assaulted her. I hadn't but Kate didn't believe it and we broke up".
"But why would the sister say something horrible like that?"
"No idea. Jealousy, hormones, spite…who knows what goes on in the mind of teenage girls."
"What a terrible thing to do. I hate it when women falsely accuse a man of something like that. It gives us all a bad name." She looked over. "Hey John, cheer up. No one who knows you would believe you capable of hurting a woman, or doing something she didn't want. Just give me her name and we'll sort her out when she gets here. She'll get the worst jobs, the grottiest accommodation Between Angel, Astra, Molly and me, we'll make her life hell".
I laughed. "Thanks Celeste, I feel better already."
On either side of the concrete ribbon we were driving along, there wasn't much to see. Grass meadows, trees, a few distant hills. I was glad that Celeste was there. I began to have the distinct impression that the most exciting

part of this journey would be the arriving. I wasn't holding my breath over that either.

I still habitually checked my mirrors but, guess what?, there was nothing behind us. The dash gauges all read normal and Maggie was positively purring along. I should have been enjoying myself. Nice truck, empty road and a beautiful woman in the passenger seat. What more could a trucker ask for? But, the shine had been taken off the day by that innocuous little parcel behind my seat. What was in it and why was it such a secret?

Again, I decided to wait until I arrived at my destination before making my decision. And, judging by the way we were eating up the miles, that wouldn't be long. The cab sat-nav and my internal one told me that I was about an hour away.

It really was the strangest feeling. One that I wasn't sure that I would get used to. On my previous trips, I had a definite destination that I could see on a road map. I could read road sign information that told me how many miles I had to travel to the major markers, like cities or motorway junctions; things like that. Here, there were no traffic signs, no barriers, no traffic and bugger all to show where I was by looking out the side windows.

I think that even Celeste was starting to get bored. She rummaged through my dvd collection and popped Dirty Dancing into the slot. I couldn't pretend that I didn't like it because it was in my collection. Because there was nothing that required my total concentration, I kept darting glances at the overhead monitor as Maggie motored on.

"Did you know that he has started giving dance lessons?" Celeste asked.

"No. Why? Are you thinking of going." Somehow I didn't fancy the idea of Patrick Swayze getting up close and personal with any of *my* girls. Ok, I know I said I wouldn't get jealous but Patrick Swayze? Come on. Get real.
"Thinking of it. Why don't you come as well? Learn a few smooth moves like your Dad"
My Dad? I was competing with my Dad now? Smooth?
"Um, not going to have much time for stuff like that" I told her. "I'm going to be as busy little trucker."
"Well, if you do get the time, you should come. The girls and I are going to go together if we can. It'll be fun." She looked over at me with a grin on her face.
I looked back at her "I guess you're just winding me up?"
"Of course" she giggled. "I love it when you get all jealous."
"Celeste? Can you get me a duster out of that Slotfer above your head?" I needed to dust my dash.
"Slotfer? What's a Slotfer?"
"It's for putting stuff into, Celeste" I told her with a straight face.
"Oh, I'll just get…..Oh you! I walked right into that one didn't I?"
She grabbed the duster and threw it at me. I pretended to lose control and swerved the trailer a bit. She screamed and grabbed her seat belt. She looked over at me and then did a double take. Pointed out of the windscreen. "John, what is that?"
I followed her finger and frowned. On the far horizon I could see something that looked like ……like what? A massive black wall? Or, as I belatedly realized, our destination?

"I guess that's our journey's end, Celeste. Welcome to Southern England State."

TWENTY ONE

" What do you think we should do with it, Beth?" Peter Tiler waved the cheque that he had taken from the envelope that came in the morning's post. It was full and final settlement from the insurance company that had insured John Slater's truck. The Renault Magnum was relatively new so the cheque Peter held was for a large amount. Not what the vehicle was worth on the open market but more than he had expected.

Probably, he thought a bit cynically, a certain amount of public relations was involved in the large and speedy settlement. After all, John Slater had died saving a lot of young lives. No company wanted to be mixed up in an adverse publicity where young lives were involved.

"Well, I think we should get it into the bank first" his ever practical wife replied. "Then pay off the funeral expenses. After that, we'll have to give it a good long thought."

Peter was just about to protest that he would settle the funeral bill when it suddenly occurred to him that it didn't matter. The bulk of the funeral costs had been donated by grateful parents. John had no family to leave his estate to. It all came to Beth and himself as they were the people John regarded as his family. The solicitor had been quite clear on that point. All of John's goods and estate came to them to do with as they saw fit.

Peter had done what he saw as his duty to his friend when he arranged his funeral. Even now other drivers came up to him and congratulated him on the spectacular yet dignified convoy of trucks that had accompanied the Kenworth showtruck and coffin it had carried from Kent to

Coventry. Where the money came from to pay for it was immaterial. Still, there would be a lot left over and Peter promised himself that he would use it, not on Beth and himself, but on some sort of memorial to John. But, that was in the future. Now, he had to get to work. Grabbing his keys and gear, he kissed his wife and climbed into his Ford Ranger pick-up truck. 'John never saw this' he thought as he started the engine and backed onto the road. 'Bet he would have laughed and teased me about my second childhood'. Well, true or not, Peter still enjoyed driving it. It was a fact of life that truck drivers preferred big cars.

The drive to his Crick depot didn't take long and he was soon entering the transport office to pick up his paperwork. The transport clerk placed his papers on the counter then put a magazine on top of it.

"Evening Peter" he greeted him. "Doncaster tonight and then back. Easy night. Might even be able to get a couple of hours in the sleeper. If you do, have a read of this" he indicated the latest copy of Trucking International "it's got a great story about your mate John and the funeral convoy in it."

Intrigued, Peter opened it to the appropriate article and saw the headline:

'John Slater: A driving force for change?

By Dave Williams.

" A little while ago I had the rare privilege of driving a heavily customized Kenworth truck on the motorway. Nothing strange in that, you might say. Plenty of K Whoppers about, thanks to Truckfest and other truck shows. What was different in this particular case was that

I was at the head of a convoy of trucks that stretched nose to tail for over five miles on the inside lane. Of course, I didn't know that at the time. I saw it on the news afterwards.

What struck me was a comment from one of the police chiefs. "This was probably the longest continuous convoy of trucks that the M1 or any other British motorway has ever seen. It was also the most well behaved with no problems whatsoever".

Peter sat down and continued reading. No way could he stop now. If he was late, he was late.

"That police chief was surprised. He was expecting trouble as soon as he heard about the convoy. Instead he found a bunch of truckers determined to show their respect for a fellow trucker in the most dignified and noticeable way they could.

Many of you know that the Kenworth I was driving carried the coffin of John Slater. John Slater was in the middle lane, just about to overtake a coach, when it lost a front wheel and swerved in front of him. That coach was full of school kids going to France on a school trip. John didn't have much time to react but he pulled to the left and applied his brakes. Motorists behind say that he was braking hard when he started to jack-knife. Now, I don't know what was going through his mind but I can guess. He must have known that a jack-knife would have caused carnage so, as witnessed by those behind, he stopped braking, straightened up and hit a bridge support.

Maybe he didn't have time to think. Maybe he acted purely on instinct. Whatever, he averted what could have resulted in a serious road accident. The coach was stopped by the central barriers, the kids were safe and, apart from a few minor fender benders, no one else was hurt. John Slater paid the ultimate price for that seemingly simple choice between steering or braking. Bad luck or a deliberate sacrifice by a professional truck driver?

I didn't know John Slater personally. I wish that I had. He seemed the kind of trucker I would have liked. I was fortunate enough to get involved with his funeral and his mate/foster dad, Peter Tiler.

Peter had know John most of his life. First as a truck-struck kid, then passenger and finally as a fully qualified truck driver. John became an owner driver on international work. Peter knew him as well as anyone could. He was John's mentor, his knowledge and his ideal. Peter told me a lot about John Slater during the time we organized his funeral. Based on that, my personal opinion is that John Slater knew exactly what he was doing when he hit that bridge support. One life for many? He wouldn't have even hesitated. He was that kind of guy.

He was also the kind of guy who cared passionately about trucking. He saw it as a profession and acted profcssionally. He wished that some of the truck drivers he saw on a daily basis felt the same way. He never saw the need to bully his way on the roads, to terrorize other motorists. To speed or drive irresponsibly. He tried to uprate the public perception of truck drivers by making a point of driving considerately and professionally. He considered it part of his job to make friends on the road rather than enemies.

There are many truckers like John on our roads. Trying in their own quiet way to drive to high standards.

Unfortunately, it is not those truck drivers who the public remember. It is the truckers who drive right up behind a car to force it out of the middle lane, who pull out without checking or caring about other motorists, that they remember. The ones who think that they have an image to live up to. But, is it the image that we truck drivers want to be associated with?

When I was at the head of that convoy, the one thing I saw and felt from the passing 'ordinary' motorists was respect. Peter Tiler was with me in that cab. He felt the same. A lot of that respect was via the news coverage that told them about the convoy and the reasons behind it. No parent could fail to admire someone who saved so many young lives.

But, the overwhelming impression I got was that they respected the way that we truckers honoured one of our own. They respected the quiet yet determined way we bonded together to accompany a fallen driver on his last journey. For that one journey, on that one day, the British driving public saw truck drivers as something else. And, I like to think, they gave us a unanimous and universal acknowledgement for the part we play on the roads. On that one day, the truck driver gained the respect that he should have and deserves but never quite attains.

Sadly, it took the death of one brave man for we truckers to achieve that. John Slater, in his own quiet way, tried on a daily basis to earn that respect for himself and all of us. Might I suggest that, as a mark of respect for this remarkable man, we continue to strive for his ideals?

How much time does it take to let someone out of a side street? How much time do you gain by driving irresponsibly and bullying other drivers?. In a single journey, how much time does a bad truck driver save against that of a professional caring driver?

If we want to achieve the status we deserve, we need to earn it. Act professionally and we will be seen as professionals. Be professional. Live up to the legacy of John Slater. Make a difference. John used to say that if every truck driver did just one good deed a day – let just one motorist out of a junction, for instance – imagine that one good deed repeated, every day, by every trucker throughout the land. That would get us noticed. Maybe once again we could then be called what truck drivers used to be called; the title the older generation of truckers had earned. The Knights of the Road

I wish that I had known John Slater. Many of you did and I envy you that. I didn't but I can speak for him and remind you of his ideals and, hopefully, his lasting legacy.

Goodbye John Slater. Truck on Good Buddy. I hope you are enjoying your Good Roads and Far Horizons. You have earnt them."

Peter Tiler looked up at the ceiling with misty eyes. "Oh, Dave, you old bugger" he whispered as he tried to swallow the lump in his throat "that's bootiful……that's just so bootiful."

"Here you are Peter" the clerk said as he pushed a box of tissue towards him. "Must be something in the air conditioning irritating the eyes. Everyone who read that articlc today had the same problem."

Peter grabbed a tissue and dabbed at his eyes. "Oh bugger off Mike. I'm going to work."

Peter Tiler did drive his truck to Doncaster and drove back to Crick. He didn't remember any of it. Reading the article had fired up his desire to do something positive with John Slater's money. Myriad ideas came and went but nothing that was practical, effective or suitable. All he knew was that there would be some sort of memorial.
When he arrived home, Beth had gone to work but had left a note on the kitchen table. 'This bloke rang. He wants to talk to you. Can you ring him back?' Not until I've had a cuppa and something to eat, he grumbled, as he switched the kettle on and put two slices in the toaster.
Half an hour later, he picked up the phone and dialed the number. 'Good morning. Steed Public Relations. How may I help you?'
"Morning. My name is Peter Tiler. I have a message to contact a Philip Steed"
'Ah yes. He is expecting you. Putting you through' Peter heard the usual transfer noise then "Mr Tiler! Phil Steed. Thank you so much for returning my call.'
"Do I know you, Mr Steed?"
"Phil, please. May I call you Peter? No Peter, you don't know me but I have been asked to contact you by one of my clients, the TMA. That stands for the Truck Manufacturers Association. Everyone in the industry is buzzing about that article in Trucking International. The TMA represents, as the name suggests, the companies who produce the trucks. Every manufacturer is a member.
Its purpose is to present a united front for the industry. Obviously it is in everyone's interests if the transport industry is seen in a good light. Since seeing the article, the various pr departments of the truck makers have been

buzzing. The good news is that together they want to meet with you and discuss several options that have been put forward. Initially, I will handle things but, if we progress, then it is hoped that there will be a joint meeting between the manufacturers and yourself. How do you feel about that, Peter?"

"A bit stunned at the moment. I've just finished work. I'm a trucker on the night shift. What would be the purpose of this meeting?"

"Yes, I know that you are trucker. In fact, I know quite a lot about you, Peter. A mutual friend, Dave Williams, has discussed this with me with my TMA hat on. Dave feels that you would like some sort of memorial, a tribute, to John Slater. He suggested I ring you and try to work something out. The TMA members would be prepared to finance a joint scheme. We just need to know what it should be. Have you any thoughts?"

"Thousands of them going round and round in my brain. Nothing immediate. Look, can I think about this? Obviously, I'm in agreement in principle but I need a sleep. Is that ok?"

"Yes, fine Peter. What are you doing tomorrow?"

"I have four days off before starting again. Why?"

"I'm only in Milton Keynes. I could be with you in an hour. Can we arrange something for tomorrow, say at around 11am?"

"Ok, I suppose. I'll see you then" Peter said unenthusiastically.

"Thank you Stewart. Look, I don't blame you for being a bit cautious. Why don't you ring Dave Williams to ask about me? Better yet, why don't you invite him as well?"

Replacing the phone, Peter walked into the lounge. He felt strangely exhilarated, curious yet cautious. Things were certainly happening fast. Maybe too fast? He rang Dave Williams and asked him if he could come round. Dave arrived ten minutes later and, within five minutes, Stewart had told him what had happened.

"You started all this, you old bugger. If it hadn't been for your article, this wouldn't have happened. Having said that, thank you for that article." Peter engulfed his friend in a hug. Dave patted his shoulder then drew back.

"Steady on, Stewart. Not been spending too much time with Mike Henshaw and Dereck, have you?" They were the gay couple who owned the Kenworth.

"No, I'm not turning" Peter laughed. "Who is this pr guy? Is he ok?"

"Phil is great. I used to work with him a lot on the manufacturer truck testing and development I used to do. You can trust him."

"Well, what do you reckon then? I am keen to get some sort of a memorial going but I am not sure about involving the truck manufacturers."

"Why not? Let them put something back. If they want to do something and are prepared to finance it, take advantage. Think of the resources they have. Not just money but an individual and a joint pr machine. A dealer network. Contacts. Plus, it is in their interest to promote a professional interest in drivers and their products."

"Humph… I didn't think of it like that. Yes, ok, we join forces. To do what? How do we start?"

"Basics, Stu. What do we want to promote? Better driving and a professional approach to truck driving? Raising the standards and making friends with the public? Some sort of scheme that rewards good drivers? An apprenticeship for wannabe truckers?"

"Yes, all of that, but how?"

"I have given it a lot of thought myself. I tried to get something off the ground in the early 90's. It didn't work then because there were only two truck manufacturers involved and they couldn't agree on anything. But, it might work now."

"What was it?" Peter was starting to get excited about the idea.

"My plan was for a manufacturer to provide a truck and exhibition trailer to go round schools, truck stops, attend exhibitions and actively promoter road safety and professional driving. Let school kids see the blind spots that trucks have and make them aware of them. Let the public look around a modern truck and see just how much skill and training it takes to drive them. Talk to people and show a presence. That's the only way to get a message across."

"Bugger, boy, I like that. You have given this some thought haven't you? But what about organizing it all? Who is going to do that?"

"The truck manufacturers, Stu, that's who. Individually, through their own pr departments and jointly through Phil Steed and the TMA. It doesn't matter whose name is on the front of the truck. So long as the logo on the truck and trailer are the same and the manufacturers are all singing from the same hymn sheet. They will be glad to do that. It promotes their product, the transport industry as a whole

and, more importantly, gives drivers the professional image they deserve and aspire to."
"I like it. Boy, do I like it. Can you be here tomorrow to help me get this across?"
"Need you ask, mate? Be proud to. And, may I make two more suggestions. How about having the logo on the truck and trailers saying something like 'The John Slater Trust: Professional, Dedicated, Caring'. And, some sort of badge that a truck driver can have on the grille of his truck to show that he is professional, dedicated and caring. Something that the good drivers are inspired by. A badge that sets them apart. Something that new drivers will strive for and feel honored to be awarded."
"I reckon you have something in mind as well, don't you?" Peter grinned.
"You bet Stu. I think you'll like it, too. A stainless steel knight on a horse. A Knight of the Road".
"A Knight of the Road" Peter was stunned. "Mate, that is genius. Do you think they'll go for it?"
"Oh, they'll go for it Peter. They'll eat your hand off. It's a Win-Win situation for everyone. And, I don't want to appear as if I'm taking over but I think you should be on the board or whatever is formed to oversee operations. That way you can help make the decisions and the format for the scheme and then make sure it does what it is supposed to do. They'll need an independent outsider and I can't think of anyone else more suited for the job."
Suddenly, Peter couldn't wait for tomorrow to come and to get started. The John Slater Trust: Professional, Dedicated, Caring. The Knights of the Road. It was just what John would have wanted and proud to be a part of. And he was

going to do his best to see that the dream became a reality.

TWENTY TWO

The reality of Southern England state became more apparent the closer we got. I guessed that we still had a few miles to go but it didn't look very inviting. Suddenly the monotony of the flat featureless plains around us seemed infinitely preferable. At least there was open sky above us and natural light. The view on the horizon seemed dark and menacing. It was like a huge, black wall rising out of the ground and up into the sky. I thought the place we had come from was depressing, when seen from the ring road, but this was even more so.
I then realized that I wasn't sure just where we had travelled from. England State was not like England. The latter had densely populated cities broken up by towns, villages and little country hamlets. England State, I was told, was one solid section of high rise habitation surrounded by open countryside. Whereas in England, I could say that I had travelled from Bradford to Brighton, here I could only say that I had come from the north to the south. Assuming that what I called north was north. It could have been just the middle. I didn't know and that, for a trucker, was a little scary.
I cruised to a halt and stopped the engine. I looked at the darkness before us then looked at Celeste. If she was worried, she didn't show it. "Why have we stopped John? Something wrong?"
"No, I suppose not. Just a bit confused, that's all"
"Oh, I'm confused all the time. You'll get used to it." She said matter of factly.

I didn't think she was joking either. I smiled, started the engine and moved off. Half an hour later, my internal sensor told me to turn right. The buildings stretched from horizon to horizon. I thought our buildings were depressing but I was wrong. It was, in Earth terms, like coming from a small town and ending up in the roughest part of London.

The junction off the concrete Ring road that I turned into was a tarmac road of sorts but it was plain to see that the buildings that towered either side were not in good shape. I drove gingerly forward. There was nothing but Astros with their myriad doorways but no windows. No people. No sign of anyone living here. I should have been used to Topside by now. I realized that I wasn't.

I powered my side window down and listened. I hadn't been mistaken. I did hear something. It was like a buzzing sound that seemed to increase in volume the further into the canyon I drove. I obeyed the little voice that told me to turn right again and the sound got much louder.

Suddenly, ahead of me I could see people. There were hundreds of them, lining the sides of the road. Even Celeste looked interested. "What's going on John?"

I wasn't sure but I had an idea. "I reckon that is our reception committee."

It was. As we drove on, the people cheered and clapped. Suddenly, my mood changed. I smiled and waved back. Celeste had her window down and was doing the Royal wave out of the window. I pulled Maggie's airhorn and they went wild. The cheering increased and everywhere people were pumping their arms up and down. It was like those scenes you see on old newsreels. People in the street

celebrating the end of the Second World War. Laughing, cheering, having a good time amongst the ruins of war torn buildings. Everywhere I heard the chant “Power, Power”. No sign of Jeremy Clarkson though. I felt like I should have been driving a tank.
Driving got trickier and trickier as people pushed and shoved each other. I was just crawling along. Then a bearded man stepped into the road right in front of me. He wasn’t very tall and had long black hair that seemed to flow seamlessly into his bushy black beard. He had a noticeboard on a pole in his hand and he held it up. The board was white and, in large red letters, told me to ‘Fllow me’. I took it to mean I had to follow him.
He turned into another side street and then directed me towards a building about halfway down. I stopped when he did, turned off the engine and climbed down. Told Celeste to stay put and locked the cab doors. People were patting my back, shaking my hand and asking dozens of questions. The little guy grabbed my hand and pulled me into a nearby building and shut the door firmly behind me.
“Sorry about that” he said in a pronounced Irish accent. He held out his hand and I shook it. “Micheal Sweeney and you must be John Slater. Noel has told me all about you. How was your journey? Any problems? Feck, it is good to see you.”
Micheal Sweeney. Noel’s mate. The guy I had to give the mysterious box to.
“No problems. I wasn’t expecting that reception though. Is there a reason?”
“A very good reason. We have had little or no power for the last two days.. Lifts aren’t working, people can’t work,

limited food, - the replicators are off-line - and it has been a confused mess. The quicker we get you unloaded and power connected the better."
"Right, let's get to it then. Where are we doing it?"
"In the yard at the side of this building. I will have to get the people cleared first. It's tight enough without that mob. You'll have drive forward and come round on a tight right hander then a hard left to get in. Noel bet me you couldn't do it in one go."
"Don't tell me. With those instructions, you have to be a trucker as well."
"Sure enough. For a long, long time. Noel said you were a clever little trucker. Something like that anyhow.
What is it with the Irish? You just have to like them. I was getting the same gut feeling about this guy as I always did with Noel but I still liked him.
"Better get started then" I said and followed him out the door. Outside the crowd was quieter and Micheal held up his arms. "You are going to have to leave now folks" He shouted. "We need the room to get the trailer into the yard. If you don't go we can't do our job and you'll have no power. Go home and get ready for the big switch on."
It took a while but gradually people started drifting off and eventually we had to place to ourselves. I got Celeste down and introduced her. Micheal took her hand, kissed it and began to Blarney her. I soon put a stop to that. Bloody Mick, coming onto my girl. Yeah right, guilty as charged. Jealous.
As he had predicted, getting in was tight. Unlike Noel's prediction, I got it right first time. Reversing an artic is completely different from a rigid. If you want the trailer to

turn left, you have to steer the tractor unit right and vice versa. Sounds complicated and it is the first time. After a while, it becomes second nature and you don't have to think about. Anyway, my trailer went into that yard like it was on rails. I got out and felt very pleased with myself.
"Yeah, not bad at all, at all." Micheal grudgingly praised. "Right, let's get your covers opened and the securing straps off."
A little while later, whilst I stowed away the ratchet straps, Micheal unloaded the batteries with an ancient forklift truck. When the last one was off, I followed him into the building. The batteries were placed end to end alongside a large piece of machinery. I guessed it was a distributor of some sort that the batteries would be connected to. I was right.
Micheal linked up the terminals on each battery and then connected the plus and negative leads onto the distributor. As Sean had said, back at base, it didn't take long and wasn't complicated. He double checked his connections then walked over to a control panel set into a cabinet at the side of the building. "Here goes" he said, crossing his fingers and pulling a switch down. Nothing happened at first, then there was cheering outside. He grinned and blew out his cheeks in a relieved manner.
Outside it didn't seem any different but then people started to come out of the buildings and shaking our hands. There were no windows but I could see that the interior hallways of the Astros were now lit up. Obviously it had worked and power was restored. We left everyone celebrating and I followed Celeste and Micheal back into the building. He

checked some gauges, pronounced himself satisfied and came over.
“Now, have you got that parcel that Noel sent?” he asked.
I walked out to Maggie, unlocked the door and reached under my seat for the parcel. I walked back and stood in front of Micheal. I kept hold of the parcel. I shook it and watched his eyes. No reaction. “What’s in it, Micheal?”
“Ah now, it’s nothing for you to worry about. Just a little something from Noel to celebrate your first trip. Your first successful trip.”
“Then you won’t mind telling me what is in it, will you?”
He seemed to change before my eyes. Got taller, tidier, more imposing. I shook my head. More tired than I thought. “You have to have faith, John” he replied in a different voice; a soft yet authorative voice. He came up close and looked into my eyes. Held out his hand.
I stared into those eyes. Felt a wave of pure happiness and love wash over me. I handed over the parcel. He took it and walked over to the distributor. Opened the parcel and took out the contents. He placed it in a niche above the quietly humming machine. Without turning round he gave a quiet command.
“Close your eyes John. You too, Celeste”.
A bright light washed over the room. It was so bright that it was painful. As it died away, I could still see after-images of the brightness before my normal vision returned. In the niche was a simple wooden cross. Of Micheal Sweeney, there was no sign.
Celeste and I held hands as we walked back to Maggie. Climbed in, shut the doors. She looked across at me. Her eyes glowed. “Take me home, John”.

I drove back the way we had come. When our part of Heaven appeared on the horizon, I felt at peace. Coming Home.

"Let's not go back to the flat tonight, John. Can I have one more night alone with you?" We parked up. I replicated a meal whilst Celeste had a shower. It was still light outside so I went to the locker in the trailer and pulled out a small table and two chairs. Out there, in the peace and the quiet, Celeste and I had our meal. We didn't say much. There didn't seem much to say.

Later, as it got dark, we sat outside under the stars. I put my arm round her and she snuggled close. Overhead, strange constellations glowed down on us. Two orange moons bathed us in their light. On the horizon, we could make out the lights of home. I turned her face up to mine and kissed her softly, gently. "Time for bed, Celeste?"

Later, after we had made long, sweet love, I held her close. Her breathing was shallow, she was on the point of sleep. I breathed into her ear. "Been quite a day, Celeste". She murmured sleepily. I moved closer to hear what she said.

"That wasn't really Micheal Sweeney, was it John?" she asked

"No Celeste, it wasn't".

Three months or so later – I still couldn't tell time accurately – I had delivered batteries to most of the distribution depots in England state. I would soon be starting on the different Europe States. My girls came with me on a rota basis. I was happy. I was in love and loved by four beautiful angels. I was doing some good. I was back on the road. I was doing what I did best. What I was born to do.

But I don't think I will ever forget my first delivery. The time when Celeste and I experienced God's infinite love for the first time.

TWENTY THREE

Three months or so later, Peter Tiler had never been happier. He was driving a top of the range Scania truck and towing a custom made exhibition trailer. The legend on the trailer proudly proclaimed: The John Slater Trust: Professional, Dedicated, Caring. In pride of place on the front grille was a shining, stainless steel image of a knight on horseback.

In those three months, he and Dave Williams had met with the truck manufacturers and rounded out the details. With Phil Steed's help and the backing of the TMA, each manufacturer provided a dedicated truck, trailer and driver. Peter was one of those full time drivers.

Each day was different. Sometimes he was at a school providing road safety instructions and hoping to implant the idea of being a trucker in those young minds. Other times he was parked up in a motorway service area talking to truckers and motorists.

The results had been almost immediate. After the Trucking International article had been published, thousands of truckers had taken up the challenge of being recognized as skilled and dedicated professionals. Motorists remarked on the change in the truck drivers. A daily newspaper reprinted Dave William's article and it snowballed from there.

Once the news of the Trust was announced, there were thousands of requests for the Knight emblem. Truckers placed the emblem on their front grilles to proudly proclaim their entry into the Knights of the Road members club. They strove to keep its high ideals and policed

themselves. If a trucker was noticed driving badly or with scant regard for other road users, he would find himself boxed in by other trucks and soon got the message.
Driver training schools were inundated with trainee truckers. A section of the John Slater Trust provided medical funds and support for injured truck drivers. Widows and families of truckers who had died on the road were given financial assistance. And, Peter reminded himself as he prepared to climb into his cab, the Trust was still growing. He had given John Slater's money to the trust. Truck, trailer and truck equipment manufacturers happily boosted the Trust's ever growing bank balance. Money enough to keep John Slater's dream and ideals in practice for many years to come.

Peter was weary as he got into his bunk and prepared to sleep. Aches and pains seemed pretty much constant companions lately. He always seemed tired nowadays but it was a tiredness that he enjoyed. 'Getting old, boy' he reminded himself as he stretched out on the bottom bunk. He closed his eyes and drifted off. As his sleep became sounder, he dreamt.

He dreamt of white mists, grassy meadows and large buildings. In his dream, he saw John standing beside his beloved truck. Gathered round him were four beautiful girls. John looked happy. Happier than he had ever seen him. John walked towards him, arms outstretched . He stopped and then shook his head. He held one hand up in salute to Peter and grinned. In his dream Peter heard his words 'Thanks mate. Here's to Good Roads and Far Horizons.'

In his bunk, Peter Tiler grew still, a little smile on his face. He dreamt on.

THE END?

Dave Furlong has been a truckdriver, an owner driver and a transport journalist. He has driven throughout the UK and Europe on international work. As a freelance transport journalist he wrote articles and road tested trucksfor the major national and international transport and driver magazines. He was also involved in the development and testing of trucks and drivelines for the truck and engine manufacturers. He is now retired but continues to write about trucks and truckers.

If you enjoyed this novel look out for more John Slater stories from Dave Furlong. Any comments, stories or if you have met me on the road at some time or some place, then you are welcome to get in touch at

dwfurlong@talktalk.net

Dalyn Publishing
Dalyn House
270 Lower Hillmorton Rd
Rugby
Warwickshire CV21 4AE

Email and submission enquiries:
dalynpublishers@talktalk.net

■■■

Printed in Great Britain
by Amazon.co.uk, Ltd.,
Marston Gate.